THE BAEN BIG BOOK

of Monsters

BAEN BOOKS EDITED
BY HANK DAVIS
❖ ❖ ❖

The Human Edge by Gordon R. Dickson

We the Underpeople by Cordwainer Smith
When the People Fell by Cordwainer Smith

The Technic Civilization Saga
The Van Rijn Method by Poul Anderson
David Falkayn: Star Trader by Poul Anderson
Rise of the Terran Empire by Poul Anderson
Young Flandry by Poul Anderson
Captain Flandry: Defender of the Terran Empire by Poul Anderson
Sir Dominic Flandry: The Last Knight of Terra by Poul Anderson
Flandry's Legacy by Poul Anderson

The Best of the Bolos: Their Finest Hour, created by Keith Laumer

A Cosmic Christmas
A Cosmic Christmas 2 You
In Space No One Can Hear You Scream
The Baen Big Book of Monsters
As Time Goes By (forthcoming)

THE BAEN BIG BOOK

of Monsters

Edited By
HANK DAVIS

THE BAEN BIG BOOK OF MONSTERS

A Baen Book

Baen Publishing Enterprises
P.O. Box 1403
Riverdale, NY 10471

ISBN 13: 978-1-4767-3699-0

Cover art by Bob Eggleton

First Baen printing, October 2014

Distributed by Simon & Schuster
1230 Avenue of the Americas
New York, NY 10020

Library of Congress Cataloging-in-Publication Data

The Baen big book of monsters / edited by Hank Davis.
     pages cm
Summary: "From the dragons of legend to Jack the Giant Killer's colleague to King Kong and Godzilla, people have found the idea of giant creatures both scary and fascinating. Here's a book crammed full of large things that you can't outrun by such writers as David Drake, Robert Bloch, Philip Wylie, Murray Leinster, H.P. Lovecraft, Larry Correia, Wen Spencer and more"-- Provided by publisher.
 ISBN 978-1-4767-3699-0 (paperback)
1. Monsters--Fiction. 2. Giants--Fiction. 3. Science fiction. 4. Horror fiction. I. Davis, Hank.
 PN6120.95.S33B34 2014
 813'.087608--dc23
                                    2014025369

Printed in the United States of America

10 9 8 7 6 5 4 3 2 1

Table of Contents

Dedication

❖ ❖ ❖

For the guys who brought big critters to
gigantic, scary life on the silver screen:

Willis O'Brien
Ray Harryhausen
Merian C. Cooper
Eiji Tsuburaya
Ishirô Honda
Haruo Nakajima
Katsumi Tezuka
Jiro Suzuki

And all the unsung heroes and heroines who painstakingly
built miniatures and puppets, sweated over special effects, and
sweated inside rubber suits.

Plus a rueful nod to Bert I. Gordon. Sorry, Mr. B.I.G.,
but filming a close up of an iguana and calling it a T-Rex doesn't cut
the giant monster mustard.

Acknowledgements

※ ※ ※

My thanks to all the contributors, as well as those who helped with advice, permissions, contact information, and other kindnesses, including Ann Behar, Cristina Concepcion, Carol Chamberlain, Martha Grenon, Jessica Reisman, Justin Bell, David Drake, Moshe Feder, Barbara Hambly and her friend, Sitemistress Deb, Vaughne Hansen, Robert C. Harrall, Rich Henshaw, Barry Malzberg, Craig Tenney, Bud Webster, Joakim Zetterberg, and probably other helpful carbon units which my decrepit memory has unforgivably overlooked. And finally, thanks to Bob Eggleton, whose idea the whole thing was. (He *loves* to do giant monster covers.)

THE BAEN BIG BOOK

of Monsters

Size Matters
INTRODUCTION

by Hank Davis

Read any good monsters lately? Here's a big book full of even bigger monsters, one in a story over a century old, others in newly written stories, and a generous helping of stories from the years between.

I don't want to rehash the points I made in my introduction to *In Space No One Can Hear You Scream*, since I'm sure you already have that book on your shelf or in your to-be-read stack. (If you somehow overlooked it, fortunately it's still available, both in dead tree and e-book versions.) As I wrote there, briefly, people who don't read science fiction but get their notion of SF from movies and TV have a tendency to think that SF equals horror. In particular, the SF movies of the 1950s, many of which were also horror movies, laid a foundation for that perception, and a lot of them involved giant critters of all sorts: revived dinosaurs, enlarged insects and spiders and at least one giant lobster from outer space (in the awesomely awful *Teenagers from Outer Space*), giant snails, giant leeches, giant amoebae, giant crabs (no jokes, please), a giant octopus, and even giant people.

That was what was playing at your local drive-in theater, but for written SF, the 1950s was a period of the genre taking itself Very Seriously (and maybe even Constructively), with the emphasis on possible futures, logical extrapolations of current social trends and realistic technologies, no more beautiful Martian princesses (*sigh*),

1

increased attention to psychology and sociology, and did I mention being Very Serious? Space opera in general was mostly confined to four minor magazines and Ace Double-Novels, while the onetime space adventure pulps *Startling Stories* and *Thrilling Wonder Stories* cut back on covers by Earle Bergey with his celebrated babes in brass bras menaced by loathsome alien creatures and instead displayed serious covers illustrating serious stories inside. Alas, it didn't help those two venerable magazines, which soon shuffled off to the pulp Valhalla accompanied by *the* space opera pulp, *Planet Stories*. Nothing gold can stay . . .

All this seriousness wasn't conducive to stories of giant monsters. For one thing, with all the attention paid to using authentic science (with rivets), any story about giant monsters had to work around what's usually called the square-cube law. If you wanted to write a story about giant ants, you had the problem that insects, including ants, breathe through holes in their chassis called spiracles that let air circulate inside. This works fine for something the size of an insect, but if an ant is somehow doubled in its size, the surface inside its air passages increases by four times (the square of the size) while the volume of its body increases by eight times (the cube of the size), so that its respiration quickly becomes less efficient. An ant the size of a man or larger would suffocate. If an author wrote about ants as big as a man, he'd have to somehow give them something like lungs (Frederik Pohl did that in his 1949 story, "Let the Ants Try"—and they did, too).

There's also the problem that instead of an internal skeleton, insects have an exoskeleton, a setup that works very well for tiny critters, but, once again, double the size of an ant, say, and the volume of its exoskeleton increases eightfold. Increase its size ten times—still much smaller than a man—and its exoskeleton's volume and weight increases a thousand times. The exoskeleton would become very heavy if an ant somehow became as big as a man. There's also the problem that the strength of a muscle is proportional to the size of its cross-section. Double the size and the muscular strength is squared, but (again) the weight of the body is cubed. That man-sized ant might not even be able to stand up on its spindly legs . . . before it fell over from suffocation.

The square-cube law works in the other direction, too, and is responsible for the apparent feats of super-strength that insects routinely demonstrate. A flea can jump a distance that corresponds to a human leaping over a tall building in a single bound (I hope that phrase isn't copyrighted). An ant can lift a pebble half its size not because it's unusually strong, but because that pebble's inside volume shrinks faster than its surface area, so it's not as proportionately heavy as it looks. An ant-sized man would be able to lift the same pebble— of course, a man that size would have problems, such as freezing because his surface area is rapidly radiating heat away from his comparatively small-volume innards, his eyes not being designed to function at such a tiny size, and other things.

Evolution has shaped insects to operate efficiently at one size and humans to operate at a much larger size, and everything is *not* relative. (By the way, I'm certain that Einstein never said that, "Everything is relative," if only because the speed of light not being relative is the basis for special relativity.)

So giant insects are impossible, really giant humans wouldn't be able to function (nor would giant apes—sorry, Kong), and if a human shrank to insect size, he'd have more immediate problems than just having to fight off regular sized insects or spiders.

But that's no fun.

Before things got so serious, stories in the SF pulps of the 1920s and into the 1940s had stories about people who had shrunk down to microscopic size, such as Paul Ernst's "The Raid on the Termites" in the June 1932 *Astounding Stories* and "He Who Shrank" by Henry Hasse, in the August 1936 *Amazing Stories*, and even subatomic size— Ray Cummings made a cottage industry of the latter, writing "The Girl in the Golden Atom," "Beyond the Vanishing Point," and others. Other stories starred enormously enlarged insects, as in Victor Rosseau's "The Beetle Horde," in the very first issue of *Astounding*. The same month, in the January 1930 *Amazing Stories*, saw a story by Miles J. Breuer, M.D., "The Hungry Guinea Pig," which was hungry because it was very, very big. (Don't get between it and a warehouse full of grain.)

Even earlier, H.G. Wells wrote *The Food of the Gods*, which is mostly about giant people, but also had a side order of giant rats and wasps, IIRC. (Maybe somebody will someday make a good movie of that novel, and we can forget about the bloody awful *three* movies that Bert I. Gordon perpetrated.) Much later, in the middle of the seriousness of the 1950s, Richard Matheson wrote *The Shrinking Man*, which opens with its microscopic protagonist running for his life from a regular-sized spider. It was published as a paperback original by Gold Medal books, a paperback line known for westerns, mysteries, suspense—but not for science fiction. Although Matheson had sold numerous stories to most of the SF magazines of the time, I doubt that any of them would have serialized the novel, even without the harsh language and controversial scenes (which read as very mild now). Damon Knight wrote a killer review of the book, bringing his heaviest artillery to bear—and it didn't matter. The novel became a popular movie, *The Incredible Shrinking Man*, with a screenplay by Matheson, and the book has been in print almost constantly for nearly sixty years, because (here's that word again) it's *fun*.

People never (well . . . hardly ever) argue that vampires, werewolves, and other things that go bump in the night actually exist (there are also ghosts, but a lot of people take them more seriously). One can enjoy a fantasy story without believing in elves, dwarfs, dragons, unicorns, or other such creatures of institutionalized fantasy. Giant monsters may be impossible or at least very unlikely without complicated reengineering, but they're fun. Vive las giant monsters. (What's French for "giant monsters," anyway?)

Some monsters have become icons. In the 1960s, before home video, when *King Kong* only occasionally appeared on TV, everybody still recognized the context of cartoons, political or otherwise, of a giant ape, or a giant something else, clinging to the Empire State building. A bumper sticker proclaiming that "King Kong Died for Your Sins" needed no explanation, nor did such jokes as "What's between King Kong's toes? Slow natives." There was even a series of bubble gum collectible cards with ol' K.K. on them. Not bad for the star of a movie more than thirty years old at the time.

And the fascination with purportedly real monsters goes back decades. The Abominable snowman and Bigfoot may not qualify as *giant* monsters, but the Loch Ness Monster does. In *The Female*

Eunuch, Germaine Greer noted a headline where "Nessy" (usually written as "Nessie") was identified as female, and cited this as an example of the contempt the mass mind had for females of the human species. Actually, she just didn't get it—people might not want to get too close to Nessie, if she (or he) exists, but they have affection for the crypto-critter, and people often refer to even unliving objects (ships, cars, planes, even outboard boat motors) as female when they have affection for them. Nessie has *fans*!

In summary, stories about giant monsters may be fantasy disguised as science fiction, but it doesn't matter, because (I'll repeat myself) giant monsters are fun! And here's a book full of such fascinating critters and equally full of that sort of fun. I hope you enjoy these guilty pleasures.

—Hank Davis
June 2014

The Shining Ones

INTRODUCTION

Sir Arthur C. Clarke (1917-2008) was known both for writing the hardest of hard science fiction stories and also for visionary far-future stories showing the influence of Olaf Stapledon. One of his passions was the sea, demonstrated by his being an enthusiastic SCUBA diver, by the nonfiction books he wrote on the subject, and such stories as "Big Game Hunt" and "The Man Who Ploughed the Sea" (both in *Tales from the White Hart*), the novelet "The Deep Range" (later incorporated in his novel with the same title), and other works, such as the story which follows this introduction.

In *Astounding Days*, his memoirlike salute to the magazine *Astounding Science-Fiction*, Clarke discusses the possibility of very large creatures of the deeps which are still unknown to us. After noting that the few specimens of the celebrated giant squid that have washed ashore may not represent full-grown adults, who might be up to one hundred and fifty feet in length according to one expert, he cited evidence that even bigger creatures might be hiding below the waves. In 1896 a badly decayed sea dweller washed ashore, weighing in at six or seven tons. It was thought to be a dead whale, and samples were taken and preserved. When one of the fragments was examined in 1971, the creature turned out to be an octopus, possibly two hundred feet in size. Incidentally (or perhaps not), shortly before I wrote this introduction, news came out about a Great White, the superstar of sharks since *Jaws*, that had been tagged with a tracking device and was suddenly pulled down into really deep water, as if grabbed by a more formidable predator. The tracking device, without the shark attached, later washed up on a beach. With that cheering thought, I leave you to Sir Arthur's story of yet another marine titan . . .

❈ ❈ ❈

Known for being one of the "Big Three" writers of modern science fiction (along with Robert A. Heinlein and Isaac Asimov), co-author of and technical advisor for the now-classic movie, *2001: A Space Odyssey*, author of many best-selling novels, commentator on CBS's coverage of the Apollo missions, and winner of numerous awards, Sir Arthur C. Clarke surely needs no introduction (though I just snuck one in anyway). In a technical paper in 1945, he was first to describe how geosynchronous satellites could relay broadcasts from the ground around the world, bringing a new era in global communications and television. His novels are too numerous to list here (but I'll plug three of my favorites: *The City and the Stars*, *Childhood's End*, and *Earthlight*), let alone his many short stories. He was equally adept at non-fiction, notably in his *The Exploration of Space* in the early 1950s, his frequently reprinted *Profiles of the Future*, and another bunch of books also too numerous to mention. So, instead of not mentioning them further, I'll just say, go thou and read.

The Shining Ones

by Arthur C. Clarke

When the switchboard said that the Soviet Embassy was on the line, my first reaction was: "Good—another job!" But the moment I heard Goncharov's voice, I knew there was trouble.

"Klaus? This is Mikhail. Can you come over at once? It's very urgent, and I can't talk on the phone."

I worried all the way to the Embassy, marshaling my defenses in case anything had gone wrong at our end. But I could think of nothing; at the moment, we had no outstanding contracts with the Russians. The last job had been completed six months ago, on time, and to their entire satisfaction.

Well, they were not satisfied with it now, as I discovered quickly enough. Mikhail Goncharov, the Commercial Attaché, was an old friend of mine; he told me all he knew, but it was not much.

"We've just had an urgent cable from Ceylon," he said. "They want you out there immediately. There's serious trouble at the hydrothermal project."

"What sort of trouble?" I asked. I knew at once, of course, that it would be the deep end, for that was the only part of the installation that had concerned us. The Russians themselves had done all the work on land, but they had had to call on us to fix those grids three thousand feet down in the Indian Ocean. There is no other firm in the world that can live up to our motto: ANY JOB, ANY DEPTH.

9

"All I know," said Mikhail, "is that the site engineers report a complete breakdown, that the Prime Minister of Ceylon is opening the plant three weeks from now, and that Moscow will be very, very unhappy if it's not working then."

My mind went rapidly through the penalty clauses in our contract. The firm seemed to be covered, because the client had signed the take-over certificate, thereby admitting that the job was up to specification. However, it was not as simple as that; if negligence on our part was proved, we might be safe from legal action—but it would be very bad for business. And it would be even worse for me, personally; for I had been project supervisor in Trinco Deep.

Don't call me a diver, please; I hate the name. I'm a deep-sea engineer, and I use diving gear about as often as an airman uses a parachute. Most of my work is done with TV and remote-controlled robots. When I do have to go down myself, I'm inside a minisub with external manipulators. We call it a lobster, because of its claws; the standard model works down to five thousand feet, but there are special versions that will operate at the bottom of the Marianas Trench. I've never been there myself, but will be glad to quote terms if you're interested. At a rough estimate, it will cost you a dollar a foot plus a thousand an hour on the job itself.

I realized that the Russians meant business when Mikhail said that a jet was waiting at Zurich, and could I be at the airport within two hours?

"Look," I said, "I can't do a thing without equipment—and the gear needed even for an inspection weighs tons. Besides, it's all at Spezia."

"I know," Mikhail answered implacably. "We'll have another jet transport there. Cable from Ceylon as soon as you know what you want: it will be on the site within twelve hours. But please don't talk to anyone about this; we prefer to keep our problems to ourselves."

I agreed with this, for it was my problem, too. As I left the office, Mikhail pointed to the wall calendar, said "Three weeks," and ran his finger around his throat. And I knew he wasn't thinking of *his* neck.

Two hours later I was climbing over the Alps, saying goodbye to the family by radio, and wondering why, like every other sensible

Swiss, I hadn't become a banker or gone into the watch business. It was all the fault of the Picards and Hannes Keller, I told myself moodily: why did they have to start this deep-sea tradition, in Switzerland of all countries? Then I settled down to sleep, knowing that I would have little enough in the days to come.

We landed at Trincomalee just after dawn, and the huge, complex harbor—whose geography I've never quite mastered—was a maze of capes, islands, interconnecting waterways, and basins large enough to hold all the navies of the world. I could see the big white control building, in a somewhat flamboyant architectural style, on a headland overlooking the Indian Ocean. The site was pure propaganda—though of course if I'd been Russian I'd have called it "public relations."

Not that I really blamed my clients; they had good reason to be proud of this, the most ambitious attempt yet made to harness the thermal energy of the sea. It was not the first attempt. There had been an unsuccessful one by the French scientist Georges Claude in the 1930s, and a much bigger one at Abidjan, on the west coast of Africa, in the 1950s.

All these projects depended on the same surprising fact: even in the tropics the sea a mile down is almost at freezing point. Where billions of tons of water are concerned, this temperature difference represents a colossal amount of energy—and a fine challenge to the engineers of power-starved countries.

Claude and his successors had tried to tap this energy with low-pressure steam engines; the Russians had used a much simpler and more direct method. For over a hundred years it had been known that electric currents flow in many materials if one end is heated and the other cooled, and ever since the 1940s Russian scientists had been working to put this "thermoelectric" effect to practical use. Their earliest devices had not been very efficient—though good enough to power thousands of radios by the heat of kerosene lamps. But in 1974 they had made a big, and still-secret, breakthrough. Though I fixed the power elements at the cold end of the system, I never really saw them; they were completely hidden in anticorrosive paint. All I know is that they formed a big grid, like lots of old-fashioned steam radiators bolted together.

I recognized most of the faces in the little crowd waiting on the Trinco airstrip; friends or enemies, they all seemed glad to see me—especially Chief Engineer Shapiro.

"Well, Lev," I said, as we drove out in the station wagon, "what's the trouble?"

"We don't know," he said frankly. "It's your job to find out—and to put it right."

"Well, what *happened?*"

"Everything worked perfectly up to the full-power tests," he answered. "Output was within five per cent of estimate until 0134 Tuesday morning." He grimaced; obviously that time was engraved on his heart. "Then the voltage started to fluctuate violently, so we cut the load and watched the meters. I thought that some idiot of a skipper had hooked the cables—you know the trouble we've taken to avoid *that* happening—so we switched on the searchlights and looked out to sea. There wasn't a ship in sight. Anyway, who would have tried to anchor just *outside* the harbor on a clear, calm night?

"There was nothing we could do except watch the instruments and keep testing; I'll show you all the graphs when we get to the office. After four minutes everything went open circuit. We can locate the break exactly, of course—and it's in the deepest part, right at the grid. It *would* be there, and not at *this* end of the system," he added gloomily, pointing out the window.

We were just driving past the Solar Pond—the equivalent of the boiler in a conventional heat engine. This was an idea that the Russians had borrowed from the Israelis. It was simply a shallow lake, blackened at the bottom, holding a concentrated solution of brine. It acts as a very efficient heat trap, and the sun's rays bring the liquid up to almost two hundred degrees Fahrenheit. Submerged in it were the "hot" grids of the thermoelectric system, every inch of two fathoms down. Massive cables connected them to my department, a hundred and fifty degrees colder and three thousand feet lower, in the undersea canyon that comes to the very entrance of Trinco harbour.

"I suppose you checked for earthquakes?" I asked, not very hopefully.

"Of course. There was nothing on the seismograph."

"What about whales? I warned you that they might give trouble."

More than a year ago, when the main conductors were being run out to sea, I'd told the engineers about the drowned sperm whale found entangled in a telegraph cable half a mile down off South America. About a dozen similar cases are known—but ours, it seemed, was not one of them.

"That was the second thing we thought of," answered Shapiro. "We got on to the Fisheries Department, the Navy, and the Air Force. No whales anywhere along the coast."

It was at that point that I stopped theorizing, because I overheard something that made me a little uncomfortable. Like all Swiss, I'm good at languages, and have picked up a fair amount of Russian. There was no need to be much of a linguist, however, to recognize the word *sabotash*.

It was spoken by Dimitri Karpukhin, the political adviser on the project. I didn't like him; nor did the engineers, who sometimes went out of their way to be rude to him. One of the old-style Communists who had never quite escaped from the shadow of Stalin, he was suspicious of everything outside the Soviet Union, and most of the things inside it. Sabotage was just the explanation that would appeal to him.

There were, of course, a great many people who would not exactly be brokenhearted if the Trinco Power Project failed. Politically, the prestige of the USSR was committed; economically, billions were involved, for if hydrothermal plants proved a success, they might compete with oil, coal, water power, and, especially, nuclear energy.

Yet I could not really believe in sabotage; after all, the Cold War was over. It was just possible that someone had made a clumsy attempt to grab a sample of the grid, but even this seemed unlikely. I could count on my fingers the number of people in the world who could tackle such a job—and half of them were on my payroll.

The underwater TV camera arrived that same evening, and by working all through the night we had cameras, monitors, and over a mile of coaxial cable loaded aboard a launch. As we pulled out of the harbor, I thought I saw a familiar figure standing on the jetty, but it was too far to be certain and I had other things on my mind.

If you must know, I am not a good sailor; I am only really happy *underneath* the sea.

We took a careful fix on the Round Island lighthouse and stationed ourselves directly above the grid. The self-propelled camera, looking like a midget bathyscape, went over the side; as we watched the monitors, we went with it in spirit.

The water was extremely clear, and extremely empty, but as we neared the bottom there were a few signs of life. A small shark came and stared at us. Then a pulsating blob of jelly went drifting by, followed by a thing like a big spider, with hundreds of hairy legs tangling and twisting together. At last the sloping canyon wall swam into view. We were right on target, for there were the thick cables running down into the depths, just as I had seen them when I made the final check of the installation six months ago.

I turned on the low-powered jets and let the camera drift down the power cables. They seemed in perfect condition, still firmly anchored by the pitons we had driven into the rock. It was not until I came to the grid itself that there was any sign of trouble.

Have you ever seen the radiator grille of a car after it's run into a lamppost? Well, one section of the grid looked very much like that. Something had battered it in, as if a madman had gone to work on it with a sledgehammer.

There were gasps of astonishment and anger from the people looking over my shoulder. I heard *sabotash* muttered again, and for the first time began to take it seriously. The only other explanation that made sense was a falling boulder, but the slopes of the canyon had been carefully checked against this very possibility.

Whatever the cause, the damaged grid had to be replaced. That could not be done until my lobster—all twenty tons of it—had been flown out from the Spezia dockyard where it was kept between jobs.

"Well," said Shapiro, when I had finished my visual inspection and photographed the sorry spectacle on the screen, "how long will it take?"

I refused to commit myself. The first thing I ever learned in the underwater business is that no job turns out as you expect. Cost and time estimates can never be firm because it's not until you're halfway through a contract that you know exactly what you're up against.

My private guess was three days. So I said: "If everything goes well, it shouldn't take more than a week."

Shapiro groaned. "Can't you do it quicker?"

"I won't tempt fate by making rash promises. Anyway, that still gives you two weeks before your deadline."

He had to be content with that, though he kept nagging at me all the way back into the harbor. When we got there, he had something else to think about.

"Morning, Joe," I said to the man who was still waiting patiently on the jetty. "I thought I recognized you on the way out. What are *you* doing here?"

"I was going to ask you the same question."

"You'd better speak to my boss. Chief Engineer Shapiro, meet Joe Watkins, science correspondent of *Time*."

Lev's response was not exactly cordial. Normally, there was nothing he liked better than talking to newsmen, who arrived at the rate of about one a week. Now, as the target date approached, they would be flying in from all directions. Including, of course, Russia. And at the present moment Tass would be just as unwelcome as *Time*.

It was amusing to see how Karpukhin took charge of the situation. From that moment, Joe had permanently attached to him as guide, philosopher, and drinking companion a smooth young public-relations type named Sergei Markov. Despite all Joe's efforts, the two were inseparable. In the middle of the afternoon, weary after a long conference in Shapiro's office, I caught up with them for a belated lunch at the government resthouse.

"What's going on here, Klaus?" Joe asked pathetically. "I smell trouble, but no one will admit anything."

I toyed with my curry, trying to separate the bits that were safe from those that would take off the top of my head.

"You can't expect me to discuss a client's affairs," I answered.

"You were talkative enough," Joe reminded me, "when you were doing the survey for the Gibraltar Dam."

"Well, yes," I admitted. "And I appreciate the write-up you gave me. But this time there are trade secrets involved. I'm—ah—making some last-minute adjustments to improve the efficiency of the system."

And that, of course, was the truth; for I was indeed hoping to raise the efficiency of the system from its present value of exactly zero.

"Hmm," said Joe sarcastically. "Thank you very much."

"Anyway," I said, trying to head him off, "what's *your* latest crackbrained theory?"

For a highly competent science writer, Joe has an odd liking for the bizarre and the improbable. Perhaps it's a form of escapism; I happen to know that he also writes science fiction, though this is a well-kept secret from his employers. He has a sneaking fondness for poltergeists and ESP and flying saucers, but lost continents are his real specialty.

"I *am* working on a couple of ideas," he admitted. "They cropped up when I was doing the research on this story."

"Go on," I said, not daring to look up from the analysis of my curry.

"The other day I came across a very old map—Ptolemy's, if you're interested—of Ceylon. It reminded me of another old map in my collection, and I turned it up. There was the same central mountain, the same arrangement of rivers flowing to the sea. But *this* was a map of Atlantis."

"Oh, no!" I groaned. "Last time we met, you convinced me that Atlantis was the western Mediterranean basin."

Joe gave his engaging grin.

"I could be wrong, couldn't I? Anyway, I've a much more striking piece of evidence. What's the old national name for Ceylon—and the modern Sinhalese one, for that matter?"

I thought for a second, then exclaimed: "Good Lord! Why Lanka, of course. Lanka—Atlantis." I rolled the names off my tongue.

"Precisely," said Joe. "But two clues, however striking, don't make a full-fledged theory; and that's as far as I've got at the moment."

"Too bad," I said, genuinely disappointed. "And your other project?"

"This will really make you sit up," Joe answered smugly. He reached into the battered briefcase he always carried and pulled out a bundle of papers.

"This happened only one hundred and eighty miles from here, and just over a century ago. The source of my information, you'll note, is about the best there is."

He handed me a photostat, and I saw that it was a page of the London *Times* for July 4, 1874. I started to read without much enthusiasm, for Joe was always producing bits of ancient newspapers, but my apathy did not last for long.

Briefly—I'd like to give the whole thing, but if you want more details your local library can dial you a facsimile in ten seconds—the clipping described how the one-hundred-and-fifty-ton schooner *Pearl* left Ceylon in early May 1874 and then fell becalmed in the Bay of Bengal. On May 10, just before nightfall, an enormous squid surfaced half a mile from the schooner, whose captain foolishly opened fire on it with his rifle.

The squid swam straight for the *Pearl*, grabbed the masts with its arms, and pulled the vessel over on her side. She sank within seconds, taking two of her crew with her. The others were rescued only by the lucky chance that the P. and O. steamer *Strathowen* was in sight and had witnessed the incident herself.

"Well," said Joe, when I'd read through it for the second time, "what do you think?"

"I don't believe in sea monsters."

"The London *Times*," Joe answered, "is not prone to sensational journalism. And giant squids exist, though the biggest *we* know about are feeble, flabby beasts and don't weigh more than a ton, even when they have arms forty feet long."

"So? An animal like that couldn't capsize a hundred-and-fifty-ton schooner."

"True—but there's a lot of evidence that the so-called *giant* squid is merely a large squid. There may be decapods in the sea that really are giants. Why, only a year after the *Pearl* incident, a sperm whale off the coast of Brazil was seen struggling inside gigantic coils which finally *dragged it down into the sea*. You'll find the incident described in the *Illustrated London News* for November 20, 1875. And then, of course, there's that chapter in *Moby-Dick*. . . ."

"What chapter?"

"Why, the one called 'Squid.' We know that Melville was a very careful observer—but here he really lets himself go. He describes a calm day when a great white mass rose out of the sea 'like a snow-slide, new slid from the hills.' And this happened here in the Indian Ocean, perhaps a thousand miles south of the *Pearl* incident. Weather conditions were identical, please note.

"What the men of the *Pequod* saw floating on the water—I know this passage by heart, I've studied it so carefully—was a 'vast pulpy mass, furlongs in length and breadth, of a glancing cream-color, innumerable long arms radiating from its center, curling and twisting like a nest of anacondas.'"

"Just a minute," said Sergei, who had been listening to all this with rapt attention. "What's a furlong?"

Joe looked slightly embarrassed.

"Actually, it's an eighth of a mile—six hundred and sixty feet." He raised his hand to stop our incredulous laughter. "Oh, I'm sure Melville didn't mean that *literally*. But here was a man who met sperm whales every day, groping for a unit of length to describe something a lot bigger. So he automatically jumped from fathoms to furlongs. That's my theory, anyway."

I pushed away the remaining untouchable portions of my curry.

"If you think you've scared me out of my job," I said, "you've failed miserably. But I promise you this—when I do meet a giant squid, I'll snip off a tentacle and bring it back as a souvenir."

Twenty-four hours later I was out there in the lobster, sinking slowly down toward the damaged grid. There was no way in which the operation could be kept secret, and Joe was an interested spectator from a nearby launch. That was the Russians' problem, not mine; I had suggested to Shapiro that they take him into their confidence, but this, of course, was vetoed by Karpukhin's suspicious Slavic mind. One could almost see him thinking: Just *why* should an American reporter turn up at this moment? And ignoring the obvious answer that Trincomalee was now big news.

There is nothing in the least exciting or glamorous about deep-water operations—if they're done properly. Excitement means lack of foresight, and that means incompetence. The incompetent do not last long in my business, nor do those who crave excitement. I went about my job with all the pent-up emotion of a plumber dealing with a leaking faucet.

The grids had been designed for easy maintenance, since sooner or later they would have to be replaced. Luckily, none of the threads had been damaged, and the securing nuts came off easily when gripped with the power wrench. Then I switched control to the heavy-duty claws, and lifted out the damaged grid without the slightest difficulty.

It's bad tactics to hurry an underwater operation. If you try to do too much at once, you are liable to make mistakes. And if things go smoothly and you finish in a day a job you said would take a week, the client feels he hasn't had his money's worth. Though I was sure I could replace the grid that same afternoon, I followed the damaged unit up to the surface and closed shop for the day.

The thermoelement was rushed off for an autopsy, and I spent the rest of the evening hiding from Joe. Trinco is a small town, but I managed to keep out of his way by visiting the local cinema, where I sat through several hours of an interminable Tamil movie in which three successive generations suffered identical domestic crises of mistaken identity, drunkenness, desertion, death, and insanity, all in Technicolor and with the sound track turned full up.

The next morning, despite a mild headache, I was at the site soon after dawn. (So was Joe, and so was Sergei, all set for a quiet day's fishing.) I cheerfully waved to them as I climbed into the lobster, and the tender's crane lowered me over the side. Over the other side, where Joe couldn't see it, went the replacement grid. A few fathoms down I lifted it out of the hoist and carried it to the bottom of Trinco Deep, where, without any trouble, it was installed by the middle of the afternoon. Before I surfaced again, the lock nuts had been secured, the conductors spot-welded, and the engineers on shore had completed their continuity tests. By the time I was back on deck, the system was under load once more, everything was back to normal, and even Karpukhin was smiling—except when he stopped to ask himself the question that no one had yet been able to answer.

I still clung to the falling-boulder theory—for want of a better. And I hoped that the Russians would accept it, so that we could stop this silly cloak-and-dagger business with Joe.

No such luck, I realized, when both Shapiro and Karpukhin came to see me with very long faces.

"Klaus," said Lev, "we want you to go down again."

"It's your money," I replied. "But what do you want me to do?"

"We've examined the damaged grid, and there's a section of the thermoelement missing. Dimitri thinks that—someone—has deliberately broken it off and carried it away."

"Then they did a damn clumsy job," I answered. "I can promise you it wasn't one of *my* men."

It was risky to make such jokes around Karpukhin, and no one was at all amused. Not even me; for by this time I was beginning to think that he had something.

The sun was setting when I began my last dive into Trinco Deep, but the end of day has no meaning down there. I fell for two thousand feet with no lights, because I like to watch the luminous creatures of the sea, as they flash and flicker in the darkness, sometimes exploding like rockets just outside the observation window. In this open water, there was no danger of a collision; in any case, I had the panoramic sonar scan running, and that gave far better warning than my eyes.

At four hundred fathoms, I knew that something was wrong. The bottom was coming into view on the vertical sounder—but it was approaching much too slowly. My rate of descent was far too slow. I could increase it easily enough by flooding another buoyancy tank—but I hesitated to do so. In my business, anything out of the ordinary needs an explanation; three times I have saved my life by waiting until I had one.

The thermometer gave me the answer. The temperature outside was five degrees higher than it should have been, and I am sorry to say that it took me several seconds to realize why.

Only a few hundred feet below me, the repaired grid was now running at full power, pouring out megawatts of heat as it tried to equalize the temperature difference between Trinco Deep and the Solar Pond up there on land. It wouldn't succeed, of course; but in the attempt it was generating electricity—and I was being swept upward in the geyser of warm water that was an incidental by-product.

When I finally reached the grid, it was quite difficult to keep the lobster in position against the upwelling current, and I began to sweat uncomfortably as the heat penetrated into the cabin. Being too hot on the sea bed was a novel experience; so also was the miragelike vision caused by the ascending water, which made my searchlights dance and tremble over the rock face I was exploring.

You must picture me, lights ablaze in that five-hundred-fathom darkness, moving slowly down the slope of the canyon, which at this spot was about as steep as the roof of a house. The missing element—*if* it was still around—could not have fallen very far before coming to rest. I would find it in ten minutes, or not at all.

After an hour's searching, I had turned up several broken light bulbs (it's astonishing how many get thrown overboard from ships—the sea beds of the world are covered with them), an empty beer bottle (same comment), and a brand-new boot. That was the last thing I found, for then I discovered that I was no longer alone.

I never switch off the sonar scan, and even when I'm not moving I always glance at the screen about once a minute to check the general situation. The situation now was that a large object—at least the size of the lobster—was approaching from the north. When I spotted it, the range was about five hundred feet and closing slowly. I switched off my lights, cut the jets I had been running at low power to hold me in the turbulent water, and drifted with the current.

Though I was tempted to call Shapiro and report that I had company, I decided to wait for more information. There were only three nations with depth ships that could operate at this level, and I was on excellent terms with all of them. It would never do to be too hasty, and to get myself involved in unnecessary political complications.

Though I felt blind without the sonar, I did not wish to advertise my presence, so I reluctantly switched it off and relied on my eyes. Anyone working at this depth would have to use lights, and I'd see them coming long before they could see me. So I waited in the hot, silent little cabin, straining my eyes into the darkness, tense and alert but not particularly worried.

First there was a dim glow, at an indefinite distance. It grew bigger and brighter, yet refused to shape itself into any pattern that my mind could recognize. The diffuse glow concentrated into myriad spots, until it seemed that a constellation was sailing toward me. Thus might the rising star clouds of the galaxy appear, from some world close to the heart of the Milky Way.

It is not true that men are frightened of the unknown; they can be frightened only of the known, the already experienced. I could not imagine what was approaching, but no creature of the sea could touch me inside six inches of good Swiss armor plate.

The thing was almost upon me, glowing with the light of its own creation, when it split into two separate clouds. Slowly they came into focus—not of my eyes, but of my understanding—and I knew that beauty and terror were rising toward me out of the abyss.

The terror came first, when I saw that the approaching beasts were squids, and all Joe's tales reverberated in my brain. Then, with a considerable sense of letdown, I realized that they were only about twenty feet long—little larger than the lobster, and a mere fraction of its weight. They could do me no harm. And quite apart from that, their indescribable beauty robbed them of all menace.

This sounds ridiculous, but it is true. In my travels I have seen most of the animals of this world, but none to match the luminous apparitions floating before me now. The colored lights that pulsed and danced along their bodies made them seem clothed with jewels, never the same for two seconds at a time. There were patches that glowed a brilliant blue, like flickering mercury arcs, then changed almost instantly to burning neon red. The tentacles seemed strings of luminous beads, trailing through the water—or the lamps along a superhighway, when you look down upon it from the air at night. Barely visible against this background glow were the enormous eyes, uncannily human and intelligent, each surrounded by a diadem of shining pearls.

I am sorry, but that is the best I can do. Only the movie camera could do justice to these living kaleidoscopes. I do not know how long I watched them, so entranced by their luminous beauty that I had almost forgotten my mission. That those delicate, whiplash tentacles could not possibly have broken the grid was already obvious. Yet the presence of these creatures here was, to say the least, very curious. Karpukhin would have called it suspicious.

I was about to call the surface when I saw something incredible. It had been before my eyes all the time, but I had not realized it until now.

The squids were talking to each other.

Those glowing, evanescent patterns were not coming and going at random. They were as meaningful, I was suddenly sure, as the illuminated signs of Broadway or Piccadilly. Every few seconds there was an image that almost made sense, but it vanished before I could interpret it. I knew, of course, that even the common octopus shows its emotions with lightning-fast color changes—but this was something of a much higher order. It was real communication: here were two living electric signs, flashing messages to one another.

When I saw an unmistakable picture of the lobster, my last doubts vanished. Though I am no scientist, at that moment I shared the feelings of a Newton or an Einstein at some moment of revelation. *This* would make me famous. . . .

Then the picture changed—in a most curious manner. There was the lobster again, but rather smaller. And there beside it, much smaller still, were two peculiar objects. Each consisted of a pair of black dots surrounded by a pattern of ten radiating lines.

Just now I said that we Swiss are good at languages. However, it required little intelligence to deduce that this was a formalized squid's-eye view of itself, and that what I was seeing was a crude sketch of the situation. But why the absurdly small size of the squids?

I had no time to puzzle that out before there was another change. A third squid symbol appeared on the living screen—and this one was enormous, completely dwarfing the others. The message shone there in the eternal night for a few seconds. Then the creature bearing it shot off at incredible speed, and left me alone with its companion.

Now the meaning was all too obvious. "My God!" I said to myself. "They feel they can't handle me. They've gone to fetch Big Brother."

And of Big Brother's capabilities, I already had better evidence than Joe Watkins, for all his research and newspaper clippings.

That was the point—you won't be surprised to hear—when I decided not to linger. But before I went, I thought I would try some talking myself.

After hanging here in darkness for so long, I had forgotten the power of my lights. They hurt my eyes, and must have been agonizing to the unfortunate squid. Transfixed by that intolerable glare, its own illumination utterly quenched, it lost all its beauty, becoming no more than a pallid bag of jelly with two black buttons for eyes. For a moment it seemed paralyzed by the shock; then it darted after its companion, while I soared upward to a world that could never be the same again.

"I've found your saboteur," I told Karpukhin, when they opened the hatch of the lobster. "If you want to know all about him, ask Joe Watkins."

I let Dimitri sweat over that for a few seconds, while I enjoyed his expression. Then I gave my slightly edited report. I implied— without actually saying so—that the squids I'd met were powerful enough to have done all the damage: and I said nothing about the conversation I'd overseen. That would only cause incredulity. Besides, I wanted time to think matters over, and to tidy up the loose ends— if I could.

Joe has been a great help, though he still knows no more than the Russians. He's told me what wonderfully developed nervous systems squids possess, and has explained how some of them can change their appearance in a flash through instantaneous three-color printing, thanks to the extraordinary network of "chromophores" covering their bodies. Presumably this evolved for camouflage; but it seems natural— even inevitable—that it should develop into a communication system.

But there's one thing that worries Joe.

"What were they *doing* around the grid?" he keeps asking me plaintively. "They're cold-blooded invertebrates. You'd expect them to dislike heat as much as they object to light."

That puzzles Joe; but it doesn't puzzle me. Indeed, I think it's the key to the whole mystery.

Those squids, I'm now certain, are in Trinco Deep for the same reason that there are men at the South Pole—or on the Moon. Pure scientific curiosity has drawn them from their icy home, to investigate this geyser of hot water welling from the sides of the canyon. Here is a strange and inexplicable phenomenon—possibly one that menaces their way of life. So they have summoned their giant cousin (servant? slave!) to bring them a sample for study. I cannot believe that they have a hope of understanding it; after all, no scientist on earth could have done so as little as a century ago. But they are trying; and that is what matters.

Tomorrow, we begin our countermeasures. I go back into Trinco Deep to fix the great lights that Shapiro hopes will keep the squids at bay. But how long will that ruse work, if intelligence is dawning in the deep?

As I dictate this, I'm sitting here below the ancient battlements of Fort Frederick, watching the Moon come up over the Indian Ocean. If everything goes well, this will serve as the opening of the book that Joe has been badgering me to write. If it doesn't—then hello, Joe, I'm talking to *you* now. Please edit this for publication, in any way you think fit, and my apologies to you and Lev for not giving you all the facts before. Now you'll understand why.

Whatever happens, please remember this: they are beautiful, wonderful creatures; try to come to terms with them if you can.

To: Ministry of Power, Moscow
From: Lev Shapiro, Chief Engineer, Trincomalee Thermoelectric Power Project

Herewith the complete transcript of the tape recording found among Herr Klaus Muller's effects after his last dive. We are much indebted to Mr. Joe Watkins, of *Time*, for assistance on several points.

You will recall that Herr Muller's last intelligible message was directed to Mr. Watkins and ran as follows: "Joe! You were right about Melville! The thing is absolutely gigan—"

All About Strange
Monsters of the Recent Past

INTRODUCTION

Speaking of giant monster movies . . . suppose they all came true and happened at once. Would mankind stand a chance? Would human bravery and ingenuity save the day? Are you *kidding?*

From this cheerfully apocalyptic yarn, it's obvious that Howard Waldrop has seen nearly every movie monster that stalked, stomped, slithered, or oozed across the silver screen in the 1950s. Having also at the time seen nearly every movie monster that etc., etc., I can state this with confidence. True, I didn't notice a walk-on by the Killer Shrews, but I might have blinked. And there were a few sly references which I couldn't nail down. Identifying all the movies referenced (not all of them with giant monsters) would be an interesting exercise for the reader, or for an academic type, though in the latter case the number of footnotes would probably triple the length of the text. The tale begins with the title character from one of the worst monster flicks from the 1950s, and ends with the overgrown things from one of the first and best of the breed.

❖ ❖ ❖

Howard Waldrop was born in Mississippi, but has spent much of his life in Texas, where he currently resides. His novelet, "The Ugly Chickens," won both the Nebula Award and the World Fantasy

Award. Most of his output consists of short stories, written in a very individual style around striking ideas. His collections of short stories include *Howard Who?*, *All About Strange Monsters of the Recent Past*, *Night of the Cooters*, *Going Home Again*, and the recent *Horse of a Different Color*. That last one's still in print, so order it quick before you have to pay collector's prices —not that it wouldn't still be worth it.

All About Strange Monsters of the Recent Past

by Howard Waldrop

It's all over for humanity, and I'm heading east.

On the seat beside me are an M1 carbine and a Thompson submachine gun. There's a special reason for the Thompson. I traded an M16 and 200 rounds of ammo for it to a guy in Barstow. He got the worst of the deal. When things get rough, carbine and .45 ammo are easier to find than the 5.56mm rounds the M16 uses. I've got more ammo for the carbine than I need, though I've had plenty of chances to use it.

There are fifty gallons of gasoline in the car, in cans. I have food for six days. (I don't know if that many are left.)

When things really fell apart, I deserted. Like anyone else with sense. When there were more of them than we could stop. I don't know what they'll do when they run out of people. Start killing each other, maybe.

Meanwhile, I'm driving 160 kph out Route 66. I have an appointment in the desert of New Mexico.

God. Japan must have gone first. They deluged the world with them; now, it's Japan's turn. You sow what you reap.

We were all a little in love with death and the atom bomb back in the 1950s. It won't do us much good now.

The road is flat ahead. I've promised myself I'll see Meteor Crater before I die. So many of them opened at Meteor Crater, largest of the astroblemes. How fitting I should go there now.

In the back seat with the ammo is a twenty-kilo bag of sugar.

It started just like the movies did. Small strangenesses in small towns, disappearances in the back woods and lonely places, tremors in the Arctic, stirrings in the jungles.

We never thought when we saw them as kids what they would someday mean. The movies. The ones with the giant lizards, grasshoppers, molluscs. We yelled when the monsters started to get theirs. We cheered when the Army arrived to fight them. We yelled for all those movies. Now they've come to eat us up.

And nobody's cheered the Army since 1965. In 1978, the Army couldn't stop the monsters.

I was in that Army. I still am, if one's left. I was one of the last draftees, with the last bunch inducted. At the Entrance Station, I copped and took three years for a guaranteed job.

I would be getting out in three months if it weren't for this.

I left my uniform under a bush as soon as I decided to get away. I'd worn it for two and a half years. Most of the Army got torn away in the first days of the fight with the monsters. I decided to go.

So I went. East.

I saw one of the giant Gila monsters this morning. There had been a car ahead of me, keeping about three kilometers between us, not letting me catch up. Maybe a family, figuring I was going to rob them or rape the women. Maybe not. It was the first car I'd seen in eighteen hours of dodging along the back roads. The car went around a turn. It looked like it slowed. I eased down, too, thinking maybe it wasn't a family but a bunch of dudes finally deciding to ambush me. Good thing I slowed.

I came around the turn and all I could see was the side of an orange and black mountain. I slammed on the brakes and skidded sideways. The Gila monster had knocked the other car off the road and was coming for me. I was shaken, but I hadn't come this far to be eaten by a lizard. Oh, no. I threw the snout of the M1 carbine out the window and blasted away at the thing's eyes. Scales flew like rain. It twitched away then started back for me. I shot it in the tongue. It went into convulsions and crawled over a small sandhill hissing and honking like a freight train. It would come back later to eat whatever was in the other car. I trundled back on the road and drove past the wreck. Nothing moved. A pool of oil was forming on the concrete. I drove down the road with the smell of cordite in my nose and the wind whipping past. There was gila monster blood on the hood of the car.

I had been a clerk in an airborne unit deployed to get the giant locusts eating up the Midwest. It is the strangest time in the history of the United States. The nights are full of meteors and lights.

At first, we thought it was a practice alert. We suited up, climbed into the C-130s with full combat gear, T-10 parachutes, lurp bags and all. At least the others had chutes. I wasn't on jump status so I went in with the heavy equipment to the nearest airbase. A lot of my buddies jumped into Illinois. I never saw them again. By the times the planes landed, the whole brigade was gone.

We landed at Chanute. By then, the plague of monsters was so bad I ended up on the airbase perimeter with the Air Policemen. We fired at the things until the barrels of the machine guns moaned with heat. The locusts kept coming, squirting brown juice when they were hit or while killing someone.

Their mandibles work all the time.

We broke and ran after a while. I caught a C-130 revving up. The field was a moving carpet of locusts as I looked behind me. They could be killed easily, as easily as could any insect with a soft abdomen. But there were so many of them. You killed and killed and they kept coming. And dying. So you had to run. We roared off the runway while they scuttled across the airfield below. Some took to the air on their rotor-sized wings. One smashed against the Hercules, tearing off part of an elevator. We flew on through a night full of meteors. A light paced us for a while but broke off and flew after a fighter plane.

We couldn't land back at Pope AFB. It was a shambles. A survivor said the saucers hit about midnight. A meteor had landed near Charlotte, and now the Martian fighting machines were drifting toward Washington, killing everything in their paths.

We roared back across country, looking for some place to land where we wouldn't be gobbled up. Fuel got lower. We came in on a wing, a prayer and fumes to Fitzee Field at Fort Ord. I had taken basic training at Ord.

A few hours later, I duffed.

I heard about New York on the radio before the stations went off. A giant lizard had come up from the Hudson submarine canyon and destroyed Manhattan. A giant octopus was ravaging San Francisco, a hundred miles north of Ord. It had already destroyed the Golden Gate Bridge. Saucers were landing everywhere. One had crashed into a sandpit behind a house nearby. A basic training unit had been sent in. They wouldn't be back, I knew. A glass-globed intelligence would see to that.

Navy ships were pulled under by the monsters that pillaged New York, by the giant octopus, by giant crabs in the South Pacific; by caterpillar-like molluscs in the Salton Sea.

The kinds of invaders seemed endless: Martian fighting machines, four or five types of aliens. The sandpit Martians, much different from the fighting machine kind. Bigheaded invaders with eyes on the backs of their hands.

A few scattered reports worldwide. No broadcasts from Japan after the first few minutes. Total annihilation, no doubt. Italy: a craft, which only existed on celluloid, brings back from Venus an egg of death. Mexico: a tyrannosaurus rex comes from the swamps for cattle and children. A giant scorpion invades from the volcanoes. South America: giant wasps, fungus disease, terrors from the earth. Britain: a monster slithers wild in Westminster Abbey, another fungus from space, radioactive mud, giant lizards again. Tibet: the yeti are on the move.

It is all over for humanity.

❖ ❖ ❖

Meteor Crater at sunset. A hole punched in the earth while ice sheets still covered Wyoming and Pennsylvania.

I can see for miles, and I have the carbine ready. I stare into the crater, thinking. This crater saw the last mammoth and the first of the Indians.

The shadow deepens and the floor goes dark. Memories of man, crater. Your friend the Grand Canyon regards you as an upstart in time. It's jealous because you came from space.

Speaking of mammoths, perhaps it's our time to join old woolly in the great land of fossil dreams. Whatever plows farms in a million years can turn up our teeth and wonder at them.

Nobody knows why the mammoth disappeared, or the dinosaur, or our salamander friend the Diplovertebron, for that matter. Racial old age. No plausible reason. So now it's our turn. Done in by our own dreams from the silver screen. Maybe we've created our own Id monsters, come to snuffle us out in nightmares.

The reason I deserted: the Air Force was going to drop an A-bomb on the Martian fighting machines. They were heading for Ord after they finished L.A. I was at the command post when one of the last B-52s went over, heading for the faraway carnage on the horizon.

"If the A-bomb doesn't stop it, Colonel," said a major to the commander, "nothing will."

How soon they forget, I thought, and headed for the perimeter.

The Great Southwest saw more scenes of monster destruction than anywhere in the world except Japan. Film producers loved it for the sterility of the desert, the hot sun, the contrasts with no gradations for their black and white cameras. In them, saucers landed, meteors hurtled down, townspeople disappeared, tracks and bones were found.

Here is where it started, was the reasoning. In the desert thirty-three years ago when the first atomic bomb was detonated, when sand was turned to glass.

So the monsters shambled, plodded, pillaged and shook the Southwest. This desert where once there was only a shallow sea. You can find clamshells atop the Sierras, if you look.

I have an appointment here, near Alamogordo. Where it started. The racial old age is on us now. Unexplained, and we'll die not knowing why, or why we lived the least time of all the dominant species on this planet.

One question keeps coming to me. Why only films of the 1950s?

Am I the only one who remembers? Have I been left alone because I'm the only one who remembers and knows what I'm doing? Am I the only one with a purpose, not just running around like a chicken with its head cut off?

The radio stations are going off one by one as I drive from the crater to Alamogordo. Emergency broadcast stations, something out of Arkansas, an Ohio station. Tonight, I'm not going to be stopped. I've got the 30-round magazine in the carbine and the 45-round drum in the Thompson. I wish I had some grenades, or even tear gas, but I have no mask (I lost it in the battle against the grasshoppers). Besides, I'm not sure tear gas will be effective for what I have in mind.

On the dying radio stations and in my mind's eye, this is what I see and hear.

The locusts reach Chicago and feast till dawn, while metal robots roam the streets looking for men to kill.

The giant lizard goes past Coney Island with no resistance.

The huge mantis, after pillaging the Arctic, reduces Washington to shambles. It has to dodge flying saucers while it pulls apart monuments, looking for goodies. The statue of Abraham Lincoln looks toward Betelgeuse and realizes that the War Between the States *was* fought in vain.

The sky is filled with meteors, saucers, a giant flying bird. Two new points of light hang in the sky: a dead star and a planet which will crash into earth in a few days. The night is beginning to be bathed in a dim bloody light.

An amorphous thing sludges its way through a movie theater, alternately flattening, thickening, devouring anything left.

The Martian fighting machines have gone up and down both coasts, moving in a crescent pivotal motion.

The octopus has been driven underwater by heat from the burning San Francisco.

So much for the rest of the country.

Here in the Southwest, a million-eyed monster has taken over the cattle and dogs for hundreds of miles.

A giant spider eats cattle and people and grows. The last Air Force fighters have given up and are looking for a place to land. Maybe one or two pilots, like me, will get away. Maybe saucers will get them. It won't be long now.

The Gila monsters roam, tongues moving, seeking the heat of people, cars, dogs.

Beings with a broken spaceship are repairing it, taking over the bodies of those not eaten by other monsters. Soon they will be back up in the sky. Benevolent monsters.

Giant columns of stone grow, break, fall, crushing all in their paths. Miles wide now, and moving toward the Colorado River, the Gulf and infinite growing bliss. No doubt they have crushed giant Gila monsters and spiders along with people, towns, and mountains.

A stranded spaceman makes it to Palomar and spends his last seconds turning the telescope toward his home star. He has already killed nineteen people in his effort to communicate.

A monster grows, feeding on the atoms of the air.

A robot cuts its way through a government installation fence, off on its own path of rampage. The two MPs fire until their 45s click dry. Bullets ricochet off the metal being. Soon a saucer will fly over and hover. They will fire at the saucer with no effect; the saucer will fire and the MPs will drift away on the wind.

(There may be none of our bones to dig up in a million years.)

All this as I drive toward the dawn, racing at me and the Southwest like the avenging eye of God. No headlights. I saw a large meteor hit back in the direction of Flagstaff; there'll be hell to pay there soon. Meanwhile, I haven't slept in two days. The car sometimes swerves toward the road edge. No time for a crack-up, so close now.

The last radio station went off at 0417.

Nothing on the dial but mother earth's own radio music, and perhaps stellar noises that left somewhere 500 million years ago, about the time our friend the Diplovertebron slithered through the mud. The east is greying. I'm almost there.

The car motor pops and groans as it cools. The wind blows steadily toward the deeper desert. Not far from here, the first A-bomb went off. Perhaps that was the challenge to the universe, and it waited thirty years to get back at us. This is where it started.

This is where it ends.

I'm drinking a hot Coke. It tastes better than any I've ever had. No uppers, downers, hash, horse or grass for me. I'm on a natural high.

I've set my things in order. All the empty bottles are filled with gasoline and the blanket's been torn up for fuses. My lighter and matches are laid out, with some cigarettes for punks. With the carbine slung over my shoulder, I wait with the Thompson in my right hand, round chambered, selector on rock and roll.

They won't die easy, but I envision a stack of them ringing my body, my bones, the car; some scorched and blackened, some shot all away, some with mandibles still working long after I'm dead.

I open the twenty-kilo bag of sugar and shake it onto the wind. It sifts into a pile a few feet away. The scent should carry right to them.

I took basic at Fort Ord. There was a tunnel we had to double-time through to get to the range. In cadence. Weird shadows on the wall as we ran. No matter how tired I was, I thought of the soldiers going into the storm drains after the giant ants in a movie I'd seen when I was six. They started here, near the first A-blast. They had to be here. The sugar would bring them.

A sound floats back up the wind like the keening of an off-angle buzz saw. Ah, they're coming. They'll be here soon, first one, then many. Maybe the whole nest will turn out. They'll rise from behind that dune, or maybe that one.

Closer now, still not in sight.

It's all over for man, but there are still some things left. Like choices, there's still that. A choice of personal monsters.

Closer now, and more sounds. Maybe ten or twenty of them. Maybe more.

End of movie soon. No chance to be James Arness and get the girl. But plenty of time to be the best James Whitmore ever. No kids to throw to safety. But a Thompson and a carbine. And Molotov cocktails.

Aha. An antenna waves in the middle distance. And—

Bigger than I thought. Take your head right off.

Eat leaden death, Hymenopterae! The Thompson blasts to life.

Screams of confusion. A flash of 100 octane and glass. High keening like an off-angle buzz saw.

I laugh. Formic acid. Cordite.

Hell of a life.

The Monster-God of Mamurth

INTRODUCTION

Weird Tales was one of the most beloved of the pulp magazines, though unfortunately not beloved by large enough numbers of readers for it ever to be successful. Still, during its initial run from 1923 to 1954 (it's been revised several times since), it published the works of now-legendary writers, such as H. P. Lovecraft, Robert E. Howard, Ray Bradbury and Edmond Hamilton. In fact, *WT* published Hamilton's first story in its August 1926 issue. That story of an explorer seeking a lost city whose vanished inhabitants worshipped a hideous gigantic creature was an auspicious debut, and still packs a wallop, which is why I included it here. Of course, the explorer was sure that "The Monster-God of Mamurth" had never actually existed. And, even if it had existed centuries ago, it surely couldn't *still* be alive . . .

❖ ❖ ❖

Edmond Hamilton (1904-1977) was one of the most prolific contributors to *Weird Tales*, which published 79 of his stories between 1926 and 1948. Unusually for a *WT* mainstay, most of his work was science fiction (or, as the magazine tagged it initially, "weird-scientific") rather than fantasy. He was also prolific outside the pages of *WT*, with stories in many other pulps, sometimes under pseudonyms. In the late 1940s, as interest in adventure SF waned, Hamilton developed a more serious style, with deeper characterizations, notably in his 1952 short story, "What's It Like Out There?" and his 1960 novel, *The Haunted*

Stars. During the 1950s, he was also a prolific writer for such D.C. comic books as *The Legion of Super-Heroes.* He continued writing into the 1970s, with stories in the SF magazines and new novels in paperback. He was a writer's writer, with a gift for tales of adventure. Some critics may have felt that such tales were insignificant, but that is their loss. Readers should be grateful for such a good and prolific writer.

The Monster-God of Mamurth

by Edmond Hamilton

Out of the desert night he came to us, stumbling into our little circle of firelight and collapsing at once. Mitchell and I sprang to our feet with startled exclamations, for men who travel alone and on foot are a strange sight in the deserts of North Africa.

For the first few minutes that we worked over him, I thought he would die at once, but gradually we brought him back to consciousness. While Mitchell held a cup of water to his cracked lips, I looked him over and saw that he was too far gone to live much longer. His clothes were in rags, and his hands and knees literally flayed, from crawling over the sands, I judged. So when he motioned feebly for more water, I gave it to him, knowing that in any case his time was short. Soon he could talk, in a dead, croaking voice.

"I'm alone," he told us, in answer to our first question; "no more out there to look for. What are you two—traders? I thought so. No, I'm an archeologist. A digger-up of the past." His voice broke for a moment. "It's not always good to dig up dead secrets. There are some things the past should be allowed to hide."

He caught the look that passed between Mitchell and me.

"No, I'm not mad," he said. "You will hear, I'll tell you the whole thing. But listen to me, you two," and in his earnestness he raised himself to a sitting position, "keep out of Igidi Desert. Remember

41

that I told you that. I had a warning, too, but I disregarded it. And I went into hell—into hell! But there, I will tell you from the beginning.

"My name—that doesn't matter now. I left Mogador more than a year ago, and came through the foot-hills of the Atlas ranges, striking out into the desert in hopes of finding some of the Carthaginian ruins the North African deserts are known to hold.

"I spent months in the search, traveling among the squalid Arab villages, now near an oasis and now far into the black, untracked desert. And as I went farther into that savage country, I found more and more of the ruins I sought, crumbled remnants of temples and fortresses, relics, almost destroyed, of the age when Carthage meant empire and ruled all of North Africa from her walled city. And then, on the side of a massive block of stone, I found that which turned me toward Igidi.

"It was an inscription in the garbled Phenician of the traders of Carthage, short enough so that I remembered it and can repeat it word for word. It read, literally, as follows:

"Merchants, go not into the city of Mamurth, which lies beyond the mountain pass. For I, San-Drabat of Carthage, entering the city with four companions in the month of Eschmoun, to trade, on the third night of our stay came priests and seized my fellows, I escaping by hiding. My companions they sacrificed to the evil god of the city, who has dwelt there from the beginning of time, and for whom the wise men of Mamurth have built a great temple the like of which is not on Earth elsewhere, where the people of Mamurth worship their god. I escaped from the city and set this warning here that others may not turn their steps to Mamurth and to death.

"Perhaps you can imagine the effect that inscription had on me. It was the last trace of a city unknown to the memory of men, a last floating spar of a civilization sunken in the sea of time. That there could have been such a city at all seemed to me quite probable. What do we know of Carthage even, but a few names? No city, no civilization was ever so completely blotted off the Earth as Carthage, when Roman Scipio ground its temples and palaces into the very dust, and plowed up the ground with salt, and the eagles of conquering Rome flew across a desert where a metropolis had been.

"It was on the outskirts of one of those wretched little Arab villages that I had found the block and its inscription, and I tried to find someone in the village to accompany me, but none would do so. I could plainly see the mountain pass, a mere crack between towering blue cliffs. In reality it was miles and miles away, but the deceptive optical qualities of the desert light made it seem very near. My maps placed that mountain range all right, as a lower branch of the Atlas, and the expanse behind the mountains was marked as 'Igidi Desert,' but that was all I got from them. All that I could reckon on as certain was that it was desert that lay on the other side of the pass, and I must carry enough supplies to meet it.

"But the Arabs knew more! Though I offered what must have been fabulous riches to those poor devils, not one would come with me when I let them know what place I was heading for. None had ever been there, they would not even ride far into the desert in that direction; but all had very definite ideas of the place beyond the mountains as a nest of devils, a haunt of evil Jinns.

"Knowing how firmly superstition is implanted in their kind, I tried no longer to persuade them, and started alone, with two scrawny camels carrying my water and supplies. So for three days I forged across the desert under a broiling sun, and on the morning of the fourth I reached the pass.

"It was only a narrow crevice to begin with, and great boulders were strewn so thickly on its floor that it was a long, hard job getting through. And the cliffs on each side towered to such a height that the space between was a place of shadows and whispers and semi-darkness. It was late in the afternoon when I finally came through, and for a moment I stood motionless; for from that side of the pass the desert sloped down into a vast basin, and at the basin's center, perhaps two miles from where I stood, gleamed the white ruins of Mamurth.

"I remember that I was very calm as I covered the two miles between myself and the ruins. I had taken the existence of the city as a fact, so much so that if the ruins had not been there I should have been vastly more surprised than at finding them.

"From the pass I had seen only a tangled mass of white fragments, but as I drew nearer, some of these began to take outline as crumbling blocks, and walls, and columns. The sand had drifted, too, and the ruins were completely buried in some sections, while nearly all were half covered.

"And then it was that I made a curious discovery. I had stopped to examine the material of the ruins, a smooth, veinless stone, much like an artificial marble or a superfine concrete. And while I looked about me, intent on this, I noticed that on almost every shaft and block, on broken cornice and column, was carved the same symbol—if it was a symbol. It was a rough picture of a queer, outlandish creature, much like an octopus, with a round, almost shapeless body, and several long tentacles or arms branching out from the body, not supple and boneless, like those of an octopus, but seemingly stiff and jointed, like a spider's legs. In fact, the thing might have been intended to represent a spider, I thought, though some of the details were wrong. I speculated for a moment on the profusion of these creatures carved on the ruins all around me, then gave it up as an enigma that was unsolvable.

"And the riddle of the city about me seemed unsolvable also. What could I find in this half-buried mass of stone fragments to throw light on the past? I could not even superficially explore the place, for the scantiness of my supplies and water would not permit a long stay. It was with a discouraged heart that I went back to the camels and, leading them to an open spot in the ruins, made my camp for the night. And when night had fallen, and I sat beside my little fire, the vast, brooding silence of this place of death was awful. There were no laughing human voices, or cries of animals, or even cries of birds or insects. There was nothing but the darkness and silence that crowded around me, flowed down upon me, beat sullenly against the glowing spears of light my little fire threw out.

"As I sat there musing, I was startled by a slight sound behind me. I turned to see its cause, and then stiffened. As I have mentioned, the space directly around my camp was clear sand, smoothed level by the winds. Well, as I stared at that flat expanse of sand, a hole several inches across suddenly appeared in its surface, yards from where I stood, but clearly visible in the firelight.

"There was nothing whatever to be seen there, not even a shadow, but there it was, one moment the level surface of the sand, the next moment a hole appearing in it, accompanied by a soft, crunching sound. As I stood gazing at it in wonder, that sound was repeated, and simultaneously another hole appeared in the sand's surface, five or six feet nearer to me than the other.

"When I saw that, ice-tipped arrows of fear seemed to shoot through me, and then, yielding to a mad impulse, I snatched a blazing piece of fuel from the fire and hurled it, a comet of red flame, at the place where the holes had appeared. There was a slight sound of scurrying and shuffling, and I felt that whatever thing had made those marks had retreated, if a living thing had made them at all. What it had been, I could not imagine, for there had been absolutely nothing in sight, one track and then another appearing magically in the clear sand, if indeed they were really tracks at all.

"The mystery of the thing haunted me. Even in sleep I found no rest, for evil dreams seemed to flow into my brain from the dead city around me. All the dusty sins of ages past, in the forgotten place, seemed to be focused on me in the dreams I had. Strange shapes walked through them, unearthly as the spawn of a distant star, half seen and vanishing again.

"It was little enough sleep I got that night, but when the sun finally came, with its first golden rays, my fears and oppressions dropped from me like a cloak. No wonder the early peoples were sun-worshippers!

"And with my renewed strength and courage, a new thought struck me. In the inscription I have quoted to you, that long-dead merchant-adventurer had mentioned the great temple of the city and dwelt on its grandeur. Where, then, were its ruins? I wondered. I decided that what time I had would be better spent in investigating the ruins of this temple, which should be prominent, if that ancient Carthaginian had been correct as to its size.

❋ ❋ ❋

"I ascended a near-by hillock and looked about me in all directions, and though I could not perceive any vast pile of ruins that might have been the temple's, I did see for the first time, far away, two great figures of stone that stood out black against the rosy flame of the sunrise. It was a discovery that filled me with excitement, and I broke camp at once, starting in the direction of those two shapes.

"They were on the very edge of the farther side of the city, and it was noon before I finally stood before them. And now I saw clearly their nature: two great, sitting figures, carved of black stone, all of fifty feet in height, and almost that far apart, facing both toward the city and toward me. They were of human shape and dressed in a queer, scaled armor, but the faces I cannot describe, for they were unhuman. The features were human, well-proportioned, even, but the face, the expression, suggested no kinship whatever with humanity as we know it. Were they carved from life? I wondered. If so, it must have been a strange sort of people who had lived in this city and set up these two statues.

"And now I tore my gaze away from them, and looked around. On each side of those shapes, the remains of what must once have been a mighty wall branched out, a long pile of crumbling ruins. But there had been no wall between the statues, that being evidently the gateway through the barrier. I wondered why the two guardians of the gate had survived, apparently entirely unharmed, while the wall and the city behind me had fallen into ruins. They were of a different material, I could see; but what was that material?

"And now I noticed for the first time the long avenue that began on the other side of the statues and stretched away into the desert for a half-mile or more. The sides of this avenue were two rows of smaller stone figures that ran in parallel lines away from the two colossi. So I started down that avenue, passing between the two great shapes that stood at its head. And as I went between them, I noticed for the first time the inscription graven on the inner side of each.

"On the pedestal of each figure, four or five feet from the ground, was a raised tablet of the same material, perhaps a yard square, and covered with strange symbols—characters, no doubt, of a lost language, undecipherable, at least to me. One symbol, though, that was especially prominent in the inscription, was not new to me. It was the carven picture of the spider, or octopus, which I have mentioned that I had found everywhere on the ruins of the city. And here it was scattered thickly among the symbols that made up the inscription. The tablet on the other statue was a replica of the first, and I could learn no more from it. So I started down the avenue, turning over in my mind the riddle of that omnipresent symbol, and then forgetting it, as I observed the things about me.

"That long street was like the avenue of sphinxes at Karnak, down which Pharaoh swung in his litter, borne to his temple on the necks of men. But the statues that made up its sides were not sphinx shaped. They were carved in strange forms, shapes of animals unknown to us, as far removed from anything we can imagine as the beasts of another world. I cannot describe them, any more than you could describe a dragon to a man who had been blind all his life. Yet they were of evil, reptilian shapes; they tore at my nerves as I looked at them.

"Down between the two rows of them I went, until I came to the end of the avenue. Standing there between the last two figures, I could see nothing before me but the yellow sands of the desert, as far as the eye could reach. I was puzzled. What had been the object of all the pains that had been taken, the wall, the two great statues, and this long avenue, if it but led into the desert?

"Gradually I began to see that there was something queer about the part of the desert that lay directly before me. It was *flat*. For an area, seemingly round in shape, that must have covered several acres, the surface of the desert seemed absolutely level. It was as though the sands within that great circle had been packed down with tremendous force, leaving not even the littlest ridge of dune on its surface. Beyond this flat area, and all around it, the desert was broken up by small hills and valleys, and traversed by whirling sand-clouds, but nothing stirred on the flat surface of the circle.

"Interested at once, I strode forward to the edge of the circle, only a few yards away. I had just reached that edge when an invisible hand seemed to strike me a great blow on the face and chest, knocking me backward in the sand.

"It was minutes before I advanced again, but I did advance, for all my curiosity was now aroused. I crawled toward the circle's edge, holding my pistol before me, pushing slowly forward.

"When the automatic in my outstretched hand reached the line of the circle, it struck against something hard, and I could push it no farther. It was exactly as if it had struck against the side of a wall, but no wall or anything else was to be seen. Reaching out my hand, I touched the same hard barrier, and in a moment I was on my feet.

"For I knew now that it was solid matter I had run into, not force. When I thrust out my hands, the edge of the circle was as far as they would go, for there they met a smooth wall, totally invisible, yet at the same time quite material. And the phenomenon was one which even I could partly understand. Somehow, in the dead past, the scientists of the city behind me, the 'wise men' mentioned in the inscription, had discovered the secret of making solid matter invisible, and had applied it to the work that I was now examining. Such a thing was far from impossible. Even our own scientists can make matter partly invisible, with the X-ray. Evidently these people had known the whole process, a secret that had been lost in the succeeding ages, like the secret of hard gold, and malleable glass, and others that we find mentioned in ancient writings. Yet I wondered how they had done this, so that, ages after those who had built the thing were wind-driven dust, it remained as invisible as ever.

"I stood back and threw pebbles into the air, toward the circle. No matter how high I threw them, when they reached the line of the circle's edge they rebounded with a clicking sound; so I knew that the wall must tower to a great height above me. I was on fire to get inside the wall, and examine the place from the inside, but how to do it? There must be an entrance, but where? And I suddenly remembered the two guardian statues at the head of the great avenue, with their carven tablets, and wondered what connection they had with this place.

"Suddenly the strangeness of the whole thing struck me like a blow. The great, unseen wall before me, the circle of sand, flat and unchanging, and myself, standing there and wondering, wondering.

A voice from out the dead city behind me seemed to sound in my heart, bidding me to turn and flee, to get away. I remembered the warning of the inscription, 'Go not to Mamurth.' And as I thought of the inscription, I had no doubt that this was the great temple described by San-Drabat. Surely he was right: the like of it was not on Earth elsewhere.

"But I would not go, I could not go, until I had examined the wall from the inside. Calmly reasoning the matter, I decided that the logical place for the gateway through the wall would be at the end of the avenue, so that those who came down the street could pass directly through the wall. And my reasoning was good, for it was at that spot that I found the entrance: an opening in the barrier, several yards wide, and running higher than I could reach, how high I had no means of telling.

"I felt my way through the gate, and stepped at once upon a floor of hard material, not as smooth as the wall's surface, but equally invisible. Inside the entrance lay a corridor of equal width, leading into the center of the circle, and I felt my way forward.

"I must have made a strange picture, had there been any there to observe it. For while I knew that all around me were the towering, invisible walls, and I knew not what else, yet all my eyes could see was the great flat circle of sand beneath me, carpeted with the afternoon sunshine. Only, I seemed to be walking a foot above the ground, in thin air. That was the thickness of the floor beneath me, and it was the weight of this great floor, I knew, that held the circle of sand under it forever flat and unchanging.

"I walked slowly down the passageway, with hands outstretched before me, and had gone but a short distance when I brought up against another smooth wall that lay directly across the corridor, seemingly making it a blind alley. But I was not discouraged now, for I knew that there must be a door somewhere, and began to feel around me in search of it.

"I found the door. In groping about the sides of the corridor my hands encountered a smoothly rounded knob set in the wall, and as

I laid my hand on this, the door opened. There was a sighing, as of a little wind, and when I again felt my way forward, the wall that had lain across the passageway was gone, and I was free to go forward. But I dared not go through at once. I went back to the knob on the wall, and found that no amount of pressing or twisting of it would close the door that had opened. Some subtle mechanism within the knob had operated, that needed only a touch of the hand to work it, and the whole end of the corridor had moved out of the way, sliding up in grooves, I think, like a portcullis, though of this I am not sure.

"But the door was safely opened, and I passed through it. Moving about, like a blind man in a strange place, I found that I was in a vast inner court, the walls of which sloped away in a great curve. When I discovered this, I came back to the spot where the corridor opened into the court, and then walked straight out into the court itself.

"It was steps that I encountered: the first broad steps of what was evidently a staircase of titanic proportions. And I went up, slowly, carefully, feeling before me every foot of the way. It was only the feel of the staircase under me that gave reality to it, for as far as I could see, I was simply climbing up into empty space. It was weird beyond telling.

"Up and up I went, until I was all of a hundred feet above the ground, and then the staircase narrowed, the sides drew together. A few more steps, and I came out on a flat floor again, which, after some groping about, I found to be a broad landing, with high, railed edges. I crawled across this landing on hands and knees, and then struck against another wall, and in it, another door. I went through this too, still crawling, and though everything about me was still invisible, I sensed that I was no longer in the open air, but in a great room.

"I stopped short, and then, as I crouched on the floor, I felt a sudden prescience of evil, of some malignant, menacing entity that was native here. Nothing I could see, or hear, but strong upon my brain beat the thought of something infinitely ancient, infinitely evil, that was a part of this place. Was it a consciousness, I wonder, of the horror that had filled the place in ages long dead? Whatever caused it, I could go no farther in the face of the terror that possessed me; so

I drew back and walked to the edge of the landing, leaning over its high, invisible railing and surveying the scene below.

"The setting sun hung like a great ball of red-hot iron in the western sky, and in its lurid rays the two great statues cast long shadows on the yellow sands. Not far away, my two camels, hobbled, moved restlessly about. To all appearances I was standing on thin air, a hundred feet or more above the ground, but in my mind's eye I had a picture of the great courts and corridors below me, through which I had felt my way.

"As I mused there in the red light, it was clear to me that this was the great temple of the city. What a sight it must have been, in the time of the city's life! I could imagine the long procession of priests and people, in somber and gorgeous robes, coming out from the city, between the great statues and down the long avenue, dragging with them, perhaps, an unhappy prisoner to sacrifice to their god in this, his temple.

"The sun was now dipping beneath the horizon, and I turned to go, but before ever I moved, I became rigid and my heart seemed to stand still. For on the farther edge of the clear stretch of sand that lay beneath the temple and the city, a hole suddenly appeared in the sand, springing into being on the desert's face exactly like the one I had seen at my campfire the night before. I watched, as fascinated as by the eyes of a snake. And before my eyes, another and another appeared, not in a straight line, but in a zigzag fashion. Two such holes would be punched down on one side, then two more on the other side, then one in the middle, making a series of tracks, perhaps two yards in width from side to side, and advancing straight toward the temple and myself. And I could see nothing!

"It was like—the comparison suddenly struck me—like the tracks a many-legged insect might make in the sand, only magnified to unheard-of proportions. And with that thought, the truth rushed on me, for I remembered the spider carved on the ruins and on the statues, and I knew now what it had signified to the dwellers in the city. What was it the inscription had said? 'The evil god of the city, who has dwelt there from the beginning of time.' And as I saw those tracks advancing toward me, I knew that the city's ancient evil god still dwelt here, and that I was in his temple, alone and unarmed.

"What strange creatures might there not have been in the dawn of time? And this one, this gigantic monster in a spider's form—had not those who built the city found it here when they came, and, in awe, taken it as the city's god, and built for it the mighty temple in which I now stood? And they, who had the wisdom and art to make this vast fane invisible, not to be seen by human eyes, had they done the same to their god, and made of him almost a true god, invisible, powerful, undying? Undying! Almost it must have been, to survive the ages, as it had done. Yet I knew that even some kinds of parrots live for centuries, and what could I know of this monstrous relic of dead ages? And when the city died and crumbled, and the victims were no longer brought to its lair in the temple, did it not live, as I thought, by ranging the desert? No wonder the Arabs had feared the country in this direction! It would be death for anything that came even within view of such a horror, that could clutch and spring and chase, and yet remain always unseen. And was it death for me?

"Such were some of the thoughts that pounded through my brain, as I watched death approach, with those steadily advancing tracks in the sand. And now the paralysis of terror that had gripped me was broken, and I ran down the great staircase, and into the court. I could think of no place in that great hall where I might hide. Imagine hiding in a place where all is invisible! But I must go some place, and finally I dashed past the foot of the great staircase until I reached a wall directly under the landing on which I had stood, and against this I crouched, praying that the deepening shadows of dusk might hide me from the gaze of the creature whose lair this was.

"I knew instantly when the thing entered the gate through which I too had come. Pad, pad, pad—that was the soft, cushioned sound of its passage. I heard the feet stop for a moment by the opened door at the end of the corridor. Perhaps it was in surprise that the door was open, I thought, for how could I know how great or little intelligence lay in that unseen creature's brain? Then, pad, pad—across the court it came, and I heard the soft sound of its passing as it ascended the staircase. Had I not been afraid to breathe, I would have almost screamed with relief.

"Yet still fear held me, and I remained crouched against the wall while the thing went up the great stairs. Imagine that scene! All around me was absolutely nothing visible, nothing but the great flat circle of sand that lay a foot below me; yet I saw the place with my mind's eye, and knew of the walls and courts that lay about me, and the thing above me, in fear of which I was crouching there in the gathering darkness.

"The sound of feet above me had ceased, and I judged that the thing had gone into the great room above, which I had feared to enter. Now, if ever, was the time to make my escape in the darkness; so I rose, with infinite carefulness, and softly walked across the court to the door that led into the corridor. But when I had walked only half of the distance, as I thought, I crashed squarely into another invisible wall across my path, and fell backward, the metal handle of the sheath-knife at my belt striking the flooring with a loud clang. God help me, I had misjudged the position of the door, and had walked straight into the wall, instead!

"I lay there, motionless, with cold fear flooding every part of my being. Then, pad, pad—the soft steps of the thing across the landing, and then silence for a moment. Could it see me from the landing? I wondered. Could it? For a moment, hope warmed me, as no sound came, but the next instant I knew that death had me by the throat, for pad, pad—down the stairs it came.

"With that sound my last vestige of self-control fled and I scrambled to my feet and made another mad dash in the direction of the door. Crash!—into another wall I went, and rose to my feet trembling. There was no sound of footsteps now, and as quietly as I could, I walked into the great court still farther, as I thought, for all my ideas of direction were hopelessly confused. God, what a weird game it was we played there on that darkened circle of sand!

"No sound whatever came from the thing that hunted me, and my hope flickered up again. And with a dreadful irony, it was at that exact moment that I walked straight into the thing. My outstretched hand touched and grasped what must have been one of its limbs, thick and cold and hairy, which was instantly torn from my grasp and then seized me again, while another and another clutched me also. The thing had stood quite still, leaving me to walk directly into its grasp—the drama of the spider and the fly!

"A moment only it held me, for that cold grasp filled me with such deep shuddering abhorrence that I wrenched myself loose and fled madly across the court, stumbling again on the first step of the great staircase. I raced up the stairs, and even as I ran I heard the thing in pursuit.

"Up I went, and across the landing, and grasped the edge of the railing, for I meant to throw myself down from there, to a clean death on the floor below. But under my hands, the top of the railing moved, one of the great blocks that evidently made up its top was loosened and rocked toward me. In a flash I grasped the great block and staggered across the landing with it in my arms, to the head of the staircase. Two men could hardly have lifted it, I think, yet I did more, in a sudden excess of mad strength; for as I heard that monster coming swiftly up the great stairs, I raised the block, invisible as ever, above my head, and sent it crashing down the staircase upon the place where I thought the thing was at that moment.

"For an instant after the crash there was silence, and then a low humming sound began, that waxed into a loud droning. And at the same time, at a spot half-way down the staircase where the block had crashed, a thin, purple liquid seemed to well out of the empty air, giving form to a few of the invisible steps as it flowed over them, and outlining, too, the block I had thrown, and a great hairy limb that lay crushed beneath it, and from which the fluid that was the monster's blood was oozing. I had not killed the thing, but had chained it down with the block that held it prisoner.

"There was a thrashing sound on the staircase, and the purple stream ran more freely, and by the outline of its splashes, I saw, dimly, the monstrous god that had been known in Mamurth in ages past. It was like a giant spider, with angled limbs that were yards long, and a hairy, repellent body. Even as I stood there, I wondered that the thing, invisible as it was, was yet visible by the life-blood in it, when that blood was spilled. Yet so it was, nor can I even suggest a reason. But one glimpse I got of its half-visible, purple-splashed outline, and then, hugging the farther side of the stairs, I descended. When I passed the thing, the intolerable odor of a crushed insect almost smothered me, and the monster itself made frantic efforts to loosen itself and spring at me. But it could not, and I got safely down, shuddering and hardly able to walk.

"Straight across the great court I went, and ran shakily through the corridor, and down the long avenue, and out between the two great statues. The moonlight shone on them, and the tablets of inscriptions stood out clearly on the sides of the statues, with their strange symbols and carved spider forms. But I knew now what their message was!

"It was well that my camels had wandered into the ruins, for such was the fear that struck through me that I would never have returned for them had they lingered by the invisible wall. All that night I rode to the north, and when morning came I did not stop, but still pushed north. And as I went through the mountain pass, one camel stumbled and fell, and in falling burst open all my water supplies that were lashed on its back.

"No water at all was left, but I still held north, killing the other camel by my constant speed, and then staggered on, afoot. On hands and knees I crawled forward, when my legs gave out, always north, away from that temple of evil and its evil god. And tonight, I had been crawling, how many miles I do not know, and I saw your fire. And that is all."

He lay back exhausted, and Mitchell and I looked at each other's faces in the firelight. Then, rising, Mitchell strode to the edge of our camp and looked for a long time at the moonlit desert, which lay toward the south. What his thoughts were, I do not know. I was nursing my own, as I watched the man who lay beside our fire.

It was early the next morning that he died, muttering about great walls around him. We wrapped his body securely, and bearing it with us held our way across the desert.

In Algiers we cabled to the friends whose address we found in his moneybelt, and arranged to ship the body to them, for such had been his only request. Later they wrote that he had been buried in the little churchyard of the New England village that had been his childhood home. I do not think that his sleep there will be troubled by dreams of that place of evil which he fled. I pray that it will not.

Often and often have Mitchell and I discussed the thing, over lonely campfires and in the inns of the seaport towns. Did he kill the invisible monster he spoke of, and is it lying now, a withered remnant, under the block on the great staircase? Or did it gnaw its way loose; does it still roam the desert and make its lair in the vast, ancient temple, as unseen as itself?

Or, different still, was the man simply crazed by the heat and thirst of the desert, and his tale but the product of a maddened mind? I do not think that this is so. I think that he told truth, yet I do not know. Nor shall I ever know, for never, Mitchell and I have decided, shall we be the ones to venture into the place of hell on Earth where that ancient god of evil may still be living, amid the invisible courts and towers, beyond the unseen wall.

Talent

INTRODUCTION

Here's a story by a man known for chilling horror stories, but also for wacky humorous fantasy yarns, in particular the Lefty Feep stories. Both sides of Robert Bloch's authorial personality are in evidence in this unsettling and sardonic tale of a very unusual orphan with a very unusual talent. . . .

✳ ✳ ✳

Robert Bloch (1917-1994) was, of course, author of the novel *Psycho*, which became the basis for the Alfred Hitchcock movie, but before that he had written many horror classics for *Weird Tales* (there's that magazine again) and other pulps, such as "Yours Truly, Jack the Ripper," and "The Cloak." On one memorable occasion, he and his friend H.P. Lovecraft wrote a story apiece for *WT*'s pages in which each killed the other off. (After all, what else are friends for?) While he didn't write the screenplay for *Psycho*, its success led to his writing many scripts for movies and TV, a considerable improvement over the one cent per word or less that the pulps paid. Still, he never forgot his early days in SF fandom where he was known for humorous pieces in fanzines. And he felt that he shouldn't be judged harshly by his horror stories. "I have the heart of a small boy," he once said. "I keep it in a jar on my desk."

T'alent

by Robert Bloch

It is perhaps a pity that nothing is known of Andrew Benson's parents.

The same reasons which prompted them to leave him as a foundling on the steps of the St. Andrews Orphanage also caused them to maintain a discreet anonymity. The event occurred on the morning of March 3rd, 1943—the war era, as you probably recall—so in a way the child may be regarded as a wartime casualty. Similar occurrences were by no means rare during those days, even in Pasadena, where the Orphanage was located.

After the usual tentative and fruitless inquiries, the good Sisters took him in. It was there that he acquired his first name, from the patron and patronymic saint of the establishment. The "Benson" was added some years later, by the couple who eventually adopted him.

It is difficult, at this late date, to determine what sort of a child Andrew was; orphanage records are sketchy, at best, and Sister Rosemarie, who acted as supervisor of the boys' dormitory, is long since dead. Sister Albertine, the primary grades teacher of the Orphanage School, is now—to put it as delicately as possible—in her senility, and her testimony is necessarily colored by knowledge of subsequent events.

That Andrew never learned to talk until he was nearly seven years old seems almost incredible; the forced gregarity and the conspicuous lack of individual attention characteristic of orphanage upbringing would make it appear as though the ability to speak is necessary for actual survival in such an environment from infancy onward. Scarcely more credible is Sister Albertine's theory that Andrew knew how to talk but merely refused to do so until he was well into his seventh year.

For what it is worth, she now remembers him as an unusually precocious youngster, who appeared to possess an intelligence and understanding far beyond his years. Instead of employing speech, however, he relied on pantomime, an art at which he was so brilliantly adept (if Sister Albertine is to be believed) that his continuing silence seemed scarcely noticeable.

"He could imitate anybody," she declares. "The other children, the Sisters, even the Mother Superior. Of course I had to punish him for that. But it was remarkable, the way he was able to pick up all the little mannerisms and facial expressions of another person, just at a glance. And that's all it took for Andrew—just a mere glance.

"Visitors' Day was Sunday. Naturally, Andrew never had any visitors, but he liked to hang around the corridor and watch them come in. And afterwards, in the dormitory at night, he'd put in a regular performance for the other boys. He could impersonate every single man, woman or child who'd come to the Orphanage that day— the way they walked, the way they moved, every action and gesture. Even though he never said a word, nobody made the mistake of thinking Andrew was mentally deficient. For a while, Dr. Clement had the idea he might be a mute."

Dr. Roger Clement is one of the few persons who might be able to furnish more objective data concerning Andrew Benson's early years. Unfortunately, he passed away in 1954; a victim of a fire which also destroyed his home and his office files.

It was Dr. Clement who attended Andrew on the night that he saw his first motion picture.

The date was 1949, some Saturday evening in the late fall of the year. The orphanage received and showed one film a week, and only children of school age were permitted to attend. Andrew's inability— or unwillingness—to speak had caused some difficulty when he entered primary grades that September, and several months went by before he was allowed to join his classmates in the auditorium for the Saturday night screenings. But it is known that he eventually did so.

The picture was the last (and probably the least) of the Marx Brothers movies. Its title was *Love Happy,* and if it is remembered by the general public at all today, that is due to the fact that the film contained a brief walk-on appearance by a then-unknown blonde bit player named Marilyn Monroe.

But the orphanage audience had other reasons for regarding it as memorable. Because *Love Happy* was the picture that sent Andrew Benson into his trance.

Long after the lights came up again in the auditorium the child sat there, immobile, his eyes staring glassily at the blank screen. When his companions noticed and sought to arouse him he did not respond; one of the Sisters (possibly Sister Rosemarie) shook him, and he promptly collapsed in a dead faint. Dr. Clement was summoned, and he administered to the patient. Andrew Benson did not recover consciousness until the following morning.

And it was then that he talked.

He talked immediately, he talked perfectly, he talked fluently— but not in the manner of a six-year-old child. The voice that issued from his lips was that of a middle-aged man. It was a nasal, rasping voice, and even without the accompanying grimaces and facial expressions it was instantaneously and unmistakably recognizable as the voice of Groucho Marx.

Andrew Benson mimicked Groucho in his *Sam Grunion* role to perfection, word for word. Then he "did" Chico Marx. After that he relapsed into silence again, mute phase. But it was an eloquent silence, and soon it became evident that he was imitating Harpo. In rapid succession, Andrew created recognizable vocal and visual portraits of Raymond Burr, Melville Cooper, Eric Blore and the other actors who played small roles in the picture. His impersonations seemed uncanny to his companions, and the Sisters were not unimpressed.

"Why, he even *looked* like Groucho," Sister Albertine insists.

Ignoring the question of how a towheaded moppet of six can

achieve a physical resemblance to Groucho Marx without benefit (or detriment) of make-up, it is nevertheless an established fact that Andrew Benson gained immediate celebrity as a mimic within the small confines of the orphanage.

And from that moment on, he talked regularly, if not freely. That is to say, he replied to direct questions, he recited his lessons in the classroom, and responded with the outward forms of politeness required by orphanage discipline. But he was never loquacious, or even communicative, in the ordinary sense. The only time he became spontaneously articulate was immediately following the showing of a weekly movie.

There was no recurrence of his initial seizure, but each Saturday night screening brought in its wake a complete dramatic recapitulation by the gifted youngster. During the fall of '49 and the winter of '50, Andrew Benson saw many movies. There was *Sorrowful Jones* with Bob Hope; *Tarzan's Magic Fountain; The Fighting O'Flynn; The Life of Riley; Little Women,* and a number of other films, current and older. Naturally, these pictures were subject to approval by the Sisters before being shown, and as a result movies depicting or emphasizing violence were not included. Still, several westerns reached the orphanage screen, and it is significant that Andrew Benson reacted in what was to become a characteristic fashion.

"Funny thing," declares Albert Dominguez, who attended the orphanage during the same period as Andrew Benson and is one of the few persons located who is willing to admit, let alone discuss the fact. "At first Andy imitated everybody—all the men, that is. He never imitated none of the women. But after he started to see westerns, it got so he was choosey, like. He just imitated the villains. I don't mean like when us guys was playing cowboys—you know, when one guy is the sheriff and one is a gunslinger. I mean he imitated villains all the time. He could talk like 'em, he could even look like 'em. We used to razz hell out of him, you know?"

It is probably as a result of the "razzing" that Andrew Benson, on the evening of May 17th, 1950, attempted to slit the throat of Frank Phillips with a table knife. Probably—although Albert Dominguez claims that the older boy offered no provocation, and that Andrew

Benson was exactly duplicating the screen role of a western desperado in an old Charles Starrett movie.

The incident was hushed up, apparently, and no action taken; we have little information on Andrew Benson's growth and development between the summer of 1950 and the autumn of 1955. Dominguez left the orphanage, nobody else appears willing to testify, and Sister Albertine had retired to a rest-home. As a result, there is nothing available concerning what may well have been Andrew's crucial, formative years. The meager records of his classwork seem satisfactory enough, and there is nothing to indicate that he was a disciplinary problem to his instructors. In June of 1955 he was photographed with the rest of his classmates upon the occasion of graduation from eighth grade. His face is a mere blur, an almost blank smudge in a sea of preadolescent countenances. What he actually looked like at that age is hard to tell.

The Bensons thought that he resembled their son, David.

Little David Benson had died of polio in 1953, and two years later his parents came to St. Andrews Orphanage seeking to adopt a boy. They had David's picture with them, and they were frank to state that they sought a physical resemblance as a guide to making their choice.

Did Andrew Benson see that photograph? Did—as has been subsequently theorized by certain irresponsible alarmists—he see certain home movies which the Bensons had taken of their child?

We must confine ourselves to the known facts, which are, simply, that Mr. and Mrs. Louis Benson, of Pasadena, California, legally adopted Andrew Benson, aged 12, on December 9th, 1955.

And Andrew Benson went to live in their home, as their son. He entered the public high school. He became the owner of a bicycle. He received an allowance of one dollar a week. And he went to the movies.

Andrew Benson went to the movies, and there were no restrictions. No restrictions at all. For several months, that is. During this period he saw comedies, dramas, westerns, musicals, melodramas. He must have seen melodramas. Was there a film, released early in 1956, in which an actor played the role of a gangster who pushed a victim out of a second-story window?

Knowing what we do today, we must suspect that there must have been. But at the time, when the actual incident occurred, Andrew Benson was virtually exonerated. He and the other boy had been "scuffling" in a classroom after school, and the boy had "accidentally fallen." At least, this is the official version of the affair. The boy—now Pvt. Raymond Schuyler, USMC—maintains to this day that Benson deliberately tried to kill him.

"He was spooky, that kid," Schuyler insists. "None of us ever really got close to him. It was like there was nothing to get close to, you know? I mean, he kept changing off so. From one day to the next you could never figure out what he was going to be like. Of course we all knew he imitated these movie actors—he was only a freshman but already he was a big shot in the dramatic club—but it was as though he imitated all the time. One minute he'd be real quiet, and the next, wham! You know that story, the one about Jekyll and Hyde? Well, that was Andrew Benson. Afternoon he grabbed me, we weren't even talking to each other. He just came up to me at the window and I swear to God he changed right before my eyes. It was as if he all of a sudden got about a foot taller and fifty pounds heavier, and his face was real wild. He pushed me out the window, without one word. Of course I was scared spitless, and maybe I just thought he changed. I mean, nobody can actually do a thing like that, can they?"

This question, if it arose at all at the time, remained unanswered. We do know that Andrew Benson was brought to the attention of Dr. Max Fahringer, child psychiatrist and part-time guidance counselor at the school, and that his initial examination disclosed no apparent abnormalities of personality or behavior patterns. Dr. Fahringer did, however, have several long talks with the Bensons, and as a result Andrew was forbidden to attend motion pictures. The following year, Dr. Fahringer voluntarily offered to examine young Andrew— undoubtedly his interest had been aroused by the amazing dramatic abilities the boy was showing in his extracurricular activities at the school.

Only one such interview ever took place, and it is to be regretted that Dr. Fahringer neither committed his findings to paper nor communicated them to the Bensons before his sudden, shocking death at the hands of an unknown assailant. It is believed (or was believed by the police, at the time) that one of his former patients, committed to an institution as a psychotic, may have been guilty of the crime.

All that we know is that it occurred some short while following a local rerun of the film *Man in the Attic*, in which Jack Palance essayed the role of Jack the Ripper. It is interesting, today, to examine some of the so-called "horror movies" of those years, including the reruns of earlier vehicles starring Boris Karloff, Bela Lugosi, Peter Lorre and a number of other actors.

We cannot say with any certainty, of course, that Andrew Benson was violating the wishes of his foster-parents and secretly attending motion pictures. But if he did, it is quite likely that he would frequent the smaller neighborhood houses, many of which specialized in reruns. And we do know, from the remarks of fellow classmates during these high school years, that "Andy" was familiar—almost omnisciently so—with the mannerisms of these performers.

The evidence is oftentimes conflicting. Joan Charters, for example, is willing to "swear on a stack of Bibles" that Andrew Benson, at the age of 15, was "a dead ringer for Peter Lorre—the same bug eyes and everything." Whereas Nick Dossinger, who attended classes with Benson a year later, insists that he "looked just like Boris Karloff."

Granted that adolescence may bring about a considerable increase in height during the period of a year, it is nevertheless difficult to imagine how a "dead ringer for Peter Lorre" could metamorphize into an asthenic Karloff type.

A mass of testimony is available concerning Andrew Benson during those years, but almost all of it deals with his phenomenal histrionic talent and his startling skill at ad-lib impersonations of motion picture actors. Apparently, he had given up mimicking his associates and contemporaries almost entirely.

"He said he liked to do actors better, because they were bigger," says Don Brady, who appeared with him in the senior play. "I asked him what he meant by 'bigger' and he said it was just that—actors were bigger on the screen, sometimes twenty feet tall. He said, 'Why bother with little people when you can be big?' Oh, he was a real offbeat character, that one."

The phrases recur. "Oddball" and "screwball" and "real gone" are picturesque, but hardly enlightening. And there seems to be little recollection of Andrew Benson as a friend or classmate, in the ordinary role of adolescence. It's the imitator who is remembered, with admiration and, frequently, with distaste bordering on actual apprehension.

"He was so good he scared you. But that's when he was doing those impersonations, of course. The rest of the time, you scarcely knew he was around."

"Classes? I guess he did all right. I didn't notice him much."

"Andrew was a fair student. He could recite when called upon, but he never volunteered. His marks were average. I got the impression he was rather withdrawn."

"No, he never dated much. Come to think of it, I don't think he went out with girls at all. I never paid much attention to him, except when he was on stage, of course."

"I wasn't really what you call close to Andy. I don't know anybody who seemed to be friends with him. He was so quiet, outside of the dramatics. And when he got up there, it was like he was a different person—he was real great, you know? We all figured he'd end up at the Pasadena Playhouse."

The reminiscences of his contemporaries are frequently apt to touch upon matters which did not directly involve Andrew Benson. The years 1956 and 1957 are still remembered, by high school students of the area in particular, as the years of the curfew. It was a voluntary curfew, of course, but it was nevertheless strictly observed by most of the female students during the period of the "werewolf murders"—that series of savage, still-unsolved crimes which terrorized the community for well over a year. Certain cannibalistic aspects of the slaying of the five young women led to the "werewolf" appellation on the part of the sensation-mongering press. The *Wolf Man* series made by Universal had been revived, and perhaps this had something to do with the association.

But to return to Andrew Benson; he grew up, went to school, and lived the normal life of a dutiful stepson. If his foster-parents were a bit strict, he made no complaints. If they punished him because they suspected he sometimes slipped out of his room at night, he made no complaint or denials. If they seemed apprehensive lest he be disobeying their set injunctions not to attend the movies, he offered no overt defiance.

The only known clash between Andrew Benson and his family came about as a result of their flat refusal to allow a television set in their home. Whether or not they were concerned about the possible encouragement of Andrew's mimicry or whether they had merely developed an allergy to Lawrence Welk and his ilk is difficult to determine. Nevertheless, they balked at the acquisition of a TV set. Andrew begged and pleaded, pointed out that he "needed" television as an aid to a future dramatic career. His argument had some justification, for in his senior year, Andrew had indeed been "scouted" by the famous Pasadena Playhouse, and there was even some talk of a future professional career without the necessity of formal training.

But the Bensons were adamant on the television question; as far as we can determine, they remained adamant right up to the day of their death.

The unfortunate circumstances occurred at Balboa, where the Bensons owned a small cottage and maintained a little cabin-cruiser. The elder Bensons and Andrew were heading for Catalina Channel when the cruiser overturned in choppy waters. Andrew managed to cling to the craft until rescued, but his foster-parents were gone. It was a common enough accident; you've probably seen something just like it in the movies a dozen times.

Andrew, just turned eighteen, was left an orphan once more—but an orphan in full possession of a lovely home, and with the expectation of coming into a sizeable inheritance when he reached twenty-one. The Benson estate was administered by the family attorney, Justin L. Fowler, and he placed young Andrew on an allowance of forty dollars a week—an amount sufficient for a recent graduate of high school to survive on, but hardly enough to maintain him in luxury.

It is to be feared that violent scenes were precipitated between the young man and his attorney. There is no point in recapitulating them here, or in condemning Fowler for what may seem—on the surface of it—to be the development of a fixation.

But up until the night that he was struck down by a hit-and-run driver in the street before his house, Attorney Fowler seemed almost obsessed with the desire to prove that the Benson lad was legally incompetent, or worse. Indeed, it was his investigation which led to the uncovering of what few facts are presently available concerning the life of Andrew Benson.

Certain other hypotheses—one hesitates to dignify them with the term "conclusions"—he apparently extrapolated from these meager findings, or fabricated them out of thin air. Unless, of course, he did manage to discover details which he never actually disclosed. Without the support of such details there is no way of authenticating what seem to be a series of fantastic conjectures.

A random sampling, as remembered from various conversations Fowler had with the authorities, will suffice.

"I don't think the kid is even human, for that matter. Just because he showed up on those orphanage steps, you call him a foundling. Changeling might be a better word for it. Yes, I know they don't believe in such things any more. And if you talk about life-forms from other planets, they laugh at you and tell you to join the Fortean Society. So happens, I'm a member.

"Changeling? It's probably a more accurate term than the narrow meaning implies. I'm talking about the way he changes when he sees these movies. No, don't take my word for it—ask anyone who's ever seen him act. Better still, ask those who never saw him on a stage, but just watched him imitate movie performers in private. You'll find out he did a lot more than just imitate. He *becomes* the actor. Yes, I mean he undergoes an actual physical transformation. Chameleon. Or some other form of life. Who can say?

"No, I don't pretend to understand it. I know it's not 'scientific' according to the way you define science. But that doesn't mean it's impossible. There are a lot of life-forms in the universe, and we can only guess at some of them. Why shouldn't there be one that's abnormally sensitive to mimicry?

"You know what effect the movies can have on so-called 'normal' human beings, under certain conditions. It's a hypnotic state, this movie-viewing, and you can ask the psychologists for confirmation. Darkness, concentration, suggestion—all the elements are present. And there's post-hypnotic suggestion, too. Again, psychiatrists will back me up on that. Most people tend to identify with various characters on the screen. That's where our hero worship comes in, that's why we have western-movie fans, and detective fans, and all the rest. Supposedly ordinary people come out of the theater and fantasy themselves as the heroes and heroines they saw up there on the screen; imitate them, too.

"That's what Andrew Benson did, of course. Only suppose he could carry it one step further? Suppose he was capable of *being* what he saw portrayed? And he chose to *be* the villains? I tell you, it's time to investigate those killings of a few years back, all of them. Not just the murder of those girls, but the murder of the two doctors who examined Benson when he was a child, and the death of his foster-parents, too. I don't think any of these things were accidents. I think some people got too close to the secret, and Benson put them out of the way.

"Why? How should I know why? Any more than I know what he's looking for when he watches the movies. But he's looking for something, I can guarantee that. Who knows what purpose such a life-form can have, or what he intends to do with his power? All I can do is warn you."

It is easy to dismiss Attorney Fowler as a paranoid type, though perhaps unfair, in that we cannot evaluate the reasons for his outburst. That he knew (or believed he knew) something is self-evident. As a matter of fact, on the very evening of his death, he was apparently about to put his findings on paper.

Deplorably, all that he ever set down was a preamble, in the form of a quotation from Eric Voegelin, concerning rigid pragmatic attitudes of "scientism," so-called:

"(1) the assumption that the mathematized science of natural phenomena is a model science to which all other sciences ought to conform; (2) that all realms of being are accessible to the methods of the sciences of phenomena; and (3) that all reality which is not accessible to sciences of phenomena is either irrelevant or, in the more radical form of the dogma, illusionary."

But Attorney Fowler is dead, and we deal with the living; with Max Schick, for example, the motion-picture and television agent who visited Andrew Benson at his home shortly after the death of the elder Bensons, and offered him an immediate contract.

"You're a natural," Schick declared. "Never mind with the Pasadena Playhouse bit. I can spot you right now, believe me! With what you got, we'll back Brando right off the map! Of course, we gotta start small, but I know just the gimmick. Main thing is to establish you in a starring slot right away. None of this stock-contract jazz, get me? The studios aren't handing 'em out anymore in the first place, and even if you landed one, you'd end up on Cloud Nowhere. No, the deal is to get you a lead and billing right off the bat. And like I said, I got the angle.

"We go to a small independent producer, get it? Must be a dozen of 'em operating right now, and all of 'em making the same thing. Only one kind of picture that combines low budgets with big grosses and that's a science fiction movie.

"Yeah, you heard me, a science fiction movie. Whaddya mean, you never saw one? Are you kidding? How about that? You mean you never saw any science fiction pictures at all?

"Oh, your folks, eh? Had to sneak out? And they only show that kind of stuff at the downtown houses? Well look, kid, it's about time, that's all I can say. It's about time! Hey, just so's you know what we're talking about, you better get on the ball and take in one right away. Sure, I'm positive, there must be one playing a downtown first run now. Why don't you go this afternoon? I got some work to finish up here at the office—run you down in my car and you can go on to the show, meet me back here when you get out.

"Sure, you can take the car after you drop me off. Be my guest."

So Andrew Benson saw his first science fiction movie. He drove there and back in Max Schick's car (coincidentally enough, it was the late afternoon of the day when Attorney Fowler became a hit-and-run victim) and Schick has good reason to remember Andrew Benson's reappearance at his office just after dusk.

"He had a look on his face that was out of this world," Schick says.

" 'How'd you like the picture?' I ask him. 'It was wonderful,' he tells me. 'Just what I've been looking for all these years. And to think I didn't know.' 'Didn't know what?' I ask. But he isn't talking to me anymore. You can see that. He's talking to himself. 'I thought there must be something like that,' he says. 'Something better than Dracula, or Frankenstein's Monster, or all the rest. Something bigger, more powerful. Something I could really be. And now I know. And now I'm going to.' "

Max Schick is unable to maintain coherency from this point on. But his direct account is not necessary. We are, unfortunately, all too well aware of what happened next.

Max Schick sat there in his chair and watched Andrew Benson *change*.

He watched him *grow*. He watched him put forth the eyes, the stalks, the writhing tentacles. He watched him twist and tower, filling the room and then *overflowing* until the flimsy stucco walls collapsed and there was nothing but the green, gigantic horror, the sixty-foot-high monstrosity that may have been born in a screenwriter's brain or may have been spawned beyond the stars, but certainly existed and drew nourishment from realms far from a three-dimensional world or three-dimensional concepts of sanity.

Max Schick will never forget that night and neither, of course, will anybody else.

That was the night the monster destroyed Los Angeles . . .

The End of the Hunt

INTRODUCTION

Science fiction often speculates on what the future might be like centuries from now, even millennia from now, but the far future, *millions* of years from now is a tougher game to play. If humans still exist, they may have drastically changed, either through evolution or through deliberate biological alteration. And other species as well may be different from their present state . . .

❖ ❖ ❖

David Drake, author of the best-selling Hammer's Slammers future mercenary series, is often referred to as the Dean of military science fiction, but is much more versatile than that label might suggest, as shown by his epic fantasy series that began with *Lord of the Isles* (Tor), and his equally popular Republic of Cinnabar Navy series of space operas (Baen) starring the indefatigable team of Leary and Mundy. His recent collection of horror and fantasy stories, *Night & Demons* (Baen) has a generous helping of monsters, several of them giant-sized. He lives near Chapel Hill, NC, with his family.

The End of the Hunt

by David Drake

Corll's eyes caught the betraying dust trail of a pebble skipping down the canyon wall ahead of him. Realizing what it meant, he flattened in mid-stride, his feet and hands braced to fling him in any direction of safety. "Shedde," he demanded, "how do we get out of here?"

"Think," replied the other. "You're admirably fitted for it."

"Shedde," Corll snarled, "there's no time for joking! They must have reached the canyon mouth behind us by now—and they're ahead of us on the rim as well!" Corll had underestimated the ants again. His self-surety had led him to scout the territory the insects claimed with their many-spired mounds. He had not known that they would go beyond it in the savage tenacity of their pursuit. The comparison of his long strides with their tiny scrambling had left him scornful even then. But Corll needed rest, needed sleep, needed to hunt for water when the supply he carried grew low in these sun-blasted badlands; and those who pursued him seemed to recognize no such necessities.

"Run for the far end of the canyon," directed Shedde.

"Won't they have it blocked by now?" Corll asked, but he sprang into motion without awaiting the answer. He had feared this sort of trap ever since he learned that the ants had ways of moving beneath the surface more swiftly than they could above it. He now had proof that their intrusions in the subsoil must penetrate far beyond their range above ground.

Once already they had ringed Corll. He had thought it was finished with him then.

"They won't have to block the end," Shedde was saying. "This is a box canyon. Yes, I remember this canyon . . . though it's been a long time. A terribly long time."

"Shedde!" Corll hissed, his brain seething with rage, "you will die with me, don't you understand? There is no time now for jokes!"

A ponderous cornice sheared from the right wall of the canyon. Corll spent a millisecond judging the trajectory of the orange-red mass, then leaped to the right, his equipment belt clanking on the wall as his fingers scrabbled and found cracks to burrow into.

"Mutated vermin," Shedde murmured in revulsion.

The ledge of rock touched an out-thrust knob twenty feet above Corll; inertia exploded the missile outward, the knob shattered with it and slashed Corll as a sleet of dust and gravel. That he ignored, waiting only for the tremble of the last murderous, head-sized fragments striking the ground before he darted off again.

"Shedde," he asked, "can we turn around and break through the canyon mouth?" Through the crawling horde that would choke the ground. Through the things that shambled instead of crawling, the giants that would have justified Corll's journey if they had left him an opportunity to warn the others of his race. It seemed quite certain now that the giants would be the ultimate cause of his failure. Only two bombs still hung from his equipment belt, and their poison had already proven ineffective against the things whose size belied their ant-like appearance.

"Keep running," Shedde directed. "They must be blocking the passage behind us for almost a mile by now."

"But—" Corll began. Fluttering jewel-flickers in the light of the great sun cut him off. There was no choice now. He lengthened his stride, freeing one of the heavy globes in either hand. Pain knifed his thigh. He ignored it, loped on. For the moment the pain was only pain, and had no margin to waste on comfort.

A ruby-carapaced ant sailed past Corll's face, twisting violently as though sheer determination would bring its mandibles the remaining inch they needed to close on Corll's flesh. The insect was scarcely an inch long itself, half mandible and entirely an engine of destruction. The warriors were light enough to drop safely from any height, ready to slash and to tear when they landed. They were pouring off the rim in a deadly shower that carpeted the canyon floor too thickly, now, for the runner to avoid. Agony tore Corll's pads and ankles a dozen times. More frightening were the ghost-light twitchings that mounted his calves. He had waited as long as he could.

Corll's right hand smashed a globular bomb against the massively-functional buckle of his crossbelt. The bomb shattered, spraying the acrid reek of its vegetable distillate about him in a blue mist. The poison cooled his body where it clung to him, but its clammy, muscle-tightening chill was infinitely preferable to the fiery horror of the warriors' jaws. No matter—he could feel the mandibles relax, see the wave of ants on the ground wither and blacken as the dense cloud oozed over them. Corll held his own breath as he ran through the sudden carnage. He knew that the fluid coating his lower limbs would protect him for a time, and he prayed that the time would be adequate.

"Not much further," Shedde remarked.

Dead ants scrunched underfoot. Jaws seared Corll briefly, then dropped away. His eyes scanned the rim of the canyon as it dog-legged, noting that the rain of warriors had paused for the moment.

A long rock hurtled down, pitched with more force than gravity could have given it. Corll's leap took him a dozen feet up the cliff wall where his legs shot him off at a flat angle, a safe angle. . . . Stone smashed on stone beside him. A feeler waved vexedly from the high rim.

The ants had very nearly caught him three days before while he dozed in the shadow of a wind-sculpted cliff, certain that his smooth pacing had left the insects far behind. Through half-closed eyelids Corll had suddenly seen that the ruddy sunlight on ruddy stone was now being picked out by tiny, blood-bright droplets that trickled toward his shelter. The first bomb had not freed him then, nor had the third. When he had darted over the nearest rise with the poison and its bitter stench lapping about him like a shroud, Corll had seen the horizon in all directions sanguine with deadly life. The ants had waited until a cold intelligence somewhere had assessed their success as certain. But that time Corll had leaped through them as a lethal ghost, wrapped in his poison and guided by Shedde's calculated guess as the the narrowest link in a chain of inobservable thickness.

If the insects or the brain that controlled them had reconsidered the capacities of their quarry, that had not caused them to slacken their pursuit.

"Their numbers aren't infinite," Shedde explained, "and they can't have laced the whole continent with their tunnels—yet. Many of them are following us, yes. But it's the ones sent on ahead that are dangerous, and with every mile we run, the more of those we're safe from. There will be some waiting for us at the end of the canyon. If we could have bypassed them, perhaps we would have escaped entirely."

Corll was stung with wordless anger at his companion's objectivity; then he rounded the canyon's bend to see the cliffs linked sharply a hundred yards in front of him. The concrete of the blockhouse that squatted at the base of the cliffs would have been magenta in the light of the waning sun, save for the warriors that clung to it like a layer of blazing fungus.

Corll halted.

"There's a door," Shedde prompted.

"I can't get through those ants on the residue of the bomb," Corll said. The whisper-whisper of feet a million times magnified echoed in his mind if not his ears.

"Use the last bomb, then. There's no choice."

Nor was there. Baying a defiant challenge, Corll charged for the structure. A stride before he reached the waiting mass, he smashed his last defense into vitreous splinters on his breast. Do the ants feel pain? he wondered, the warriors only a dying blur at the edges of his mind. Then, expecting it to slam open, he hit the portal in a bound— and recoiled from it. The metal door fit its jambs without a seam, refuge if open but otherwise a cruel jest.

"To the right," Shedde directed. "There should be a pressure plate."

The tapestry of ants, linked even in death, still hung in swathes across the blockhouse. Corll's hands groped through the insects desperately, feeling the desiccated bodies crumble as easily as the ashes of an ancient fire. The door swung open on a lighted room.

Corll sprang inside. "The inner plate is also a lock," his companion said. "Touch to open, touch to close. But only the touch of your kind." Corll slammed the door and palmed the device.

They were in a narrow anteroom, softly lighted by a strip in the ceiling. At the back was another metal door, half closed. The only furnishings of the anteroom were a pair of objects fixed to the wall to either side of the rear door. In general shape they resembled sockets for flambeaux, but they were thrust out horizontally rather than vertically. Corll's quick eyes flicked over them, but he did not move closer.

"Now what?" he asked.

"Now we wait, of course," replied Shedde. "If the systems are still working, there should be water inside." There was a pause before he concluded acidly, "And Hargen built to last."

Corll eased open the door. The inner room was much larger, but it was almost filled with dull, black machinery. Against the far wall stood the framework of a chair in a clear semi-circle. It was backed against another door, this one open onto darkness. On the floor before the chair sprawled a skeleton.

The outer door of the blockhouse clanged as something heavy struck it.

"Who is Hargen?" Corll demanded. Half-consciously he backed against the inner door of the anteroom, shutting it against the gong-notes echoing through the building. His breath still came in short, quick sobs. "Shedde, what is this place?"

"Hargen," Shedde repeated with a whisper of hatred. "Hargen was a genetic engineer. As a technician, as a craftsman, he may have had no equal . . . though perhaps the men who built his instruments, they were brilliant in their own right. But tools of metal weren't enough for Hargen—he had his dream, he said, for the new Mankind."

Corll eyed the room. He was uneasy because he had never before known such vicious intensity in his companion. A pencil of water spurted from one corner of the ceiling down into a metal basin from which it then drained. Corll tested a drop of the fluid with his tongue before drinking deeply.

"He had to change us, Corll," continued Shedde. "Cut into genes, weld them, treat the unformed flesh as a sculptor does stone. 'Your children will live forever!' he said. 'Your children will live forever!'

"Have we lived forever, Corll?"

The echoes that flooded the building changed note, warning Corll that the outer door was sagging. He quickly squeezed empty the long waterbag of intestine looped across his shoulders, then refilled it from the falling stream.

"Where does the other door lead, Shedde?"

"A tunnel. Try it."

Pretending to ignore the undertone of his companion's voice, Corll attempted to leap the chair. Something caught him in mid-air and flung him back into the room.

"You see?" Shedde giggled. "Hargen wasn't just a genius, he had a sense of humor. He could sit there and control every machine in the building—and no man could touch him without his permission. Do you want to leave that way, Corll?"

"If they can batter down the outer door, they can get through this one," Corll noted with the tense desperation of a fighter at bay. The sound of metal ripping underscored his words. "Shedde, what do we do?"

Suddenly calmer, Shedde replied, "The weapons should have manual controls. There, beside the door."

Staring at the pair of hand-sized plates flanking the anteroom door, Corll realized what unfamiliarity had hidden from him: both plates displayed shrunken perspectives of the anteroom itself and the wreckage of the outer door. Joystick controls were set beneath the plates. When Corll twitched one of the rods, it moved the black dot he had thought was a flaw in the screen.

"If you push the top of the control rod," Shedde said, "it fires. "

The outer door of the blockhouse squealed again as it was rent completely away. A pair of giants that seemed ants in all but size stood framed in the doorway, their forelegs bowed a little to allow them to peer inside. Uncertain of what he was doing, Corll squeezed his thumb down on the stick.

The dazzling spatter of light blasted powder from the concrete, vapor from the outer doorjamb. Corll's reflex slashed the fierce beam sideways across one of the giants. The creature separated along the line of contact.

The light blinked off when Corll raised the thumbswitch. The remaining giant was scrambling backwards. Corll flicked the control. The dot moved in the direction opposite to his expectations. He moved it the other way and squeezed, chuckling in wonder as the glare sawed lethally across the second monster as well.

"They're hollow," he exclaimed as he squinted at the jerking bodies.

"I wonder how they fuel them?" Shedde mused. "The exoskeleton would give adequate area for muscle attachment without the mass of digestive organs to contend with. Even the vermin seem to have their genetic geniuses."

"How long will this weapon burn?" Corll asked, caution tempering his elation.

"Perhaps forever," the other replied. "Near enough that neither of us needs be concerned. Hargen never took half measures.

"I stood here before," Shedde continued, "to plead with him. I had been one of the first, you see. 'You don't know what you're doing,' I told him. 'You call it freedom from the tyranny of the body, a chance for the children of the race to have the immortality that was only vicarious before. But it's the death of those you change! We don't breed, we won't breed—it's not worth personal immortality to me to know that I'll never have a son.' And Hargen laughed at me, and he said, 'I have stayed here in this fortress for seventy-four years without leaving, so you think that I am ignorant. You can breed, little man; if the will is lacking, my knives didn't cut it out of you.'

"I shouted at him then; but before his servants pushed me out, Hargen stood and stretched his long bones, those bones that lie there in the dust, and he said, 'Come back in twenty thousand, come back in two hundred thousand years if it takes that long—come back and tell my bones then that I did not know.' " Shedde paused for so long that Corll thought he was done speaking, but at last he continued, "Well, you were right, Hargen. If we failed to breed, then so did the men you didn't change—and yes, you knew it. Just as you knew what would come of the race you formed and called, 'mere adjuncts to human immortality. . . .' Gods, how you must have hated Man!"

Corll said nothing, leaning over the weapon control and watching the smear of tiny red forms thicken on the wreckage of the giants.

"But perhaps even you forgot the ants," Shedde concluded bitterly.

The warriors surged forward in a solid wave that covered all four faces of the anteroom. Corll zig-zagged his flame through them, but there was no thrill in watching a black line razor across an attack condensed in the sights to an amorphous stain. More of the insects flowed over a surface pitted by earlier destruction. Corll did not raise his thumb, but the ants crawled forward more quickly than he could traverse his weapon across their rectangular advance.

Shedde, answering the question Corll had been too harried to ask, said, "The small ones can't smash open the door, but they'll be able to short out the weapon heads."

Corll whipped his control about in a frenzy. With someone to fight the right-hand beam as well, the wave could have been stopped. But—a scarlet runnel leaked across the wall toward the other wire-framed gun muzzle, and Corll realized the same thing must be happening in the dead area too close to his own weapon to be swept by its fire. A moment later the beam of deadly light vanished in coruscance and a thunder-clap that shook the blockhouse and flung the remains of the first dead giant a dozen yards from the entrance. Corll leaped for the other control. He was not quick enough. As soon as he touched the firing stud, the right-hand weapon also shorted explosively.

The sighting displays still worked. A third giant ant scrabbled noisily into the anteroom, its feelers stiff before it. Held easily between its mandibles was a huge fragment of stone.

"Shedde," Corll hissed, "this door won't hold any longer than the other one did. How can we get out of here?"

"You can leave any time through the tunnel," Shedde replied calmly. "Hargen must have kept a vehicle of some sort there."

Corll hurled himself again toward the low doorway. Again the unseen barrier slammed him back. The anteroom door clanged, denting inward slightly.

"It throws me back!"

"It throws me back," Shedde corrected gently. "Hargen's sense of humor, you see. Unstrap me and get away from here."

The door rang again. Flakes spalled off from the inside.

Corll seized a machine of unguessed precision and smashed it into the quivering metal. "I carried you since the day my father died!" he shouted. "My stomach fed you, my lungs gave you air, my kidneys cleared your wastes. Shedde, my blood is your blood!"

"Your family has served my needs for more years than even I can remember," Shedde stated, utterly calm. "Now that you can no longer serve me, serve yourself and your own race. Quickly now, the door can't hold much longer."

The panel banged inward again.

Corll cringed back, in horror rather than in fear. "Shedde," he pleaded, "you are the last."

"Somebody had to be. This is as good a place as any, where the end began. Set me down and go."

Keening deep in his throat, Corll fumbled at the massive crossbuckle he had unfastened only once before, while his father shuddered into death after a thirty-foot fall. "Shedde. . . ."

"Go!"

The upper door-hinge popped like a frost-cracked boulder as it sheared.

Sphincter muscles clamped shut the tiny valve in Corll's back as the tube pulled out of it. Only a single drop of blood escaped to glint within his bristling fur. He carefully swung Shedde to the floor, trying as he did so not to look at his burden: the tiny limbs, the abdomen without intestines and with lungs of no capacity beyond what was needed to squeak words through the vocal cords. In the center, flopping loosely, was an appendage that looked like an umbilicus and had served Shedde in that function for millenia. The genitalia were functional, but anything they had spawned would have had to be transferred to a host body for gestation.

The skull was fully the size of Hargen's, which leered vacuously from the floor. Shedde's eyes were placid and as blue as was nothing else remaining on the Earth.

"Good luck against the ants, Corll," the half-formed travesty of a man wheezed. "But I'm afraid Hargen may not have seen as clearly as he believed he did when he planned his new race."

Corll clenched his fingers, ("To hold tools for your children," Hargen had said so long ago) and sprang upright. "A stupid servant is a useless servant"—Hargen had said that too, and Corll's forehead bulged with a brain to equal that of the man he had carried. But in Corll's eyes bled a rage that was the heritage of the wolf and had not been totally expunged from the most pampered of lap dogs.

But the man on the floor whispered, "Go, my friend."

And as the first of the giants smashed into the room, Corll whirled and leaped for the tunnel door and darkness.

Ooze

INTRODUCTION

Here's another venerable yarn, this one appearing in the very first issue of *Weird Tales*, the issue dated March 1923. The invention of the microscope in the sixteenth century revealed a micro-jungle all around us, full of tiny predators, of which the amoeba was particularly fascinating, with its shapelessness and its way of engulfing its prey, then dissolving it. It was inevitable that someone would wonder what would happen if an amoeba could grow to *much* larger than normal size . . .

❖ ❖ ❖

Not a great deal is known about Anthony Melville Rud (1893-1942), though with that middle name, he must have been destined to be a writer. Born in Chicago, he contributed stories to such pulps as *Weird Tales*, *Munsey's Magazine* and *Blue Book*, as well as nonfiction pieces to such magazines as *Scientific American*. He was also a pulp magazine editor, and in one biographical note said that he had written movies. He wrote at least one borderline SF novel, *The Stuffed Men*, described by *The Encyclopedia of Science Fiction* as a "Sax Rohmer-esque fantasy." And "Ooze," the story you are about to read, was one of H.P. Lovecraft's favorite stories.

Ooze

by Anthony N. Rud

❊ I ❊

In the heart of a second-growth piney-woods jungle of southern Alabama, a region sparsely settled by back-woods blacks and Cajans—that queer, half-wild people descended from Acadian exiles of the middle eighteenth century—stands a strange, enormous ruin.

Interminable trailers of Cherokee rose, white-laden during a single month of spring, have climbed the heights of its three remaining walls. Palmetto fans rise knee high above the base. A dozen scattered live oaks, now belying their nomenclature because of choking tufts of gray, Spanish moss and two-foot circlets of mistletoe parasite which have stripped bare of foliage the gnarled, knotted limbs, lean fantastic beards against the crumbling brick.

Immediately beyond, where the ground becomes soggier and lower—dropping away hopelessly into the tangle of dogwood, holly, poison sumac and pitcher plants that is Moccasin Swamp—undergrowth of ti-ti and annis has formed a protecting wall impenetrable to all save the furtive ones. Some few outcasts utilize the stinking depths of that sinister swamp, distilling "shinny" of "pure cawn" liquor for illicit trade.

Tradition states that this is the case, at least—a tradition which antedates that of the premature ruin by many decades. I believe it, for during evenings intervening between investigations of the awesome spot I often was approached as a possible customer by wood-billies who could not fathom how anyone dared venture near without plenteous fortification of liquid courage.

I knew "shinny," therefore I did not purchase it for personal consumption. A dozen times I bought a quart or two, merely to establish credit among the Cajans, pouring away the vile stuff immediately into the sodden ground. It seemed then that only through filtration and condensation of their dozens of weird tales regarding "Daid House" could I arrive at understanding of the mystery and weight of horror hanging about the place.

Certain it is that out of all the superstitious cautioning, head-wagging and whispered nonsensities I obtained only two indisputable facts. The first was that no money, and no supporting battery of ten-gauge shotguns loaded with chilled shot, could induce either Cajan or darky of the region to approach within five hundred yards of that flowering wall! The second fact I shall dwell upon later.

Perhaps it would be as well, as I am only a mouthpiece in this chronicle, to relate in brief why I came to Alabama on this mission.

I am a scribbler of general fact articles, no fiction writer as was Lee Cranmer—though doubtless the confession is superfluous. Lee was my roommate during college days. I knew his family well, admiring John Corliss Cranmer even more than I admired the son and friend—and almost as much as Peggy Breede whom Lee married. Peggy liked me, but that was all. I cherish sanctified memory of her for just that much, as no other woman before or since has granted this gangling dyspeptic even a hint of joyous and sorrowful intimacy.

Work kept me to the city. Lee, on the other hand, coming of wealthy family—and, from the first, earning from his short-stories and novel royalties more than I wrested from editorial coffers—needed no anchorage. He and Peggy honeymooned a four-month trip to Alaska, visited Honolulu next winter, fished for salmon on Cain's River, New Brunswick, and generally enjoyed the outdoors at all seasons.

They kept an apartment in Wilmette, near Chicago, yet, during the few spring and fall seasons they were "home," both preferred to rent a suite at one of the country clubs to which Lee belonged. I suppose they spent thrice or five times the amount Lee actually earned, yet for my part I only honored that the two should find such great happiness in life and still accomplish artistic triumph.

They were honest, zestful young Americans, the type—and pretty nearly the only type—two million dollars cannot spoil. John Corliss Cranmer, father of Lee, though as different from his boy as a microscope is different from a painting by Remington, was even further from being dollar conscious. He lived in a world bounded only by the widening horizon of biological science—and his love for the two who would carry on that Cranmer name.

Many a time I used to wonder how it could be that as gentle, clean-souled and lovable a gentleman as John Corliss Cranmer could have ventured so far into scientific research without attaining small-caliber atheism. Few do. He believed both in God and human kind. To accuse him of murdering his boy and the girl wife who had come to be loved as the mother of baby Elsie—as well as blood and flesh of his own family—was a gruesome, terrible absurdity! Yes, even when John Corliss Cranmer was declared unmistakably insane!

Lacking a relative in the world, baby Elsie was given to me—and the middle-aged couple who had accompanied the three as servants about half of the known world. Elsie would be Peggy over again. I worshiped her, knowing that if my stewardship of her interests could make of her a woman of Peggy's loveliness and worth I should not have lived in vain. And at four Elsie stretched out her arms to me after a vain attempt to jerk out the bobbed tail of Lord Dick, my tolerant old Airedale—and called me "papa."

I felt a deep-down choking . . . yes, those strangely long black lashes some day might droop in fun or coquetry, but now baby Elsie held a wistful, trusting seriousness in depths of ultramarine eyes—that same seriousness which only Lee had brought to Peggy.

Responsibility in one instant became double. That she might come to love me as more than foster parent was my dearest wish. Still, through selfishness I could not rob her of rightful heritage; she must know in after years. And the tale that I would tell her must not be the horrible suspicion which had been bandied about in common talk!

I went to Alabama, leaving Elsie in the competent hands of Mrs. Daniels and her husband, who had helped care for her since birth.

In my possession, prior to the trip, were the scant facts known to authorities at the time of John Corliss Cranmer's escape and disappearance. They were incredible enough.

For conducting biological research upon forms of protozoan life, John Corliss Cranmer had hit upon this region of Alabama. Near a great swamp teeming with microscopic organisms, and situated in a semitropical belt where freezing weather rarely intruded to harden the bogs, the spot seemed ideal for his purpose.

Through Mobile he could secure supplies daily by truck. The isolation suited. With only an octoroon man to act as chef, house man and valet for the times he entertained no visitors, he brought down scientific apparatus, occupying temporary quarters in the village of Burdett's Corners while his woods house was in process of construction.

By all accounts the Lodge, as he termed it, was a substantial affair of eight or nine rooms, built of logs and planed lumber bought at Oak Grove. Lee and Peggy were expected to spend a portion of each year with him; quail, wild turkey and deer abounded, which fact made such a vacation certain to please the pair. At other times all save four rooms was closed.

This was in 1907, the year of Lee's marriage. Six years later when I came down, no sign of a house remained except certain mangled and rotting timbers projecting from viscid soil—or what seemed like soil. And a twelve-foot wall of brick had been built to enclose the house completely! One portion of this had fallen *inward!*

✱ II ✲

I wasted weeks of time at first, interviewing officials of the police department at Mobile, the town marshals and county sheriffs of Washington and Mobile counties, and officials of the psychopathic hospital from which Cranmer made his escape.

In substance the story was one of baseless homicidal mania. Cranmer the elder had been away until late fall, attending two scientific conferences in the North, and then going abroad to compare certain of his findings with those of a Dr. Gemmler of Prague University. Unfortunately, Gemmler was assassinated by a religious fanatic shortly afterward. The fanatic voiced virulent objection to all Mendelian research as blasphemous. This was his only defense. He was hanged.

Search of Gemmler's notes and effects revealed nothing save an immense amount of laboratory data on karyokinesis —the process of chromosome arrangement occurring in first growing cells of higher animal embryos. Apparently Cranmer had hoped to develop some similarities, or point out differences between hereditary factors occurring in lower forms of life and those half-demonstrated in the cat and monkey. The authorities had found nothing that helped me. Cranmer had gone crazy; was that not sufficient explanation?

Perhaps it was for them, but not for me—and Elsie. But to the slim basis of fact I was able to unearth: No one wondered when a fortnight passed without appearance of any person from the Lodge. Why should anyone worry? A provision salesman in Mobile called up twice, but failed to complete a connection. He merely shrugged. The Cranmers had gone away somewhere on a trip. In a week, a month, a year they would be back. Meanwhile he lost commissions, but what of it? He had no responsibility for these queer nuts up there in the piney-woods. Crazy? Of course! Why should any guy with millions to spend shut himself up among the Cajans and draw microscope-enlarged notebook pictures of—what the salesman called—"germs"?

A stir was aroused at the end of the fortnight, but the commotion confined itself to building circles. Twenty carloads of building brick, fifty bricklayers, and a quarter acre of fine-meshed wire—the sort used for screening off pens of rodents and small marsupials in a zoological garden—were ordered, *damn expense, hurry!* by an unshaved, tattered man who identified himself with difficulty as John Corliss Cranmer.

He looked strange, even then. A certified check for the total amount, given in advance, and another check of absurd size slung toward a labor *entrepreneur*, silenced objection, however. These millionaires were apt to be flighty. When they wanted something they wanted it at tap of the bell. Well, why not drag down the big profits? A poorer man would have been jacked up in a day. Cranmer's fluid gold bathed him in immunity to criticism.

The encircling wall was built, and roofed with wire netting which drooped about the squat-pitch of the Lodge. Curious inquiries of workmen went unanswered until the final day.

Then Cranmer, a strange, intense apparition who showed himself more shabby than a quay derelict, assembled every man jack of the workmen. In one hand he grasped a wad of blue slips—fifty-six of them. In the other he held a Luger automatic.

"I offer each man a thousand dollars for *silence!*" he announced. "As an alternative—*death!* You know little. Will all of you consent to swear upon your honor that nothing which has occurred here will be mentioned elsewhere? By this I mean *absolute* silence! You will not come back here to investigate anything. You will not tell your wives. You will not open your mouths even upon the witness stand in case you are called! My price is one thousand apiece.

"In case one of you betrays me *I give you my word that this man shall die!* I am rich. I can hire men to do murder. Well, what do you say?"

The men glanced apprehensively about. The threatening Luger decided them. To a man they accepted the blue slips—and, save for one witness who lost all sense of fear and morality in drink, none of the fifty-six has broken his pledge, as far as I know. That one bricklayer died later in delirium tremens.

It might have been different had not John Corliss Cranmer escaped.

⊰ III ⊱

They found him the first time, mouthing meaningless phrases concerning an amoeba—one of the tiny forms of protoplasmic life he was known to have studied. Also he leaped into a hysteria of self-accusation. He had murdered two innocent people! The tragedy was his crime. He had drowned them in ooze! Ah, God!

Unfortunately for all concerned, Cranmer, dazed and indubitably stark insane, chose to perform a strange travesty on fishing four miles to the west of his lodge—on the further border of Moccasin Swamp. His clothing had been torn to shreds, his hat was gone, and he was coated from head to foot with gluey mire. It was far from strange that the good folk of Shanksville, who never had glimpsed the eccentric millionaire, failed to associate him with Cranmer.

They took him in, searched his pockets—finding no sign save an inordinate sum of money—and then put him under medical care. Two precious weeks elapsed before Dr. Quirk reluctantly acknowledged that he could do nothing more for this patient, and notified the proper authorities.

Then much more time was wasted. Hot April and half of still hotter May passed by before the loose ends were connected. Then it did little good to know that this raving unfortunate was Cranmer, or that the two persons of whom he shouted in disconnected delirium actually had disappeared. Alienists absolved him of responsibility. He was confined in a cell reserved for the violent.

Meanwhile, strange things occurred back at the Lodge—which now, for good and sufficient reason, was becoming known to dwellers of the woods as Dead House. Until one of the walls fell in, however, there had been no chance to see—unless one possessed the temerity to climb either one of the tall live oaks, or mount the barrier itself. No doors or opening of any sort had been placed in that hastily-constructed wall!

By the time the western side of the wall fell, not a native for miles around but feared the spot far more than even the bottomless, snake-infested bogs which lay to west and north.

The single statement was all John Corliss Cranmer ever gave to the world. It proved sufficient. An immediate search was instituted. It showed that less than three weeks before the day of initial reckoning, his son and Peggy had come to visit him for the second time that winter—leaving Elsie behind in company of the Daniels pair. They had rented a pair of Gordons for quail hunting, and had gone out. That was the last anyone had seen of them.

The backwoods Negro who glimpsed them stalking a covey behind their two pointing dogs had known no more—even when sweated through twelve hours of third degree. Certain suspicious circumstances (having to do only with his regular pursuit of "shinny" transportation) had caused him to fall under suspicion at first. He was dropped.

Two days later the scientist himself was apprehended—a gibbering idiot who sloughed his pole—holding on to the baited hook—into a marsh where nothing save moccasins, an errant alligator, or amphibian life could have been snared.

His mind was three-quarters dead. Cranmer then was in the state of the dope fiend who rouses to a sitting position to ask seriously how many Bolshevists were killed by Julius Caesar before he was stabbed by Brutus, or why it was that Roller canaries sang only on Wednesday evenings. He knew that tragedy of the most sinister sort had stalked through his life—but little more, at first.

Later the police obtained that one statement that he had murdered two human beings, but never could means or motive be established. Official guess as to the means was no more than wild conjecture; it mentioned enticing the victims to the noisome depths of Moccasin Swamp, there to let them flounder and sink.

The two were his son and daughter-in-law, Lee and Peggy!

❖ IV ❖

By feigning coma—then awakening with suddenness to assault three attendants with incredible ferocity and strength—John Corliss Cranmer escaped from Elizabeth Ritter Hospital.

How he hid, how he managed to traverse sixty-odd intervening miles and still balk detection, remains a minor mystery to be explained only by the assumption that maniacal cunning sufficed to outwit saner intellects.

Traverse these miles he did, though until I was fortunate enough to uncover evidence to this effect, it was supposed generally that he had made his escape as stowaway on one of the banana boats, or had buried himself in some portion of the nearer woods where he was unknown. The truth ought to be welcome to householders of Shanksville, Burdett's Corners and vicinage—those excusably prudent ones who to this day keep loaded shotguns handy and barricade their doors at nightfall.

The first ten days of my investigation may be touched upon in brief. I made headquarters in Burdett's Corners, and drove out each morning, carrying lunch and returning for my grits and piney-woods pork or mutton before nightfall. My first plan had been to camp out at the edge of the swamp, for opportunity to enjoy the outdoors comes rarely in my direction. Yet after one cursory examination of the premises, I abandoned the idea. I did not want to camp alone there. And I am less superstitious than a real estate agent.

It was, perhaps, psychic warning; more probably the queer, faint, salty odor as of fish left to decay, which hung about the ruin, made too unpleasant an impression upon my olfactory sense. I experienced a distinct chill every time the lengthening shadows caught me near Dead House.

The smell impressed me. In newspaper reports of the case one ingenious explanation had been worked out. To the rear of the spot where Dead House had stood—inside the wall—was a swampy hollow circular in shape. Only a little real mud lay in the bottom of the bowllike depression now, but one reporter on the staff of *The Mobile Register* guessed that during the tenancy of the lodge it had been a fishpool. Drying up of the water had killed the fish, who now permeated the remnant of mud with this foul odor.

The possibility that Cranmer had needed to keep fresh fish at hand for some of his experiments silenced the natural objection that in a country where every stream holds gar pike, bass, catfish and many other edible varieties, no one would dream of stocking a stagnant puddle.

After tramping about the enclosure, testing the queerly brittle, desiccated top stratum of earth within and speculating concerning the possible purpose of the wall, I cut off a long limb of chinaberry and probed the mud. One fragment of fish spine would confirm the guess of that imaginative reporter.

I found nothing resembling a piscal skeleton, but established several facts. First, this mud crater had definite bottom only three or four feet below the surface of remaining ooze. Second, the fishy stench became stronger as I stirred. Third, at one time the mud, water, or whatever had comprised the balance of content, had reached the rim of the bowl. The last showed by certain marks plain enough when the crusty, two-inch stratum of upper coating was broken away. It was puzzling.

The nature of that thin, desiccated effluvium which seemed to cover everything even to the lower foot or two of brick, came in for next inspection. It was strange stuff, unlike any earth I ever had seen, though undoubtedly some form of scum drained in from the swamp at the time of river floods or cloudbursts (which in this section are common enough in spring and fall). It crumbled beneath the fingers. When I walked over it, the stuff crunched hollowly. In fainter degree it possessed the fishy odor also.

I took some samples where it lay thickest upon the ground, and also a few where there seemed to be no more than a depth of a sheet of paper. Later I would have a laboratory analysis made.

Apart from any possible bearing the stuff might have upon the disappearance of my three friends, I felt the tug of article interest— that wonder over anything strange or seemingly inexplicable which lends the hunt for fact a certain glamour and romance all its own. To myself I was going to have to explain sooner or later just why this layer covered the entire space within the walls and was not perceptible *anywhere* outside! The enigma could wait, however—or so I decided.

Far more interesting were the traces of violence apparent on wall and what once had been a house. The latter seemed to have been ripped from its foundations by a giant hand, crushed out of semblance to a dwelling, and then cast in fragments about the base of wall—mainly on the south side, where heaps of twisted, broken timbers lay in profusion. On the opposite side there had been such heaps once, but now only charred sticks, coated with that gray-black, omnipresent coat of desiccation, remained. These piles of charcoal had been sifted and examined most carefully by the authorities, as one theory had been advanced that Cranmer had burned the bodies of his victims. Yet no sign whatever of human remains was discovered.

The fire, however, pointed out one odd fact which controverted the reconstructions made by detectives months before. The latter, suggesting the dried scum to have drained in from the swamp, believed that the house timbers had floated out to the sides of the wall—there to arrange themselves in a series of piles! The absurdity of such a theory showed even more plainly in the fact that *if* the scum had filtered through in such a flood, the timbers most certainly had been dragged into piles *previously!* Some had burned—*and the scum coated their charred surfaces!*

What had been the force which had torn the lodge to bits as if in spiteful fury? Why had the parts of the wreckage been burned, the rest to escape?

Right here I felt was the keynote to the mystery, yet I could imagine no explanation. That John Corliss Cranmer himself—physically sound, yet a man who for decades had led a sedentary life—could have accomplished such destruction, unaided, was difficult to believe.

❧ V ❧

I turned my attention to the wall, hoping for evidence which might suggest another theory.

That wall had been an example of the worst snide construction. Though little more than a year old, the parts left standing showed evidence that they had begun to decay the day the last brick was laid. The mortar had fallen from the interstices. Here and there a brick had cracked and dropped out. Fibrils of the climbing vines had penetrated crevices, working for early destruction.

And one side already had fallen.

It was here that the first glimmering suspicion of the terrible truth was forced upon me. The scattered bricks, even those which had rolled inward toward the gaping foundation lodge, *had not been coated with scum!* This was curious, yet it could be explained by surmise that the flood itself had undermined this weakest portion of the wall. I cleared away a mass of brick from the spot on which the structure had stood; to my surprise I found it exceptionally firm! Hard red clay lay beneath! The flood conception was faulty; only some great force, exerted from inside or outside, could have wreaked such destruction.

When careful measurement, analysis and deduction convinced me—mainly from the fact that the lowermost layers of brick all had fallen outward, while the upper portions toppled in—I began to link up this mysterious and horrific force with the one which had rent the Lodge asunder. It looked as though a typhoon or gigantic centrifuge had needed elbow room in ripping down the wooden structure.

But I got nowhere with the theory, though in ordinary affairs I am called a man of too great imaginative tendencies. No less than three editors have cautioned me on this point. Perhaps it was the narrowing influence of great personal sympathy—yes, and love. I make no excuses, though beyond a dim understanding that some terrific, implacable force must have made this spot his playground, I ended my ninth day of note-taking and investigation almost as much in the dark as I had been while a thousand miles away in Chicago.

Then I started among the darkies and Cajans. A whole day I listened to yarns of the days which preceded Cranmer's escape from Elizabeth Ritter Hospital—days in which furtive men sniffed poisoned air for miles around Dead House, finding the odor intolerable. Days in which it seemed none possessed nerve enough to approach close. Days when the most fanciful tales of medieval superstitions were spun. These tales I shall not give; the truth is incredible enough.

At noon upon the eleventh day I chanced upon Rori Pailleron, a Cajan—and one of the least prepossessing of all with whom I had come in contact. "Chanced" perhaps is a bad word. I had listed every dweller of the woods within a five mile radius. Rori was sixteenth on my list. I went to him only after interviewing all four of the Crabiers and two whole families of Pichons. And Rori regarded me with the utmost suspicion until I made him a present of the two quarts of "shinny" purchased of the Pichons.

Because long practice has perfected me in the technique of seeming to drink another man's awful liquor—no, I'm not an absolute prohibitionist; fine wine or twelve-year-in-cask Bourbon whiskey arouses my definite interest—I fooled Pailleron from the start. I shall omit preliminaries, and leap to the first admission from him that he knew more concerning Dead House and its former inmates than any of the other darkies or Cajans roundabout.

"... But I ain't talkin'. *Sacre!* If I should open my gab, what might fly out? It is for keeping silent, y'r damn right! ..."

I agreed. He was a wise man—educated to some extent in the queer schools and churches maintained exclusively by Cajans in the depths of the woods, yet naive withal.

We drank. And I never had to ask another leading question. The liquor made him want to interest me; and the only extraordinary topic in this whole neck of the woods was the Dead House.

Three-quarters of a pint of acrid, nauseous fluid, and he hinted darkly. A pint, and he told me something I scarcely could believe. Another half-pint. ... But I shall give his confession in condensed form.

He had known Joe Sibley, the octoroon chef, houseman and valet who served Cranmer. Through Joe, Rori had furnished certain indispensables in way of food to the Cranmer household. At first, these salable articles had been exclusively vegetable—white and yellow turnip, sweet potatoes, corn and beans—but later, *meat!*

Yes, meat especially—whole lambs, slaughtered and quartered, the coarsest variety of piney-woods pork and beef, all in immense quantity!

⁂ VI ⁂

In December of the fatal winter Lee and his wife stopped down at the Lodge for ten days or thereabouts.

They were en route to Cuba at the time, intending to be away five or six weeks. Their original plan had been only to wait over a day or so in the piney-woods, but something caused an amendment to the scheme.

The two dallied. Lee seemed to have become vastly absorbed in something—so much absorbed that it was only when Peggy insisted upon continuing their trip that he could tear himself away.

It was during those ten days that he began buying meat. Meager bits of it at first—a rabbit, a pair of squirrels, or perhaps a few quail beyond the number he and Peggy shot. Rori furnished the game, thinking nothing of it except that Lee paid double prices—and insisted upon keeping the purchases secret from other members of the household.

"I'm putting it across on the Governor, Rori!" he said once with a wink. "Going to give him the shock of his life. So you mustn't let on, even to Joe about what I want you to do. Maybe it won't work out, but if it does . . . ! Dad'll have the scientific world at his feet! He doesn't blow his own horn anywhere near enough, you know."

Rori didn't know. Hadn't a suspicion what Lee was talking about. Still, if this rich, young idiot wanted to pay him a half dollar in good silver coin for a quail that anyone—himself included—could knock down with a five-cent shell, Rori was well satisfied to keep his mouth shut. Each evening he brought some of the small game. And each day Lee Cranmer seemed to have use for an additional quail or so. . . .

When he was ready to leave for Cuba, Lee came forward with the strangest of propositions. He fairly whispered his vehemence and desire for secrecy! He would tell Rori, and would pay the Cajan five hundred dollars—half in advance, and half at the end of five weeks when Lee himself would return from Cuba—provided Rori agreed to adhere absolutely to a certain secret program! The money was more than a fortune to Rori; it was undreamt-of affluence. The Cajan acceded.

"He wuz tellin' me then how the ol' man had raised some kind of pet," Rori confided, "an' wanted to get shet of it. So he give it to Lee, tellin' him to kill it, but Lee was sot on foolin' him. W'at I ask yer is, w'at kind of a pet is it w'at lives down in a mud sink an' *eats a couple hawgs every night?*"

I couldn't imagine, so I pressed him for further details. Here at last was something which sounded like a clue!

He really knew too little. The agreement with Lee provided that if Rori carried out the provisions exactly, he should be paid extra and at his exorbitant scale of all additional outlay, when Lee returned.

The young man gave him a daily schedule which Rori showed. Each evening he was to procure, slaughter and cut up a definite—and growing—amount of meat. Every item was checked, and I saw that they ran from five pounds up to *forty!*

"What, in heaven's name, did you do with it?" I demanded, excited now and pouring him an additional drink for fear caution might return to him.

"Took it through the bushes in back an' slung it in the mud sink there! An' suthin' come up an' drug it down!"

"A 'gator?"

"*Diablo!* How should I know? It was dark. I wouldn't go close." He shuddered, and the fingers which lifted his glass shook as with sudden chill. "Mebbe you'd of done it, huh? Not me, though! The young fellah tole me to sling it in, an' I slung it.

"A couple times I come around in the light, but there wasn't nuthin' there you could see. Jes' mud, an' some water. Mebbe the thing didn't come out in daytimes. . . ."

"Perhaps not," I agreed, straining every mental resource to imagine what Lee's sinister pet could have been. "But you said something about *two hogs a day?* What did you mean by that? This paper, proof enough that you're telling the truth so far, states that on the thirty-fifth day you were to throw forty pounds of meat—any kind—into the sink. Two hogs, even the piney-woods variety, weigh a lot more than forty pounds!"

"Them was after—after he come back!"

From this point onward, Rori's tale became more and more enmeshed in the vagaries induced by bad liquor. His tongue thickened. I shall give his story without attempt to reproduce further verbal barbarities, or the occasional prodding I had to give in order to keep him from maundering into foolish jargon.

Lee had paid munificently. His only objection to the manner in which Rori had carried out his orders was that the orders themselves had been deficient. The pet, he said had grown enormously. It was hungry, ravenous. Lee himself had supplemented the fare with huge pails of scraps from the kitchen.

From that day Lee purchased from Rori whole sheep and hogs! The Cajan continued to bring the carcasses at nightfall, but no longer did Lee permit him to approach the pool. The young man appeared chronically excited now. He had a tremendous secret—one the extent of which even his father did not guess, and one which would astonish the world! Only a week or two more and he would spring it. First he would have to arrange certain data.

Then came the day when everyone disappeared from Dead House. Rori came around several times, but concluded that all of the occupants had folded tents and departed—doubtless taking their mysterious "pet" along. Only when he saw from a distance Joe, the octoroon servant, returning along the road on foot toward the Lodge, did his slow mental processes begin to ferment. That afternoon Rori visited the strange place for the next to last time.

He did not go to the Lodge itself—and there were reasons. While still some hundreds of yards away from the place a terrible, sustained screaming reached his ears! It was faint, yet unmistakably the voice of Joe! Throwing a pair of number two shells into the breech of his shotgun, Rori hurried on, taking his usual path through the brush at the back.

He saw—and as he told me even "shinny" drunkenness fled his chattering tones—Joe, the octoroon. Aye, he stood in the yard, far from the pool into which Rori had thrown the carcasses—and Joe could not move!

Rori failed to explain in full, but something, a slimy, amorphous something, which glistened in the sunlight, already engulfed the man to his shoulders! Breath was cut off. Joe's contorted face writhed with horror and beginning suffocation. One hand—all that was free of the rest of him!—beat feebly upon the rubbery, translucent thing that was engulfing his body!

Then Joe sank from sight. . . .

❧ VII ❧

Five days of liquored indulgence passed before Rori, alone in his shaky cabin, convinced himself that he had seen a phantasy born of alcohol. He came back the last time—to find a high wall of brick surrounding the Lodge, and including the pool of mud into which he had thrown the meat!

While he hesitated, circling the place without discovering an opening—which he would not have dared to use, even had he found it—a crashing, tearing of timbers, and persistent sound of awesome destruction came from within. He swung himself into one of the oaks near the wall. And he was just in time to see the last supporting stanchions of the Lodge give way *outward!*

The whole structure came apart. The roof fell in yet seemed to move after it had fallen! Logs of wall deserted retaining grasp of their spikes like layers of plywood in the grasp of the shearing machine!

That was all. Soddenly intoxicated now, Rori mumbled more phrases, giving me the idea that on another day when he became sober once more, he might add to his statements, but I—numbed to the soul—scarcely cared. If that which he related was true, what nightmare of madness must have been consummated here!

I could envision some things now which concerned Lee and Peggy, horrible things. Only remembrance of Elsie kept me faced forward in the search—for now it seemed almost that the handiwork of a madman must be preferred to what Rori claimed to have seen! What had been that sinister, translucent thing? That glistening thing which jumped upward about a man, smothering, engulfing?

Queerly enough, though such a theory as came most easily to mind now would have outraged reason in me if suggested concerning total strangers, I asked myself only what details of Rori's revelation had been exaggerated by fright and fumes of liquor. And as I sat on the creaking bench in his cabin, staring unseeing as he lurched down to the floor, fumbling with a lock box of green tin which lay under his cot, and muttering, the answer to all my questions lay within reach!

It was not until next day, however, that I made the discovery. Heavy of heart I had reexamined the spot where the Lodge had stood, then made my way to the Cajan's cabin again, seeking sober confirmation of what he had told me during intoxication.

In imagining that such a spree for Rori would be ended by a single night, however, I was mistaken. He lay sprawled almost as I had left him. Only two factors were changed. No "shinny" was left—and lying open, with its miscellaneous contents strewed about, was the tin box. Rori somehow had managed to open it with the tiny key still clutched in his hand.

Concern for his safety alone was what made me notice the box. It was a receptacle for small fishing tackle of the sort carried here and there by any sportsman. Tangles of Dowagiac minnows, spoon hooks ranging in size to silver-backed number eights; three reels still carrying line of different weights, spinners, casting plugs, wobblers, floating baits, were spilled out upon the rough plank flooring where they might snag Rori badly if he rolled. I gathered them, intending to save him an accident.

With the miscellaneous assortment in my hands, however, I stopped dead. Something had caught my eye—something lying flush with the bottom of the lock box! I stared, and then swiftly tossed the hooks and other impedimenta upon the table. What I had glimpsed there in the box was a loose-leaf notebook of the sort used for recording laboratory data! And Rori scarcely could read let alone *write!*

Feverishly, a riot of recognition, surmise, hope and fear bubbling in my brain, I grabbed the book and threw it open. At once I knew that this was the end. The pages were scribbled in pencil, but the handwriting was that precise chirography I knew as belonging to John Corliss Cranmer, the scientist!

"*. . . Could he not have obeyed my instructions! Oh, God! This . . .*"

❖ ❖ ❖

These were the words at top of the first page which met my eye.

Because knowledge of the circumstances, the relation of which I pried out of the reluctant Rori only some days later when I had him in Mobile as a police witness for the sake of my friend's vindication, is necessary to understanding, I shall interpolate.

Rori had not told me everything. On his late visit to the vicinage of Dead House he saw more. A crouching figure, seated Turk fashion on top of the wall, appeared to be writing industriously. Rori recognized the man as Cranmer, yet did not hail him. He had no opportunity.

Just as the Cajan came near, Cranmer rose, thrust the notebook, which had rested across his knees, into the box. Then he turned, tossed outside the wall both the locked box and a ribbon to which was attached the key.

Then his arms raised toward heavens. For five seconds he seemed to invoke the mercy of Power beyond all of man's scientific prying. And finally he leaped, *inside* !

Rori did not climb to investigate. He knew that directly below this portion of wall lay the mud sink into which he had thrown the chunks of meat!

❋ VIII ❋

This is a true transcription of the statement I inscribed, telling the sequence of actual events at Dead House. The original of the statement now lies in the archives of the detective department.

Cranmer's notebook, though written in a precise hand, yet betrayed the man's insanity by incoherence and frequent repetitions. My statement has been accepted now, both by alienists and by detectives who had entertained different theories in respect to the case. It quashes the noisome hints and suspicions regarding three of the finest Americans who ever lived—and also one queer supposition dealing with supposed criminal tendencies in poor Joe, the octoroon.

John Corliss Cranmer *went* insane for sufficient cause!

❖ ❖ ❖

As readers of popular fiction know well, Lee Cranmer's *forte* was the writing of what is called—among fellows in the craft—the pseudo scientific story. In plain words, this means a yarn, based upon solid fact in the field of astronomy, chemistry, anthropology or whatnot, which carries to logical conclusion improved theories of men who devote their lives to searching out further nadirs of fact.

In certain fashion these men are allies of science. Often they visualize something which has not been imagined even by the best of men from whom they secure data, thus opening new horizons of possibility. In a large way Jules Verne was one of these men in his day; Lee Cranmer bade fair to carry on the work in worthy fashion— work taken up for a period by an Englishman named Wells, but abandoned for stories of a different—and, in my humble opinion, less absorbing—type.

Lee wrote three novels, all published, which dealt with such subjects—two of the three secured from his own father's labors, and the other speculating upon the discovery and possible uses of inter-atomic energy. Upon John Corliss Cranmer's return from Prague that fatal winter, the father informed Lee that a greater subject than any with which the young man had dealt, now could be tapped.

Cranmer, senior, had devised a way in which the limiting factors in protozoic life and growth, could be nullified; in time, and with cooperation of biologists who specialized upon karyokinesis and embryology of higher forms, he hoped—to put the theory in pragmatic terms—to be able to grow swine the size of elephants, quail or woodcock with breasts from which a hundredweight of white meat could be cut away, and steers whose dehorned heads might butt at the third story of a skyscraper!

Such result would revolutionize the methods of food supply, of course. It also would hold out hope for all undersized specimens of humanity—provided only that if factors inhibiting growth could be deleted, some methods of stopping gianthood also could be developed.

Cranmer the elder, through use of an undescribed (in the notebook) growth medium of which one constituent was agar-agar, and the use of radium emanations, had succeeded in bringing about apparently unrestricted growth in the paramoecium protozoan, certain of the vegetable growths (among which were bacteria), and in the amorphous cell of protoplasm known as the amoeba—the last a single cell containing only neucleolus, neucleus, and a space known as the contractile vacuole which somehow aided in throwing off particles impossible to assimilate directly. This point may be remembered in respect to the piles of lumber left near the outside walls surrounding Dead House!

When Lee Cranmer and his wife came south to visit, John Corliss Cranmer showed his son an amoeba—normally an organism visible under low-power microscope—which he had absolved from natural growth inhibitions. This amoeba, a rubbery, amorphous mass of protoplasm, was of the size then of a large beef liver. It could have been held in two cupped hands, placed side by side.

"How large could it grow?" asked Lee, wide-eyed and interested.

"So far as I know," answered his father, "there is no limit—now! It might, if it got food enough, grow to be as big as the Masonic Temple!

"But take it out and kill it. Destroy the organism utterly—burning the fragments—else there is no telling what might happen. The amoeba, as I have explained, reproduces by simple division. Any fragment remaining might be dangerous."

Lee took the rubbery, translucent giant cell—but he did not obey orders. Instead of destroying it as his father had directed, Lee thought out a plan. Suppose he should grow this organism to tremendous size? Suppose, when the tale of his father's accomplishment were spread, an amoeba of many tons weight could be shown in evidence? Lee, of somewhat sensational cast of mind, determined instantly to keep secret the fact that he was not destroying the organism, but encouraging its further growth. Thought of possible peril never crossed his mind.

He arranged to have the thing fed—allowing for normal increase of size in an abnormal thing. It fooled him only in growing much more rapidly. When he came back from Cuba the amoeba practically filled the whole of the mud sink hollow. He had to give it much greater supplies. . . .

The giant cell came to absorb as much as two hogs in a single day. During daylight, while hunger still was appeased, it never emerged, however. That remained for the time that it could secure no more food near at hand to satisfy its ravenous and increasing appetite.

Only instinct for the sensational kept Lee from telling Peggy, his wife, all about the matter. Lee hoped to spring a *coup* which would immortalize his father, and surprise his wife terrifically. Therefore, he kept his own counsel—and made bargains with the Cajan, Rori, who supplied food daily for the shapeless monster of the pool.

The tragedy itself came suddenly and unexpectedly. Peggy, feeding the two Gordon setters that Lee and she used for quail hunting, was in the Lodge yard before sunset. She romped alone, as Lee himself was dressing.

Of a sudden her screams cut the still air! Without her knowledge, ten-foot pseudopods—those flowing tentacles of protoplasm sent forth by the sinister occupant of the pool—slid out and around her putteed ankles.

For a moment she did not understand. Then, at first suspicion of the horrid truth, her cries rent the air. Lee, at that time struggling to lace a pair of high shoes, straightened, paled, and grabbed a revolver as he dashed out.

In another room a scientist, absorbed in his note-taking, glanced up, frowned, and then—recognizing the voice—shed his white gown and came out. He was too late to do aught but gasp with horror.

In the yard Peggy was half engulfed in a squamous, rubbery something which at first he could not analyze.

Lee, his boy, was fighting with the sticky folds, and slowly, surely, losing his own grip upon the earth!

⚔ IX ⚔

John Corliss Cranmer was by no means a coward, he stared, cried aloud, then ran indoors, seizing the first two weapons which came to hand—a shotgun and hunting knife which lay in sheath in a cartridged belt across hook of the hall-tree. The knife was ten inches in length and razor keen.

Cranmer rushed out again. He saw an indecent fluid something—which as yet he had not had time to classify—lumping itself into a six-foot-high center before his very eyes!

It looked like one of the micro-organisms he had studied! One grown to frightful dimensions. An amoeba!

There, some minutes suffocated in the rubbery folds—yet still apparent beneath the glistening ooze of this monster—were two bodies.

They were dead. He knew it. Nevertheless he attacked the flowing, senseless monster with his knife. Shot would do no good. And he found that even the deep, terrific slashes made by his knife closed together in a moment and healed. The monster was invulnerable to ordinary attack!

A pair of *pseudopods* sought out his ankles, attempting to bring him low. Both of these he severed   and escaped. Why did he try? He did not know. The two whom he had sought to rescue were dead, buried under folds of this horrid thing he knew to be his own discovery and fabrication.

Then it was that revulsion and insanity came upon him.

There ended the story of John Corliss Cranmer, save for one hastily scribbled paragraph—evidently written at the time Rori had seen him atop the wall.

May we not supply with assurance the intervening steps?

Cranmer was known to have purchased a whole pen of hogs a day or two following the tragedy. These animals never were seen again. During the time the wall was being constructed is it not reasonable to assume that he fed the giant organism within—to keep it quiet? His scientist brain must have visualized clearly the havoc and horror which could be wrought by the loathsome thing if it ever were driven by hunger to flow away from the Lodge and prey upon the countryside!

With the wall once in place, he evidently figured that starvation or some other means which he could supply would kill the thing. One of the means had been made by setting fire to several piles of the disgorged timbers; probably this had no effect whatever.

The amoeba was to accomplish still more destruction. In the throes of hunger it threw its gigantic, formless strength against the house walls from the inside; then every edible morsel within was assimilated, the logs, rafters and other fragments being worked out through the contractile vacuole.

During some of its last struggles, undoubtedly, the side wall of brick was weakened—not to collapse, however, until the giant amoeba no longer could take advantage of the breach.

In final death lassitude, the amoeba stretched itself out in a thin layer over the ground. There it succumbed, though there is no means of estimating how long a time intervened.

The last paragraph in Cranmer's notebook, scrawled so badly that it is possible some words I have not deciphered correctly, read as follows:

> *"In my work I have found the means of creating a monster. The unnatural thing, in turn, has destroyed my work and those whom I held dear. It is in vain that I assure myself of innocence of spirit. Mine is the crime of presumption. Now, as expiation— worthless though that may be—I give myself. . . ."*

It is better not to think of that last leap, and the struggle of an insane man in the grip of the dying monster.

The Valley of the Worm

INTRODUCTION

Originally published in the February 1934 issue of *Weird Tales*, this story by the celebrated creator of Conan the barbarian and King Kull of Atlantis gives us a tale of a huge monster which might have been created by Howard's friend and correspondent, H.P. Lovecraft. This time, however, the nameless thing is up against one of Howard's mighty-thewed barbarians, and the final score is not necessarily going to read eldritch horror 1, human(s) 0.

❖ ❖ ❖

Texan Robert E. Howard (1906-1936) is often credited with inventing the fantasy subgenre of sword and sorcery (though that name was applied to the field somewhat later by Fritz Leiber), and while he wrote much more than his now-classic tales of Conan the barbarian, and also much more than sword and sorcery, it's Conan, star of the pulps, paperbacks, comic books, movies, and TV shows who has proven Howard's most enduring creation. And they are likely to endure as long as readers continue to enjoy fast-moving action-adventure stories with a hero who is free of conflicted desires or neurotic hangups. As L. Sprague de Camp put it, the stories are pure *fun*.

The Valley of the Worm

by Robert E. Howard

I will tell you of Niord and the Worm. You have heard the tale before in many guises wherein the hero was named Tyr, or Perseus, or Siegfried, or Beowulf, or Saint George. But it was Niord who met the loathly demoniac thing that crawled hideously up from hell, and from which meeting sprang the cycle of hero-tales that revolves down the ages until the very substance of the truth is lost and passes into the limbo of all forgotten legends. I know whereof I speak, for I was Niord.

As I lie here awaiting death, which creeps slowly upon me like a blind slug, my dreams are filled with glittering visions and the pageantry of glory. It is not of the drab, disease-racked life of James Allison I dream, but all the gleaming figures of the mighty pageantry that have passed before, and shall come after; for I have faintly glimpsed, not merely the shapes that trail out behind, but shapes that come after, as a man in a long parade glimpses, far ahead, the line of figures that precede him winding over a distant hill, etched shadow like against the sky. I am one and all the pageantry of shapes and guises and masks which have been, are, and shall be the visible manifestations of that illusive, intangible, but vitally existent spirit now promenading under the brief and temporary name of James Allison.

Each man on earth, each woman, is part and all of a similar

caravan of shapes and beings. But they can not remember—their minds can not bridge the brief, awful gulfs of blackness which lie between those unstable shapes, and which the spirit, soul or ego, in spanning, shakes off its fleshy masks. I remember. Why I can remember is the strangest tale of all; but as I lie here with death's black wings slowly unfolding over me, all the dim folds of my previous lives are shaken out before my eyes, and I see myself in many forms and guises—braggart, swaggering, fearful, loving, foolish, all that men— have been or will be.

I have been Man in many lands and many conditions; yet—and here is another strange thing—my line of reincarnation runs straight down one unerring channel. I have never been any but a man of that restless race men once called Nordheimr and later Aryans, and today named by many names and designations. Their history is my history, from the first mewling wail of a hairless white ape cub in the wastes of the arctic, to the death-cry of the last degenerate product of ultimate civilization, in some dim and unguessed future age.

My name has been Hialmar, Tyr, Bragi, Bran, Horsa, Eric, and John: I strode red-handed through the deserted streets of Rome behind the yellow-maned Brennus; I wandered through the violated plantations with Alaric and his Goths when the flame of burning villas lit the land like day and an empire was gasping its last under our sandalled feet; I waded sword in hand through the foaming surf from Hengist's galley to lay the foundations of England in blood and pillage; when Leif the Lucky sighted the broad white beaches of an unguessed world, I stood beside him in the bows of the dragonship, my golden beard blowing in the wind; and when Godfrey of Bouillon led his Crusaders over the walls of Jerusalem, I was among them in steel cap and brigandine.

But it is of none of these things I would speak: I would take you back with me into an age beside which that of Brennus and Rome is as yesterday. I would take you back through, not merely centuries and millenniums, but epochs and dim ages unguessed by the wildest philosopher. Oh far, far and far will you fare into the nighted Past before you win beyond the boundaries of my race, blue-eyed, yellow-haired, wanderers, slayers, lovers, mighty in rapine and wayfaring.

It is the adventure of Niord Worm's-bane of which I speak—the root-stem of a whole cycle of hero-tales which has not yet reached its end, the grisly underlying reality that lurks behind time-distorted myths of dragons, fiends and monsters.

Yet it is not alone with the mouth of Niord that I will speak. I am James Allison no less than I was Niord, and as I unfold the tale, I will interpret some of his thoughts and dreams and deeds from the mouth of the modern I, so that the saga of Niord shall not be a meaningless chaos to you. His blood is your blood, who are sons of Aryan; but wide misty gulfs of eons lie horrifically between, and the deeds and dreams of Niord seem as alien to your deeds and dreams as the primordial and lion-haunted forest seems alien to the white-walled city street.

It was a strange world in which Niord lived and loved and fought, so long ago that even my eon-spanning memory can not recognize landmarks. Since then the surface of the earth has changed, not once but a score of times; continents have risen and sunk, seas have changed their beds and rivers their courses, glaciers have waxed and waned, and the very stars and constellations have altered and shifted.

It was so long ago that the cradle-land of my race was still in Nordheim. But the epic drifts of my people had already begun, and blue-eyed, yellow-maned tribes flowed eastward and southward and westward, on century-long treks that carried them around the world and left their bones and their traces in strange lands and wild waste places. On one of these drifts I grew from infancy to manhood. My knowledge of that northern homeland was dim memories, like half-remembered dreams, of blinding white snow plains and ice fields, of great fires roaring in the circle of hide tents, of yellow manes flying in great winds, and a sun setting in a lurid wallow of crimson clouds, blazing on trampled snow where still dark forms lay in pools that were redder than the sunset.

That last memory stands out clearer than the others. It was the field of Jotunheim, I was told in later years, whereon had just been fought that terrible battle which was the Armageddon of the Esirfolk, the subject of a cycle of hero-songs for long ages, and which still lives today in dim dreams of Ragnarok and Goetterdaemmerung. I looked on that battle as a mewling infant; so I must have lived about—but I will not name the age, for I would be called a madman, and historians and geologists alike would rise to refute me.

But my memories of Nordheim were few and dim, paled by memories of that long, long trek upon which I had spent my life. We had not kept to a straight course, but our trend had been for ever southward. Sometimes we had bided for a while in fertile upland valleys or rich river-traversed plains, but always we took up the trail again, and not always because of drouth or famine. Often we left countries teeming with game and wild grain to push into wastelands. On our trail we moved endlessly, driven only by our restless whim, yet blindly following a cosmic law, the workings of which we never guessed, any more than the wild geese guess in their flights around the world. So at last we came into the Country of the Worm.

I will take up the tale at the time when we came into jungle-clad hills reeking with rot and teeming with spawning life, where the tom-toms of a savage people pulsed incessantly through the hot breathless night. These people came forth to dispute our way—short, strongly built men, black-haired, painted, ferocious, but indisputably white men. We knew their breed of old. They were Picts, and of all alien races the fiercest. We had met their kind before in thick forests, and in upland valleys beside mountain lakes. But many moons had passed since those meetings.

I believe this particular tribe represented the easternmost drift of the race. They were the most primitive and ferocious of any I ever met. Already they were exhibiting hints of characteristics I have noted among black savages in jungle countries, though they had dwelt in these environs only a few generations. The abysmal jungle was engulfing them, was obliterating their pristine characteristics and shaping them in its own horrific mold. They were drifting into head-hunting, and cannibalism was but a step which I believe they must have taken before they became extinct. These things are natural adjuncts to the jungle; the Picts did not learn them from the black people, for then there were no blacks among those hills. In later years they came up from the south, and the Picts first enslaved and then were absorbed by them. But with that my saga of Niord is not concerned.

We came into that brutish hill country, with its squalling abysms of savagery and black primitiveness. We were—a whole tribe marching on foot, old men, wolfish with their long beards and gaunt limbs, giant warriors in their prime, naked children running along the line of march, women with tousled yellow locks carrying babies which never cried—unless it were to scream from pure rage. I do not remember our numbers, except, that there were some five hundred fighting-men—and by fighting-men I mean all males, from the child just strong enough to lift a bow, to the oldest of the old men. In that madly ferocious age all were fighters. Our women fought, when brought to bay, like tigresses, and I have seen a babe, not yet old enough to stammer articulate words, twist its head and sink its tiny teeth in the foot that stamped out its life.

Oh, we were fighters! Let me speak of Niord. I am proud of him, the more when I consider the paltry crippled body of James Allison, the unstable mask I now wear. Niord was tall, with great shoulders, lean hips and mighty limbs. His muscles were long and swelling, denoting endurance and speed as well as strength. He could run all day without tiring, and he possessed a co-ordination that made his movements a blur of blinding speed. If I told you his full strength, you would brand me a liar. But there is no man on earth today strong enough to bend the bow Niord handled with ease. The longest arrow-flight on record is that of a Turkish archer who sent a shaft 482 yards. There was not a stripling in my tribe who could not have bettered that flight.

As we entered the jungle country we heard the tomtoms booming across the mysterious valleys that slumbered between the brutish hills, and in a broad, open plateau we met our enemies. I do not believe these Picts knew us, even by legends, or they had never rushed so openly to the onset, though they outnumbered us. But there was no attempt at ambush. They swarmed out of the trees, dancing and singing their war-songs, yelling their barbarous threats. Our heads should hang in their idol-hut and our yellow-haired women should bear their sons. Ho! ho! ho! By Ymir, it was Niord who laughed then, not James Allison. Just so we of the Aesir laughed to hear their threats—deep thunderous laughter from broad and mighty chests: Our trail was laid in blood and embers through many lands. We were the slayers and ravishers, striding sword in hand across the world, and that these folk threatened us woke our rugged humor. We went to meet them, naked but for our wolfhides, swinging our bronze swords, and our singing was like rolling thunder in the hills. They sent their arrows among us, and we gave back their fire. They could not match us in archery. Our arrows hissed in blinding clouds among them, dropping them like autumn leaves, until they howled and frothed like mad dogs and charged to hand-grips. And we, mad with the fighting joy, dropped our bows and ran to meet them, as a lover runs to his love.

By Ymir, it was a battle to madden and make drunken with the slaughter and the fury. The Picts were as ferocious as we, but ours was the superior physique, the keener wit, the more highly developed fighting-brain. We won because we were a superior race, but it was no easy victory. Corpses littered the blood-soaked earth; but at last they broke, and we cut them down as they ran, to the very edge of the trees. I tell of that fight in a few bald words. I can not paint the madness, the reek of sweat and blood, the panting, muscle-straining effort, the splintering of bones under mighty blows, the rending and hewing of quivering sentient flesh; above all the merciless abysmal savagery of the whole affair, in which there was neither rule nor order, each man fighting as he would or could. If I might do so, you would recoil in horror; even the modern I, cognizant of my close kinship with those times, stand aghast as I review that butchery.

Mercy was yet unborn, save as some individual's whim, and rules of warfare were as yet undreamed of. It was an age in which each tribe and each human fought tooth and fang from birth to death, and neither gave nor expected mercy.

So we cut down the fleeing Picts, and our women came out on the field to brain the wounded enemies with stones, or cut their throats with copper knives. We did not torture. We were no more cruel than life demanded.

The rule of life was ruthlessness, but there is more wanton cruelty today than ever we dreamed of. It was not wanton bloodthirstiness that made us butcher wounded and captive foes. It was because we knew our chances of survival increased with each enemy slain.

Yet there was occasionally a touch of individual mercy, and so it was in this fight. I had been occupied with a duel with an especially valiant enemy. His tousled thatch of black hair scarcely came above my chin, but he was a solid knot of steel-spring muscles, than which lightning scarcely moved faster. He had an iron sword and a hidecovered buckler. I had a knotty-headed bludgeon. That fight was one that glutted even my battle-lusting soul. I was bleeding from a score of flesh wounds before one of my terrible, slashing strokes smashed his shield like cardboard, and an instant later my bludgeon glanced from his unprotected head. Ymir! Even now I stop to laugh and marvel at the hardness of that Pict's skull. Men of that age were assuredly built on a rugged plan! That blow should have spattered his brains like water. It did lay his scalp open horribly, dashing him senseless to the earth, where I let him lie, supposing him to be dead, as I joined in the slaughter of the fleeing warriors.

When I returned reeking with sweat and blood, my club horridly clotted with blood and brains, I noticed that my antagonist was regaining consciousness, and that a naked tousle-headed girl was preparing to give him the finishing touch with a stone she could scarcely lift: A vagrant whim caused me to check the blow. I had enjoyed the fight, and I admired the adamantine quality of his skull.

We made camp a short distance away, burned our dead on a great pyre, and after looting the corpses of the enemy, we dragged them across the plateau and cast them down in a valley to make a feast for the hyenas, jackals and vultures which were already gathering. We kept close watch that night, but we were not attacked, though far away through the jungle we could make out the red gleam of fires, and could faintly hear, when the wind veered, the throb of tom-toms and demoniac screams and yells—keenings for the slain or mere animal squallings of fury.

Nor did they attack us in the days that followed. We bandaged our captive's wounds and quickly learned his primitive tongue, which, however, was so different from ours that I can not conceive of the two languages having ever had a common source.

His name was Grom, and he was a great hunter and fighter, he boasted. He talked freely and held no grudge, grinning broadly and showing tusk-like teeth, his beady eyes glittering from under the tangled black mane that fell over his low forehead. His limbs were almost apelike in their thickness.

He was vastly interested in his captors, though he could never understand why he had been spared; to the end it remained an inexplicable mystery to him. The Picts obeyed the law of survival even more rigidly than did the Aesir. They were the more practical, as shown by their more settled habits. They never roamed as far or as blindly as we. Yet in every line we were the superior race.

Grom, impressed by our intelligence and fighting qualities, volunteered to go into the hills and make peace for us with his people. It was immaterial to us, but we let him go. Slavery had not yet been dreamed of.

So Grom went back to his people, and we forgot about him, except that I went a trifle more cautiously about my hunting, expecting him to be lying in wait to put an arrow through my back. Then one day we heard a rattle of tom-toms, and Grom appeared at the edge of the jungle, his face split in his gorilla-grin, with the painted, skinclad, feather-bedecked chiefs of the clans. Our ferocity had awed them, and our sparing of Grom further impressed them. They could not understand leniency; evidently—we valued them too cheaply to bother about killing one when he was in our power.

So peace was made with much pow-wow, and sworn to with many strange oaths and rituals we swore only by Ymir, and an Aesir never broke that vow. But they swore by the elements, by the idol which sat in the fetish-hut where fires burned for ever and a withered crone slapped a leather-covered drum all night long, and by another being too terrible to be named.

Then we all sat around the fires and gnawed meatbones, and drank a fiery concoction they brewed from wild grain, and the wonder is that the feast did not end in a general massacre; for that liquor had devils in it and made maggots writhe in our brains. But no harm came of our vast drunkenness, and thereafter we dwelt at peace with our barbarous neighbors. They taught us many things, and learned many more from us. But they taught us iron-workings; into which they had been forced by the lack of copper in those hills, and we quickly excelled them.

We went freely among their villages—mud-walled clusters of huts in hilltop clearings, overshadowed by giant trees—and we allowed them to come at will among our camps—straggling lines of hide tents on the plateau where the battle had been fought. Our young men cared not for their squat beady-eyed women, and our rangy clean-limbed girls with their tousled yellow heads were not drawn to the hairy-breasted savages. Familiarity over a period of years would have reduced the repulsion on either side, until the two races would have flowed together to form one hybrid people, but long before that time the Aesir rose and departed, vanishing into the mysterious hazes of the haunted south. But before that exodus there came to pass the horror of the Worm.

I hunted with Grom and he led me into brooding, uninhabited valleys and up into silence-haunted hills where no men had set foot before us. But there was one valley, off in the mazes of the southwest, into which he would not go. Stumps of shattered columns, relics of a forgotten civilization, stood among the trees on the valley floor. Grom showed them to me, as we stood on the cliffs that flanked the mysterious vale, but he would not go down into it, and he dissuaded me when I would have gone alone. He would not speak plainly of the danger that lurked there, but it was greater than that of serpent or tiger, or the trumpeting elephants which occasionally wandered up in devastating droves from the south.

Of all beasts, Grom told me in the gutturals of his tongue, the Picts feared only Satha, the great snake, and they shunned the jungle where he lived. But there was another thing they feared, and it was connected in some manner with the Valley of Broken Stones, as the Picts called the crumbling pillars. Long ago, when his ancestors had first come into the country, they had dared that grim vale, and a whole clan of them had perished, suddenly, horribly, and unexplainably. At least Grom did not explain. The horror had come up out of the earth, somehow, and it was not good to talk of it, since it was believed that It might be summoned by speaking of It—whatever It was.

But Grom was ready to hunt with me anywhere else; for he was the greatest hunter among the Picts, and many and fearful were our adventures. Once I killed, with the iron sword I had forged with my own hands, that most terrible of all beasts—old saber-tooth, which men today call a tiger because he was more like a tiger than anything else. In reality he was almost as much like a bear in build, save for his unmistakably feline head. Saber-tooth was massive-limbed, with a low-hung, great, heavy body, and he vanished from the earth because he was too terrible a fighter, even for that grim age. As his muscles and ferocity grew, his brain dwindled until at last even the instinct of self-preservation vanished. Nature, who maintains her balance in such things, destroyed him because, had his super-fighting powers been allied with an intelligent brain, he would have destroyed all other forms of life on earth. He was a freak on the road of evolution— organic development gone mad and run to fangs and talons, to slaughter and destruction.

I killed saber-tooth in a battle that would make a saga in itself, and for months afterward I lay semi-delirious with ghastly wounds that made the toughest warriors shake their heads. The Picts said that never before had a man killed a saber-tooth single-handed. Yet I recovered, to the wonder of all.

While I lay at the doors of death there was a secession from the tribe. It was a peaceful secession, such as continually occurred and contributed greatly to the peopling of the world by yellow-haired tribes. Forty-five of the young men took themselves mates simultaneously and wandered off to found a clan of their own. There was no revolt; it was a racial custom which bore fruits in all the later ages, when tribes sprung from the same roots met, after centuries of separation, and cut one another's throats with joyous abandon. The tendency of the Aryan and the pre-Aryan was always toward disunity, clans splitting off the main stem, and scattering.

So these young men, led by one Bragi, my brother-in-arms, took their girls and venturing to the southwest, took up their abode in the Valley of Broken Stones. The Picts expostulated, hinting vaguely of a monstrous doom that haunted the vale, but the Aesir laughed. We had left our own demons and weirds in the icy wastes of the far blue north, and the devils of other races did not much impress us:

When my full strength was returned, and the grisly wounds were only scars, I girt on my weapons and strode over the plateau to visit Bragi's clan. Grom did not accompany me. He had not been in the Aesir camp for several days. But I knew the way. I remembered well the valley, from the cliffs of which I had looked down and seen the lake at the upper end, the trees thickening into forest at the lower extremity. The sides of the valley were high sheer cliffs, and a steep broad ridge at either end cut it off from the surrounding country. It was toward the lower or southwestern end that the valley-floor was dotted thickly with ruined columns, some towering high among the trees, some fallen into heaps of lichenclad stones. What race reared them none knew. But Grom had hinted fearsomely of a hairy, apish monstrosity dancing loathsomely under the moon to a demoniac piping that induced horror and madness.

I crossed the plateau whereon our camp was pitched, descended the slope, traversed a shallow vegetation-choked valley, climbed another slope, and plunged into the hills. A half-day's leisurely travel brought me to the ridge on, the other side of which lay the valley of the pillars. For many miles I had seen no sign of human life. The settlements of the Picts all lay many miles to the east. I topped the ridge and looked down into the dreaming valley with its still blue lake, its brooding cliffs and its broken columns jutting among the trees. I looked for smoke. I saw none, but I saw vultures wheeling in the sky over a cluster of tents on the lake shore.

I came down the ridge warily and approached the silent camp. In it I halted, frozen with horror. I was not easily moved. I had seen death in many forms, and had fled from or taken part in red massacres that spilled blood like water and heaped the earth with corpses. But here I was confronted with an organic devastation that staggered and appalled me: Of Bragi's embryonic clan, not one remained alive, and not one corpse was whole. Some of the hide tents still stood erect. Others were mashed down and flattened out, as if crushed by some monstrous weight, so that at first I wondered if a drove of elephants had stampeded across the camp. But no elephants ever wrought such destruction as I saw strewn on the bloody ground. The camp was a shambles, littered with bits of flesh and fragments of bodies—hands, feet, heads, pieces of human debris. Weapons lay about, some of them stained with a greenish slime like that which spurts from a crushed caterpillar.

No human foe could have committed this ghastly atrocity. I looked at the lake, wondering if nameless amphibian monsters had crawled from the calm waters whose deep blue told of unfathomed depths. Then I saw a print left by the destroyer. It was a track such as a titanic worm might leave, yards broad, winding back down the valley. The grass lay flat where it ran, and bushes and small trees had been crushed down into the earth, all horribly smeared with blood and greenish slime.

With berserk fury in my soul I drew my sword and started to follow it, when a call attracted me. I wheeled, to see a stocky form approaching me from the ridge. It was Grom the Pict, and when I think of the courage it must have taken for him to have overcome all the instincts planted in him by traditional teachings and personal experience, I realize the full depths of his friendship for me.

Squatting on the lake shore, spear in his hands, his black eyes ever roving fearfully down the brooding treewaving reaches of the valley, Grom told me of the horror that had come upon Bragi's clan under the moon. But first he told me of it, as his sires had told the tale to him: Long ago the Picts had drifted down from the northwest on a long, long trek, finally reaching these jungle covered hills, where, because they were weary, and because the game and fruit were plentiful and there were no hostile tribes, they halted and built their mud-walled villages.

Some of them, a whole clan of that numerous tribe, took up their abode in the Valley of the Broken Stones. They found the columns and a great ruined temple back in the trees, and in that temple there was no shrine or altar, but the mouth of a shaft that vanished deep into the black earth, and in which there were no steps such as a human being would make and use. They built their village in the valley, and in the night, under the moon, horror came upon them and left only broken walls and bits of slime-smeared flesh.

In those days the Picts feared nothing. The warriors of the other clans gathered and sang their war-songs and danced their war-dances, and followed a broad track of blood and slime to the shaft-mouth in the temple. They howled defiance and hurled down boulders which were never heard to strike bottom. Then began a thin demoniac piping, and up from the well pranced a hideous anthropomorphic figure dancing to the weird strains of a pipe it held in its monstrous hands. The horror of its aspect froze the fierce Picts with amazement, and close behind it a vast white bulk heaved up from the subterranean darkness. Out of the shaft came a slavering mad nightmare which arrows pierced but could not check, which swords carved but could not slay. It fell slobbering upon the warriors, crushing them to crimson pulp, tearing them to bits as an octopus might tear small fishes, sucking their blood from their mangled limbs and devouring them even as they screamed and struggled. The survivors fled, pursued to the very ridge, up which, apparently, the monster could not propel its quaking mountainous bulk. After that they did not dare the silent valley. But the dead came to their shamans and old men in dreams and told them strange and terrible secrets. They spoke of an ancient, ancient race of semihuman beings which once inhabited that valley and reared those columns for their own weird inexplicable purposes. The white monster in the pits was their god, summoned up from the nighted abysses of mid-earth uncounted fathoms below the black mold, by sorcery unknown to the sons of men. The hairy anthropomorphic being was its servant, created to serve the god, a formless elemental spirit drawn up from below and cased in flesh, organic but beyond the understanding of humanity. The Old Ones had long vanished into the limbo from whence they crawled in the black dawn of the universe; but their bestial god and his inhuman slave lived on. Yet both were organic after a fashion, and could be wounded, though no human weapon had been found potent enough to slay them.

Bragi and his clan had dwelt for weeks in the valley before the horror struck. Only the night before, Grom, hunting above the cliffs, and by that token daring greatly, had been paralyzed by a high-pitched demon piping, and then by a mad clamor of human screaming. Stretched face down in the dirt, hiding his head in a tangle of grass, he had not dared to move, even when the shrieks died away in the slobbering, repulsive sounds of a hideous feast. When dawn broke he had crept shuddering to the cliffs to look down into the valley, and the sight of the devastation, even when seen from afar, had driven him in yammering flight far into the hills. But it had occurred to him, finally, that he should warn the rest of the tribe, and returning, on his way to the camp on the plateau, he had seen me entering the valley.

So spoke Grom, while I sat and brooded darkly, my chin on my mighty fist. I can not frame in modern words the clan-feeling that in those days was a living vital part of every man and woman. In a world where talon and fang were lifted on every hand, and the hands of all men raised against an individual, except those of his own clan, tribal instinct was more than the phrase it is today. It was as much a part of a man as was his heart or his right hand. This was necessary, for only thus banded together in unbreakable groups could mankind have survived in the terrible environments of the primitive world. So now the personal grief I felt for Bragi and the clean-limbed young men and laughing white-skinned girls was drowned in a deeper sea of grief and fury that was cosmic in its depth and intensity. I sat grimly, while the Pict squatted anxiously beside me, his gaze roving from me to the menacing deeps of the valley where the accursed columns loomed like broken teeth of cackling hags among the waving leafy reaches.

I, Niord, was not one to use my brain over-much. I lived in a physical world, and there were the old men of the tribe to do my thinking. But I was one of a race destined to become dominant mentally as well as physically, and I was no mere muscular animal. So as I sat there there came dimly and then clearly a thought to me that brought a short fierce laugh from my lips.

Rising, I bade Grom aid me, and we built a pyre on the lake shore of dried wood, the ridge-poles of the tents, and the broken shafts of spears. Then we collected the grisly fragments that had been parts of Bragi's band, and we laid them on the pile, and struck flint and steel to it.

The thick sad smoke crawled serpent-like into the sky, and turning to Grom, I made him guide me to the jungle where lurked that scaly horror, Satha, the great serpent. Grom gaped at me; not the greatest hunters among the Picts sought out the mighty crawling one. But my will was like a wind that swept him along my course, and at last he led the way. We left the valley by the upper end, crossing the ridge, skirting the tall cliffs, and plunged into the fastnesses of the south, which was peopled only by the grim denizens of the jungle. Deep into the jungle we went, until we came to a low-lying expanse, dank and dark beneath the great creeper-festooned trees, where our feet sank deep into the spongy silt, carpeted by rotting vegetation, and slimy moisture oozed up beneath their pressure. This, Grom told me, was the realm haunted by Satha, the great serpent.

Let me speak of Satha. There is nothing like him on earth today, nor has there been for countless ages: Like the meat-eating dinosaur, like old saber-tooth, he was too terrible to exist. Even then he was a survival of a grimmer age when life and its forms were cruder and more hideous. There were not many of his kind then, though they may have existed in great numbers in the reeking ooze of the vast jungle-tangled swamps still farther south. He was larger than any python of modern ages, and his fangs dripped with poison a thousand times more deadly than that of a king cobra.

He was never worshipped by the pure-blood Picts, though the blacks that came later deified him, and that adoration persisted in the hybrid race that sprang from the Negroes and their white conquerors.

But to other peoples he was the nadir of evil horror, and tales of him became twisted into demonology; so in later ages Satha became the veritable devil of the white races, and the Stygians first worshipped, and then, when they became Egyptians, abhorred him under the name of Set, the Old Serpent, while to the Semites he became Leviathan and Satan. He was terrible enough to be a god, for he was a crawling death. I had seen a bull elephant fall dead in his tracks from Satha's bite. I had seen him, had glimpsed him writhing his horrific way through the dense jungle, had seen him take his prey, but I had never hunted him. He was too grim, even for the slayer of old saber-tooth.

But now I hunted him, plunging farther and farther into the hot, breathless reek of his jungle, even when friendship for me could not drive Grom farther: He urged me to paint my body and sing my death-song before I advanced farther, but I pushed on unheeding.

In a natural runway that wound between the shouldering trees, I set a trap. I found a large tree, soft and spongy of fiber, but thick-boled and heavy, and I hacked through its base close to the ground with my great sword, directing its fall so that, when it toppled, its top crashed into the branches of a smaller tree, leaving it leaning across the runway, one end resting on the earth, the other caught in the small tree. Then I cut away the branches on the under side, and cutting a slim tough sapling I trimmed it and stuck it upright like a prop-pole under the leaning tree. Then, cutting away the tree which supported it, I left the great trunk poised precariously on the prop-pole, to which I fastened a long vine, as thick as my wrist.

Then I went alone through that primordial twilight jungle until an overpowering fetid odor assailed my nostrils, and from the rank vegetation in front of me, Satha reared up his hideous head, swaying lethally from side to side, while his forked tongue jetted in and out, and his great yellow terrible eyes burned icily on me with all the evil wisdom of the black elder world that was when man was not. I backed away, feeling no fear, only an icy sensation along my spine, and Satha came sinuously after me, his shining eighty-foot barrel rippling over the rotting vegetation in mesmeric silence. His wedge-shaped head was bigger than the head of the hugest stallion, his trunk was thicker than a man's body, and his scales shimmered with a thousand changing scintillations. I was to Satha as a mouse is to a king cobra, but I was fanged as no mouse ever was. Quick as I was, I knew I could not avoid the lightning stroke of that great triangular head; so I dared not let him come too close. Subtly I fled down the runway; and behind me the rush of the great supple body was like the sweep of wind through the grass.

He was not far behind me when I raced beneath the deadfall, and as the great shining length glided under the trap, I gripped the vine with both hands and jerked desperately. With a crash the great trunk fell across Satha's scaly back, some six feet back of his wedge-shaped head.

I had hoped to break his spine but I do not think it did, for the great body coiled and knotted, the mighty tail lashed and thrashed, mowing down the bushes as if with a giant flail. At the instant of the fall, the huge head had whipped about and struck the tree with a terrific impact, the mighty fangs shearing through bark and wood like scimitars. Now, as if aware he fought an inanimate foe, Satha turned on me, standing out of his reach. The scaly neck writhed and arched, the mighty jaws gaped, disclosing fangs a foot in length, from which dripped venom that might have burned through solid stone.

I believe, what of his stupendous strength, that Satha would have writhed from under the trunk, but for a broken branch that had been driven deep into his side, holding him like a barb. The sound of his hissing filled the jungle and his eyes glared at me with such concentrated evil that I shook despite myself. Oh, he knew it was I who had trapped him! Now I came as close as I dared, and with a sudden powerful cast of my spear, transfixed his neck just below the gaping jaws, nailing him to the tree-trunk. Then I dared greatly, for he was far from dead, and I knew he would in an instant tear the spear from the wood and be free to strike. But in that instant I ran in, and swinging my sword with all my great power, I hewed off his terrible head.

The heavings and contortions of Satha's prisoned form in life were naught to the convulsions of his headless length in death. I retreated, dragging the gigantic head after me with a crooked pole, and at a safe distance from the lashing, flying tail, I set to work. I worked with naked death then, and no man ever toiled more gingerly than did I. For I cut out the poison sacs at the base of the great fangs, and in the terrible venom I soaked the heads of eleven arrows, being careful that only the bronze points were in the liquid, which else had corroded away the wood of the tough shafts. While I was doing this, Grom, driven by comradeship and curiosity, came stealing nervously through the jungle, and his mouth gaped as he looked on the head of Satha.

For hours I steeped the arrowheads in the poison, until they were caked with a horrible green scum, and showed tiny flecks of corrosion where the venom had eaten into the solid bronze. He wrapped them carefully in broad, thick, rubber-like leaves, and then, though night had fallen and the hunting beasts were roaring on every hand, I went back through the jungled hills, Grom with me, until at dawn we came again to the high cliffs that loomed above the Valley of Broken Stones.

At the mouth of the valley I broke my spear, and I took all the unpoisoned shafts from my quiver, and snapped them. I painted my face and limbs as the Aesir painted themselves only when they went forth to certain doom, and I sang my death-song to the sun as it rose over the cliffs, my yellow mane blowing in the morning wind. Then I went down into the valley, bow in hand.

Grom could not drive himself to follow me. He lay on his belly in the dust and howled like a dying dog.

I passed the lake and the silent camp where the pyre-ashes still smoldered, and came under the thickening trees beyond. About me the columns loomed, mere shapeless heaps from the ravages of staggering eons. The trees grew more dense, and under their vast leafy branches the very light was dusky and evil. As in twilight shadow I saw the ruined temple, cyclopean walls staggering up from masses of decaying masonry and fallen blocks of stone. About six hundred yards in front of it a great column reared up in an open glade, eighty or ninety feet in height. It was so worn and pitted by weather and time that any child of my tribe could have climbed it, and I marked it and changed my plan.

I came to the ruins and saw huge crumbling walls upholding a domed roof from which many stones had fallen, so that it seemed like the lichen-grown ribs of some mythical monster's skeleton arching above me. Titanic columns flanked the open doorway through which ten elephants could have stalked abreast. Once there might have been inscriptions and hieroglyphics on the pillars and walls, but they were long worn away. Around the great room, on the inner side, ran columns in better state of preservation. On each of these columns was a flat pedestal, and some dim instinctive memory vaguely resurrected a shadowy scene wherein black drums roared madly, and on these pedestals monstrous beings squatted loathsomely in inexplicable rituals rooted in the black dawn of the universe.

There was no altar—only the mouth of a great welllike shaft in the stone floor, with strange obscene carvings all about the rim. I tore great pieces of stone from the rotting floor and cast them down the shaft which slanted down into utter darkness. I heard them bound along the side, but I did not hear them strike bottom. I cast down stone after stone, each with a searing curse, and at last I heard a sound that was not the dwindling rumble of the falling stones. Up from the well floated a weird demon-piping that was a symphony of madness. Far down in the darkness I glimpsed the faint fearful glimmering of a vast white bulk.

I retreated slowly as the piping grew louder, falling back through the broad doorway. I heard a scratching, scrambling noise, and up from the shaft and out of the doorway between the colossal columns came a prancing incredible figure. It went erect like a man, but it was covered with fur, that was shaggiest where its face should have been. If it had ears, nose and a mouth I did not discover them. Only a pair of staring red eyes leered from the furry mask. Its misshapen hands held a strange set of pipes, on which it blew weirdly as it pranced toward me with many a grotesque caper and leap.

Behind it I heard a repulsive obscene noise as of a quaking unstable mass heaving up out of a well. Then I nocked an arrow, drew the cord and sent the shaft singing through the furry breast of the dancing monstrosity. It went down as though struck by a thunderbolt, but to my horror the piping continued, though the pipes had fallen from the malformed hands. Then I turned and ran fleetly to the column, up which I swarmed before I looked back. When I reached the pinnacle I looked, and because of the shock and surprise of what I saw, I almost fell from my dizzy perch.

Out of the temple the monstrous dweller in the darkness had come, and I, who had expected a horror yet cast in some terrestrial mold, looked on the spawn of nightmare. From what subterranean hell it crawled in the long ago I know not, nor what black age it represented. But it was not a beast, as humanity knows beasts. I call it a worm for lack of a better term. There is no earthly language which has a name for it. I can only say that it looked somewhat more like a worm than it did an octopus, a serpent or a dinosaur.

It was white and pulpy, and drew its quaking bulk along the ground, worm-fashion. But it had wide flat tentacles, and fleshly feelers, and other adjuncts the use of which I am unable to explain. And it had a long proboscis which it curled and uncurled like an elephant's trunk. Its forty eyes, set in a horrific circle, were composed of thousands of facets of as many scintillant colors which changed and altered in never-ending transmutation. But through all interplay of hue and glint, they retained their evil intelligence—intelligence there was behind those flickering facets, not human nor yet bestial, but a nightborn demoniac intelligence such as men in dreams vaguely sense throbbing titanically in the black gulfs outside our material universe. In size the monster was mountainous; its bulk would have dwarfed a mastodon.

But even as I shook with the cosmic horror of the thing, I drew a feathered shaft to my ear and arched it singing on its way. Grass and bushes were crushed flat as the monster came toward me like a moving mountain and shaft after shaft I sent with terrific force and deadly precision. I could not miss so huge a target. The arrows sank to the feathers or clear out of sight in the unstable bulk, each bearing enough poison to have stricken dead a bull elephant. Yet on it came; swiftly, appallingly, apparently heedless of both the shafts and the venom in which they were steeped. And all the time the hideous music played a maddening accompaniment, whining thinly from the pipes that lay untouched on the ground.

My confidence faded; even the poison of Satha was futile against this uncanny being. I drove my last shaft almost straight downward into the quaking white mountain, so close was the monster under my perch; then suddenly its color altered. A wave of ghastly blue surged over it, and the vast hulk heaved in earthquake-like convulsions. With a terrible plunge it struck the lower part of the column, which crashed to falling shards of stone. But even with the impact, I leaped far out and fell through the empty air full upon the monster's back.

The spongy skin yielded and gave beneath my feet, and I drove my sword hilt-deep, dragging it through the pulpy flesh, ripping a horrible yard-long wound, from which oozed a green slime. Then a flip of a cable-like tentacle flicked me from the titan's back and spun me three hundred feet through the air to crash among a cluster of giant trees.

The impact must have splintered half the bones in my frame, for when I sought to grasp my sword again and crawl anew to the combat, I could not move hand or foot, could only writhe helplessly with my broken back. But I could see the monster and I knew that I had won, even in defeat. The mountainous bulk was heaving and billowing, the tentacles were lashing madly, the antennae writhing and knotting, and the nauseous whiteness had changed to a pale and grisly green. It turned ponderously and lurched back toward the temple, rolling like a crippled ship in a heavy swell. Trees crashed and splintered as it lumbered against them.

I wept with pure fury because I could not catch up my sword and rush in to die glutting my berserk madness in mighty strokes. But the worm-god was deathstricken and needed not my futile sword. The demon pipes on the ground kept up their infernal tune, and it was like the fiend's death-dirge. Then as the monster veered and floundered, I saw it catch up the corpse of its hairy slave. For an instant the apish form dangled in midair, gripped round by the trunk-like proboscis, then was dashed against the temple wall with a force that reduced the hairy body to a mere shapeless pulp. At that the pipes screamed out horribly, and fell silent for ever.

The titan staggered on the brink of the shaft; then another change came over it—a frightful transfiguration the nature of which I can not yet describe. Even now when I try to think of it clearly, I am only chaotically conscious of a blasphemous, unnatural transmutation of form and substance, shocking and indescribable. Then the strangely altered bulk tumbled into the shaft to roll down into the ultimate darkness from whence it came, and I knew that it was dead. And as it vanished into the well, with a rending, grinding groan the ruined walls quivered from dome to base. They bent inward and buckled with deafening reverberation, the columns splintered, and with a cataclysmic crash the dome itself came thundering down. For an instant the air seemed veiled with flying debris and stone-dust, through which the treetops lashed madly as in a storm or an earthquake convulsion. Then all was clear again and I stared, shaking the blood from my eyes. Where the temple had stood there lay only a colossal pile of shattered masonry and broken stones, and every column in the valley had fallen, to lie in crumbling shards.

In the silence that followed I heard Grom wailing a dirge over me. I bade him lay my sword in my hand, and he did so, and bent close to hear what I had to say, for I was passing swiftly.

"Let my tribe remember," I said, speaking slowly. "Let the tale be told from village to village, from camp to camp, from tribe to tribe, so that men may know that not man nor beast nor devil may prey in safety on the golden-haired people of Asgard. Let them build me a cairn where I lie and lay me therein with my bow and sword at hand, to guard this valley for ever; so if the ghost of the god I slew comes up from below, my ghost will ever be ready to give it battle."

And while Grom howled and beat his hairy breast, death came to me in the Valley of the Worm.

Whoever Fights Monsters

INTRODUCTION

While the Great Orm of Loch Ness gets most of the publicity, other lakes have their own legendary monsters, including Lake George in New York state, though that one was supposedly an early 20th Century hoax. Lake Champlain, a lake shared by NY state and Vermont, with a small protrusion into Quebec, has another cryptozoic critter, nicknamed "Champ," though the Native American legends of the creature called it "Tatoskok." Sightings of it in historical times go back at least to 1609. Interestingly, "Champ" is the mascot of Vermont's Minor League Baseball team, the Vermont Lake Monsters. (Let's see Nessie top *that*.) As it happens, the two lakes are connected, and Wen Spencer considers the possibility of there being a real lake monster. This one might not make a good mascot for a sports team . . .

❖ ❖ ❖

John W. Campbell Award Winner Wen Spencer resides in paradise in Hilo, Hawaii with two volcanoes overlooking her home. Spencer says that she often wakes up and exclaims "Oh my god, I live on an island in the middle of the Pacific!" This, says Spencer, is a far cry from her twenty years of living in land-locked Pittsburgh. According to Spencer, she lives with "my Dalai Lama-like husband, my autistic teenage son, and two cats (one of which is recovering from mental illness). All of which makes for very odd home life at times." Spencer's love of Japanese anime and manga flavors her writing. The Elfhome series opener, *Tinker*, won the 2003 Sapphire Award for Best Science Fiction Romance and was a finalist for the *Romantic Times* Reviewers' Choice Award for Fantasy Novel. *Wolf Who Rules*, the sequel to *Tinker*, was chosen as a Top Pick by *Romantic Times* and given their top rating of four and a half stars. Other Baen books include the SF adventure thriller *Endless Blue*, and the third and fourth Elfhome novels, *Elfhome* and *Wood Sprites*, as well as the standalone fantasy novel, *Eight Million Gods*.

Whoever Fights Monsters

by Wen Spencer

As an insurance field-claims adjustor, Tuck Bagans had seen some very odd accidents. In fact, he was starting to suspect someone in the main office had decided he was the go-to man for strange claims. This one, though, won the "weird" category, hands down. He eyed the smoldering house, the pickup truck frozen in a block of ice, the massive barn timbers scattered like Lincoln Logs, and the half-eaten yak dangling in the upper branches of a hundred-year-old oak tree. Sighing, he looked back down at the form his office supplied. After all the important case identifiers there was "cause of damage."

"Not a clue" was not an acceptable answer.

This was the part of the job he hated. There were three ways this could go, and the company claiming "act of God" and not covering the damage was the most likely. The other direction was claiming insurance fraud and trying to have the poor customer arrested. It was going to take a great deal of careful working to make sure that the owner of the Fairy Water Petting Zoo got his money, because it obviously wasn't either of the first two.

Bernd Schnitker was said owner. The tall, red-haired man was slowly working his way across the yard to Tuck. All the pygmy goats were loose and hungry. They crowded around the man, giving a new meaning to "a trip of goats."

"Poor Genevieve," Bernd Schnitker said as a greeting once Tuck introduced himself and handed over his business card as proof of his identity.

"Genevieve?" Tuck had been told the family had been at town, dining out, when . . . whatever . . . hit.

"Genevieve Gorder." Schnitker pointed up at the half-eaten yak. "She was supposed to be our star animal. I thought she'd do well here, being able to take the cold and all. Couldn't ask for a sweeter, gentler beast." He sighed and spread his hands in tired dismay. "She scared the daylights out of the city kids. Too big. Too hairy scary."

"Tianzhu white yak?" Tuck guessed from the color of the long shaggy coat. A true white yak would be more expensive since they were much more rare. Schnitker had hefty coverage that indicated either a lot of animals or a handful of irreplaceable specimens.

"I was working on breeding her for yarn. White seemed easier to dye than black. We planned to sell it at my sister-in-law's craft boutique in town; New Yorkers drop a ton of money in it for anything labeled organic."

"You have paperwork for her purchase? Photographs? If you can't prove that she was actually a full-blooded Tianzhu, I can only okay replacement cost of a standard yak, which is about eight hundred dollars."

Schnitker waved toward the smoldering house. "Everything is in a fireproof safe. They say I wasn't to touch anything until you and the fire marshal had a good look-see."

Tuck relaxed slightly. Documentation and a claimant who was following instructions made it easier to force the main office to cough up money. "Are your other animals all accounted for?"

"I think the alpaca headed into the park land." He waved a hand to the north. "Where one goes, they all go. My wife and her family are out looking for them. She grew up here; she's related to half the town."

"You're a very lucky man." Tuck blushed as his envious slip earned him a bewildered look. "I know that this is rough. I—I've seen people lose so much. But you got to remember that the important thing is that your family is alive and well. Things aren't important. People are."

It was the wrong thing to say, no matter how true. It led of course to the inevitable listing of irreplaceable items that had been in the house. The land had been in the family for over a hundred years, back when the label of "millionaire" had the same power as "billionaire" of current reckoning. The smoldering structure had been the carriage house of a much grander mansion (ironically enough, destroyed by a freak storm on nearly the same day fifty years earlier). Despite its lowly origin, the carriage house had been handcrafted with quality materials and was one of only three houses on Lake George on the National Historic Register. Schnitker had split his lifetime between being miserable in his parents' Manhattan apartment (a cold, stark temple to modern architecture) and happy summers on the lake, surrounded by the bric-a-brac of dead (but extremely wealthy) relatives.

Cha-ching. Cha-ching. Cha-ching. Tuck's involvement in the claim became clearer and clearer. He nodded silently to Schnitker's outpouring. He should have known better not to say it to someone that hadn't lived through the destruction. For some reason, the people that came home to a ruined house only focused on the material losses. They never seemed to get beyond the rubble to realize how lucky they were. A minute or two of utter terror did wonders for perspective.

Scknitker had devolved into explaining how he'd talked his father (a Wall Street investment banker who was still alive and vastly annoyed at the turn of events) into giving him the land after deciding to quit law school and become an organic farmer. "It takes three years of compliance before you can get USDA-certified as organic, so the petting zoo is only a way to bring in revenue."

The well of information ran abruptly dry, and they stood a moment in silence with the baby goats trying to eat their clothes.

"I'm—I'm going to see if I can find something for these little guys to eat." Schnitker waved vaguely toward the scattered barn timbers.

Tuck freed the man with a nod. "I'm going to walk your fence line and take some pictures. I'll e-mail in the paperwork. The main office has the final decision, but I don't see them having any trouble with this. It seems fairly open and shut." Except that Tuck still had no idea what had caused all the damage.

❖ ❖ ❖

The trail of destruction led through an old orchard to the fieldstone foundations of a massive house perched at the edge of a steep hillside. From the paved veranda, he could see the blue of the lake peeking through the green foliage. Whatever had hit the petting zoo, it cut the same path as the freak storm fifty years earlier. Like last night, though, the family had survived unharmed and unaware how lucky they'd been. The happy summers at the lake continued, blithely collecting more valuable stuff to clutter up their lives.

Tuck sensed someone looking at him and turned. There was a very tall, muscular African-American man standing in the shadow of the nearest tree. He had dreadlocks, a neatly trimmed goatee, and sunglasses. His entire outfit was black and form-fitting, making it clear he probably could snap Tuck in half without much effort.

Normally very tall men made Tuck aware that he was a fairly short person. This man, however, made Tuck feel like he was rabbit. Next to a pissed-off grizzly bear.

Tuck was considering playing dead when the man reached up and slid his sunglasses down to peer over the top of them at Tuck.

"What are you?" the man asked.

"I'm—I'm the field adjustor." Tuck fumbled his business card out of his shirt's breast pocket. He held the card and tried to ignore the fact his hand was shaking. "Mr. Schnitker has several insurance policies with my company. Life. Vehicle. Commercial. Homeowners."

The man stalked forward, making no noise in the dry bracken. He snapped the card from Tuck's fingers and stepped back several feet while he eyed it.

"Homeowners?" The man indicated the smoking house and shattered barn across the open pasture. "You're kind of far from the *home*."

"His policy covers damage to livestock, fences, outbuildings, trees . . ." Tuck trailed off. "Who exactly are you?"

The man ignored the question. "Have you seen a lot of this?"

"No. Are—are you a cop? Or something like that?"

That got Tuck another look over the top of the sunglasses but no answer. Mr. Dreadlocks made the business card vanish and snatched the clipboard from Tuck's other hand.

"Wet microburst?" He read what Tuck had put down under cause of damage. "Is that what you think caused all this damage?"

"I need to put something down." Tuck tracked the path of destruction with his hand. "Something big stomped through here and smacked the barn hard as it went through."

Mr. Dreadlocks studied the direction Tuck was pointing and then gave him another over-the-sunglasses glare.

Someone else had joined in on the staring game. Tuck turned around to discover there was an equally tall, black-clad African-American woman watching from the shadows.

"What did you find, Oz?" She kept to the shadows.

"Not sure." Apparently Mr. Dreadlocks' name was Oz. The man caught Tuck by the shoulder and spun him around and around and around. "Tell me again, what caused this?"

"Hey! Stop!" Even when Oz finally stopped, the world continued to spin. "I don't know!"

"Come on. What did you say before?"

"Something big stomped through here." Tuck pointed out the path of destruction. "It hit the house dead center of the back door. The fire was from the water heater igniting a gas leak when the kitchen stove was knocked into the living room, along with most of the kitchen. It did something to the truck to freeze it into a block of ice. That part I can't explain. Then it hit the barn hard and took the yak. Maybe more than the yak; it took out Schnitker's paddock, and his animals are scattered all through the neighborhood."

"And?"

The world at least stopped spinning, but at some point Tuck had lost the logic of the conversation. He peered up at the man in confusion. "A-a-and?"

"And then it . . . ?"

"It left." Tuck waved toward the fence line that was a line of uprooted fence posts and a tangle of barbwire. "There wasn't any more damage reported in the area, so it followed the ravine to the lake."

The woman made a slight noise of surprise. "Type two?"

"I'm thinking a type three." The black man gazed toward the lake that was still out of sight by a matter of a mile or two. "Maybe a four."

"A four? We wouldn't get so lucky."

The man flicked out a twenty dollar bill.

The woman glanced at Tuck and then eyed the torn-up fence post. "Yeah, I'm in."

Without a nod or a wave or a word of dismissal, they took off in long, ground-eating strides, dark and silent as black jaguars.

Type four what?

It had been a weird day, but Tuck couldn't get the parting phrase out of his head. The conversation played in a loop like a catchy earworm. It unsettled him, leaving him in need of some serious comfort food.

Generally he tried to watch what he ate and exercise when he could, swimming at hotels with pools. Living on the road, though, meant there was little to comfort the psyche at the end of a hard day. No familiar living room with an overstuffed chair. No pet to welcome you home. No friends nearby to hang out with. Even the order of the TV stations was scrambled. Why was Channel 11 on three and Channel 7 on eleven?

The joy of being in a tourist town like Lake George Village was the abundance of good restaurants that offered Americana dishes. Betty's was a small diner on Lake Shore Road, tucked between a quilt shop and a souvenir store. Betty's didn't have a lake-front view, but the pickup trucks in the parking lot behind the diner proclaimed it as a local favorite. He took a booth by the front window so he could look out onto the street.

He ordered the meatloaf. When it came, it had a thick crust of Heinz ketchup baked across the top exactly like his grandmother used to make. The mashed potatoes were Yukon golds and whipped up with local organic milk and real butter. Baby peas cooked to perfection and flakey biscuits straight from the oven. They did wonders for his sense of normalcy. He ate slowly, enjoying the flavors of his food, and watched the people walking up and down the wide sidewalks. Just by their long hurried stride, it was easy to spot the rich New Yorker tourists.

He hadn't noticed as he drove in, but across the street was a big white building with gothic arched windows on the second story and a cupola roof. It looked vaguely like the top floor of the Bates hotel had been cut in half and dropped onto a standard storefront. Large red letters over the front door proclaimed it as the House of Frankenstein Wax Museum. Any place else in America, it would probably stand out like a sore thumb, but the village clung hard to its turn-of-century architecture. The only reason he noticed it was because it was neatly framed by the diner's window. Still, a wax museum seemed an odd choice of business for such a little town.

"Meatloaf and mashed potatoes!" The mysterious black man with the dreadlocks slid into the booth's opposite bench seat. He picked up the spoon that Tuck hadn't used yet and sampled the mashed potatoes. "Oh, those are good spuds."

"Hey! No!" Tuck cried as the man took another spoonful with the now dirty utensil. "What are you doing?" He lost some the anger when the woman sat down beside Tuck and he was suddenly reminded that both of them towered over him. One little rabbit between two dangerous predators.

The man loaded up the spoon with mashed potatoes. "Hiked all over that creek bottom, didn't find anything."

"What were you looking for?" Tuck cried. "A storm cell?"

"Something a little more . . ." The man waved his stolen spoon.

"Physical," the woman said.

"Like what?" Tuck asked. "Godzilla?"

The man glanced over his sunglasses at Tuck even as he also helped himself to Tuck's meatloaf. His dark eyes were piercing. His eyebrows were thin and underscored a wide expansive forehead that led up to the wild forest of his deadlocks. Somehow he seemed very intelligent and primally deadly at the same time.

Tuck pushed his plate across the table. Feeding bears might be a bad idea, but it was better than leaving them hungry. "Who are you people?"

"I'm Lylove Sutter. The bottomless pit is Osmyn Walcott." She snorted when Osmyn gave her a hard look. "You stole the man's dinner. He should at least know your name."

"This is seriously good food." Osmyn indicated the entire plate by a circle of his stolen spoon.

"We're with the government." Lylove ignored Osmyn. "We're investigating the damage at the farm."

"Why?"

"It's our job." Osmyn grunted and then tried the biscuit, ignoring the fact that there were two bites taken out of it already. "Why isn't this place on Yelp?"

Lylove frowned slightly and took out her phone. She accessed an app, and then, realizing Tuck was watching, stood and walked away.

Osmyn seemed not to notice that his partner had left. "We investigate unusual—insurance—claims."

"You're not a very good liar," Tuck said.

Osmyn licked his spoon and leaned out to rap Tuck on the forehead. "You . . . !"

"Hey!" Tuck jerked back.

". . . should be more careful who you call a liar."

And the rabbit-versus-grizzly-bear impression was back in force.

Tuck glanced around for the waitress. He would need his check for his expense report, otherwise he'd just toss money down and leave. Lylove, he noticed, was going through the swinging door into the kitchen. Apparently the partners both had problems with observing rules of politeness.

"This is just one freak storm or something." Tuck tried to steer the conversation back to safe ground.

"You don't really think it's a storm." Osmyn went back to eating Tuck's dinner.

"No, but I don't really need to know what it was. It was a freak occurrence, not caused by the homeowner, and unlikely to happen again."

Osmyn studied him over the sunglasses for a painfully long minute. "To him." He focused back on his food. "What about one of his neighbors? We're here doing a risk assessment."

Oddly enough, that sounded completely truthful.

Lylove returned from the kitchen and sat back down beside Tuck. "Have you eaten here before?"

"No. I thought it looked homey." He glanced toward the swinging door. The waitress was peering fearfully through the window in the door. "What did you . . ." He caught himself before he said "do" and changed it to ". . . find in the kitchen?"

Lylove sighed and held out two twenties to Osmyn. "You're right."

"I am? Cool beans." Osmyn snatched the twenties out of Lylove's hand.

She shook her head. "I told you not to say that, makes you sound like a dork."

"What is he right about?" Tuck asked.

"That our job just got a whole lot easier." Osmyn slipped the twenties into his jacket.

"How? And what's a type four?"

The two exchanged a look.

Lylove half turned in her seat to gaze down at him. "What has struck you as significant—other than the unnaturally good food that this place has to offer?"

"Unnatural? It's meatloaf and mashed potatoes. The beef is grass-fed, and everything in the potatoes is local and organic."

"Focus!" she growled.

Her skin was the color of dark chocolate and her teeth were blazing white, only visible as she talked because otherwise she kept her lips pressed tightly together. The only makeup she wore was eyeliner and a shade of lipstick so close to the color of her skin it might have been just lip gloss. She probably was beautiful, but Tuck was slightly too scared to judge in those terms. If Osmyn was a grizzly bear, she was more a black jaguar.

"S-s-significant?" Tuck stammered.

"Pft." Osmyn waved Lylove off. "What has caught your eye since you came to town? Other than this place."

They weren't going to let him alone until he played whatever game they were setting up for him. He glanced around and then pointed at the building across the street, neatly framed by the window. A storm front had rolled in and cloaked the tower with dark clouds. Lightning flickered as if cued. "The wax museum."

Tuck had hoped that they would leave him alone after that, but next thing he knew, he was being firmly escorted across the street.

They'd let him collect his check and pay it. Then, with each agent holding one of his elbows, they all but frog marched him across the street. Thunder rumbled ominously, and the sky flickered with distant lightning.

"Why are we going to the wax museum?" Tuck hated haunted houses. When his grandfather was still alive, he'd been dragged to every one within driving distance. He never understood the attraction.

"Not a clue," Osmyn stated cheerfully.

"We're following a lead," Lylove said.

"What lead?" Tuck said.

The two didn't answer, merely opened the double doors and propelled him into the lobby.

The ticket booth was an elaborate steel cage. A bored teenaged girl sat behind the bars. She wore a Babymetal T-shirt and pigtails; she was listening to metal rock so loud that the music leaked out of her headphones. She droned "our restrooms are for our customers only" without looking up from the manga she was reading.

"Three adults." Lylove pushed money across the counter and took the tickets.

"The entrance is through those doors." The girl pointed and flipped the page of her manga.

And thus—much against his will—he found himself entering a haunted house filled with wax figures of monsters.

"What lead?" Tuck asked again as he was dragged down a pitch-dark hallway while eerie organ music played over a hidden loudspeaker. "You simply asked what caught my eye. This-this-this is a wax museum! You can't call this a . . ."

Something lurched out of the darkness with a menacing hiss. He registered gleaming red eyes and a mouthful of sharp teeth before suddenly being jerked backwards by Lylove while Osmyn opened fire.

"What in God's name are you doing?" Tuck shouted over the thunder of Osmyn's gunshots. "It's a wax figure! We're in a wax museum!"

Osmyn continued to point his smoking gun at the figure. "You can never be too careful."

"Yes, you can! That is too careful!" Tuck pointed at the wax zombie that was now missing an eye and had an impressive close grouping of holes in the chest where a heart should have been. "Do you have any idea how much it's going to cost to fix this? A basic mannequin costs in the neighborhood of two hundred dollars. Add in a custom paint job and . . ."

Osmyn turned to glare down at Tuck. His gun, at least, remained trained on the zombie. Tuck noticed that Lylove also held a gun leveled at the mannequin. He was in a dark building filled with simulated murder scenes with two very jumpy, heavily armed strangers.

"Shutting up now," Tuck said. Thunder rumbled loudly overhead, and the lights flickered.

Osmyn turned back to the zombie. "I think the bullet holes add a touch of realism." He put his pistol away and led the way into the dimness.

They stumbled through the maze of dark corridors, past a half-dozen horror-themed dioramas. Frankenstein lab. The pit and pendulum. A guillotine beheading. A vampire staking. A crystal-ball séance. While the two agents lingered beside all of them, as if waiting for something noteworthy to jump out for them to shoot, Tuck hurried on through. The sooner they were out of the museum, the sooner, hopefully, he could escape the two. The last featured a plesiosaur guarding a nest of eggs.

"What in the world?" Tuck paused to read the placard. "George, the Lake George Monster? Why would they give it a male name?"

"Why would you think it's female?" Osmyn bent to check the sex of the monster.

Tuck sighed and pointed at the sprawling nest. "Because of the eggs."

"Eggs?" both agents asked.

"What? These?" Osmyn reached over the barricade and picked one up.

"Don't touch those!" Tuck skittered back. "Seriously, do you people have no respect? You can't just go around shooting up places and messing with fragile things."

"Fragile?" Osmyn held the large gray egg out to Tuck. " It's freaking heavy. Here. It looks like river rock to me."

Tuck hit the walls and edged sideways, hands up above his head. "I'm not touching it. I don't want my fingerprints all over it! I don't want to bring trouble down on my head."

He hit the doorway and slipped through it while both agents climbed into the diorama with the plesiosaur. He was at full run by the time he hit the foyer door. He'd checked into his motel before dinner. If he packed up fast, though, he could be in Saratoga Springs before nightfall.

When he had picked out the Tiki Resort motel, it'd seemed charming. The place had been built to look like a series of little tiki huts, all strung together. He wasn't sure what moved people to mix together Easter Island moai statues, Polynesian tiki huts, and Hawaiian hula dancing in the middle of upstate New York, but it seemed harmless. He had no idea that it was the tip of the huge iceberg of weirdness.

The luau floorshow was in full swing when he hit the lobby. Grass-skirted hula girls came giggling out of the dining area, and the drums started a heavy beat. He was almost to his room when two women started to sing a duet. He paused, cocking his head as he recognized the song: the *Shobijin* summoning of Mothra.

"Why?" he cried unlocking his door. "Why that song? Why the wax museum? What the hell was that all about? How did they ever even find me at the diner?"

That truly was the most disturbing question. He paused again in the middle of gathering together all his "home comfort" items he'd scattered about his room to help de-stress after dinner. His yellow Mini Cooper was fairly distinctive, but he'd parked in back of the diner, between two massive pickup trucks. Had Agents Walcott and Sutter just happened to see him sitting by the window—he was in plain view of anyone that drove down main street—or had they somehow tracked him? Like with his phone? They were government agents. At least they claimed to be—they never said for what department. And he'd given Agent Walcott his business card!

Why had he given such a dangerous man his card?

Bugging out to Saratoga Springs seemed better and better as he reconsidered the last few hours. Or maybe he should go as far as Albany.

He'd picked up the box from Cold Hollow and realized he'd need a luggage cart to get everything out to his car. Maybe he had gone overboard at making his motel rooms homey. He started out traveling with just one small bag. It hadn't made sense, though, to continue paying for his grandparents' big old Victorian when he rarely slept there. It had been at once too cluttered and echoingly empty. So he'd sold everything, all the bric-a-brac of dead people that Schnitker was now mourning. Tuck had felt free at first, stripped of all worldly possessions, living like a nomadic monk. Lately, though, he felt more like a lost balloon, drifting off to its doom. All the little home comforts had started to grow, like he'd desperately tried to anchor himself someplace. Anyplace.

A demanding knock on the door startled him

Three years of living on the road, and no one had ever knocked on his hotel room door before.

He crept to the door and rose up onto his tiptoes to use the spyhole.

The two agents stood outside his room, looking as if they were considering ways to break in.

Osmyn beat on the door again with a gloved fist. "I can hear you breathing!"

Tuck stumbled backwards. His room was on the ground floor. Maybe he could go out a window. He was halfway across the room when his lock clicked and the door opened.

"Safety tip." Osmyn walked into the room. "Always use the chain on the door, because you never know who has a copy of the keys to these old motel rooms."

"I was just . . ." Maybe telling him that he was leaving was a bad idea.

Osmyn took the Cold Hollow box out of Tuck's hand and opened it up. "Hmm!" He helped himself to the donuts inside.

"That's—that's—" probably a bad thing to complain about.

Lylove made a sound of disgust. "Oz, don't take the man's . . ."

Osmyn pulled a piece of donut off and popped it into Lylove's mouth.

"Oh my god, what are those?" Lylove reached for the rest.

"I think they're apple." Osmyn helped himself to another.

"They're apple cider donuts from Cold Hollow Cider Mill." Tuck considered fleeing without even his suitcase. "I stopped in Waterbury, Vermont, early this morning on the way to here. They're better hot and fresh."

Lylove took out her phone and murmured, "Check out Waterbury, Vermont. The cider mill bakery."

Tuck realized that Osmyn had drifted to block the room's only window while Lylove leaned against the door. The two agents had guessed that he'd bolt if given half a chance. "What is it that you want?"

"There is no Lake George monster." Osmyn dropped the now empty donut box into the trashcan.

"Huh?" Tuck looked back and forth between them in confusion.

"According to wax museum staff, the monster was a hoax," Lylove said in slightly accusing tone. "In 1904, two summer residents named Harry Waltrous and Colonel William Mann played a series of practical jokes on each other. Mann had tricked Waltrous during a trout fishing competition by pretending to catch a massive fish. He mounted a huge *wooden* fish in his home with the furniture arranged so guests couldn't examine the trout closely. That triggered Waltrous to build a lake monster and had it attack Mann while he was out on the lake. After that, he used it to terrorize random boaters until the town threatened to lynch him for nearly ruining the tourist trade."

The two agents were looking at him as if he'd lied about something.

"I never said there was a monster!" He threw up his hands. None of this made any sense. They were the ones who had forced him to go to the wax museum. "All of that was made up! Nothing in that museum was real. There are no such things as monsters. Why would you even think there's a monster in Lake George?"

"What do you think caused all the damage at the petting zoo?"

Osmyn spotted Tuck's thermoelectric cooler. He leaned down and flipped up the lid. "My God, you know how to eat! Chocolate truffles. Cheddar cheese. Cider jelly? Where are the crackers?"

"Yes, please, help yourself!" Tuck cried since Osmyn had produced a wicked-looking foot-long knife and was already slicing the Cabot Private Stock Cheddar and smearing it with the cider jelly from Cold Hollow. "There are seven billion people on the planet playing with everything from jet planes to mining equipment! Statistically anything can happen, and sometimes weird shit does! It's my job to go from one accident to another and figure out how to help the survivors. You would not believe some of the things I've seen."

"So why did you freak out over these?" Lylove swung a bag off her back and pulled out one of the eggs.

"What in God's name?" Tuck backed away from the female agent. "Did you steal that from the museum?"

"We didn't steal them." Osmyn waggled the knife at him. "We're government agents; we *confiscated* them."

"Why?" Tuck cried as he edged toward the bathroom, which was the farthest point he could get from both of them. It didn't have a window, but it did have a door. "Wait. Them? As in 'all of' them?"

"You never get anywhere if you do things half-ass." Osmyn tried one of the Lake Champlain Chocolate truffles. "Damn, you have great food."

"The rest are out in our truck." Lylove stepped closer, holding out the egg. "But if there's no Lake George monster, the question becomes: What is this?"

"What—what? I don't know! How should I know? I'm field insurance adjustor! They look like river rock, but they could be man-made stone or even resin."

Lylove snorted and checked her cell phone. "Oh!"

Osmyn stopped feasting on Tuck's comfort food to look at her sharply. "What?"

"Research says according to the Iroquois and Abenaki tribes, Lake Champlain has a monster. The Abenaki called it Tatoskok. The two lakes are connected by a short waterway at Ticonderoga . . ."

"And?" Tuck asked.

Both agents, though, had gone silent, listening to an odd rumble outside.

"Did you feel that?" Osmyn asked.

Lylove breathed out a curse word and tapped on her phone and whispered another harsher curse. "We've got incoming!"

Osmyn sheathed his giant knife and grabbed the egg from Lylove. "Get him!"

Tuck had about three seconds to wonder "Get who?" before he found himself being dragged through the motel at high speed. "Wait! Wait! Where are you taking me?"

"Lake Champlain apparently loaned Lake George its monster!" Lylove shouted.

"There's no such things as monsters!" Tuck cried.

The end of the hallway suddenly vanished. In the vast empty space that had been the hall, there came a noise. "Very loud" didn't do justice to the sound level. It started out like an elephant trumpeting and ended with a rumbling that sounded much more like a house-size lion growling.

Tuck somehow wriggled free of Lylove's hold and headed the other direction without even knowing how he'd done it. At the lobby, he veered into the restaurant and into the kitchen beyond. It wasn't until he came skittering out on the kitchen's loading dock that he remembered that because of the dinner crowd, he'd parked beside it.

There was, however, a large black SUV blocking his yellow Mini Cooper in.

"Oh, God! Why is the only other car in the lot blocking me?"

"Because we didn't want you leaving!" Lylove burst out of the kitchen behind him.

"We've got to put some distance between us and it," Osmyn shouted.

"*We? We?*" Tuck cried. "How did I get mixed up in this?"

"Because it's chasing you!" Osmyn picked him up and shoved him into the back of the SUV.

"Not me!" Tuck realized he was sitting among duffel bags full of all the river rock from the museum. "You! You have the eggs! You brought the eggs to me!"

The weird roaring noise sounded again—louder now that there was no building to mute it. In the rain-shrouded dark, something massive moved. It was sleek, with patches of white but with very articulated back legs supporting a bipedal body.

"That is not a plesiosaur!" Tuck pointed at the creature that in no way resembled the extinct dinosaur.

"Never said it was." Osmyn peeled the SUV out of the parking lot as the creature turned one of the Easter Island moai to a block of ice.

Lylove's phone buzzed again. "Research says that based on the monster's size and the dates of the sightings, that it most likely has a life cycle like salmon, where it spawns in lakes but lives in the Arctic Ocean, undetected, for most of its life."

"Where are you going?" Tuck cried as he realized that they were heading into town. "Not this way! Think of the collateral property damage! Don't drag the thing through town!"

Osmyn slammed the SUV through a 180 turn. "Does Research have any suggestion on how to kill it?"

"Kill it?" Tuck cried. "No! Just give it back the eggs! Put them where the museum took them from and everything will go back to 'there's no lake monster.'"

The two agents exchanged looks in the front seat.

"Type six?" Lylove murmured.

"Maybe. Ask Research to find out where the museum found the eggs."

"It's going to be somewhere on the lake's shore." Tuck leaned over the back of the seat to point at the upcoming intersection with West Brook Road. "Turn-turn-turn-turn! This is all parkland on the right. We can get to the marina without dragging it through town. If we can get it out on the water, there's going to be nothing for it to stomp on."

"At this point the only thing I'm worried about getting stomped on is us." But Osmyn still took the turn at high speed.

The marina was small, with only three boats at the dock. Big boats. Steam paddleboats. One was lit up like a Chinese lantern, casting a warm glow over the dark water. Its steam engine idled, huffing like a giant beast. *Minne Ha Ha* was printed in three-feet-high letters across its top deck railing.

Osmyn slid the SUV to a stop a foot from the gangplank of the sternwheeler.

"No!" Tuck pointed at the *Minne Ha Ha* as the agents leapt out of the SUV. "No! No! You are not stealing that."

"We're government agents," Osmyn stated. "We're commandeering it."

"Do you have any idea what something like that is worth?" He escaped the SUV, but he was torn between running and trying to be a voice of reason in the madness. "If they don't have adequate insurance, you would be bankrupting this company."

Lylove grabbed his wrist and yanked him into a fireman carry. "Acceptable loss."

"Wait! Why are you taking me with you? I am an insurance adjustor. I know nothing about monsters!"

"Because Research says there's a hundred and nine miles of shoreline."

"Yes, it's a very big lake." Tuck found himself babbling, trying to figure out how to talk himself out of this mess. "Its got like four hundred islands. The staff from the wax museum could have taken a boat out and raided an island."

"So it's more like two or three hundred miles of shoreline?" Lylove asked.

"Yes!" Maybe that wasn't the right answer. "Possibly."

"Then you're definitely coming with us." She carried him up the gangplank while Osmyn transferred the duffel bags.

"You can't do this!" Tuck cried.

"If you haven't noticed, we can and we are." Lylove carried him up to the third level, where a small wheelhouse perched between twin tall black smokestacks.

"Do you even know how to drive a boat this size?"

"All agents are certified in several different types of boats and aircraft." She eyed the wheel and the range of controls. "Ah, it really is a steamboat."

There was some yelling on the dock, indicating that someone was strenuously objecting to the boat being commandeered.

Lylove consulted her phone and shouted out the open door. "Oz! Four hundred meters and closing!"

The conversation on the dock ended abruptly with a splash.

"Did he just throw that man into the water?" Tuck cried.

"Standard operating procedure: clear the area of civilians."

"Throwing him into the water is not *safely* clearing the area!"

Lylove dropped into a tall chair beside the wheel. "Stay." She pointed at him so there could be no misunderstanding. "Try to run and I'll hurt you . . ." She paused for the threat to sink fully in. "And then handcuff you to that chair."

"Yes, ma'am."

The monster roared somewhere in the darkness as Lylove backed the *Minne Ha Ha* away from the dock. Downstairs the engines thumped quietly and the red-painted paddlewheel in the stern of the boat churned up the dark lake water.

Osmyn appeared at the doorway. "That monster is going to be faster in the water than on land."

"It's a steamboat, not a speedboat." Lylove calmly spun the wheel, bringing the nose around as she took the engines to full power. The paddlewheel furiously beat the water, but they didn't seem to be moving much faster.

"We should take a smaller boat," Tuck murmured while there was time to change to something less irreplaceable.

Osmyn snorted. "I've seen *Jaws*. We'll need the bigger boat."

Tuck's phone rang, making him yelp in surprise. He blushed and took it out of his pants pocket. "Hello, this is Tuck Bagans." He spoke on automatic, amazed at how calm his voice was.

"Tuck, this is Wayne Sexsmith; I'm the night shift supervisor. Sorry to call you so late, but I've got a claim that I need to check while you're still in the Lake George area." Sexsmith laughed. "This one is straight up your alley; some idiot got his Lamborghini stuck *in* a tree. A million dollar sports car and it's twenty feet up this big old oak tree. He's e-mailed pictures as if this proves something beyond being an idiot. He's claiming it's a freak ice storm."

The beast roared.

Tuck flinched down in the wheelhouse and peered out toward the dock. It was a small pool of light surrounded by darkness. Apparently they were going faster than he thought. "The weather is really . . . weird right now."

"Yeah." Wayne used a tone that indicated that he didn't believe Tuck. "That Schnitker claim? We're delaying that until the case can be investigated for arson."

"What?"

"We ran a credit check and found that he was turned down for a loan to build a resort spa on his land."

"A spa?" That didn't match anything with the eco-warrior he'd met. "Are you sure the fraud department pulled the right Social Security number?"

"There's a mineral spring on his land. It's the only one in the area, but similar quality to ones farther south at Saratoga Springs. He wants to do a low-impact eco resort spa. Yurts. Organic food. Massages. A mineral spring-fed indoor/outdoor swimming pool. The whole works complete with boat access to Lake George."

Boat access? A millionaire's summer estate probably would have had boat access to the lake. It probably lay at the bottom of the steep hill, downhill of the old ruins of the mansion. "I didn't see any mineral springs."

"*Fairy Water* Petting Zoo!" Sexsmith cried as if Tuck were stupid and not being chased by a giant monster. "The mineral springs is on his land; he has full water rights to it. If he torched his house, he's not going to mention what he's going to do with the money. Don't worry about it; not your job any more. Actually it never was your job. I'm sending you the files on the Lamborghini case. Nip over to it first thing in the morning, and then you need to be in Rhode Island. Sent you files on that, too. Ciao!"

Sexsmith hung up before Tuck could form any coherent answer.

Behind them, all the lights at the dock suddenly winked out. A deep rumbling growl echoed over the lake.

This was not going to end well for him. He carried two Ziploc baggies in his wallet for such times as this. He sealed his phone into one and his wallet into the other. His wristwatch was already waterproof and shock absorbent.

"Which way?" Lylove shouted.

It took Tuck a moment to realize that she was asking him. "What?"

"Where are we going?" Lylove asked.

"You kidnapped me! Remember?"

She gave him a hard, dark stare.

Don't make the woman with a gun angry. Think! Where did the eggs come from?

"If it spawns like salmon, then it has a nesting site it's coming back to every so many . . ." Tuck paused and cocked his head. "Oh geez, Fairy Water! Salmon have an olfactory impression of their birth stream; they smell their way back to the place where they were born. Fifty years ago, the main house at Fairy Water got stomped on by something big."

Lylove glanced at her phone. "Oz! Six o'clock dead on! Twenty meters! Slow it down!"

There was a deep cough from the second floor aft deck. Something splashed into the lake and then there was a bloom of brightness within the liquid darkness. Water fountained upwards.

For several minutes there was only the thumping wheeze of the steam engine.

"Is it moving?" Osmyn broke the silence.

"Not yet," Lylove called back. "Telemetry says it's still alive, though. It's generating an inertia field. Armory says its probably only stunned. Research doesn't believe we have anything with us that can kill it."

"Oh, this is going to be fun." Osmyn disappeared back into the night.

Some type of flotation device suddenly seemed expedient. The *Minne Ha Ha* would be a classed as a T-Boat; it had to have life jackets someplace on board. Tuck slipped unnoticed from the room. He felt bad that he had to break into the supply room on the first floor to find one. The likelihood, though, of the boat coming out unscathed was diminishing every minute. He was pulling on one of the jackets when Lylove called out bearings, and a moment later another flash-bang grenade exploded under water.

"I've only got one more," Osmyn reported in the darkness of the aft deck.

"We've got another two miles at least."

They were not going to make it. Tuck supposed with the theft of the steamboat, the multiple explosions, and the giant monster roaring like a pack of elephant-lion hybrids that someone on shore was aware that they were out on the lake. Somehow he doubted, though, there were rescue teams standing by.

He picked up two extra lifejackets. On the shelf below the lifejackets were two self-inflating life rafts packed in hard cases. He stared at them. Even though it was summer, the lake water would be dangerously cold. If the monster tore apart the *Minne Ha Ha*, though, a life raft would be nothing but a small chew toy in comparison.

The last flash-bang grenade exploded, this only a dozen feet to the starboard of the ship. In the sudden brilliance, the monster was highlighted in the dark waters. It dwarfed the *Minne Ha Ha*.

Tuck dropped the life jackets and snatched up the canisters. The monster was chasing the eggs. There was no other way to explain how it tracked them to the hotel and then to the dock. As long as they had the eggs, the monster was going to chase them. Just lobbing the eggs overboard probably might just piss off the monster more, but *floating* them away from the *Minne Ha Ha* might work.

The duffel bags with the eggs were where Osmyn dropped them, a foot from the gangplank. Tuck opened the hatch on the life raft canister, grabbed hold of the D-ring, and pulled the release cable out a foot. Then, lifting the canister, he flung it over the side, keeping hold of the D-ring. The release cable fed out and then hit the end and jerked. With a hiss and a pop, the life raft exploded out of the canister housing, inflating in seconds. He used the release cable to tie it to the railing so it was being towed beside the *Minne Ha Ha*.

He couldn't lift the duffel bags. Growling, he unzipped them. The agent had taken every bloody rock-like thing at the museum. "Oh, you've got to be kidding me! Any idiot can tell if you just pay attention. The rocks are rough." He lifted out the plain river rock and flung it overboard. "The eggs are smooth." He picked up the egg and carefully tossed it down into the life raft. A dozen more rocks followed the first. "Don't tell me all this is for just one egg? Oh, here's another."

Five in all, hidden within the normal rocks. It seemed a tiny number compared to the amount a salmon would lay, but considering the end size of the beast, probably a good thing.

"Here it comes!" Lylove shouted, warning that the beast was no longer stunned.

Tuck glanced behind him. The beast was coming, a dark runnel outlined by a roiling white wake, straight at the *Minne Ha Ha*. He loosed the life raft and, grabbing the other canister, ran up the stairs. If this went the way he thought it was going to go, he needed to be on the top deck before the ship went under, or he'd be pinned under the boat.

With a loud crash, the monster struck the *Minne Ha Ha*. The boat shuddered and pitched hard to starboard. He stumbled on the stairs, clinging tightly to the canister.

There was the roar of the monster and the splintering, cracking of wood, and the thunder of guns.

"Stop! No! You're just pissing it off more!" Tuck shouted. He came out of the stairwell on the top level and discovered it put him eye-to-eye with the beast.

It was a very big eye.

Huge mouth.

Lots and lots and lots of sharp teeth.

He wheeled around and ran back down the stairs. He felt the rush of wind as it took a deep breath. He hit the last step and turned sharply, scurrying to a protected corner.

Ice filled the staircase.

Time to get off the boat.

He turned and ran to the railing of the second deck. He opened the release panel, grabbed the D-ring and flung the canister as far out into the night as he could. The release cord unraveled, and when it hit the end, the life raft expanded. Groaning and cracking, the boat shuddered and pitched even more to starboard.

Holding tight to the release cord, Tuck dove from the boat. The water was a sudden confusion of dark and cold and muted thundering noises. There was the rhythmic chop of the paddlewheel, the deep groan of tortured metal, and a muffled roar of the monster.

He came up to the surface. The massive boat was rolling toward him even as its nose started its deadly dive to the bottom of the lake. Turning, he sighted up on the distant lights of houses on the shore and started to swim, towing the life raft after him.

He stopped swimming when he realized that the night had gotten silent. Treading water, he turned in a circle. There was no sign of the *Minne Ha Ha*. The monster was a wake of water, barely visible in the starlight, heading northwest. The life raft loaded with the eggs trailed behind it, apparently being towed by its release cord. He was totally alone in the water.

"Shit," he whispered, because he was scared that the monster would come back and eat him. Where were the agents? What happened to them? "Shit. Shit. Shit. Shit. Shit."

It was like he was seven again, covered in blood on the side of the highway, no idea where his parents had gone or how he'd gotten there. The familiar sense of guilt and dread filled him.

"Pull it together. You're not seven anymore. You know everything there is to know about boat accidents." There wasn't much else to do in hotel rooms but study in his monk-like devotion. The *Minne Ha Ha* had been traveling northwest, fast as its engines could take it, so it would continue on that course even as it sank. Any trapped air in the cabin would be escaping as a disturbance in the water . . . There!

He dove blindly into the darkness. It was hopeless, but he had to at least try.

Against all odds, he found them. Lylove floundered under Osmyn's unconscious weight. Tuck pushed her up toward the surface and caught Osmyn in a lifeguard hold. It was like dragging a grizzly bear up out of the depths. His lungs were burning when they broke the surface of the lake.

Once he got them into the raft, and Osmyn was breathing again, he bound a long gash on Lylove's leg. He flopped onto his back in the raft, panting. The thunderstorm had blown over and stars blazed overhead, cold and remote. The raft bobbed on the rough lake waters. The lap of the waves drowned out everything but his hammering heartbeat.

He should call someone. Tell them that he was fine. The question of "who" echoed as empty as his grandparents' house after they'd died. Something about nearly dying stripped away the lies he'd been telling himself. He hadn't sold the house because he rarely slept there. Or even because everything in the big old house held memories. The sheer emptiness of it made the truth inescapable: he was completely and totally alone. If he stayed in one town, the fact that he knew no one would be unbearable. He traveled town to town, state to state, because then there was nothing odd about being constantly surrounded by strangers.

But it wasn't working. He was just as lonely as before. All he'd done was rob himself of all the comforts of the familiar. He needed to stop moving, take root. Get a house and fill it with comfortable furniture. Learn the bedroom layout well enough that he could walk around in the dark without kicking something. Get a cat or maybe a dog. Join a club (although he wasn't sure what kind of club) but something non-religious that didn't require him to play a sport.

His phone buzzed into his wet pants pocket. He pulled out the Ziploc baggie holding his phone and undid the seal.

"Hello?"

"Bagans? Sorry to bother you so late—again. Got more work at Lake George. I really didn't quite get what the nature of the claim, but it's a steamboat company that runs cruises. Something about men with guns and a big animal running amuck and one of their boats is missing and possibly a fire."

Tuck glanced toward the Southern shore. There were fire engines and emergency vehicles clustered around it, lights flashing. The two other big boats were moving hastily away from the area. As he watched, a flame flickered higher and higher from the fuel dock. "Oh," he said. "Yes. Definitely a fire." If he showed up at the cruise company in the *Minne Ha Ha* life raft, he was going to get arrested. Any proof that the now unconscious agents used force on him—like security-camera footage showing Lylove carrying him aboard—was about go up in flames.

"Hold on," Sexsmith said. "I just got another e-mail. There's a Tiki Motel . . ." the rest was lost under a sudden explosion on shore. ". . . Easter Island—Easter Island thing—damaged by ice. What's going on up there?"

Tuck opened and closed his mouth a couple of times. What had Osmyn said about doing things half-assed? "You're going to have to send someone else. I quit." He hung up. Immediately his phone rang again with Sexsmith calling him back. He considered his phone for several minutes as it cycled through falling silent and starting to ring again.

The two agents had tracked him to the diner and his motel room. With the lake monster mollified, they might leave him alone. Maybe.

"Oh well, I've been wanting a new phone anyhow." He flung the still ringing cell phone out across the water. It skipped five times before landing with a quiet "ploink." He assembled one of the paddles and pulled in the sea anchor. First he had to get the agents someplace where they'd receive medical attention. After that, he needed a new phone, a new job, and a place to live. Someplace as far from any lake as he could get. And a dog. Definitely a dog.

Deviation from a Theme

INTRODUCTION

Here's one of the most celebrated giant monsters of all in an unusual virtual reality setting. Or maybe not so virtual after all . . .

❖   ❖   ❖

Steven Utley (1948-2013) published his first story in 1972, and went on to write well and often, though he once referred to himself as an "internationally unknown author." Gardner Dozois concurred in a way, writing that Utley "may be the most under-rated science fiction writer alive." He also commented that Utley was a writer "of strength, suppleness, and seemingly endless resource." Utley was probably best known for his unusual time travel series, the SilurianT, chronicling a project with a time tunnel back to what might be considered one of the least interesting periods in Earth's past, but nonetheless made fascinating by Utley's writing skill and his gift for strong characterization. All of the Silurian Tales have been collected in two volumes: *The 400-Million-Year Itch* and *Invisible Kingdoms*. He probably intended to write more stories in the setting, but cancer didn't give him the time.

Deviation from a Theme

Steven Utley

Teacher Payeph wagged her wattles in exasperation as she surveyed the shambles I had made of my first continuum.

"How many times must I tell you?" she demanded. "The smaller, the better! Random factors produce effects which spread outward in waves in all directions! Subtlety, Ellease! Subtlety is called for in order to have a smoothly running continuum."

I bent a spine into the apologetic position and said, "I am abjectly sorry, Teacher."

"I'm certain the fact that you're sorry will console all the life-forms suffering in your continuum." She settled at my side and became solicitous, stroking my frill with her whiskers. That egg-gummer Myosa looked up from her continuum and snickered on my private frequency.

Payeph always feels warmth for the retards.

Expel it from your nether vents, I told Myosa, and shut her off.

Payeph punched MEDIUM REDUCTION on my console slate and picked up my continuum. It hung in her pincers like a punctured bagaloon. I colored and clamped the lids shut on my dorsal vents, lest my embarrassment offend.

"What is wrong?" Payeph asked as she returned my limp creation to its mount. "Are you having trouble with your vision? Can't you perceive fine details? Or is it that you simply don't care?"

"Oh, no. It's just...I'm clumsy, Teacher. I *try* to work on a small scale, but every time I attempt to manipulate my life-forms, I accidentally gouge the side off a mountain or punch a hole clean through the planet. Once, I missed altogether and ruptured the sun."

Payeph looked sad. "I think you need more practice, Ellease, before I turn you loose on another continuum of your own. Come over to mine."

I risked a glance at Myosa. She was smoking with envy. It was no secret that Payeph's continuum was the best in existence. Her decision to let me practice there was an undeniable show of favor. I rose and followed my teacher past Myosa, at whom I surreptitiously twitched a nipple.

When we came to her continuum, Payeph punched MEDIUM REDUCTION. Everything became gray shading into black or white.

"Of course," said Payeph, "I can't simply turn you loose on my pride and joy."

"Of course, Teacher." My hearts sank.

"But I am going to allot you control of a quasi-world."

I cocked a spine at her. "A quasi-world, Teacher?"

"A sort of alternate reality which the life-forms in this sector have erected and preserved on light-sensitive film. The absence of color disconcerts you, Ellease? You'll soon become accustomed to it. The process by which images are preserved is rather primitive at this point in my life-forms' development as a technological race. But they learn quickly. They're imaginative, after a fashion. Now I want you to review everything here, and then I'll let you practice handling the random factors."

"Yes, Teacher."

I reviewed the material. Payeph's creations' creations were two-dimensional in addition to being monochromatic, but I nevertheless found them fascinating. My teacher's five-pointed life-forms had grasped the rudiments of continuum-building and, while keeping within the limitations of their technology, had constructed neat, succinct worlds wherein everything contrived to move itself from this point to that. It was rather like a primer in construction.

"I think I have it now," I finally told Payeph.

"You may begin. Just remember to be subtle when selecting your variables."

And I began.

Time was running in circles now, doubling back and catching up with itself, enfolding Ann Darrow in a scramble of images. A skull-shaped mountain rising through the fog. Black hands lashing her between the weathered stone pillars. Monsters crashing through the jungle, blundering into one another in their eagerness to get at her.

It had been a harrowing night for Ann, a night of bad dreams come true, of fearful childhood imaginings spilling over into reality. She had no way of telling how long or how far she had been carried in her monstrous abductor's paw. She could no longer scream. Her throat was raw. She had lost and regained consciousness more times than she could number, and, always, the awakening had been the same.

In the limbo separating nightmare-filled consciousness and total awakening, she tramped the sidewalks of New York City, moving mindlessly, mechanically, like a zombie. She was tired and hungry, but she had no money, no job, no place to go, and it was cold, so very cold.

But the fetid stench in the air was that of decaying vegetation, not automobile-exhaust fumes and ripening garbage. Her clothes were pasted to her skin with perspiration. And a far greater horror than exhaustion or hunger bore her in its hand as though she were a doll.

In the limbo between unconsciousness and awakening, Ann prayed for deliverance.

Make the bad dream go away!

Don't let me—

Please, somebody, save me! Save me!

But the awakening was always the same.

"Ah," said Teacher Payeph. "I'm impressed, Ellease. You reveal a distinct talent for subjectivity."

I retracted my mandibles, a sign of profound thanks, and then, carefully, nervously, started restructuring events in the quasi-world.

❖ ❖ ❖

Tyrannosaurus sniffed the hot, damp air and began to move through the jungle. The sky was just beginning to lighten, but a thick mist was rising, keeping visibility to a minimum. The dinosaur ploughed through the gloom unconcernedly, letting his acute sense of smell guide him.

Prey-scent was abundant. He crossed the cooling spoor of a nocturnal stegosaurus at one point and, further on, followed the trail of a swamp-dwelling giant until the ground fell off sharply into a bog. Unable to proceed into the swamp, Tyrannosaurus roared out his frustration and swung his twenty-meter length about to seek food elsewhere.

He was aptly named, this Tyrant Lizard; a striding maw of a creature, with teeth like carving knives and jaw muscles like steel cable. He walked on his splayed, talon-tipped toes and held his small forearms close to his scaly chest. He hardly needed the forearms. He did his killing with his jaws and the weight behind those jaws.

He was aptly named, this Tyrannosaurus, and the other denizens of his world feared and respected him accordingly. In their marshes, the thunder lizards headed for deeper water when he approached on the shore. The pterodactyls climbed into the sky. The stegosaurs crouched under their rows of dorsal plates and flicked their spiked tails in alarm.

Tyrannosaurus paused abruptly and listened. He heard a muffled roar in the distance, followed by a series of thin shrieks and a dull crash. There was a sound of large branches snapping. Then the slowly moving air of the jungle brought a faint scent which evoked a fleeting impression, a dim flash of recognition, in the dinosaur's mind: ape.

The Tyrant Lizard began to move again, uprooting saplings and tearing up great clumps of sodden earth as he walked. A lesser scent, intermingled with that of the ape, impinged upon his nostrils. It was a completely unfamiliar odor. Vaguely perplexed, the carnivore slowed his advance. He came to the edge of a clearing and tensed for the attack, for the ape-scent was thick there.

But there was no ape in sight.

A high, plaintive screech brought Tyrannosaurus' head around.

His glistening eye fastened upon a strange white thing wedged into the fork of a lightning-blasted tree at the far side of the clearing.

It seemed hardly more than a mouthful, hardly worth the trouble, but its noise was annoying. He hissed and strode forward, and he was almost upon the wailing thing when an enormous ape burst into the clearing like a black mountain on legs.

Tyrannosaurus immediately forgot about the irritating white creature as he wheeled to meet the ape's attack. The simian was as tall as the dinosaur and, though considerably less heavy, very powerfully built. Jaws distended, the reptile lunged. His opponent ducked under his head and clamped its shaggy arms around his neck. He raked his teeth across the beast's broad back, shredding flesh.

Back and forth across the clearing they raged, biting, tearing, kicking, clawing. Locked together, they crashed against the dead tree, felling it. The ape lost its hold on the dinosaur and went down on top of the tree.

Before the mammal could rise, Tyrannosaurus planted an enormous foot upon its stomach, bent down and bit out its throat.

Payeph fluttered her wattles approvingly. "Very good," she said, "but don't forget that the alterations you've made will have a direct bearing on everything which follows."

"Of course. Teacher."

She awoke with a splitting headache. She was pinned beneath the fallen bole, with only a short, thick nub of branch holding it away from her. For several seconds, she could not remember where she was. Through a rift in the jungle canopy, she could see that the stars had faded from the sky, but the effort required to keep her eyes open and focused served only to worsen the agony behind them. She closed her eyes and pressed her cheek into the warm mud.

Then a basso profundo grunt shook her out of her daze. She twisted around as best she could and gave a short, sharp scream.

Her erstwhile captor's inert mass was sprawled across the trunk.

The giant ape was dead. Looming over it was the monster to end all monsters.

Blood dripping from his jaws and dewlap, Tyrannosaurus looked up from his meal when he heard the scream. He peered down at the strange white creature. A growl started to rumble up from his long, deep chest.

It had been a bad night for Ann Darrow. A worse day was dawning.

"Not at all bad, Ellease. See how simple it is?"

"Yes, Teacher."

"All you have to do is exercise the same meticulous care on a cosmic scale. Take your time. Pay attention to details." She clacked her mandibles. "And watch out for your own elbows."

"Yes, Teacher."

"Do you think you've got the hang of it now? Or would you like to practice with another alternate reality?"

I turned to have another look at the gray quasi-world and quite accidentally ground Tyrannosaurus to mush underfoot just as he was about to nip off Ann Darrow's head and shoulders. Payeph moaned.

I pulled my head down into my carapace. "Er, should I fix it all back the way it was at first?"

"No! I mean, no, Ellease. Let's, uh, leave well enough alone."

"Yes, Teacher." I backed out of the quasi-world as she punched MEDIUM REDUCTION on her console slate. Several of my feet became entangled in something. I gave a tug and pulled free. "Teacher, won't the life-forms who constructed that quasi-world notice the changes I made?"

Payeph made a hooting sound and inflated her wattles in dismay. "I think they have more serious matters to consider now."

I looked into her continuum and groaned. Pulling my feet free, I had broken something else.

"Ellease," Payeph said, "perhaps you should try another line of work."

I stared disconsolately at the mess I had created. Stars were blossoming like variegated flowers. For a brief moment, an entire galaxy flared up into a bouquet.

"Yes, Teacher," I said.

The Eggs from Lake Tanganyika

INTRODUCTION

The first magazine to publish only science fiction was *Amazing Stories*, commencing with the April 1926 issue, founded by Hugo Gernsback, after whom the coveted Hugo Award is nicknamed. At the time, the phrase "science fiction" was not in use, and Gernsback described the magazine's contents as "scientifiction," an amalgamation of "scientific" and "fiction." The third issue had an eye-catching cover of men in naval uniforms on the deck of a (presumably German) ship, frantically firing rifles and aiming a deck gun at an enormous fly zooming toward them. While the author of that cover story didn't get his name on the cover alongside such luminaries as H.G. Wells, Jules Verne, and Garrett P. Serviss (the magazine relied heavily on reprints at first), Curt Siodmak would later gain fame in a different venue. Though editor Gernsback praised the story as "the best scientifiction story so far of 1926," I'm not sure that Siodmak intended it as a serious story, giving the characters names like Meyer-Maier, Schmidt-Schmitt, and my favorite, Pritzel-Wilzell. Joseph Heller's Major Major Major wouldn't be out of place here.

❖ ❖ ❖

Curt Siodmak (1902-2000) was born in Dresden, Germany. He wrote many novels and screenplays, including the 1932 SF novel *F.P.1 Antwortet Nicht* (*F.P.1 Doesn't Answer*, where "F.P." stands for "floating platform," a mid-ocean refueling station for trans-oceanic aircraft), which became a popular movie. After moving to the U.S. in 1937, he wrote the screenplay for *The Wolf Man*, and the rest was history. Some of his other notable horror movies were *Frankenstein Meets the Wolf Man*, *The Beast with Five Fingers*, and *I Walked with a Zombie*. His 1942 novel *Donovan's Brain* was an international bestseller, and has been adapted for radio and at least three movie versions, of which the best is the second version from 1952, also notable for starring an actress named Nancy Davis (no relation), who later became First Lady Nancy Reagan.

The Eggs from Lake Tanganyika

by Curt Siodmak

Professor Meyer-Maier drew a sharp needle out of the cushion, carfully picked up with the pincers the fly lying in front of him, and stuck it carefully upon a piece of white paper. He looked over the rim of his glasses, dipped his pen in the ink and wrote under the specimen:

> *Glossina Palpalis*, specimen from Tsetsefly River.
> In the aboriginal language termed *nsi-nsi*. Usually
> found on river course and lakes in West Africa.
> Bearer of the malady Negana (Tse-tse sickness—
> "sleeping sickness.")

He laid down the pen and took up a powerful magnifying glass for a closer examination. "A horrible creature," he murmured and shivered involuntarily. On each side of the head of the flying horror, there was a monstrous eye surrounded by many sharp lashes and divided up into a hundred thousand flashing facets. An ugly proboscis thickly studded with curved barbs or hooks grew out of the lower side of the head. The wings were small and pointed, the legs armed with thorns, spines and claws. The thorax was muscular like that of a prize fighter. The abdomen was thin and looked like India rubber. It could take in a great quantity of blood and expand like a balloon. On the whole, the flying horror, resembling a pre-historic flying dragon, was not very pleasant looking—Prof. Meyer-Maier took a pin and transfixed the body of the fly. It seemed to him that a vicious sheen of light emanated from the eyes and that the proboscis rolled up. Quicly he picked up the magnifying glass, but it was an optical illusion—the thing was dead with all its poison still within its body.

Memories of the Expedition to Africa

With a deep sigh he laid aside pincers and magnifying glass and sank into a deep reverie. The clock struck 12. 1-2-3-4-5, counted Professor Meyer-Maier.

In Udjidi, a village on lake Tanganyika, the natives had told him of gigantic flies inhabiting the interior further north. These monsters were three times as big as the giants composing the giant bodyguard of the Prince of Ssuggi, who all had to be of at least standard height. Meyer-Maier laughed over this Negro fable, but the Negroes were obstinate. They refused to follow him to the northern part of Lake Tanganyika. Even Msu-uru, his black servant, who otherwise made an intelligent impression, trembled with excitement and begged to be left out of the expedition—because there enormous flies and bees were to be found—that let no man approach. They drank the river dry and guarded the valley of the elephants. "The Valley of the Elephants" where the old pachyderms withdrew to die. "It is inexplicable," soliloquized Meyer-Maier, "that no one ever found a dead elephant."

The clock struck 6-7-8.

The natives had come along on the expedition much against their will. Meyer-Maier had trouble to keep the caravan moving up to the day when he found four great, strange looking eggs, larger than ostrich eggs. The Negroes were seized with a panic, half of them deserting in the night, in spite of the great distance from the coast. The other half could only be kept there by tremendous efforts. He had to make up his mind finally, to go back, but he secretly put the eggs he had found into his camping chest to solve their riddle.

Now they were here in his Berlin home in his workroom. He had not found time as yet to examine them, for he had brought much material home to be worked over.

The clock struck 9-10.

Meyer-Maier kept thinking of the ugly head of the tse-tse fly that he had seen through the magnifying glass. A strange thought occurred to him and made him smile. Suppose the stories of the Negroes were true and the giant flies—butterflies and beetles as big as elephants did exist! And suppose that they propagated as flies do!—each one laying eighty million eggs a year! He laughed aloud and pictured to himself how such a creature would stalk through the streets.

A Strange Sound and the Hatching of an Egg

He broke off suddenly, in the midst of his laughter. A sound reached his ear, an earsplitting buzzing like that of a thousand flies, a deafening hum, as if a swarm of bees were entering the room; it burst out like a blast of wind through the room and then stopped. Meyer-Maier jerked the door open. Nothing. All was quiet.

"I must relax for a while," said he, and opened the window. He turned on the light and threw back the lid of the big chest, which contained the giant eggs. Suddenly he grew pale as death and staggered back. A creature was crawling out, a creature as big as a police dog—a frightful creature, with wings—a muscular body, and six hairy legs with claws. It crept slowly, raised its incandescent head to the light and polished its wings with its hind legs. Faint with fright, Meyer-Maier pressed against the wall with outspread arms. A loud buzzing—the creature swept across the room, climbed up on the windowsill and was gone.

Meyer-Maier came slowly to himself. "My nerves are deceiving me. Did I dream?" He whispered and dragged himself to the camp-chest. But he became frozen with horror. One egg was broken open. "It breaks out of its shell like a chicken, it does not change into a chrysalis," he thought mechanically. At last his mind cleared and he awoke to the emergency. He sprang to the desk, snatched up his revolver, ran downstairs and out into the street. He saw no trace of the escaped giant insect. Meyer-Maier looked up at the lighted windows of his home. Suddenly the light became dim. "The other eggs"—like a blow came the thought—"the other eggs too have broken." He raced back up the stairs. A deafening buzzing filled the room. He jerked his door open and fired—once, twice, until the magazine was empty—the room was silent. Through the window he saw three silhouettes sweeping high across the night sky and disappearing in the direction of the great woods in the West. In the chest there lay the four broken giant eggs.

A Call for His Colleague

Meyer-Maier sank upon a chair. "It's against all logic," he thought and glanced at the empty revolver in his hand. "My delirium has taken wings and crawled out of the egg. What should I do? Shall I call the police? They will send me to an alienist! Keep quiet about it? Look for the creatures? I'll call up my colleague, Schmidt-Schmitt!" He dragged himself to the telephone and got a connection. Schmidt-Schmitt was at home! "This is Meyer-Maier," sounded a tired voice. "Come over at once!"

"What's the trouble?" asked Schmidt-Schmitt.

"My African giant eggs have burst," lisped Meyer-Maier with a failing voice. "You must come at once!"

"Your nerves are out of order," answered Schmidt-Schmitt. "Have you still got the creatures?"

"They've gone," whispered Meyer-Maier—he thought he would collapse—"flew out of the window."

"There, there," laughed Schmidt-Schmitt. "Now, we are getting to the truth—of course they're aren't there. Anyhow, I'll come over. Meanwhile, take a cognac and put on a cold pack."

"Take your car, and say nothing about what I told you."

Professor Meyer-Maier hung up the receiver.

It was incredible. He pressed his hand to his forehead. "If the empty shells were not irrefutable evidence, he would have been inclined to think of hallucinations.

He helped himself to some brandy and after the second glass he felt better. "I wish Professor Schmidt-Schmitt would come. He ought to be here by now. He will have an explanation and will help me to get myself in hand again. The day of ghosts and miracles is long past. But why isn't he here? He ought to have come by this time."

Meyer-Maier looked out of the window. A car came tearing through the dark street and stopped with squeaking brakes in front of Meyer-Maier's residence. A form jumped out like an India rubber ball, ran up the steps, burst into Meyer-Maier's study, and collapsed into a chair.

"How awful," he gasped.

"It seems to me, you are even more excited over it than I," said Professer Meyer-Maier dispiritedly while he watched his shaking friend.

"Absolutely terrible," Professor Schmmidt-Schmitt wiped his forehead with a silk handkerchief. "You were not suffering from nerves, you had no hallucinations. Just now I saw a fly-creature as large as a heifer falling upon a horse. The monster grew big and heavy, while the horse collapsed, and the fly flew away. I examined the horse. Its veins and arteries were empty. Not a drop of blood was left in its body. The driver fainted with fright and has not come to yet. It is a world catastrophe."

Notifying the Police

"We must notify the police at once."

A quick telephone connection was obtained. The police Lieutenant in charge himself answered.

"This is Professor Meyer-Maier talking! Please believe what I am going to tell you. I am neither drunk nor crazy. Four poisonous gigantic flies, as large as horses, are at large in the city. They must be destroyed at all costs."

"What are you trying to do? Kid me?" the lieutenant came back in an angry voice.

"Believe me—for God's sake," yelled Meyer-Maier, reaching the end of his nervous strength.

"Hold the wire." The Lieutenant turned to the desk of the sergeant. "What is up now?"

"A cab driver has been here who says that his horse was killed by a gigantic bird on Karlstrasse."

"Get the men of the second platoon ready for immediate action," he ordered the sergeant, and turned back to the telephone. "Hello, Professor! Are you still there? Please come over as quickly as possible. What you told me is true. One of these giant insects has been seen."

Professor Meyer-Maier hung up. He loaded his revolver and put a Browning pistol into his colleague's hand. "Is your car still downstairs?"

"Yes, I took the little limousine."

"Excellent—then the monster cannot attack us." They rushed on through the night.

"What can happen now?" inquired Professor Schmidt-Schmitt.

"These giant flies may propagate and multiply in the manner of the housefly. And in that case, due to their strength and poisonous qualities," continued Professor Meyer-Maier, "the whole human race will perish in a few weeks. When they crept from the shell they were as large as dogs. They grew to the size of a horse within an hour. God knows what will happen next. Let us hope and pray that we will be able to find and kill the four flies and destroy the eggs which they have laid in the meantime, within fourteen days."

The car came to a stop in front of the Police Station. A policeman armed with a steel helmet and hand trench bombs swinging from his belt tore open the limousine door. The Lieutenant hastened out and conducted the scientists into the station house.

"Any more news?" inquired Meyer-Maier.

"the West Precinct station just called up. One of their patrolmen saw a giant animal fly over the Teutoburger Forest. Luckily we had war tanks near there which immediately set out in search of the creature."

The telephone bell rang. The Lieutenant rushed to the phone.

"Central Police Station."

"East Station talking. Report comes from Lake Wieler, that a gigantic fly has attacked two motor boats."

"Put small trench mortars on the police-boat and go out on the lake. Shoot when the beast gets near you."

The door of the Station House opened and the city commissioner entered. "I have just heard some fabulous stories," he said, and approached the visitors. "Professor Meyer-Maier? Major Pritzel-Wilzell! Can you explain all this?"

"I brought home with me four large eggs from my African expedition. Tonight these eggs broke open. Four great flies came out —a sort of tse-tse fly, such as is found in Lake Tanganyika. The creatures escaped through the window and we must make every endeavor to kill them at once."

The telephone bell rang as if possessed.

"This is the Central Broadcasting Station. A giant bird has been caught in the high voltage lines. It has fallen down and lies on the street."

"Close the street at once." The Major took up the instrument. "Call up the Second company. Let all four flying companies go off with munition and gasoline for three days. Come with me, my friends. We will get at least one of them!"

One of the Giant Flies is Electrocuted

Although it was five o'clock in the morning, the square in front of the broadcasting station was black with people. The police kept a space clear in the center, where monstrously large and ugly lay the dead giant fly. Its wings were burnt, its proboscis extended, while the legs, with their claws, were drawn up against the body. The abdomen was a great ball, full of bright red liquid. "that is certainly the creature that killed the horse," said Schmidt-Schmitt, and pointed at the thick abdomen. He then walked around the creature. "*Glossina palpalis*. A monstrous tse-tse fly."

"Will you please send the monster to the zoological laboratory?" The Major nodded assent. The firemen, prepared for service, pushed poles under the insect and tried to lift it up from the ground. Out of the air came a droning sound. An airplane squadron dropped out of the clouds and again disappeared. A bright body with vibrating wings flew across the sky. The airplanes dropped on it. The noise of the machine guns started. The bright body fell in a spiral course to the ground. Crying and screaming, the people fled from the street and crowded into the houses. They couldn't tell where the insect would fall and they were afraid for their heads. The street was empty in an instant. The body of the monster fell directly in front of the armored car and lay there, stiff. In its fall it carried away a lot of aerial cable and now it lay on the pavement as if caught in a net, the head torn by the machine gun bullets. It looked like a strange gleaming cactus.

"Take me to my home, Major," groaned Meyer-Maier. "I can't stand it any longer. The excitement is too much for me."

In the Hospital

The armored car started noisily into motion. Meyer-Maier fell from the seat, senseless, upon the floor of the tonneau. When he came to himself, he lay in a strange bed. His gaze fell upon a bell which swung to and fro above his face. In his head there was a humming like an airplane motor. He made no attempt, even to think. His finger pressed the pushbutton and he never released it until half a dozen attendants came rushing into the room. One figure stood out in dark colors in the group of white-clad interns. It was his colleague, Schmidt-Schmitt.

"You're awake?" said he, and stepped to his bed. "How are you feeling?"

"My head is buzzing as if there were a swarm of hornets living in it. How many hours have I lain here?"

"Hours?" Schmidt-Schmitt dwelt upon the word. "Today is the fifteenth day that you are lying in Professor Stiebling's sanitorium. It was a difficult case. You always woke up at mealtime and without saying a word, went to sleep again."

"Fifteen days!" cried Meyer-Maier excitedly. "And the insects? Have they been killed?"

"I'll tell you the whole story when you are well again," aid Schmidt-Schmitt, quieting him. "Lie as you are quietly—any excitement may hurt you."

"They must not come into the room!" he screamed out to an excited messenger, who breathlessly pulled the door open.

"Professor!"—the man was in deadly fear—"the Central Police station has given out the news that a swarm of giant flies are descending upon the city."

"Barricade all windows at once!"

"You wasted precious time," screamed Meyer-Maier, and jumped out of the bed. "Let me go to my house. I must solve the riddle as how to get at the insects. Don't touch me," he raved. He snatched a coat from the rack, ran out of the house, and jumped into Schmidt-Schmitt's automobile which stood at the gate, and went like the wind to his home. The door of his house was ajar. He rushed up four flights and in delirious haste rushed into his workroom. The telephone bell rang.

Meyer-Maier snatched up the receiver. He got the consoling message from the city police-commissioner. "The danger is over, Professor. Our air squadron has destroyed the swarm with a cloud of poison gas. Only two of the insects escaped death. Those we have caught in a net and are taking them to the zoological gardens."

"And if they have left eggs behind them?"

"We are going to search the woods systematically and will inject Lysol into any eggs we find. I think that will help," laughed the Major. "Shall I send some of them to you for examination?"

"No," cried Meyer-Maier in fright. "Keep them off my neck."

He sat down at his work table. There seemed a vicious smile on the face of the transfixed dead tse-tse fly. "You frightful ghost," murmured the professor with palid lips, and threw a book on the insect. His head was in a daze. He tried his best to think clearly. An axiom of science came to him: if the flies are as large as elephants, they can only propagate as fast as elephants do. They can't have a million young ones, but only a few. "I can't be wrong," he murmured. "I'll look up the confirmation."

He took up the telephone and called the city Commissioner. "Major, how many insects were in the swarm?"

"Thirteen. Eleven are dead. The other two will never escape alive. They are fed up with the poison gas."

"Thank you." Meyer-Maier hung up the receiver. "Very well," he murmured, "now there can be no question of any danger, for each fly can only lay three or four eggs at once—not a million."

An immense weariness overcame him. He went into his bedroom and fell exhausted on his bed. "It is well that there is a supreme wisdom which controls the laws of nature. Otherwise the world would be subject to the strangest surprises," he thought of the monsters and crept anxiously under the bedclothes. "I'll entrust Schmidt-Schmitt with the investigation of the creature phenomenon. I simply can't stand further excitement."

And sleep spread the mantle of well-deserved quiet over him.

The Dunwich Horror

INTRODUCTION

H.P. Lovcraft (1890-1937) was, of course, one of the most influential horror writers of the twentieth century, and this story is one of his best, and one of the major reasons for that influence. The basic thesis of most of Lovecraft's stories is that the Earth was once ruled by things too horrible for the human mind to perceive and remain sane. Though they have left the Earth, some of them wish to return, which would be very bad news for the puny humans who have infested the globe since their departure. This is a story of an attempt to open a gateway for that return, an attempt which results in a creature which is very big, very dangerous . . . and invisible . . .

❖ ❖ ❖

Though H.P. Lovecraft died in 1937, at that time almost unknown outside the pages of *Weird Tales*, which published most of his output while he was alive, and a substantial amount after his death, and had his writing dismissed by critics as varied as Damon Knight and Edmund Wilson, he is now considered a major American writer, with numerous paperback editions of his writing, and a two-volume set of his works by the Library of America. (Maybe dying well is the second best revenge.) He was a prolific writer of letters to a circle of friends and correspondents, many of them fellow writers to whom he generously gave advice, and I'm very happy that in addition to a story by HPL, this book includes stories by three of his friends: Robert Bloch, Robert E. Howard, and Henry Kuttner. The Lovecraft Circle lives!

The Dunwich Horror

by H. P. Lovecraft

"Gorgons, and Hydras, and Chimaeras—dire stories of Celaeno and
the Harpies—may reproduce themselves in the brain of
superstition—*but they were there before.* They are transcripts, types—
the archetypes are in us, and eternal. How else should the recital of
that which we know in a waking sense to be false come to affect us at
all? Is it that we naturally conceive terror from such objects,
considered in their capacity of being able to inflict upon us bodily
injury? O, least of all! *These terrors are of older standing. They date
beyond body*—or without the body, they would have been the same.
. . . That the kind of fear here treated is purely spiritual—that it is
strong in proportion as it is objectless on earth, that it predominates
in the period of our sinless infancy—are difficulties the solution of
which might afford some probable insight into our ante-mundane
condition, and a peep at least into the shadowland of pre-existence."
—*Charles Lamb:* "Witches and Other Night-Fears"

❧ I ❧

When a traveller in north central Massachusetts takes the wrong fork
at the junction of the Aylesbury pike just beyond Dean's Corners he

comes upon a lonely and curious country. The ground gets higher, and the brier-bordered stone walls press closer and closer against the ruts of the dusty, curving road. The trees of the frequent forest belts seem too large, and the wild weeds, brambles, and grasses attain a luxuriance not often found in settled regions. At the same time the planted fields appear singularly few and barren; while the sparsely scattered houses wear a surprisingly uniform aspect of age, squalor, and dilapidation. Without knowing why, one hesitates to ask directions from the gnarled, solitary figures spied now and then on crumbling doorsteps or on the sloping, rock-strown meadows. Those figures are so silent and furtive that one feels somehow confronted by forbidden things, with which it would be better to have nothing to do. When a rise in the road brings the mountains in view above the deep woods, the feeling of strange uneasiness is increased. The summits are too rounded and symmetrical to give a sense of comfort and naturalness, and sometimes the sky silhouettes with especial clearness the queer circles of tall stone pillars with which most of them are crowned.

Gorges and ravines of problematical depth intersect the way, and the crude wooden bridges always seem of dubious safety. When the road dips again there are stretches of marshland that one instinctively dislikes, and indeed almost fears at evening when unseen whippoorwills chatter and the fireflies come out in abnormal profusion to dance to the raucous, creepily insistent rhythms of stridently piping bull-frogs. The thin, shining line of the Miskatonic's upper reaches has an oddly serpent-like suggestion as it winds close to the feet of the domed hills among which it rises.

As the hills draw nearer, one heeds their wooded sides more than their stone-crowned tops. Those sides loom up so darkly and precipitously that one wishes they would keep their distance, but there is no road by which to escape them. Across a covered bridge one sees a small village huddled between the stream and the vertical slope of Round Mountain, and wonders at the cluster of rotting gambrel roofs bespeaking an earlier architectural period than that of the neighbouring region. It is not reassuring to see, on a closer glance, that most of the houses are deserted and falling to ruin, and that the broken-steepled church now harbours the one slovenly mercantile establishment of the hamlet. One dreads to trust the tenebrous tunnel of the bridge, yet there is no way to avoid it. Once across, it is hard to prevent the impression of a faint, malign odour about the village street, as of the massed mould and decay of centuries. It is always a relief to get clear of the place, and to follow the narrow road around the base of the hills and across the level country beyond till it rejoins the Aylesbury pike. Afterward one sometimes learns that one has been through Dunwich.

Outsiders visit Dunwich as seldom as possible, and since a certain season of horror all the signboards pointing toward it have been taken down. The scenery, judged by any ordinary aesthetic canon, is more than commonly beautiful; yet there is no influx of artists or summer tourists. Two centuries ago, when talk of witch-blood, Satan-worship, and strange forest presences was not laughed at, it was the custom to give reasons for avoiding the locality. In our sensible age—since the Dunwich horror of 1928 was hushed up by those who had the town's and the world's welfare at heart—people shun it without knowing exactly why. Perhaps one reason—though it cannot apply to uninformed strangers—is that the natives are now repellently decadent, having gone far along that path of retrogression so common in many New England backwaters. They have come to form a race by themselves, with the well-defined mental and physical stigmata of degeneracy and inbreeding. The average of their intelligence is woefully low, whilst their annals reek of overt viciousness and of half-hidden murders, incests, and deeds of almost unnamable violence and perversity. The old gentry, representing the two or three armigerous families which came from Salem in 1692, have kept somewhat above the general level of decay; though many branches are sunk into the sordid populace so deeply that only their names remain as a key to the origin they disgrace. Some of the Whateleys and Bishops still send their eldest sons to Harvard and Miskatonic, though those sons seldom return to the mouldering gambrel roofs under which they and their ancestors were born.

No one, even those who have the facts concerning the recent horror, can say just what is the matter with Dunwich; though old legends speak of unhallowed rites and conclaves of the Indians, amidst which they called forbidden shapes of shadow out of the great rounded hills, and made wild orgiastic prayers that were answered by loud crackings and rumblings from the ground below. In 1747 the Reverend Abijah Hoadley, newly come to the Congregational Church at Dunwich Village, preached a memorable sermon on the close presence of Satan and his imps; in which he said:

> "It must be allow'd, that these Blasphemies of an infernall Train of Daemons are Matters of too common Knowledge to be deny'd; the cursed Voices of *Azazel* and *Buzrael,* of *Beelzebub* and *Belial,* being heard now from under Ground by above a Score of credible Witnesses now living. I my self did not more than a Fortnight ago catch a very plain Discourse of evill Powers in the Hill behind my House; wherein there were a Rattling and Rolling, Groaning, Screeching, and Hissing, such as no Things of this Earth cou'd raise up, and which must needs have come from those Caves that only black Magick can discover, and only the Divell unlock."

Mr. Hoadley disappeared soon after delivering this sermon; but the text, printed in Springfield, is still extant. Noises in the hills continued to be reported from year to year, and still form a puzzle to geologists and physiographers.

Other traditions tell of foul odours near the hill-crowning circles of stone pillars, and of rushing airy presences to be heard faintly at certain hours from stated points at the bottom of the great ravines; while still others try to explain the Devil's Hop Yard—a bleak, blasted hillside where no tree, shrub, or grass-blade will grow. Then too, the natives are mortally afraid of the numerous whippoorwills which grow vocal on warm nights. It is vowed that the birds are psychopomps lying in wait for the souls of the dying, and that they time their eerie cries in unison with the sufferer's struggling breath. If they can catch the fleeing soul when it leaves the body, they instantly flutter away chittering in daemoniac laughter; but if they fail, they subside gradually into a disappointed silence.

These tales, of course, are obsolete and ridiculous; because they come down from very old times. Dunwich is indeed ridiculously old—older by far than any of the communities within thirty miles of it. South of the village one may still spy the cellar walls and chimney of the ancient Bishop house, which was built before 1700; whilst the ruins of the mill at the falls, built in 1806, form the most modern piece of architecture to be seen. Industry did not flourish here, and the nineteenth-century factory movement proved short-lived. Oldest of all are the great rings of rough-hewn stone columns on the hill-tops, but these are more generally attributed to the Indians than to the settlers. Deposits of skulls and bones, found within these circles and around the sizeable table-like rock on Sentinel Hill, sustain the popular belief that such spots were once the burial-places of the Pocumtucks; even though many ethnologists, disregarding the absurd improbability of such a theory, persist in believing the remains Caucasian.

❧ II ❧

It was in the township of Dunwich, in a large and partly inhabited farmhouse set against a hillside four miles from the village and a mile and a half from any other dwelling, that Wilbur Whateley was born at 5 A.M. on Sunday, the second of February, 1913. This date was recalled because it was Candlemas, which people in Dunwich curiously observe under another name; and because the noises in the hills had sounded, and all the dogs of the countryside had barked persistently, throughout the night before. Less worthy of notice was the fact that the mother was one of the decadent Whateleys, a somewhat deformed, unattractive albino woman of thirty-five, living with an aged and half-insane father about whom the most frightful tales of wizardry had been whispered in his youth. Lavinia Whateley had no known husband, but according to the custom of the region made no attempt to disavow the child; concerning the other side of whose ancestry the country folk might—and did—speculate as widely as they chose. On the contrary, she seemed strangely proud of the dark, goatish-looking infant who formed such a contrast to her own sickly and pink-eyed albinism, and was heard to mutter many curious prophecies about its unusual powers and tremendous future.

Lavinia was one who would be apt to mutter such things, for she was a lone creature given to wandering amidst thunderstorms in the hills and trying to read the great odorous books which her father had inherited through two centuries of Whateleys, and which were fast falling to pieces with age and worm-holes. She had never been to school, but was filled with disjointed scraps of ancient lore that Old Whateley had taught her. The remote farmhouse had always been feared because of Old Whateley's reputation for black magic, and the unexplained death by violence of Mrs. Whateley when Lavinia was twelve years old had not helped to make the place popular. Isolated among strange influences, Lavinia was fond of wild and grandiose day-dreams and singular occupations; nor was her leisure much taken up by household cares in a home from which all standards of order and cleanliness had long since disappeared.

There was a hideous screaming which echoed above even the hill noises and the dogs' barking on the night Wilbur was born, but no known doctor or midwife presided at his coming. Neighbours knew nothing of him till a week afterward, when Old Whateley drove his sleigh through the snow into Dunwich Village and discoursed incoherently to the group of loungers at Osborn's general store. There seemed to be a change in the old man—an added element of furtiveness in the clouded brain which subtly transformed him from an object to a subject of fear—though he was not one to be perturbed by any common family event. Amidst it all he shewed some trace of the pride later noticed in his daughter, and what he said of the child's paternity was remembered by many of his hearers years afterward.

"I dun't keer what folks think—ef Lavinny's boy looked like his pa, he wouldn't look like nothin' ye expeck. Ye needn't think the only folks is the folks hereabaouts. Lavinny's read some, an' has seed some things the most o' ye only tell abaout. I calc'late her man is as good a husban' as ye kin find this side of Aylesbury; an' ef ye knowed as much abaout the hills as I dew, ye wouldn't ast no better church weddin' nor her'n. Let me tell ye suthin'—*some day yew folks'll hear a child o' Lavinny's a-callin' its father's name on the top o' Sentinel Hill!"*

The only persons who saw Wilbur during the first month of his life were old Zechariah Whateley, of the undecayed Whateleys, and Earl Sawyer's common-law wife, Mamie Bishop. Mamie's visit was frankly one of curiosity, and her subsequent tales did justice to her observations; but Zechariah came to lead a pair of Alderney cows which Old Whateley had bought of his son Curtis. This marked the beginning of a course of cattle-buying on the part of small Wilbur's family which ended only in 1928, when the Dunwich horror came and went; yet at no time did the ramshackle Whateley barn seem overcrowded with livestock. There came a period when people were curious enough to steal up and count the herd that grazed precariously on the steep hillside above the old farmhouse, and they could never find more than ten or twelve anaemic, bloodless-looking specimens. Evidently some blight or distemper, perhaps sprung from the unwholesome pasturage or the diseased fungi and timbers of the filthy barn, caused a heavy mortality amongst the Whateley animals. Odd wounds or sores, having something of the aspect of incisions, seemed to afflict the visible cattle; and once or twice during the earlier months certain callers fancied they could discern similar sores about the throats of the grey, unshaven old man and his slatternly, crinkly-haired albino daughter.

In the spring after Wilbur's birth Lavinia resumed her customary rambles in the hills, bearing in her misproportioned arms the swarthy child. Public interest in the Whateleys subsided after most of the country folk had seen the baby, and no one bothered to comment on the swift development which that newcomer seemed every day to exhibit. Wilbur's growth was indeed phenomenal, for within three months of his birth he had attained a size and muscular power not usually found in infants under a full year of age. His motions and even his vocal sounds shewed a restraint and deliberateness highly peculiar in an infant, and no one was really unprepared when, at seven months, he began to walk unassisted, with falterings which another month was sufficient to remove.

It was somewhat after this time—on Hallowe'en—that a great

blaze was seen at midnight on the top of Sentinel Hill where the old table-like stone stands amidst its tumulus of ancient bones. Considerable talk was started when Silas Bishop—of the undecayed Bishops—mentioned having seen the boy running sturdily up that hill ahead of his mother about an hour before the blaze was remarked. Silas was rounding up a stray heifer, but he nearly forgot his mission when he fleetingly spied the two figures in the dim light of his lantern. They darted almost noiselessly through the underbrush, and the astonished watcher seemed to think they were entirely unclothed. Afterward he could not be sure about the boy, who may have had some kind of a fringed belt and a pair of dark trunks or trousers on. Wilbur was never subsequently seen alive and conscious without complete and tightly buttoned attire, the disarrangement or threatened disarrangement of which always seemed to fill him with anger and alarm. His contrast with his squalid mother and grandfather in this respect was thought very notable until the horror of 1928 suggested the most valid of reasons.

The next January gossips were mildly interested in the fact that "Lavinny's black brat" had commenced to talk, and at the age of only eleven months. His speech was somewhat remarkable both because of its difference from the ordinary accents of the region, and because it displayed a freedom from infantile lisping of which many children of three or four might well be proud. The boy was not talkative, yet when he spoke he seemed to reflect some elusive element wholly unpossessed by Dunwich and its denizens. The strangeness did not reside in what he said, or even in the simple idioms he used; but seemed vaguely linked with his intonation or with the internal organs that produced the spoken sounds. His facial aspect, too, was remarkable for its maturity; for though he shared his mother's and grandfather's chinlessness, his firm and precociously shaped nose united with the expression of his large, dark, almost Latin eyes to give him an air of quasi-adulthood and well-nigh preternatural intelligence. He was, however, exceedingly ugly despite his appearance of brilliancy; there being something almost goatish or animalistic about his thick lips, large-pored, yellowish skin, coarse crinkly hair, and oddly elongated ears. He was soon disliked even more decidedly than his mother and grandsire, and all conjectures about him were spiced with references to the bygone magic of Old Whateley, and how the hills once shook when he shrieked the dreadful name of *Yog-Sothoth* in the midst of a circle of stones with a great book open in his arms before him. Dogs abhorred the boy, and he was always obliged to take various defensive measures against their barking menace.

❖ III ❖

Meanwhile Old Whateley continued to buy cattle without measurably increasing the size of his herd. He also cut timber and began to repair the unused parts of his house—a spacious, peaked-roofed affair whose rear end was buried entirely in the rocky hillside, and whose three least-ruined ground-floor rooms had always been sufficient for himself and his daughter. There must have been prodigious reserves of strength in the old man to enable him to accomplish so much hard labour; and though he still babbled dementedly at times, his carpentry seemed to shew the effects of sound calculation. It had already begun as soon as Wilbur was born, when one of the many tool-sheds had been put suddenly in order, clapboarded, and fitted with a stout fresh lock. Now, in restoring the abandoned upper story of the house, he was a no less thorough craftsman. His mania shewed itself only in his tight boarding-up of all the windows in the reclaimed section—though many declared that it was a crazy thing to bother with the reclamation at all. Less inexplicable was his fitting up of another downstairs room for his new grandson—a room which several callers saw, though no one was ever admitted to the closely boarded upper story. This chamber he lined with tall, firm shelving; along which he began gradually to arrange, in apparently careful order, all the rotting ancient books and parts of books which during his own day had been heaped promiscuously in odd corners of the various rooms.

"I made some use of 'em," he would say as he tried to mend a torn black-letter page with paste prepared on the rusty kitchen stove, "but the boy's fitten to make better use of 'em. He'd orter hev 'em as well sot as he kin, for they're goin' to be all of his larnin'."

When Wilbur was a year and seven months old—in September of 1914—his size and accomplishments were almost alarming. He had grown as large as a child of four, and was a fluent and incredibly intelligent talker. He ran freely about the fields and hills, and accompanied his mother on all her wanderings. At home he would pore diligently over the queer pictures and charts in his grandfather's books, while Old Whateley would instruct and catechise him through long, hushed afternoons. By this time the restoration of the house was finished, and those who watched it wondered why one of the upper windows had been made into a solid plank door. It was a window in the rear of the east gable end, close against the hill; and no one could imagine why a cleated wooden runway was built up to it from the ground. About the period of this work's completion people noticed that the old tool-house, tightly locked and windowlessly clapboarded since Wilbur's birth, had been abandoned again. The door swung listlessly open, and when Earl Sawyer once stepped within after a cattle-selling call on Old Whateley he was quite discomposed by the singular odour he encountered—such a stench, he averred, as he had never before smelt in all his life except near the Indian circles on the hills, and which could not come from anything sane or of this earth. But then, the homes and sheds of Dunwich folk have never been remarkable for olfactory immaculateness.

The following months were void of visible events, save that everyone swore to a slow but steady increase in the mysterious hill noises. On May-Eve of 1915 there were tremors which even the Aylesbury people felt, whilst the following Hallowe'en produced an underground rumbling queerly synchronised with bursts of flame— "them witch Whateleys' doin's"—from the summit of Sentinel Hill. Wilbur was growing up uncannily, so that he looked like a boy of ten as he entered his fourth year. He read avidly by himself now; but talked much less than formerly. A settled taciturnity was absorbing him, and for the first time people began to speak specifically of the dawning look of evil in his goatish face. He would sometimes mutter an unfamiliar jargon, and chant in bizarre rhythms which chilled the listener with a sense of unexplainable terror. The aversion displayed toward him by dogs had now become a matter of wide remark, and he was obliged to carry a pistol in order to traverse the countryside in safety. His occasional use of the weapon did not enhance his popularity amongst the owners of canine guardians.

The few callers at the house would often find Lavinia alone on the ground floor, while odd cries and footsteps resounded in the boarded-up second story. She would never tell what her father and the boy were doing up there, though once she turned pale and displayed an abnormal degree of fear when a jocose fish-peddler tried the locked door leading to the stairway. That peddler told the store loungers at Dunwich Village that he thought he heard a horse stamping on that floor above. The loungers reflected, thinking of the door and runway, and of the cattle that so swiftly disappeared. Then they shuddered as they recalled tales of Old Whateley's youth, and of the strange things that are called out of the earth when a bullock is sacrificed at the proper time to certain heathen gods. It had for some time been noticed that dogs had begun to hate and fear the whole Whateley place as violently as they hated and feared young Wilbur personally.

In 1917 the war came, and Squire Sawyer Whateley, as chairman of the local draft board, had hard work finding a quota of young Dunwich men fit even to be sent to a development camp. The government, alarmed at such signs of wholesale regional decadence, sent several officers and medical experts to investigate; conducting a survey which New England newspaper readers may still recall. It was the publicity attending this investigation which set reporters on the track of the Whateleys, and caused the *Boston Globe* and *Arkham Advertiser* to print flamboyant Sunday stories of young Wilbur's precociousness, Old Whateley's black magic, the shelves of strange books, the sealed second story of the ancient farmhouse, and the weirdness of the whole region and its hill noises. Wilbur was four and a half then, and looked like a lad of fifteen. His lips and cheeks were fuzzy with a coarse dark down, and his voice had begun to break.

Earl Sawyer went out to the Whateley place with both sets of reporters and camera men, and called their attention to the queer stench which now seemed to trickle down from the sealed upper spaces. It was, he said, exactly like a smell he had found in the tool-shed abandoned when the house was finally repaired; and like the faint odours which he sometimes thought he caught near the stone circles on the mountains. Dunwich folk read the stories when they appeared, and grinned over the obvious mistakes. They wondered, too, why the writers made so much of the fact that Old Whateley always paid for his cattle in gold pieces of extremely ancient date. The Whateleys had received their visitors with ill-concealed distaste, though they did not dare court further publicity by violent resistance or refusal to talk.

❖ IV ❖

For a decade the annals of the Whateleys sink indistinguishably into the general life of a morbid community used to their queer ways and hardened to their May-Eve and All-Hallows orgies. Twice a year they would light fires on the top of Sentinel Hill, at which times the mountain rumblings would recur with greater and greater violence; while at all seasons there were strange and portentous doings at the lonely farmhouse. In the course of time callers professed to hear sounds in the sealed upper story even when all the family were downstairs, and they wondered how swiftly or how lingeringly a cow or bullock was usually sacrificed. There was talk of a complaint to the Society for the Prevention of Cruelty to Animals; but nothing ever came of it, since Dunwich folk are never anxious to call the outside world's attention to themselves.

About 1923, when Wilbur was a boy of ten whose mind, voice, stature, and bearded face gave all the impressions of maturity, a second great siege of carpentry went on at the old house. It was all inside the sealed upper part, and from bits of discarded lumber people concluded that the youth and his grandfather had knocked out all the partitions and even removed the attic floor, leaving only one vast open void between the ground story and the peaked roof. They had torn down the great central chimney, too, and fitted the rusty range with a flimsy outside tin stovepipe.

In the spring after this event Old Whateley noticed the growing number of whippoorwills that would come out of Cold Spring Glen to chirp under his window at night. He seemed to regard the circumstance as one of great significance, and told the loungers at Osborn's that he thought his time had almost come.

"They whistle jest in tune with my breathin' naow," he said, "an' I guess they're gittin' ready to ketch my soul. They know it's a-goin' aout, and dun't calc'late to miss it. Yew'll know, boys, arter I'm gone, whether they git me er not. Ef they dew, they'll keep up a-singin' an' laffin' till break o' day. Ef they dun't they'll kinder quiet daown like. I expeck them an' the souls they hunts fer hev some pretty tough tussles sometimes."

On Lammas Night, 1924, Dr. Houghton of Aylesbury was hastily summoned by Wilbur Whateley, who had lashed his one remaining horse through the darkness and telephoned from Osborn's in the village. He found Old Whateley in a very grave state, with a cardiac action and stertorous breathing that told of an end not far off. The shapeless albino daughter and oddly bearded grandson stood by the bedside, whilst from the vacant abyss overhead there came a disquieting suggestion of rhythmical surging or lapping, as of the waves on some level beach. The doctor, though, was chiefly disturbed by the chattering night birds outside; a seemingly limitless legion of whippoorwills that cried their endless message in repetitions timed diabolically to the wheezing gasps of the dying man. It was uncanny and unnatural—too much, thought Dr. Houghton, like the whole of the region he had entered so reluctantly in response to the urgent call.

Toward one o'clock Old Whateley gained consciousness, and interrupted his wheezing to choke out a few words to his grandson.

"More space, Willy, more space soon. Yew grows—an' *that* grows faster. It'll be ready to sarve ye soon, boy. Open up the gates to Yog-Sothoth with the long chant that ye'll find on page 751 *of the complete edition,* an' *then* put a match to the prison. Fire from airth can't burn it nohaow."

He was obviously quite mad. After a pause, during which the flock of whippoorwills outside adjusted their cries to the altered tempo while some indications of the strange hill noises came from afar off, he added another sentence or two.

"Feed it reg'lar, Willy, an' mind the quantity; but dun't let it grow too fast fer the place, fer ef it busts quarters or gits aout afore ye opens to Yog-Sothoth, it's all over an' no use. Only them from beyont kin make it multiply an' work. . . . Only them, the old uns as wants to come back. . . ."

But speech gave place to gasps again, and Lavinia screamed at the way the whippoorwills followed the change. It was the same for more than an hour, when the final throaty rattle came. Dr. Houghton drew shrunken lids over the glazing grey eyes as the tumult of birds faded imperceptibly to silence. Lavinia sobbed, but Wilbur only chuckled whilst the hill noises rumbled faintly.

"They didn't git him," he muttered in his heavy bass voice.

Wilbur was by this time a scholar of really tremendous erudition in his one-sided way, and was quietly known by correspondence to many librarians in distant places where rare and forbidden books of old days are kept. He was more and more hated and dreaded around Dunwich because of certain youthful disappearances which suspicion laid vaguely at his door; but was always able to silence inquiry through fear or through use of that fund of old-time gold which still, as in his grandfather's time, went forth regularly and increasingly for cattle-buying. He was now tremendously mature of aspect, and his height, having reached the normal adult limit, seemed inclined to wax beyond that figure. In 1925, when a scholarly correspondent from Miskatonic University called upon him one day and departed pale and puzzled, he was fully six and three-quarters feet tall.

Through all the years Wilbur had treated his half-deformed albino mother with a growing contempt, finally forbidding her to go to the hills with him on May-Eve and Hallowmass; and in 1926 the poor creature complained to Mamie Bishop of being afraid of him.

"They's more abaout him as I knows than I kin tell ye, Mamie," she said, "an' naowadays they's more nor what I know myself. I vaow afur Gawd, I dun't know what he wants nor what he's a-tryin' to dew."

That Hallowe'en the hill noises sounded louder than ever, and fire burned on Sentinel Hill as usual; but people paid more attention to the rhythmical screaming of vast flocks of unnaturally belated whippoorwills which seemed to be assembled near the unlighted Whateley farmhouse. After midnight their shrill notes burst into a kind of pandaemoniac cachinnation which filled all the countryside, and not until dawn did they finally quiet down. Then they vanished, hurrying southward where they were fully a month overdue. What this meant, no one could quite be certain till later. None of the country folk seemed to have died—but poor Lavinia Whateley, the twisted albino, was never seen again.

In the summer of 1927 Wilbur repaired two sheds in the farmyard and began moving his books and effects out to them. Soon afterward Earl Sawyer told the loungers at Osborn's that more carpentry was going on in the Whateley farmhouse. Wilbur was closing all the doors and windows on the ground floor, and seemed to be taking out partitions as he and his grandfather had done upstairs four years before. He was living in one of the sheds, and Sawyer thought he seemed unusually worried and tremulous. People generally suspected him of knowing something about his mother's disappearance, and very few ever approached his neighbourhood now. His height had increased to more than seven feet, and shewed no signs of ceasing its development.

❦ V ❦

The following winter brought an event no less strange than Wilbur's first trip outside the Dunwich region. Correspondence with the Widener Library at Harvard, the Bibliothèque Nationale in Paris, the British Museum, the University of Buenos Ayres, and the Library of Miskatonic University of Arkham had failed to get him the loan of a book he desperately wanted; so at length he set out in person, shabby, dirty, bearded, and uncouth of dialect, to consult the copy at Miskatonic, which was the nearest to him geographically. Almost eight feet tall, and carrying a cheap new valise from Osborn's general store, this dark and goatish gargoyle appeared one day in Arkham in quest of the dreaded volume kept under lock and key at the college library—the hideous *Necronomicon* of the mad Arab Abdul Alhazred in Olaus Wormius' Latin version, as printed in Spain in the seventeenth century. He had never seen a city before, but had no thought save to find his way to the university grounds; where, indeed, he passed heedlessly by the great white-fanged watchdog that barked with unnatural fury and enmity, and tugged frantically at its stout chain.

Wilbur had with him the priceless but imperfect copy of Dr. Dee's English version which his grandfather had bequeathed him, and upon receiving access to the Latin copy he at once began to collate the two texts with the aim of discovering a certain passage which would have come on the 751st page of his own defective volume. This much he could not civilly refrain from telling the librarian—the same erudite Henry Armitage (A.M. Miskatonic, Ph.D. Princeton, Litt.D. Johns Hopkins) who had once called at the farm, and who now politely plied him with questions. He was looking, he had to admit, for a kind of formula or incantation containing the frightful name *Yog-Sothoth*, and it puzzled him to find discrepancies, duplications, and ambiguities which made the matter of determination far from easy. As he copied the formula he finally chose, Dr. Armitage looked involuntarily over his shoulder at the open pages; the left-hand one of which, in the Latin version, contained such monstrous threats to the peace and sanity of the world.

"Nor is it to be thought," ran the text as Armitage mentally translated it, "that man is either the oldest or the last of earth's masters, or that the common bulk of life and substance walks alone. The Old Ones were, the Old Ones are, and the Old Ones shall be. Not in the spaces we know, but *between* them, They walk serene and primal, undimensioned and to us unseen. *Yog-Sothoth* knows the gate. *Yog-Sothoth* is the gate. *Yog-Sothoth* is the key and guardian of the gate. Past, present, future, all are one in *Yog-Sothoth*. He knows where the Old Ones broke through of old, and where They shall break through again. He knows where They have trod earth's fields, and where They still tread them, and why no one can behold Them as They tread. By Their smell can men sometimes know Them near, but of Their semblance can no man know, *saving only in the features of those They have begotten on mankind;* and of those are there many sorts, differing in likeness from man's truest eidolon to that shape without sight or substance which is *Them.* They walk unseen and foul in lonely places where the Words have been spoken and the Rites howled through at their Seasons. The wind gibbers with Their voices, and the earth mutters with Their consciousness. They bend the forest and crush the city, yet may not forest or city behold the hand that smites. Kadath in the cold waste hath known Them, and what man knows Kadath? The ice desert of the South and the sunken isles of Ocean hold stones whereon Their seal is engraven, but who hath seen the deep frozen city or the sealed tower long garlanded with seaweed and barnacles? Great Cthulhu is Their cousin, yet can he spy Them only dimly. *Iä! Shub-Niggurath!* As a foulness shall ye know Them. Their hand is at your throats, yet ye see Them not; and Their habitation is even one with your guarded threshold. *Yog-Sothoth* is the key to the gate, whereby the spheres meet. Man rules now where They ruled once; They shall soon rule where Man rules now. After summer is winter, and after winter summer. They wait patient and potent, for here shall They reign again."

Dr. Armitage, associating what he was reading with what he had heard of Dunwich and its brooding presences, and of Wilbur Whateley and his dim, hideous aura that stretched from a dubious birth to a cloud of probable matricide, felt a wave of fright as tangible as a draught of the tomb's cold clamminess. The bent, goatish giant before him seemed like the spawn of another planet or dimension; like something only partly of mankind, and linked to black gulfs of essence and entity that stretch like titan phantasms beyond all spheres of force and matter, space and time. Presently Wilbur raised his head and began speaking in that strange, resonant fashion which hinted at sound-producing organs unlike the run of mankind's.

"Mr. Armitage," he said, "I calc'late I've got to take that book home. They's things in it I've got to try under sarten conditions that I can't git here, an' it 'ud be a mortal sin to let a red-tape rule hold me up. Let me take it along, Sir, an' I'll swar they wun't nobody know the difference. I dun't need to tell ye I'll take good keer of it. It wa'n't me that put this Dee copy in the shape it is. . . ."

He stopped as he saw firm denial on the librarian's face, and his own goatish features grew crafty. Armitage, half-ready to tell him he might make a copy of what parts he needed, thought suddenly of the possible consequences and checked himself. There was too much responsibility in giving such a being the key to such blasphemous outer spheres. Whateley saw how things stood, and tried to answer lightly.

"Wal, all right, ef ye feel that way abaout it. Maybe Harvard wun't be so fussy as yew be." And without saying more he rose and strode out of the building, stooping at each doorway.

Armitage heard the savage yelping of the great watchdog, and studied Whateley's gorilla-like lope as he crossed the bit of campus visible from the window. He thought of the wild tales he had heard, and recalled the old Sunday stories in the *Advertiser;* these things, and the lore he had picked up from Dunwich rustics and villagers during his one visit there. Unseen things not of earth—or at least not of tri-dimensional earth—rushed foetid and horrible through New England's glens, and brooded obscenely on the mountain-tops. Of this he had long felt certain. Now he seemed to sense the close presence of some terrible part of the intruding horror, and to glimpse a hellish advance in the black dominion of the ancient and once passive nightmare. He locked away the *Necronomicon* with a shudder of disgust, but the room still reeked with an unholy and unidentifiable stench. "As a foulness shall ye know them," he quoted. Yes—the odour was the same as that which had sickened him at the Whateley farmhouse less than three years before. He thought of Wilbur, goatish and ominous, once again, and laughed mockingly at the village rumours of his parentage.

"Inbreeding?" Armitage muttered half-aloud to himself. "Great God, what simpletons! Shew them Arthur Machen's Great God Pan and they'll think it a common Dunwich scandal! But what thing—what cursed shapeless influence on or off this three-dimensioned earth—was Wilbur Whateley's father? Born on Candlemas—nine months after May-Eve of 1912, when the talk about the queer earth noises reached clear to Arkham—What walked on the mountains that May-Night? What Roodmas horror fastened itself on the world in half-human flesh and blood?"

During the ensuing weeks Dr. Armitage set about to collect all possible data on Wilbur Whateley and the formless presences around Dunwich. He got in communication with Dr Houghton of Aylesbury, who had attended Old Whateley in his last illness, and found much to ponder over in the grandfather's last words as quoted by the physician. A visit to Dunwich Village failed to bring out much that was new; but a close survey of the *Necronomicon,* in those parts which Wilbur had sought so avidly, seemed to supply new and terrible clues to the nature, methods, and desires of the strange evil so vaguely threatening this planet. Talks with several students of archaic lore in Boston, and letters to many others elsewhere, gave him a growing amazement which passed slowly through varied degrees of alarm to a state of really acute spiritual fear. As the summer drew on he felt dimly that something ought to be done about the lurking terrors of the upper Miskatonic valley, and about the monstrous being known to the human world as Wilbur Whateley.

⚜ VI ⚜

The Dunwich horror itself came between Lammas and the equinox in 1928, and Dr. Armitage was among those who witnessed its monstrous prologue. He had heard, meanwhile, of Whateley's grotesque trip to Cambridge, and of his frantic efforts to borrow or copy from the *Necronomicon* at the Widener Library. Those efforts had been in vain, since Armitage had issued warnings of the keenest intensity to all librarians having charge of the dreaded volume. Wilbur had been shockingly nervous at Cambridge; anxious for the book, yet almost equally anxious to get home again, as if he feared the results of being away long.

Early in August the half-expected outcome developed, and in the small hours of the 3rd Dr. Armitage was awakened suddenly by the wild, fierce cries of the savage watchdog on the college campus. Deep and terrible, the snarling, half-mad growls and barks continued; always in mounting volume, but with hideously significant pauses. Then there rang out a scream from a wholly different throat—such a scream as roused half the sleepers of Arkham and haunted their dreams ever afterward—such a scream as could come from no being born of earth, or wholly of earth.

Armitage, hastening into some clothing and rushing across the street and lawn to the college buildings, saw that others were ahead of him; and heard the echoes of a burglar-alarm still shrilling from the library. An open window shewed black and gaping in the moonlight. What had come had indeed completed its entrance; for the barking and the screaming, now fast fading into a mixed growling and moaning, proceeded unmistakably from within. Some instinct warned Armitage that what was taking place was not a thing for unfortified eyes to see, so he brushed back the crowd with authority as he unlocked the vestibule door. Among the others he saw Professor Warren Rice and Dr. Francis Morgan, men to whom he had told some of his conjectures and misgivings; and these two he motioned to accompany him inside. The inward sounds, except for a watchful, droning whine from the dog, had by this time quite subsided; but Armitage now perceived with a sudden start that a loud chorus of whippoorwills among the shrubbery had commenced a damnably rhythmical piping, as if in unison with the last breaths of a dying man.

The building was full of a frightful stench which Dr. Armitage knew too well, and the three men rushed across the hall to the small genealogical reading-room whence the low whining came. For a second nobody dared to turn on the light, then Armitage summoned up his courage and snapped the switch. One of the three—it is not certain which—shrieked aloud at what sprawled before them among disordered tables and overturned chairs. Professor Rice declares that he wholly lost consciousness for an instant, though he did not stumble or fall.

The thing that lay half-bent on its side in a foetid pool of greenish-yellow ichor and tarry stickiness was almost nine feet tall, and the dog had torn off all the clothing and some of the skin. It was not quite dead, but twitched silently and spasmodically while its chest heaved in monstrous unison with the mad piping of the expectant whippoorwills outside. Bits of shoe-leather and fragments of apparel were scattered about the room, and just inside the window an empty canvas sack lay where it had evidently been thrown. Near the central desk a revolver had fallen, a dented but undischarged cartridge later explaining why it had not been fired. The thing itself, however, crowded out all other images at the time. It would be trite and not wholly accurate to say that no human pen could describe it, but one may properly say that it could not be vividly visualised by anyone whose ideas of aspect and contour are too closely bound up with the common life-forms of this planet and of the three known dimensions. It was partly human, beyond a doubt, with very man-like hands and head, and the goatish, chinless face had the stamp of the Whateleys upon it. But the torso and lower parts of the body were teratologically fabulous, so that only generous clothing could ever have enabled it to walk on earth unchallenged or uneradicated.

Above the waist it was semi-anthropomorphic; though its chest, where the dog's rending paws still rested watchfully, had the leathery, reticulated hide of a crocodile or alligator. The back was piebald with yellow and black, and dimly suggested the squamous covering of certain snakes. Below the waist, though, it was the worst; for here all human resemblance left off and sheer phantasy began. The skin was thickly covered with coarse black fur, and from the abdomen a score of long greenish-grey tentacles with red sucking mouths protruded limply. Their arrangement was odd, and seemed to follow the symmetries of some cosmic geometry unknown to earth or the solar system. On each of the hips, deep set in a kind of pinkish, ciliated orbit, was what seemed to be a rudimentary eye; whilst in lieu of a tail there depended a kind of trunk or feeler with purple annular markings, and with many evidences of being an undeveloped mouth or throat. The limbs, save for their black fur, roughly resembled the hind legs of prehistoric earth's giant saurians; and terminated in ridgy-veined pads that were neither hooves nor claws. When the thing breathed, its tail and tentacles rhythmically changed colour, as if from some circulatory cause normal to the non-human side of its ancestry. In the tentacles this was observable as a deepening of the greenish tinge, whilst in the tail it was manifest as a yellowish appearance which alternated with a sickly greyish-white in the spaces between the purple rings. Of genuine blood there was none; only the foetid greenish-yellow ichor which trickled along the painted floor beyond the radius of the stickiness, and left a curious discolouration behind it.

As the presence of the three men seemed to rouse the dying thing, it began to mumble without turning or raising its head. Dr. Armitage made no written record of its mouthings, but asserts confidently that nothing in English was uttered. At first the syllables defied all correlation with any speech of earth, but toward the last there came some disjointed fragments evidently taken from the *Necronomicon*, that monstrous blasphemy in quest of which the thing had perished. These fragments, as Armitage recalls them, ran something like "*N'gai, n'gha'ghaa, bugg-shoggog, y'hah; Yog-Sothoth, Yog-Sothoth. . . .*" They trailed off into nothingness as the whippoorwills shrieked in rhythmical crescendoes of unholy anticipation.

Then came a halt in the gasping, and the dog raised its head in a long, lugubrious howl. A change came over the yellow, goatish face of the prostrate thing, and the great black eyes fell in appallingly. Outside the window the shrilling of the whippoorwills had suddenly ceased, and above the murmurs of the gathering crowd there came the sound of a panic-struck whirring and fluttering. Against the moon vast clouds of feathery watchers rose and raced from sight, frantic at that which they had sought for prey.

All at once the dog started up abruptly, gave a frightened bark, and leaped nervously out of the window by which it had entered. A cry rose from the crowd, and Dr. Armitage shouted to the men outside that no one must be admitted till the police or medical examiner came. He was thankful that the windows were just too high to permit of peering in, and drew the dark curtains carefully down over each one. By this time two policemen had arrived; and Dr. Morgan, meeting them in the vestibule, was urging them for their own sakes to postpone entrance to the stench-filled reading-room till the examiner came and the prostrate thing could be covered up.

Meanwhile frightful changes were taking place on the floor. One need not describe the *kind* and *rate* of shrinkage and disintegration that occurred before the eyes of Dr. Armitage and Professor Rice; but it is permissible to say that, aside from the external appearance of face and hands, the really human element in Wilbur Whateley must have been very small. When the medical examiner came, there was only a sticky whitish mass on the painted boards, and the monstrous odour had nearly disappeared. Apparently Whateley had had no skull or bony skeleton; at least, in any true or stable sense. He had taken somewhat after his unknown father.

❖ VII ❖

Yet all this was only the prologue of the actual Dunwich horror. Formalities were gone through by bewildered officials, abnormal details were duly kept from press and public, and men were sent to Dunwich and Aylesbury to look up property and notify any who might be heirs of the late Wilbur Whateley. They found the countryside in great agitation, both because of the growing rumblings beneath the domed hills, and because of the unwonted stench and the surging, lapping sounds which came increasingly from the great empty shell formed by Whateley's boarded-up farmhouse. Earl

Sawyer, who tended the horse and cattle during Wilbur's absence, had developed a woefully acute case of nerves. The officials devised excuses not to enter the noisome boarded place; and were glad to confine their survey of the deceased's living quarters, the newly mended sheds, to a single visit. They filed a ponderous report at the court-house in Aylesbury, and litigations concerning heirship are said to be still in progress amongst the innumerable Whateleys, decayed and undecayed, of the upper Miskatonic valley.

An almost interminable manuscript in strange characters, written in a huge ledger and adjudged a sort of diary because of the spacing and the variations in ink and penmanship, presented a baffling puzzle to those who found it on the old bureau which served as its owner's desk. After a week of debate it was sent to Miskatonic University, together with the deceased's collection of strange books, for study and possible translation; but even the best linguists soon saw that it was not likely to be unriddled with ease. No trace of the ancient gold with which Wilbur and Old Whateley always paid their debts has yet been discovered.

It was in the dark of September 9th that the horror broke loose. The hill noises had been very pronounced during the evening, and dogs barked frantically all night. Early risers on the 10th noticed a peculiar stench in the air. About seven o'clock Luther Brown, the hired boy at George Corey's, between Cold Spring Glen and the village, rushed frenziedly back from his morning trip to Ten-Acre Meadow with the cows. He was almost convulsed with fright as he stumbled into the kitchen; and in the yard outside the no less frightened herd were pawing and lowing pitifully, having followed the boy back in the panic they shared with him. Between gasps Luther tried to stammer out his tale to Mrs. Corey.

"Up thar in the rud beyont the glen, Mis' Corey—they's suthin' ben thar! It smells like thunder, an' all the bushes an' little trees is pushed back from the rud like they'd a haouse ben moved along of it. An' that ain't the wust, nuther. They's *prints* in the rud, Mis' Corey— great raound prints as big as barrel-heads, all sunk daown deep like a elephant had ben along, *only they's a sight more nor four feet could make!* I looked at one or two afore I run, an' I see every one was covered with lines spreadin' aout from one place, like as if big palm-leaf fans—twict or three times as big as any they is—hed of ben paounded daown into the rud. An' the smell was awful, like what it is araound Wizard Whateley's ol' haouse. . . ."

Here he faltered, and seemed to shiver afresh with the fright that had sent him flying home. Mrs. Corey, unable to extract more information, began telephoning the neighbours; thus starting on its rounds the overture of panic that heralded the major terrors. When she got Sally Sawyer, housekeeper at Seth Bishop's, the nearest place to Whateley's, it became her turn to listen instead of transmit; for Sally's boy Chauncey, who slept poorly, had been up on the hill toward Whateley's, and had dashed back in terror after one look at the place, and at the pasturage where Mr. Bishop's cows had been left out all night.

"Yes, Mis' Corey," came Sally's tremulous voice over the party wire, "Cha'ncey he just come back a-postin', and couldn't haff talk fer bein' scairt! He says Ol' Whateley's haouse is all blowed up, with the timbers scattered raound like they'd ben dynamite inside; only the bottom floor ain't through, but is all covered with a kind o' tar-like stuff that smells awful an' drips daown offen the aidges onto the graoun' whar the side timbers is blowed away. An' they's awful kinder marks in the yard, tew—great raound marks bigger raound than a hogshead, an' all sticky with stuff like is on the blowed-up haouse. Cha'ncey he says they leads off into the medders, whar a great swath wider'n a barn is matted daown, an' all the stun walls tumbled every whichway wherever it goes.

"An' he says, says he, Mis' Corey, as haow he sot to look fer Seth's caows, frighted ez he was; an' faound 'em in the upper pasture nigh the Devil's Hop Yard in an awful shape. Haff on 'em's clean gone, an' nigh haff o' them that's left is sucked most dry o' blood, with sores on 'em like they's ben on Whateley's cattle ever senct Lavinny's black brat was born. Seth he's gone aout naow to look at 'em, though I'll vaow he wun't keer ter git very nigh Wizard Whateley's! Cha'ncey didn't look keerful ter see whar the big matted-daown swath led arter it leff the pasturage, but he says he thinks it p'inted towards the glen rud to the village.

"I tell ye, Mis' Corey, they's suthin' abroad as hadn't orter be abroad, an' I for one think that black Wilbur Whateley, as come to the bad eend he desarved, is at the bottom of the breedin' of it. He wa'n't all human hisself, I allus says to everybody; an' I think he an' Ol' Whateley must a raised suthin' in that there nailed-up haouse as ain't even so human as he was. They's allus ben unseen things araound Dunwich—livin' things—as ain't human an' ain't good fer human folks.

"The graoun' was a-talkin' lass night, an' towards mornin' Cha'ncey he heerd the whippoorwills so laoud in Col' Spring Glen he couldn't sleep nun. Then he thought he heerd another faint-like saound over towards Wizard Whateley's—a kinder rippin' or tearin' o' wood, like some big box er crate was bein' opened fur off. What with this an' that, he didn't git to sleep at all till sunup, an' no sooner was he up this mornin', but he's got to go over to Whateley's an' see what's the matter. He see enough, I tell ye, Mis' Corey! This dun't mean no good, an' I think as all the men-folks ought to git up a party an' do suthin'. I know suthin' awful's abaout, an' feel my time is nigh, though only Gawd knows jest what it is.

"Did your Luther take accaount o' whar them big tracks led tew? No? Wal, Mis' Corey, ef they was on the glen rud this side o' the glen, an' ain't got to your haouse yet, I calc'late they must go into the glen itself. They would do that. I allus says Col' Spring Glen ain't no healthy nor decent place. The whippoorwills an' fireflies there never did act like they was creaters o' Gawd, an' they's them as says ye kin hear strange things a-rushin' an' a-talkin' in the air daown thar ef ye stand in the right place, atween the rock falls an' Bear's Den."

By that noon fully three-quarters of the men and boys of Dunwich were trooping over the roads and meadows between the new-made Whateley ruins and Cold Spring Glen, examining in horror the vast, monstrous prints, the maimed Bishop cattle, the strange, noisome wreck of the farmhouse, and the bruised, matted vegetation of the fields and roadsides. Whatever had burst loose upon the world had assuredly gone down into the great sinister ravine; for all the trees on the banks were bent and broken, and a great avenue had been gouged in the precipice-hanging underbrush. It was as though a house, launched by an avalanche, had slid down through the tangled growths of the almost vertical slope. From below no sound came, but only a distant, undefinable foetor; and it is not to be wondered at that the men preferred to stay on the edge and argue, rather than descend and beard the unknown Cyclopean horror in its lair. Three dogs that were with the party had barked furiously at first, but seemed cowed and reluctant when near the glen. Someone telephoned the news to the *Aylesbury Transcript;* but the editor, accustomed to wild tales from Dunwich, did no more than concoct a humorous paragraph about it; an item soon afterward reproduced by the Associated Press.

That night everyone went home, and every house and barn was barricaded as stoutly as possible. Needless to say, no cattle were allowed to remain in open pasturage. About two in the morning a frightful stench and the savage barking of the dogs awakened the household at Elmer Frye's, on the eastern edge of Cold Spring Glen, and all agreed that they could hear a sort of muffled swishing or lapping sound from somewhere outside. Mrs. Frye proposed telephoning the neighbours, and Elmer was about to agree when the noise of splintering wood burst in upon their deliberations. It came, apparently, from the barn; and was quickly followed by a hideous screaming and stamping amongst the cattle. The dogs slavered and crouched close to the feet of the fear-numbed family. Frye lit a lantern through force of habit, but knew it would be death to go out into that black farmyard. The children and the womenfolk whimpered, kept from screaming by some obscure, vestigial instinct of defence which told them their lives depended on silence. At last the noise of the cattle subsided to a pitiful moaning, and a great snapping, crashing, and crackling ensued. The Fryes, huddled together in the sitting-room, did not dare to move until the last echoes died away far down in Cold Spring Glen. Then, amidst the dismal moans from the stable and the daemoniac piping of late whippoorwills in the glen, Selina Frye tottered to the telephone and spread what news she could of the second phase of the horror.

The next day all the countryside was in a panic; and cowed, uncommunicative groups came and went where the fiendish thing had occurred. Two titan paths of destruction stretched from the glen to the Frye farmyard, monstrous prints covered the bare patches of ground, and one side of the old red barn had completely caved in. Of the cattle, only a quarter could be found and identified. Some of these were in curious fragments, and all that survived had to be shot. Earl Sawyer suggested that help be asked from Aylesbury or Arkham, but others maintained it would be of no use. Old Zebulon Whateley, of a branch that hovered about half way between soundness and decadence, made darkly wild suggestions about rites that ought to be practiced on the hill-tops. He came of a line where tradition ran strong, and his memories of chantings in the great stone circles were not altogether connected with Wilbur and his grandfather.

Darkness fell upon a stricken countryside too passive to organise for real defence. In a few cases closely related families would band together and watch in the gloom under one roof; but in general there was only a repetition of the barricading of the night before, and a futile, ineffective gesture of loading muskets and setting pitchforks handily about. Nothing, however, occurred except some hill noises; and when the day came there were many who hoped that the new horror had gone as swiftly as it had come. There were even bold souls who proposed an offensive expedition down in the glen, though they did not venture to set an actual example to the still reluctant majority.

When night came again the barricading was repeated, though there was less huddling together of families. In the morning both the Frye and the Seth Bishop households reported excitement among the dogs and vague sounds and stenches from afar, while early explorers noted with horror a fresh set of the monstrous tracks in the road skirting Sentinel Hill. As before, the sides of the road shewed a bruising indicative of the blasphemously stupendous bulk of the horror; whilst the conformation of the tracks seemed to argue a passage in two directions, as if the moving mountain had come from Cold Spring Glen and returned to it along the same path. At the base of the hill a thirty-foot swath of crushed shrubbery saplings led steeply upward, and the seekers gasped when they saw that even the most perpendicular places did not deflect the inexorable trail. Whatever the horror was, it could scale a sheer stony cliff of almost complete verticality; and as the investigators climbed around to the hill's summit by safer routes they saw that the trail ended—or rather, reversed—there.

It was here that the Whateleys used to build their hellish fires and chant their hellish rituals by the table-like stone on May-Eve and Hallowmass. Now that very stone formed the centre of a vast space thrashed around by the mountainous horror, whilst upon its slightly concave surface was a thick and foetid deposit of the same tarry stickiness observed on the floor of the ruined Whateley farmhouse when the horror escaped. Men looked at one another and muttered. Then they looked down the hill. Apparently the horror had descended by a route much the same as that of its ascent. To speculate was futile. Reason, logic, and normal ideas of motivation stood confounded. Only old Zebulon, who was not with the group, could have done justice to the situation or suggested a plausible explanation.

Thursday night began much like the others, but it ended less happily. The whippoorwills in the glen had screamed with such unusual persistence that many could not sleep, and about 3 A.M. all the party telephones rang tremulously. Those who took down their receivers heard a fright-mad voice shriek out, "Help, oh, my Gawd! . . ." and some thought a crashing sound followed the breaking off of the exclamation. There was nothing more. No one dared do anything, and no one knew till morning whence the call came. Then those who had heard it called everyone on the line, and found that only the Fryes did not reply. The truth appeared an hour later, when a hastily assembled group of armed men trudged out to the Frye place at the head of the glen. It was horrible, yet hardly a surprise. There were more swaths and monstrous prints, but there was no longer any house. It had caved in like an egg-shell, and amongst the ruins nothing living or dead could be discovered. Only a stench and a tarry stickiness. The Elmer Fryes had been erased from Dunwich.

❦ VIII ❦

In the meantime a quieter yet even more spiritually poignant phase of the horror had been blackly unwinding itself behind the closed door of a shelf-lined room in Arkham. The curious manuscript record or diary of Wilbur Whateley, delivered to Miskatonic University for translation, had caused much worry and bafflement among the experts in languages both ancient and modern; its very alphabet, notwithstanding a general resemblance to the heavily shaded Arabic used in Mesopotamia, being absolutely unknown to any available authority. The final conclusion of the linguists was that the text represented an artificial alphabet, giving the effect of a cipher; though none of the usual methods of cryptographic solution seemed to furnish any clue, even when applied on the basis of every tongue the writer might conceivably have used. The ancient books taken from Whateley's quarters, while absorbingly interesting and in several cases promising to open up new and terrible lines of research among philosophers and men of science, were of no assistance whatever in this matter. One of them, a heavy tome with an iron clasp, was in another unknown alphabet—this one of a very different cast, and resembling Sanscrit more than anything else. The old ledger was at length given wholly into the charge of Dr. Armitage, both because of his peculiar interest in the Whateley matter, and because of his wide linguistic learning and skill in the mystical formulae of antiquity and the Middle Ages.

Armitage had an idea that the alphabet might be something esoterically used by certain forbidden cults which have come down from old times, and which have inherited many forms and traditions from the wizards of the Saracenic world. That question, however, he did not deem vital; since it would be unnecessary to know the origin of the symbols if, as he suspected, they were used as a cipher in a modern language. It was his belief that, considering the great amount of text involved, the writer would scarcely have wished the trouble of using another speech than his own, save perhaps in certain special formulae and incantations. Accordingly he attacked the manuscript with the preliminary assumption that the bulk of it was in English.

Dr. Armitage knew, from the repeated failures of his colleagues, that the riddle was a deep and complex one; and that no simple mode of solution could merit even a trial. All through late August he fortified himself with the massed lore of cryptography; drawing upon the fullest resources of his own library, and wading night after night amidst the arcana of Trithemius' *Poligraphia,* Giambattista Porta's *De Furtivis Literarum Notis,* De Vigenère's *Traité des Chiffres,* Falconer's *Cryptomenysis Patefacta,* Davys' and Thicknesse's eighteenth-century treatises, and such fairly modern authorities as Blair, von Marten, and Klüber's *Kryptographik.* He interspersed his study of the books with attacks on the manuscript itself, and in time became convinced that he had to deal with one of those subtlest and most ingenious of cryptograms, in which many separate lists of corresponding letters are arranged like the multiplication table, and the message built up with arbitrary key-words known only to the initiated. The older authorities seemed rather more helpful than the newer ones, and Armitage concluded that the code of the manuscript was one of great antiquity, no doubt handed down through a long line of mystical experimenters. Several times he seemed near daylight, only to be set back by some unforeseen obstacle. Then, as September approached, the clouds began to clear. Certain letters, as used in certain parts of the manuscript, emerged definitely and unmistakably; and it became obvious that the text was indeed in English.

On the evening of September 2nd the last major barrier gave way, and Dr. Armitage read for the first time a continuous passage of Wilbur Whateley's annals. It was in truth a diary, as all had thought; and it was couched in a style clearly shewing the mixed occult erudition and general illiteracy of the strange being who wrote it. Almost the first long passage that Armitage deciphered, an entry dated November 26, 1916, proved highly startling and disquieting. It was written, he remembered, by a child of three and a half who looked like a lad of twelve or thirteen.

"Today learned the Aklo for the Sabaoth," it ran, "which did not like, it being answerable from the hill and not from the air. That upstairs more ahead of me than I had thought it would be, and is not like to have much earth brain. Shot Elam Hutchins' collie Jack when he went to bite me, and Elam says he would kill me if he dast. I guess he won't.

Grandfather kept me saying the Dho formula last night, and I think I saw the inner city at the 2 magnetic poles. I shall go to those poles when the earth is cleared off, if I can't break through with the Dho-Hna formula when I commit it. They from the air told me at Sabbat that it will be years before I can clear off the earth, and I guess grandfather will be dead then, so I shall have to learn all the angles of the planes and all the formulas between the Yr and Nhhngr. They from outside will help, but they cannot take body without human blood. That upstairs looks it will have the right cast. I can see it a little when I make the Voorish sign or blow the powder of Ibn Ghazi at it, and it is near like them at May-Eve on the Hill. The other face may wear off some. I wonder how I shall look when the earth is cleared and there are no earth beings on it. He that came with the Aklo Sabaoth said I may be transfigured, there being much of outside to work on."

Morning found Dr. Armitage in a cold sweat of terror and a frenzy of wakeful concentration. He had not left the manuscript all night, but sat at his table under the electric light turning page after page with shaking hands as fast as he could decipher the cryptic text. He had nervously telephoned his wife he would not be home, and when she brought him a breakfast from the house he could scarcely dispose of a mouthful. All that day he read on, now and then halted maddeningly as a reapplication of the complex key became necessary. Lunch and dinner were brought him, but he ate only the smallest fraction of either. Toward the middle of the next night he drowsed off in his chair, but soon woke out of a tangle of nightmares almost as hideous as the truths and menaces to man's existence that he had uncovered.

On the morning of September 4th Professor Rice and Dr. Morgan insisted on seeing him for a while, and departed trembling and ashen-grey. That evening he went to bed, but slept only fitfully. Wednesday—the next day—he was back at the manuscript, and began to take copious notes both from the current sections and from those he had already deciphered. In the small hours of that night he slept a little in an easy-chair in his office, but was at the manuscript again before dawn. Some time before noon his physician, Dr. Hartwell, called to see him and insisted that he cease work. He refused; intimating that it was of the most vital importance for him to complete the reading of the diary, and promising an explanation in due course of time.

That evening, just as twilight fell, he finished his terrible perusal and sank back exhausted. His wife, bringing his dinner, found him in a half-comatose state; but he was conscious enough to warn her off with a sharp cry when he saw her eyes wander toward the notes he had taken. Weakly rising, he gathered up the scribbled papers and sealed them all in a great envelope, which he immediately placed in his inside coat pocket. He had sufficient strength to get home, but was so clearly in need of medical aid that Dr. Hartwell was summoned at once. As the doctor put him to bed he could only mutter over and over again, *"But what, in God's name, can we do?"*

Dr. Armitage slept, but was partly delirious the next day. He made no explanations to Hartwell, but in his calmer moments spoke of the imperative need of a long conference with Rice and Morgan. His wilder wanderings were very startling indeed, including frantic appeals that something in a boarded-up farmhouse be destroyed, and fantastic references to some plan for the extirpation of the entire human race and all animal and vegetable life from the earth by some terrible elder race of beings from another dimension. He would shout that the world was in danger, since the Elder Things wished to strip it and drag it away from the solar system and cosmos of matter into some other plane or phase of entity from which it had once fallen, vigintillions of aeons ago. At other times he would call for the dreaded *Necronomicon* and the *Daemonolatreia* of Remigius, in which he seemed hopeful of finding some formula to check the peril he conjured up.

"Stop them, stop them!" he would shout. "Those Whateleys meant to let them in, and the worst of all is left! Tell Rice and Morgan we must do something—it's a blind business, but I know how to make the powder. . . . It hasn't been fed since the second of August, when Wilbur came here to his death, and at that rate. . . ."

But Armitage had a sound physique despite his seventy-three years, and slept off his disorder that night without developing any real fever. He woke late Friday, clear of head, though sober with a gnawing fear and tremendous sense of responsibility. Saturday afternoon he felt able to go over to the library and summon Rice and Morgan for a conference, and the rest of that day and evening the three men tortured their brains in the wildest speculation and the most desperate debate. Strange and terrible books were drawn voluminously from the stack shelves and from secure places of storage; and diagrams and formulae were copied with feverish haste and in bewildering abundance. Of scepticism there was none. All three had seen the body of Wilbur Whateley as it lay on the floor in a room of that very building, and after that not one of them could feel even slightly inclined to treat the diary as a madman's raving.

Opinions were divided as to notifying the Massachusetts State Police, and the negative finally won. There were things involved which simply could not be believed by those who had not seen a sample, as indeed was made clear during certain subsequent investigations. Late at night the conference disbanded without having developed a definite plan, but all day Sunday Armitage was busy comparing formulae and mixing chemicals obtained from the college laboratory. The more he reflected on the hellish diary, the more he was inclined to doubt the efficacy of any material agent in stamping out the entity which Wilbur Whateley had left behind him—the earth-threatening entity which, unknown to him, was to burst forth in a few hours and become the memorable Dunwich horror.

Monday was a repetition of Sunday with Dr. Armitage, for the task in hand required an infinity of research and experiment. Further consultations of the monstrous diary brought about various changes of plan, and he knew that even in the end a large amount of uncertainty must remain. By Tuesday he had a definite line of action mapped out, and believed he would try a trip to Dunwich within a week. Then, on Wednesday, the great shock came. Tucked obscurely away in a corner of the *Arkham Advertiser* was a facetious little item from the Associated Press, telling what a record-breaking monster the bootleg whiskey of Dunwich had raised up. Armitage, half stunned, could only telephone for Rice and Morgan. Far into the night they discussed, and the next day was a whirlwind of preparation on the part of them all. Armitage knew he would be meddling with terrible powers, yet saw that there was no other way to annul the deeper and more malign meddling which others had done before him.

❖ IX ❖

Friday morning Armitage, Rice, and Morgan set out by motor for Dunwich, arriving at the village about one in the afternoon. The day was pleasant, but even in the brightest sunlight a kind of quiet dread and portent seemed to hover about the strangely domed hills and the deep, shadowy ravines of the stricken region. Now and then on some mountain-top a gaunt circle of stones could be glimpsed against the sky. From the air of hushed fright at Osborn's store they knew something hideous had happened, and soon learned of the annihilation of the Elmer Frye house and family. Throughout that afternoon they rode around Dunwich; questioning the natives concerning all that had occurred, and seeing for themselves with rising pangs of horror the drear Frye ruins with their lingering traces of the tarry stickiness, the blasphemous tracks in the Frye yard, the wounded Seth Bishop cattle, and the enormous swaths of disturbed vegetation in various places. The trail up and down Sentinel Hill seemed to Armitage of almost cataclysmic significance, and he looked long at the sinister altar-like stone on the summit.

At length the visitors, apprised of a party of State Police which had come from Aylesbury that morning in response to the first telephone reports of the Frye tragedy, decided to seek out the officers and compare notes as far as practicable. This, however, they found more easily planned than performed; since no sign of the party could be found in any direction. There had been five of them in a car, but now the car stood empty near the ruins in the Frye yard. The natives, all of whom had talked with the policemen, seemed at first as perplexed as Armitage and his companions. Then old Sam Hutchins thought of something and turned pale, nudging Fred Farr and pointing to the dank, deep hollow that yawned close by.

"Gawd," he gasped, "I telled 'em not ter go daown into the glen, an' I never thought nobody'd dew it with them tracks an' that smell an' the whippoorwills a-screechin' daown thar in the dark o' noonday. . . ."

A cold shudder ran through natives and visitors alike, and every ear seemed strained in a kind of instinctive, unconscious listening. Armitage, now that he had actually come upon the horror and its monstrous work, trembled with the responsibility he felt to be his. Night would soon fall, and it was then that the mountainous blasphemy lumbered upon its eldritch course. *Negotium perambulans in tenebris. . . .* The old librarian rehearsed the formulae he had memorised, and clutched the paper containing the alternative one he had not memorised. He saw that his electric flashlight was in working order. Rice, beside him, took from a valise a metal sprayer of the sort used in combating insects; whilst Morgan uncased the big-game rifle on which he relied despite his colleague's warnings that no material weapon would be of help.

Armitage, having read the hideous diary, knew painfully well what kind of a manifestation to expect; but he did not add to the fright of the Dunwich people by giving any hints or clues. He hoped that it might be conquered without any revelation to the world of the monstrous thing it had escaped. As the shadows gathered, the natives commenced to disperse homeward, anxious to bar themselves indoors despite the present evidence that all human locks and bolts were useless before a force that could bend trees and crush houses when it chose. They shook their heads at the visitors' plan to stand guard at the Frye ruins near the glen; and as they left, had little expectancy of ever seeing the watchers again.

There were rumblings under the hills that night, and the whippoorwills piped threateningly. Once in a while a wind, sweeping up out of Cold Spring Glen, would bring a touch of ineffable foetor to the heavy night air; such a foetor as all three of the watchers had smelled once before, when they stood above a dying thing that had passed for fifteen years and a half as a human being. But the looked-for terror did not appear. Whatever was down there in the glen was biding its time, and Armitage told his colleagues it would be suicidal to try to attack it in the dark.

Morning came wanly, and the night-sounds ceased. It was a grey, bleak day, with now and then a drizzle of rain; and heavier and heavier clouds seemed to be piling themselves up beyond the hills to the northwest. The men from Arkham were undecided what to do. Seeking shelter from the increasing rainfall beneath one of the few undestroyed Frye outbuildings, they debated the wisdom of waiting, or of taking the aggressive and going down into the glen in quest of their nameless, monstrous quarry. The downpour waxed in heaviness, and distant peals of thunder sounded from far horizons. Sheet lightning shimmered, and then a forky bolt flashed near at hand, as if descending into the accursed glen itself. The sky grew very dark, and the watchers hoped that the storm would prove a short, sharp one followed by clear weather.

It was still gruesomely dark when, not much over an hour later, a confused babel of voices sounded down the road. Another moment brought to view a frightened group of more than a dozen men, running, shouting, and even whimpering hysterically. Someone in the lead began sobbing out words, and the Arkham men started violently when those words developed a coherent form.

"Oh, my Gawd, my Gawd," the voice choked out. "It's a-goin' agin, *an' this time by day!* It's aout—it's aout an' a-movin' this very minute, an' only the Lord knows when it'll be on us all!"

The speaker panted into silence, but another took up his message.

"Nigh on a haour ago Zeb Whateley here heerd the 'phone a-ringin', an' it was Mis' Corey, George's wife, that lives daown by the junction. She says the hired boy Luther was aout drivin' in the caows from the storm arter the big bolt, when he see all the trees a-bendin' at the maouth o' the glen—opposite side ter this—an' smelt the same awful smell like he smelt when he faound the big tracks las' Monday mornin'. An' she says he says they was a swishin', lappin' saound, more nor what the bendin' trees an' bushes could make, an' all on a suddent the trees along the rud begun ter git pushed one side, an' they was a awful stompin' an' splashin' in the mud. But mind ye, Luther he didn't see nothin' at all, only just the bendin' trees an' underbrush.

"Then fur ahead where Bishop's Brook goes under the rud he heerd a awful creakin' an' strainin' on the bridge, an' says he could tell the saound o' wood a-startin' to crack an' split. An' all the whiles he never see a thing, only them trees an' bushes a-bendin'. An' when the swishin' saound got very fur off—on the rud towards Wizard Whateley's an' Sentinel Hill—Luther he had the guts ter step up whar he'd heerd it furst an' look at the graound. It was all mud an' water, an' the sky was dark, an' the rain was wipin' aout all tracks abaout as fast as could be; but beginnin' at the glen maouth, whar the trees had moved, they was still some o' them awful prints big as bar'ls like he seen Monday."

At this point the first excited speaker interrupted.

"But *that* ain't the trouble naow—that was only the start. Zeb here was callin' folks up an' everybody was a-listenin' in when a call from Seth Bishop's cut in. His haousekeeper Sally was carryin' on fit ter kill—she'd jest seed the trees a-bendin' beside the rud, an' says they was a kind o' mushy saound, like a elephant puffin' an' treadin', a-headin' fer the haouse. Then she up an' spoke suddent of a fearful smell, an' says her boy Cha'ncey was a-screamin' as haow it was jest like what he smelt up to the Whateley rewins Monday mornin'. An' the dogs was all barkin' an' whinin' awful.

"An' then she let aout a turrible yell, an' says the shed daown the rud had jest caved in like the storm hed blowed it over, only the wind wa'n't strong enough to dew that. Everybody was a-listenin', an' we could hear lots o' folks on the wire a-gaspin'. All to onct Sally she yelled agin, an' says the front yard picket fence hed just crumbled up, though they wa'n't no sign o' what done it. Then everybody on the line could hear Cha'ncey an' ol' Seth Bishop a-yellin' tew, an' Sally was shriekin' aout that suthin' heavy hed struck the haouse—not lightnin' nor nothin', but suthin' heavy agin the front, that kep' a-launchin' itself agin an' agin, though ye couldn't see nothin' aout the front winders. An' then . . . an' then . . ."

Lines of fright deepened on every face; and Armitage, shaken as he was, had barely poise enough to prompt the speaker.

"An' then . . . Sally she yelled aout, 'O help, the haouse is a-cavin' in' . . . an' on the wire we could hear a turrible crashin', an' a hull flock o' screamin' . . . jest like when Elmer Frye's place was took, only wuss. . . .'"

The man paused, and another of the crowd spoke.

"That's all—not a saound nor squeak over the 'phone arter that. Jest still-like. We that heerd it got aout Fords an' wagons an' raounded up as many able-bodied menfolks as we could git, at Corey's place, an' come up here ter see what yew thought best ter dew. Not but what I think it's the Lord's jedgment fer our iniquities, that no mortal kin ever set aside."

Armitage saw that the time for positive action had come, and spoke decisively to the faltering group of frightened rustics.

"We must follow it, boys." He made his voice as reassuring as possible. "I believe there's a chance of putting it out of business. You men know that those Whateleys were wizards—well, this thing is a thing of wizardry, and must be put down by the same means. I've seen Wilbur Whateley's diary and read some of the strange old books he used to read; and I think I know the right kind of spell to recite to make the thing fade away. Of course, one can't be sure, but we can always take a chance. It's invisible—I knew it would be—but there's a powder in this long-distance sprayer that might make it shew up for a second. Later on we'll try it. It's a frightful thing to have alive, but it isn't as bad as what Wilbur would have let in if he'd lived longer. You'll never know what the world has escaped. Now we've only this one thing to fight, and it can't multiply. It can, though, do a lot of harm; so we mustn't hesitate to rid the community of it.

"We must follow it—and the way to begin is to go to the place that has just been wrecked. Let somebody lead the way—I don't know your roads very well, but I've got an idea there might be a shorter cut across lots. How about it?"

The men shuffled about a moment, and then Earl Sawyer spoke softly, pointing with a grimy finger through the steadily lessening rain.

"I guess ye kin git to Seth Bishop's quickest by cuttin' acrost lower medder here, wadin' the brook at the low place, an' climbin' through Carrier's mowin' an' the timber-lot beyont. That comes aout on the upper rud mighty nigh Seth's—a leetle t'other side."

Armitage, with Rice and Morgan, started to walk in the direction indicated; and most of the natives followed slowly. The sky was growing lighter, and there were signs that the storm had worn itself away. When Armitage inadvertently took a wrong direction, Joe Osborn warned him and walked ahead to shew the right one. Courage and confidence were mounting; though the twilight of the almost perpendicular wooded hill which lay toward the end of their short cut, and among whose fantastic ancient trees they had to scramble as if up a ladder, put these qualities to a severe test.

At length they emerged on a muddy road to find the sun coming out. They were a little beyond the Seth Bishop place, but bent trees and hideously unmistakable tracks shewed what had passed by. Only a few moments were consumed in surveying the ruins just around the bend. It was the Frye incident all over again, and nothing dead or living was found in either of the collapsed shells which had been the Bishop house and barn. No one cared to remain there amidst the stench and tarry stickiness, but all turned instinctively to the line of horrible prints leading on toward the wrecked Whateley farmhouse and the altar-crowned slopes of Sentinel Hill.

As the men passed the site of Wilbur Whateley's abode they shuddered visibly, and seemed again to mix hesitancy with their zeal. It was no joke tracking down something as big as a house that one could not see, but that had all the vicious malevolence of a daemon. Opposite the base of Sentinel Hill the tracks left the road, and there was a fresh bending and matting visible along the broad swath marking the monster's former route to and from the summit.

Armitage produced a pocket telescope of considerable power and scanned the steep green side of the hill. Then he handed the instrument to Morgan, whose sight was keener. After a moment of gazing Morgan cried out sharply, passing the glass to Earl Sawyer and indicating a certain spot on the slope with his finger. Sawyer, as clumsy as most non-users of optical devices are, fumbled a while; but eventually focussed the lenses with Armitage's aid. When he did so his cry was less restrained than Morgan's had been.

"Gawd almighty, the grass an' bushes is a-movin'! It's a-goin' up—slow-like—creepin' up ter the top this minute, heaven only knows what fur!"

Then the germ of panic seemed to spread among the seekers. It was one thing to chase the nameless entity, but quite another to find it. Spells might be all right—but suppose they weren't? Voices began questioning Armitage about what he knew of the thing, and no reply seemed quite to satisfy. Everyone seemed to feel himself in close proximity to phases of Nature and of being utterly forbidden, and wholly outside the sane experience of mankind.

⊷ X ⊷

In the end the three men from Arkham—old, white-bearded Dr. Armitage, stocky, iron grey Professor Rice, and lean, youngish Dr. Morgan—ascended the mountain alone. After much patient instruction regarding its focussing and use, they left the telescope with the frightened group that remained in the road; and as they climbed they were watched closely by those among whom the glass was passed around. It was hard going, and Armitage had to be helped more than once. High above the toiling group the great swath trembled as its hellish maker re-passed with snail-like deliberateness. Then it was obvious that the pursuers were gaining.

Curtis Whateley—of the undecayed branch—was holding the telescope when the Arkham party detoured radically from the swath. He told the crowd that the men were evidently trying to get to a subordinate peak which overlooked the swath at a point considerably ahead of where the shrubbery was now bending. This, indeed, proved to be true; and the party were seen to gain the minor elevation only a short time after the invisible blasphemy had passed it.

Then Wesley Corey, who had taken the glass, cried out that Armitage was adjusting the sprayer which Rice held, and that something must be about to happen. The crowd stirred uneasily, recalling that this sprayer was expected to give the unseen horror a moment of visibility. Two or three men shut their eyes, but Curtis Whateley snatched back the telescope and strained his vision to the utmost. He saw that Rice, from the party's point of vantage above and behind the entity, had an excellent chance of spreading the potent powder with marvellous effect.

Those without the telescope saw only an instant's flash of grey cloud—a cloud about the size of a moderately large building—near the top of the mountain. Curtis, who had held the instrument, dropped it with a piercing shriek into the ankle-deep mud of the road. He reeled, and would have crumpled to the ground had not two or three others seized and steadied him. All he could do was moan half-inaudibly,

"Oh, oh, great Gawd . . . *that . . . that . . .*"

There was a pandemonium of questioning, and only Henry Wheeler thought to rescue the fallen telescope and wipe it clean of mud. Curtis was past all coherence, and even isolated replies were almost too much for him.

"Bigger'n a barn . . . all made o' squirmin' ropes . . . hull thing sort o' shaped like a hen's egg bigger'n anything, with dozens o' legs like hogsheads that haff shut up when they step . . . nothin' solid abaout it—all like jelly, an' made o' sep'rit wrigglin' ropes pushed clost together . . . great bulgin' eyes all over it . . . ten or twenty maouths or trunks a-stickin' aout all along the sides, big as stovepipes, an' all a-tossin' an' openin' an' shuttin' . . . all grey, with kinder blue or purple rings . . . *an' Gawd in heaven—that haff face on top! . . .*"

This final memory, whatever it was, proved too much for poor Curtis; and he collapsed completely before he could say more. Fred Farr and Will Hutchins carried him to the roadside and laid him on the damp grass. Henry Wheeler, trembling, turned the rescued telescope on the mountain to see what he might. Through the lenses were discernible three tiny figures, apparently running toward the summit as fast as the steep incline allowed. Only these—nothing more. Then everyone noticed a strangely unseasonable noise in the deep valley behind, and even in the underbrush of Sentinel Hill itself. It was the piping of unnumbered whippoorwills, and in their shrill chorus there seemed to lurk a note of tense and evil expectancy.

Earl Sawyer now took the telescope and reported the three figures as standing on the topmost ridge, virtually level with the altar-stone but at a considerable distance from it. One figure, he said, seemed to be raising its hands above its head at rhythmic intervals; and as Sawyer mentioned the circumstance the crowd seemed to hear a faint, half-musical sound from the distance, as if a loud chant were accompanying the gestures. The weird silhouette on that remote peak must have been a spectacle of infinite grotesqueness and impressiveness, but no observer was in a mood for aesthetic appreciation. "I guess he's sayin' the spell," whispered Wheeler as he snatched back the telescope. The whippoorwills were piping wildly, and in a singularly curious irregular rhythm quite unlike that of the visible ritual.

Suddenly the sunshine seemed to lessen without the intervention of any discernible cloud. It was a very peculiar phenomenon, and was plainly marked by all. A rumbling sound brewing beneath the hills, mixed strangely with a concordant rumbling which clearly came from the sky. Lightning flashed aloft, and the wondering crowd looked in vain for the portents of storm. The chanting of the men from Arkham now became unmistakable, and Wheeler saw through the glass that they were all raising their arms in the rhythmic incantation. From some farmhouse far away came the frantic barking of dogs.

The change in the quality of the daylight increased, and the crowd gazed about the horizon in wonder. A purplish darkness, born of nothing more than a spectral deepening of the sky's blue, pressed down upon the rumbling hills. Then the lightning flashed again, somewhat brighter than before, and the crowd fancied that it had shewed a certain mistiness around the altar-stone on the distant height. No one, however, had been using the telescope at that instant. The whippoorwills continued their irregular pulsation, and the men of Dunwich braced themselves tensely against some imponderable menace with which the atmosphere seemed surcharged.

Without warning came those deep, cracked, raucous vocal sounds which will never leave the memory of the stricken group who heard them. Not from any human throat were they born, for the organs of man can yield no such acoustic perversions. Rather would one have said they came from the pit itself, had not their source been so unmistakably the altar-stone on the peak. It is almost erroneous to call them *sounds* at all, since so much of their ghastly, infra-bass timbre spoke to dim seats of consciousness and terror far subtler than the ear; yet one must do so, since their form was indisputably though vaguely that of half-articulate *words*. They were loud—loud as the rumblings and the thunder above which they echoed—yet did they come from no visible being. And because imagination might suggest a conjectural source in the world of non-visible beings, the huddled crowd at the mountain's base huddled still closer, and winced as if in expectation of a blow.

"*Ygnaiih . . . ygnaiih . . . thflthkh'ngha . . . Yog-Sothoth . . .*" rang the hideous croaking out of space. "*Y'bthnk . . . h'ehye—n'grkdl'lh. . . .*"

The speaking impulse seemed to falter here, as if some frightful psychic struggle were going on. Henry Wheeler strained his eye at the telescope, but saw only the three grotesquely silhouetted human figures on the peak, all moving their arms furiously in strange gestures as their incantation drew near its culmination. From what black wells of Acherontic fear or feeling, from what unplumbed gulfs of extra-cosmic consciousness or obscure, long-latent heredity, were those half-articulate thunder-croakings drawn? Presently they began to gather renewed force and coherence as they grew in stark, utter, ultimate frenzy.

"*Eh-ya-ya-ya-yahaah—e'yayayayaaaa . . . ngh'aaaaa . . . ngh'aaaa . . .* h'yuh . . . h'yuh . . . HELP! HELP! . . . *ff—ff—ff—* FATHER! FATHER! YOG-SOTHOTH! . . .*"

But that was all. The pallid group in the road, still reeling at the *indisputably English* syllables that had poured thickly and thunderously down from the frantic vacancy beside that shocking altar-stone, were never to hear such syllables again. Instead, they jumped violently at the terrific report which seemed to rend the hills; the deafening, cataclysmic peal whose source, be it inner earth or sky, no hearer was ever able to place. A single lightning-bolt shot from the purple zenith to the altar-stone, and a great tidal wave of viewless force and indescribable stench swept down from the hill to all the countryside. Trees, grass, and underbrush were whipped into a fury; and the frightened crowd at the mountain's base, weakened by the lethal foetor that seemed about to asphyxiate them, were almost hurled off their feet. Dogs howled from the distance, green grass and foliage wilted to a curious, sickly yellow-grey, and over field and forest were scattered the bodies of dead whippoorwills.

The stench left quickly, but the vegetation never came right again. To this day there is something queer and unholy about the growths on and around that fearsome hill. Curtis Whateley was only just regaining consciousness when the Arkham men came slowly down the mountain in the beams of a sunlight once more brilliant and untainted. They were grave and quiet, and seemed shaken by memories and reflections even more terrible than those which had reduced the group of natives to a state of cowed quivering. In reply to a jumble of questions they only shook their heads and reaffirmed one vital fact.

"The thing has gone forever," Armitage said. "It has been split up into what it was originally made of, and can never exist again. It was an impossibility in a normal world. Only the least fraction was really matter in any sense we know. It was like its father—and most of it has gone back to him in some vague realm or dimension outside our material universe; some vague abyss out of which only the most accursed rites of human blasphemy could ever have called him for a moment on the hills."

There was a brief silence, and in that pause the scattered senses of poor Curtis Whateley began to knit back into a sort of continuity; so that he put his hands to his head with a moan. Memory seemed to pick itself up where it had left off, and the horror of the sight that had prostrated him burst in upon him again.

"Oh, oh, my Gawd, that haff face—that haff face on top of it . . . that face with the red eyes an' crinkly albino hair, an' no chin, like the Whateleys. . . . It was a octopus, centipede, spider kind o' thing, but they was a haff-shaped man's face on top of it, an' it looked like Wizard Whateley's, only it was yards an' yards acrost. . . ."

He paused, exhausted, as the whole group of natives stared in a bewilderment not quite crystallised into fresh terror. Only old

Zebulon Whateley, who wanderingly remembered ancient things but who had been silent heretofore, spoke aloud.

"Fifteen year' gone," he rambled, "I heerd Ol' Whateley say as haow some day we'd hear a child o' Lavinny's a-callin' its father's name on the top o' Sentinel Hill. . . ."

But Joe Osborn interrupted him to question the Arkham men anew.

"*What was it anyhaow,* an' haowever did young Wizard Whateley call it aout o' the air it come from?"

Armitage chose his words very carefully.

"It was—well, it was mostly a kind of force that doesn't belong in our part of space; a kind of force that acts and grows and shapes itself by other laws than those of our sort of Nature. We have no business calling in such things from outside, and only very wicked people and very wicked cults ever try to. There was some of it in Wilbur Whateley himself—enough to make a devil and a precocious monster of him, and to make his passing out a pretty terrible sight. I'm going to burn his accursed diary, and if you men are wise you'll dynamite that altar-stone up there, and pull down all the rings of standing stones on the other hills. Things like that brought down the beings those Whateleys were so fond of—the beings they were going to let in tangibly to wipe out the human race and drag the earth off to some nameless place for some nameless purpose.

"But as to this thing we've just sent back—the Whateleys raised it for a terrible part in the doings that were to come. It grew fast and big from the same reason that Wilbur grew fast and big—but it beat him because it had a greater share of the *outsideness* in it. You needn't ask how Wilbur called it out of the air. He didn't call it out. *It was his twin brother, but it looked more like the father than he did.*"

From Out The Fire

INTRODUCTION

Snails have the good grace to hide most of their boneless bodies inside a neat shell, unlike slugs, which are fully exposed to view, but they still are kinda creepy . . . eyes on stalks, sliding on a layer of slime, and all that. Sarah A. Hoyt, who finds them *very* creepy, tells a story of snails which are not only giant-sized, but also have another trick to play. And putting salt on them won't help. Nor trying bicarbonate of soda . . .

❖ ❖ ❖

Sarah A. Hoyt won the Prometheus Award for her novel *Darkship Thieves*, published by Baen, and has authored *Darkship Renegades* (nominated for the following year's Prometheus Award) and *A Few Good Men*, two more novels set in the same universe, as was "Angel in Flight," a story in the first installment of *A Cosmic Christmas*. She has written numerous short stories and novels in science fiction, fantasy, mystery, historical novels and historical mysteries, many under a number of pseudonyms, and has been published—among other places—in *Analog*, *Asimov's* and *Amazing*. For Baen, she has also written three books in her popular shape-shifter fantasy series, *Draw One in the Dark*, *Gentleman Takes a Chance*, and *Noah's Boy*. Her *According to Hoyt* is one of the most interesting blogs on the internet. Originally from Portugal, she lives in Colorado with her husband, two sons and the surfeit of cats necessary to a die-hard Heinlein fan.

From Out The Fire

by Sarah A. Hoyt

"What do you mean fire snails?" I said. "Do you mean . . . living creatures?"

We were in gear to go out, in blessed camo, and armed per regulation: .45 automatic, of our own manufacture, every part blessed in making, though often cursed in use, and an M4 with grenade launcher—and of course the Super Soaker of holy water at our back, and the blessed salt in our pockets, too. Those were regulation.

There were six of us, myself and Nerio, arguably my best friend in the outfit. Not that we had friends as such. Or not very often. At least you learned fast not to have them, because we lost so many people in each of our operations. The rest of the group were people I didn't know well. New recruits. I knew their names, of course, because we never had too many of them at one time, and they were introduced in meeting every Monday: Manfred, a muscular blond German, who looked far too young to have been able to swear the oath, much less to risk his life in an operation; Ropharz, slim and dark, who spoke with a marked French accent and smoked the stinkiest cigarettes I'd ever smelled; Daria, with dark hair, blue eyes, and an Eastern European accent, and Lilly, blond and slim and looking much like she should have been anywhere but here, and be wearing anything but combat fatigues, blessed or not. Except when you looked in her eyes, what looked back was blankness. Not as though there were no one there, but as though she had disciplined herself, through the years, to show absolutely nothing. You couldn't even see her magical power, and in most new recruits you could see it bright and clear, and estimate exactly the limits of their ability. It was only later they learned to veil and obscure. Because if your colleagues could see it, so could other things. The enemy.

Lilly might be . . . interesting. The others—

Nerio and I traded a look that said there was hardly any point learning the kids' names. They wouldn't be around long enough to matter. We'd seen them come, and we'd seen them go: blown up, burned, stabbed, shot, and sometimes just made to vanish.

It was said that The Magical Legion was the last place you came to. This was often literal. In our chapter house in Colorado, the names of our lost brethren were engraved into the crystalline walls of Memory Hall, just like the row upon row of names engraved in the smoke-dark walls of a tavern in Ye Olde England, and the row upon row of names on brass plaques in the marble halls of our Sorrentino chapter. We all knew eventually our names would grace a wall, somewhere. Because you didn't leave the legion. You died casting your last spell.

The Magical Legion was the last place you came to, and they buried you. But it was also the last place you came to, when you'd run out of places to hide. As I had.

Nerio had got his tobacco pouch out and was rolling a cigarette. I suspected it was some Italian peasant habit, from wherever and whenever he'd started out. He did it all the time, particularly when he was trying to pay attention. But even with papers and tobacco, he didn't manage to make as stinky a cigarette as Ropharz smoked.

He rolled the paper reflexively and looked at the person briefing us. "What in heaven's name are Fire Snails, anyway?"

Einar Agi sighed. He was big and must at one time have been blond. He was now some indeterminate shade between white and a yellowish gray. He was—for lack of a better term, since none of our units had a permanent structure, let alone a proper command—our commander, or perhaps our grand master, for the Colorado chapter.

When there was any problem, any call for our intervention, other units got in touch with him.

Part of the problem—or perhaps the strength—of the organization was that it consisted of fighting units and magical units, the magical units planning, deciding operations, and studying threats, and the fighting units fighting.

Mind you, fighting units were magical, too. Had to be for what we dealt with. But we hadn't made a study of magic as such. We just were. I was in a fighting unit. We fought. So was Nerio. We'd been friends for two decades. Neither of us did much thinking about possible threats until they were brought to our attention. And we certainly knew nothing of the creatures of magic and the many ways they could go wrong. Until they did. Then we used our powers and our strength. And we fought.

Einar, as I said, was different. He turned, with a sigh, and pressed buttons on the wall. The room went dark, and into that dark room, projected just behind Einar, came the image of a common garden snail. Not a flat projection, but a hologram, hideously magnified, showing glistening skin, questing antennae, and the trail of slime. I shuddered.

When I was young, more years ago than I care to mention, when the first good Queen Bess sat on the throne of England, I'd formed my first impression of snails by that trail of slime. In my mind, they were forever tagged as unclean and repulsive.

I watched in horror as this hologram—or whatever the magical equivalent was, since most apparatus in the legion were dual science and magic—of the repulsive mollusk moved around, and listened to Einar's voice with the odd Scandinavian accent say, "We all know the common land snail. There are water snails, also. What most people in the world, what most people we are supposed to protect don't know is that there are also fire snails." The hologram vanished, replaced almost instantly with . . .

I held my breath. I didn't like snails, hadn't liked them since the first time I'd seen them, when I must have been all of three or four, eating their way through my mother's garden. But this was both unmistakably a snail and breathtakingly beautiful. The skin was vitreous, shining and translucent, and through that skin there shone the reflected glory of flames. All of it was topped with a dead-black shell that shimmered like polished stone.

Einar made a gesture like slicing, midair, and the creature was sheered in half longitudinally, displaying a drawing of what its insides would look like. There was fire and something molten and red.

"They are filled with lava," he said. "Snails have an open circulatory system, and these snails have lava instead of blood."

"But they are magical?" Ropharz asked.

"How else do you think they could exist?" Einar said. "They are also . . . large. The adults can be up to fifty feet long. The babies start out at ten."

"Whoa," Lilly said, under her breath but audible.

"Yes," Einar said. "They don't occur very often. They require a great deal of magic, and they can only be invoked by a great witch or a great sorcerer."

"They've . . ." Lilly swallowed. "How long have they existed? And why has nothing been written about them?"

"Ah. Because the three previous fire snail hatchings have been stopped before they could get too far and be widely seen. All three were stopped by our people. Two were recent, but we don't have any records of the operations."

"Sir," Ropharz said. "Why not?"

"Because every one of the Magical Legionnaires died. We know they succeeded, because the snails were destroyed. But all we got back were their bodies. Or the ashes."

"And the other?"

"Ah. Pompeii," he said. "We don't have records, because they were lost when we had to move the chapter house in Rome in the fifteenth century."

"Pompeii?" Nerio said. He looked uncomfortable. I wasn't sure why.

Einar nodded. "Yes. You know how land snails reproduce? I mean, how they lay eggs?"

"Can't say I do, sir," Nerio said.

"They dig little tunnels in the ground, from which the snails emerge, cannibalizing the eggs of their siblings who are tardy in hatching, and then they erupt from the ground eating everything in sight. Most land snails are slow growers, but the carnivorous ones grow very fast indeed . . ."

"They lay eggs in volcanos?" Nerio asked and swallowed, as though worried. "I ask because Pompeii."

Einar rocked his head side to side in a gesture that was not so much confirmation or denial, but a sort of acquiescence. "They don't lay eggs. To our knowledge, unless we're very wrong, there are no adult fire snails, and there have never been."

"But? If there are no adult fire snails, how can there be eggs?"

"A . . . powerful witch from a particular line can by magic cause a normal snail to lay fire snail eggs."

"A particular line?" I said, and only realized I'd spoken after saying it.

"Yes. It seems to require a descendant of Circe," he said. "Or perhaps Circe left instructions on how to do it, still handed down in the family."

I didn't look at Nerio. I had heard him mention a witch descended from Circe before. How he had to leave her, to be able to call his soul his own. But you didn't ask questions too closely, in the legion, not even of your very best friends.

"Not exactly. But if the eggs are near an area of volcanic instability . . . well, they grow for about a century or so, and when they erupt . . ."

"They cause a volcanic eruption?" I asked.

Einar nodded and started to open his mouth, but my mind had already jumped ahead. What was the most disastrous place in which the eggs of these giant fire snails might have been laid? A place that would justify calling on the Colorado Chapter for intervention?

"Yellowstone," I said, thinking of the giant caldera. "If it goes off—"

"Most of the Western United States will be covered in lava and ash, yes. And the resulting nuclear winter might kill off most life on Earth."

"Perhaps that's why there are no populations of giant fire snails," Ropharz said. "Perhaps they self-roast on emerging."

"No. We should be so lucky. They are, as far as we can tell, fireproof," Einar said. "They are also carnivorous."

Our units are transported in varying ways. Sometimes, a striking party of witches will fly on brooms to the location. And sometimes, when the party is mostly male, and mostly not drilled in the ancient disciplines, we are transported in other ways. In this case, it was a black helicopter, though the legion can also use mechano-magical vehicles, which I suspect are responsible for most of the legends of UFOs.

This time we flew at night in a helicopter and were dropped off in a green, verdant area. The Yellowstone River was to our right, and the rim of the caldera ahead. There were tremors underfoot, but I wasn't sure if there were more than the usual tremors for a geologically interesting region. I'd never been particularly interested in it. There was a time, in the mid oughts, when I'd been having trouble sleeping during the day and spent a lot of time reading conspiracy theories about the Yellowstone super volcano.

We had magically spelled glasses which made the night landscape as clear as day, but we'd be mostly invisible to any observer.

Ropharz was ahead of us, and there were other units from other chapters throughout the west. I was vaguely aware of helicopters landing and disgorging legionnaires, and of a party of witches arriving on broomsticks. Probably from the Albuquerque Chapter. They were almost all female.

The Denver chapter is odd. Most of us are not magically learned. Ropharz was the only sensitive in this unit. At least the only trained sensitive.

For once, he didn't have his cigarettes, though a smell of them hung about him. He looked odd, as he usually did when he was working magically. His olive skin looked strangely pale, and had a suggestion of translucence about it, and his eyes were half closed. "Ahead," he said, and pointed. "That way. I'm getting communications from the other units, too. I can sense the first snail is making its way to the surface already. We will have to kill it as it emerges, and probably another three or four of them, then get down the hole they leave and kill the eggs before any more hatch. The one emerging now was close enough to the surface it will not disturb the volcano. But if the deeper ones emerge, they will form a tunnel that will allow the river to spill into the magma, and then . . ."

"And then?" Lilly asked. "Won't it cool the lava, or something?"

He shook his head. "No. If it hits just right or just wrong . . ." He made a gesture with his hands. "Kaboom." And then he gestured again, running his hands in a flat gesture, palm down, as if to indicate the quietness of death.

Well, at least it would be quick for us.

Ahead, I could see the ground humping, the green turf rising, a little, then a little again.

Something long and tentacular poked through the grass. There was a scream, and the unit closest to it—I thought it was the New Mexico witches, did something that threw a flash of light into the air. Those women worked mostly with magic, so I wasn't sure what I had seen.

Another antenna emerged, and then suddenly the entire snail head was out, and it grabbed a woman in its jaws and . . .

"Kill it," someone near me said. "Kill it with fire." It was Ropharz. A grenade flew from his grenade launcher. It must have hit the snail, because we heard it blow, and we all took cover. But when we looked back, the snail was fully out of the hole and had grabbed some guy from one of the other units. A shapeshifter, he must be, because in the jaws of the creature he was a blur of fur, claws, human hands, and human voice screaming "Ahhhhhh."

"Fall back, fall back" was called from one of the other units. But Ropharz, who was technically in charge of this operation for our group, was standing still, blinking. I heard him say, "But it was blessed!"

Like most sensitives, he didn't have the resilience to change midstream. Likely we'd have to go on without him. I looked at Ropharz. He had the .45 automatic out.

"You're not going to get close enough to fire that!" I said. "And look at how the grenade did nothing."

He hesitated. Fortunately for us, Daria had run up, firing.

Nothing happened. Well, nothing she would want to happen. The snail lurched. Snails shouldn't be able to lurch. They shouldn't be able to move fast. Clearly no one had told this to fire snails. It lurched so fast the eye couldn't follow, and it took Daria. I saw what she did with her last bullet. Another name for the wall.

And now there were two snails out, and our people were moving back and back and back.

"Listen," Lilly said as we ran back. "Listen. We have to stop these things. See, another one is coming up." She pointed at antennae coming out of the ground. "We must get in there and neutralize the rest of the clutch, before they hatch, or we, the United States, and the rest of the world are going down for the long count."

"How do you propose to do that?" I said, as the next snail emerged.

"Ropharz," Nerio barked. "Ropharz. How close to the surface are other hatching snails?"

"Uh." His eyes seemed to cross, the way sensitives did, when he was trying to feel something. He still looked shocked. "Uh . . . Not that close. More are hatching, but they are deep down. If they don't make their way up—"

"How long do we have?" Nerio said impatiently. Discipline wasn't very good in the Magical Legion. Or at least it wasn't very good in our unit. Most of us had been lone hunters for a long time before recruitment. If we could avoid killing each other, it was counted as a win.

Ropharz didn't even try to assert any authority. He wouldn't have been able to. He was much too young compared to Nerio. Instead he waggled his hand in the ancient sign of "this much, that much." "Half an hour," he said. "Maybe. Of course, they move fast, and if they don't stop to snack on their brethren too often, it could be any minute."

All the time we were talking, we were falling back, trotting backwards, and the damn fire snails were moving closer and closer. There were four of us, now: Ropharz and Lilly, and myself and Nerio.

Ropharz brought out his super soaker, as the snail advanced towards us, and he said, "Fall back without me," then he let out a stream of holy water at the creature. It sizzled as it hit, but I figured that was because the snails had lava for blood.

The nearest one lurched. Ropharz screamed. "Idiot," Nerio spat. "If the blessing on the grenade didn't work . . ."

It would have to stand for an epitaph for Ropharz, but it might stand for an epitaph for us, too, because the snail was so close I could smell it, an odor like heated pumice, and I thought there would be nothing to prevent us being the next snacks. I had a feeling if we turned and ran, it would just get closer.

"I'm going to go neutralize the eggs," Nerio said. "You two create a diversion so the snails will chase you."

"How do you plan to neutralize them?" Lilly asked, pitching her voice to a scream to be heard above the sound of the approaching snail, which was exactly like a train at full steam.

I think what Nerio said—Well . . . it didn't make any sense, but I swear what he said was, "I plan to eat them," even as he ran fast toward the river.

The snail turned antennae that way, and Lilly and I traded a look. She was flushed, which gave color to her pale face. Yes, I know it's damn stupid in a moment when we might die at any minute, but I couldn't help responding with an appreciative look and a smile.

"I run that way," she said, very fast. "And you that way. There's only one snail paying attention. It can't go in three directions."

I nodded. Well, really, we didn't know it couldn't go in three directions, but I'd give them a sporting chance. My kind are after all much harder to kill than just humans. Oh, sure, fire will destroy us. At least technically. But a few drops of blood, and there was at least a chance I'd come back.

I wished my parents had been papists, because I felt a strong need to cross myself. Nerio was always crossing himself, and it seemed to give him no end of comfort. But I couldn't. It had not been trained into me, and at any rate in my current state it might be worse than fire snails. Though I could handle blessed ammo and camo and salt.

I waited till Lilly was running and the snail started to follow, and I did this sort of dance in place. If I was right, it was the vibrations that attracted them first. It turned toward me, and I started running, fast enough it wouldn't catch me, but not so fast it would give up.

Come on, snail, I thought. I needed to get it close enough that I could pull the one trick my kind can always count on, but not so close it would eat me.

It came, and it took all my speed of movement to get me far enough ahead. We don't really turn into bats. I have no idea how that idiocy got started, except that it was probably someone who chased one of us into a cave. Our ability to move super-fast, suddenly, and the fact the idiot probably disturbed a bat colony were enough, I'm sure. Particularly if the one of my kind being pursued did what I did now— I dropped behind a slight incline in the terrain, lay very still, and willed myself to project utter non-existence. Look, I had no body heat to give me away. And if fire snails had night vision, it was probably no better than our enhanced magical vision. I could fool that well enough.

I closed my eyes and willed invisibility, even as various people ran near me, screaming. I expected at any minute to feel the crunch of very hot jaws, and wondered what it would feel like. Snails didn't have teeth, this I knew, but maybe one giant tooth, beak-like. I wished I'd looked closer at that specimen Einar had shown. And then I felt more than heard the snail go by me, and heard a high-pitched feminine scream behind me.

And then I heard a female voice, amused. "So, this is what you do? Interesting. I do something similar."

Lilly stood near me. Her eyes glimmered with amusement.

"You do?"

She grinned. "So, now, while our friend is snacking on other people . . . what do we do?"

"We?" I said.

There was movement under our feet. The other snails. "Nerio—" I said.

"Might or might not succeed. But whatever he can do, I'm sure he's not capable of destroying the already hatched snails, and that's the problem." She arched an eyebrow. "By the way, what is he?"

I frowned at her. "Shapeshifter," I said. "Of some sort. At least he once told me he was safe from any bullets that weren't silver. I've never seen him shifted, but I think werewolf?"

"Then think again. Unless wolves eat fire."

I made a face. "Right," I said. And then. "He might very well be dead by now." A wave of loss hit me.

"Like that?" she said, and the eyebrow rose higher.

"We've been friends since we met twenty-five years ago," I said.

She nodded. "Legionnaires shouldn't make friends."

"No."

"And still," she said as a stronger tremor beneath us threw us both to our knees. "How do we kill the things?"

"Salt," I said. "Blessed salt. I thought of it when—"

"The blessing won't work," she said. "It's obvious, or the grenade would have done. Or the blessed camo, for that matter. I think they're creatures more of the material world than of the supernatural one, even if magic is required for them to exist. And the salt won't work. It works on normal snails because it dries them up all to their insides, but these are made of some sort of glass."

I looked at her. Glass. I thought of my father, who had been a deacon, reading the Good Book of an evening. It had been a long time ago, but they say you never lose the childhood memories. The rest blends and blurs and passes, but those early memories are clear as day.

"Instruments," I said. "We need trumpets." And unbidden from my mouth came the unerring quote, "Now the gates of Jericho were securely barred because of the Israelites. No one went out and no one came in. Then the Lord said to Joshua, "'See, I have delivered Jericho into your hands, along with its king and its fighting men. March around the city once with all the armed men. Do this for six days. Have seven priests carry trumpets of rams' horns in front of the ark. On the seventh day, march around the city seven times, with the priests blowing the trumpets. When you hear them sound a long blast on the trumpets, have the whole army give a loud shout; then the wall of the city will collapse and the army will go up, everyone straight in.'"

Around us, people screamed, and the fire snails must have been close, because I could smell hot pumice. Things were about to get interesting. And the ground trembled behind our feet, which gave me the impression that whatever Nerio had done hadn't worked that well.

She looked at me, and the eyebrow went up again. "It could work," she said, and tilted her head. And then she made a gesture of some kind, and suddenly she was holding— It looked like a harp made with two animal horns and strung with silver.

A snail appeared behind her, its horn—tooth—glistening and bloodied.

I was about to tell her that a harp couldn't hold that long, sustained a note. And then I was going to scream and run very fast.

Lilly struck the harp. Whatever the sound was, it made my teeth vibrate. The snail stood still, and the second note hit. Then a third, fourth, fifth, sixth, seventh, each higher than the other. My hands went up involuntarily to cover my ears.

Which was good, because there was a sound like a hundred fingernails running across a hundred chalkboards, and then a loud crack.

Lilly reacted when I was still stunned by the sound. She grabbed my arm and pulled as she jumped. She was stronger than she had any right to be, given her size. We landed on the grass a few feet away from where the flow of lava from inside the snail fizzled and solidified suddenly, into a black rock.

As though called by our actions, rain started, a soft, gentle rain. It sizzled on the lava.

I don't know how long we sat there, but I finally woke enough to say, "I wonder if it took care of the eggs and the snails underground, too?"

Lilly shrugged. "Should have. And the ground hasn't trembled. Should we go check?"

"Yeah." I didn't say I wanted to know if Nerio was alive, too.

We walked to where the hole had been, where the snails had emerged. It took a long time, because I was walking in something like a dream. Everything seemed very distant, and my legs hurt like hell. I would need to feed. I would need to feed sooner than later. Otherwise I'd just keep feeling more and more tired. But right then tiredness was good. It prevented my feeling as anxious for Nerio's fate as I otherwise would have. Poor Nerio. If only I'd thought of the Jericho trick before he had gone off to destroy the nest.

As we approached the hole, I was more sure than ever he'd met his death. It was a yawning depression in the ground, and there was no movement at all.

Lilly was carrying her harp. She put her hand in mine, for only a minute. It felt very hot, even when you consider I'm ambient temperature. "I still have the harp," she said, apparently mistaking my hesitation for fear.

I opened my mouth to protest, but before I could, two hands appeared at the edge of the hole, and then Nerio pulled himself up by the force of his arms and dragged himself to the grass above. Where he lay for a few minutes, drawing deep breaths. He was stark naked. I said the first thing that came to mind. "You're naked!"

His voice came in a slow drawl. "Yeah. The clothes burned when I shifted."

Lilly giggled. "Are you wounded?" I asked, worried at his lying immobile.

"Oh, no," he said. And dragged himself to sitting. "But no one should eat that much at one sitting, and when I do the memories of my childhood demand I take a nap. I'm not going to, though. There is a witchy minx I must find."

"What?" I said.

"He's a salamander!" Lilly said. "You know, fire spirit. It's the only thing that could have eaten those fire snail eggs. Or at least their life."

Nerio smiled at her. "Smart girl," he said. "Fortunately, though, you guys killed the already hatched snails. Not much I could do about them once they were moving and fully conscious. Well, as much as a snail is." He raked me with a casual look. "Fortunately for all concerned I prefer my girls dumb. Dumb enough to hatch fire snails as a way to get me back. Now I must find her, and show her the error of her ways."

Something clicked in my mind. "The descendant of Circe."

"Right," he said. "She must be somewhere around here. She would be to try to attract me. And I'd bet she has a fire lit, too. So I can find her."

"You can't desert," I said. "If you do, they'll come for you."

"I'm not even going to be late," he said. "I can transport to any flame. As for deserting . . . I'm recruiting her."

"But after all the lives she cost—" Lilly started to say.

"The best way to neutralize a threat is to make it a legionnaire," Nerio said, and his eyes met mine briefly. "We only kill them if we have no other choice."

I nodded and ran my tongue over my fangs and remembered when Nerio and a unit of the Magical Legion had run me to ground and dragged me in. There had been a choice. The stake or the Legion.

It seemed so long ago. It was so long ago. It was like another life. One I didn't wish to revisit.

I didn't see Lilly—or Nerio—for a long while after that. The massive deaths in various units caused a reshuffling, and a restructuring. Nerio was transferred to Albuquerque, but I couldn't hear whether or not he'd dragged his witch back with him.

For a while, I thought Lilly must have been transferred to Albuquerque, too, because they had a strong pro-female bias and they'd lost a great part of their strike party.

But two months later, between assignments, as I was drinking my lunch in the general cafeteria, she dropped across the table from me and said, "Hello, stranger."

I put my glass down. "Lilly," I said.

She smiled. "Ah, you do remember me."

"I've been trying to—" I said. "But I couldn't find you. Then there was this kachina doll that became animated, in—"

"Yeah," she said. Her voice was pleasing and musical. "I know. And I was dealing with a genii in NYC. I wish we could screen those sort of illegal immigrants better."

"Yeah," I said. My mouth was unaccountably dry, and I didn't know what to say. "My . . . I mean, you're still in the Colorado chapter, I guess."

"Oh, yes. I was just loaned out, but now I'm back to stay."

"Good," I said. "Good. You know the worst about me. Some of it everyone does. I . . . I was wondering if we could see rather a lot of each other anyway?"

She laughed. One of the servers came and set a plate of pancakes in front of her, and she looked up from them and at me with a smile. "I know. Legionnaires shouldn't befriend other legionnaires. But for you, Mr. Marlowe, I'll make an exception."

I made a face at her. "Call me Kit," I said. "And you know that thing about . . . I mean . . . it's not . . . not as it was made to appear . . ."

"Nothing is as it is made to appear," she said. "Not in the legion. And it might not be a—ah—material consideration anyway."

"Oh?" I said. And I had the impression that this relationship might very well turn out more fiery than Nerio's. Even if he was a salamander and his girlfriend conjured fire snails.

Beauty and the Beast

INTRODUCTION

In days of yore, a science fiction magazine would often buy a painting of a fantastic scene, then assign a writer to write a story around the cover, a practice that lasted at least until the 1960s. This may have been the case with the April 1940 issue of *Thrilling Wonder Stories*, whose cover showed a Godzilla-sized dinosaurlike creature kicking the U.S. Capitol building to bits, while tiny humans aim a futuristic-looking death ray apparatus at it. If Henry Kuttner did write the story around a pre-existing cover, he probably decided to have some fun with the image, since this time around, the monster is the good guy. Of course, no good deed goes unpunished . . .

⁂ ⁂ ⁂

Henry Kuttner (1915-1958) began his writing career with an unforgettable horror story in a 1936 *Weird Tales*, "The Graveyard Rats," then almost ended it (according to SF historian Sam Moskowitz) by writing lurid (for the time—very mild now) and sexy stories for a short-lived "spicy" science fiction magazine. He continued writing under a number of pseudonyms, and after he married the equally talented C(atherine). L. Moore, whose remarkable story "Shambleau" had instantly made her reputation, they often collaborated under more pseudonyms, notably Lewis Padgett and Lawrence O'Donnell. Recently, some have absurdly claimed that C.L. Moore was the only talented half of the partnership in spite of statements by L. Sprague de Camp, Ray Bradbury and other writers who watched the two at work, that one would type rapidly, writing part of a story, then take a break with the story unfinished, at which point the other would sit down at the typewriter and continue the story. The two stated that later they were unable to say who did which part of the story. In any case, "Beauty and the Beast" was published (as by Kuttner) early enough in 1940, the year that Kuttner and Moore married, that the story is likely all Kuttner's work, unless the couple had pre-marital relations on paper. In the 1950s, they wrote less SF, concentrating on mystery novels (probably because mysteries paid better), then the partnership came to an end in 1958 when Kuttner died of a heart attack. Moore mostly wrote TV and movie scripts thereafter, but no SF. Another golden age had ended.

Beauty and the Beast

by Henry Kuttner

Jared Kirth saw the meteor as he lay under the pines, staring up at the stars. He was on the verge of slumber, and the sleeping bag that wrapped his lean body was warm and comfortable.

Kirth was feeling well satisfied with himself, his stomach bulged with crisp, freshly caught trout, and there was still a week left of the fortnight's vacation he had allowed himself. So he lay quietly, watching the night sky, and the meteor shrieked its death agony in that last incandescent plunge through the atmosphere.

But before it went out of sight, the luminous body seemed to turn and arc in midair. That was queer enough. And even stranger was the shape of the thing, an elongated ovoid. Vaguely recalling that meteors sometimes contained precious ores, Kirth marked the spot where the flaming thunderbolt fell beyond a high ridge. And the next morning he shouldered his fishing tackle and hiked in that direction.

So he found the wrecked spaceship. It lay among the pines, a broken giant, its hull fused in many places by the heat of friction.

Kirth's pinched, rather mean mouth tightened as he looked down at the vessel. He was remembering that two months before a man named Jay Arden had left the Earth on the first interplanetary voyage.

Arden had been lost in space—so the papers had said. But now, apparently, his ship had returned, and Kirth's gaunt, gray-stubbled face was eager as he hastened down the slope.

He walked around the ship, slipping on sharp rocks and cursing once or twice before he found the port. But the metal surrounding it had fused and melted, so that entry was impossible at this point. The gray, pitted, rough metal of the craft defied the tentative ax-blows Kirth gave it. Curiosity mounted within him.

He examined the ship more closely. The sun, rising above the eastern ridge, showed a factor he had previously overlooked. There were windows, circular deadlights, so fused and burned that they were as opaque as the metallic hull. Yet they were unmistakably of glass or some similar substance.

It was not ordinary glass. It did not shatter under the ax. But a small chip flew, and Kirth battered away diligently until he had made a small hole. Vapor gushed out of this, foul, stale, and mephitic, and Kirth fell back and waited.

Then he returned to his labors. The glass was easier to shatter now, for some reason, and it was not long before Kirth had chopped away a hole large enough to permit the entry of his lean body. First, however, he took a small flashlight from his belt and held it at arm's length within the ship.

There was but one room, and this was a shambles. It was a mass of wreckage. Yet the air had cleared, and there seemed to be no danger. Cautiously Kirth squirmed through the deadlight.

So this was a spaceship! Kirth recognized the chamber from newspaper pictures he had seen months before.

In 1942 the ship had been new, shining, and perfect. Now, only a few months later, it was a ruin. The controls were hopelessly wrecked. Metal kits and canisters were scattered about the floor, broken straps on the walls showing whence they had fallen. And on the floor, too, lay the body of Jay Arden.

Kirth made a useless examination. The man was dead. His skin was blue and cyanosed, and his neck was obviously broken. Scattered about his corpse were a few cellulose-wrapped parcels that had spilled from a broken canister nearby. Through the transparent envelopes

Kirth detected small black objects, smaller than peas, that resembled seeds.

Protruding from one of Arden's pockets was a notebook. As Kirth drew it forth, a wrapped parcel fell to the floor. Kirth hesitated, put the notebook aside, and opened the package.

Something fell from it into his palm. The man gasped in sheer wonder.

It was a jewel. Oval, large as an egg, the gem flamed gloriously in the light of the electric torch. It had no color, and yet seemed to partake of all the hues of the spectrum.

It seemed to draw into itself a thousand myriad hues— men would have died for such a jewel. Lovely it was, beyond imagination, and it was—unearthly.

Finally Kirth tore his gaze from the thing and opened the notebook. The light was too dim, so he carried it to the broken deadlight. Arden, seemingly, had not kept a diary, and his notes were broken and disconnected. But from the book, several photographs fluttered, and Kirth caught them as they fell.

The snapshots were blurred and discolored, but certain details showed with fair clarity. One showed a thick bar with rounded ends, white against blackness. This was a picture of the planet Venus, taken from outer space, though Kirth did not realize it. He examined the others.

Ruins. Cyclopean, strange, and alien in contour, half-destroyed shapes of stone were blurred against a dim background. One thing, however, was clear. The spaceship was visible in the picture—and Kirth gasped.

For the great ship was dwarfed by the gigantic ruins. Taller than the vast Temple of Karnak, monstrously large were the stones that had once been cities and buildings. Vague and murky as the pictures were, Kirth managed to form some conception of the gargantuan size of the structures shown in them. Too, he noticed that the geometry seemed oddly wrong. There were no stairs visible, only inclined planes. And a certain primeval crudeness, a lack of the delicacy noticeable even in the earlier Egyptian artifacts, was significant.

Most of the other photographs showed similar scenes. One,

however, was different. It depicted a field of flowers, such flowers as Kirth had never before seen. Despite the lack of color, it was evident that the blossoms were lovely with a bizarre, unearthly beauty. Kirth turned to the notebook.

He learned something from it, though not much. He read:

"Venus seems to be a dead planet. The atmosphere is breathable, but only plant life exists. The flowers, somewhat resembling orchids, are everywhere. The ground beneath them is covered with their seeds. I have collected a great many of these. . . .

"Since I found the jewel in one of the ruined structures, I have made another discovery. An intelligent race once lived on Venus—the ruins themselves denote that fact. But any inscriptions they might have left have been long since eroded by the foggy, wet atmosphere and the eternal rains. So I thought, till this morning, when in a subterranean chamber I discovered a bas-relief almost buried in mud.

"It took me hours to clear away the muck, and even then there was not much to see. But the pictures are more significant than any inscription in the ancient Venusian language could have been. I recognized, quite clearly, the jewel I previously discovered. From what I have been able to make out, there were many of these, artificially created. And they were something more than mere gems.

"Unbelievable as it seems, they are—to use a familiar parallel— eggs. There is life in them. Under the proper conditions of heat and sunlight—so I interpret the bas-reliefs—they will hatch. . . ."

There were a few other notes in the book, but these were technical in nature and of no interest to Kirth, save for one which mentioned the existence of a diary Arden had kept. He again searched the ship, and this time found the diary. But it was half incinerated by its proximity to the fused port, and utterly illegible.

Pondering, Kirth examined the various containers. Some were empty; others had dusty cinders in them and emitted a burned, unpleasant odor when opened. The spoils of Arden's voyage were, apparently, only the seeds and the jewel.

Now Jared Kirth, though shrewd, was not intelligent in the true sense of the word. Born on a New England farm, he had fought his way up by dint of hard, bitter persistence and a continual insistence upon his own rights. As a result, he owned a few farms and a small village store, and permitted himself one brief vacation a year. On this furlough neither his wife nor his daughter accompanied him. He was fifty, a tall, spare, gray man, with cold eyes and a tight mouth that was generally compressed as though in denial.

It is scarcely wonderful, therefore, that Kirth began to wonder how he might turn this discovery to serve his own ends. He knew that no reward had been offered for the finding of the spaceship, supposedly lost in the airless void. If there had been treasure of any sort in the vessel, he would have appropriated it, on the principle of "finder's keepers." There was nothing, save for the seeds and the gem, and Kirth had these in his pockets as he left the vessel.

The ship would not be found for some time, since this was wilderness country. Meanwhile, Kirth took with him Arden's notebook, to be destroyed at a more opportune moment. Though skeptical, he thought more than once of Arden's comparison of the jewel with an egg, and, for a man who owned several farms, the conclusion was inevitable. If this "egg" could be hatched, despite the unlikeliness of the idea, the result might be interesting. Even more— it might be profitable.

Kirth decided to cut short his vacation, and two days later he arrived at his home. He did not stay there, however, but went to one of his farms, taking with him his wife and daughter.

Heat and sunlight. A topless, electrically warmed incubator was the logical answer. At night, Kirth used a sunlamp on the jewel. Meanwhile, he waited.

Intrinsically the gem might have value. Kirth could, perhaps, have sold it for a large sum to some jeweler. But he thought better of this, and planted some of the Venusian seeds instead.

And, in the strange jewel, alien life stirred. Heat warmed it—heat that did not now exist on gloomy, rainswept Venus. From the sun poured energy, cosmic rays and other rays that for eons had been barred from the stone by the thick cloud barrier that shrouded Venus.

Into the heart of the gem stole energy that set certain forces in motion. Life came, and dim realization.

There, on the straw of a filthy incubator, lay the visitant from another world. Unknown ages ago, it had been created, for a definite purpose. And now—life returned.

Kirth saw the hatching. At midday he stood beside the incubator, gnawing on a battered pipe, scratching the gray stubble on his jaw. His daughter was beside him, a lean, underfed girl of thirteen with sallow skin and hair.

"It ain't an egg, Pa," she said in a high, nasal voice. "You don't really expect that thing to hatch, do you?"

"Hush," Kirth grunted. "Don't keep pestering me. I—hey! Look at that thing! Something's—"

Something was indeed happening. On the straw the jewel lay, flaming bright. It seemed to suck sunlight into itself thirstily. The dim radiance that had come to surround it of late pulsed and waned— pulsed once more. The glow waxed—

Waxed brighter! An opaque cloud formed suddenly, hiding the gem. There came a high-pitched tinkling sound, almost above the threshold of hearing. It faded and was gone.

The gray mist fled. Where the jewel had been was nothing, Nothing, that is, save for a round, grayish ball that squirmed and shuddered weakly. . . .

"That ain't a chick," the girl said, her jaw hanging. "Pa—" There was fright in her eyes.

"Hush!" Kirth said again. He bent down and gingerly prodded the thing. It seemed to writhe open, with an odd motion of uncoiling, and a tiny creature like a lizard lay there, its small mouth open as it sucked in air.

"I'll be damned," Kirth said slowly. "A dirty little lizard!" He felt vaguely sick. The jewel he might have sold at a good price, but this creature—what could be done with it? Who could want it?

Yet it was strange enough. It was shaped like a miniature kangaroo, almost, and like no lizard Kirth had ever seen before. Perhaps he might sell it after all.

"Go git a box," he said to his daughter, and, when she had obeyed, he picked up the reptile gingerly and deposited it in the impromptu prison.

As he carried it into the house, he glanced at the plot of ground where he had planted some of the seeds. A few yellowish, small spears were sprouting up. Kirth nodded approvingly and scratched his jaw.

Mrs. Kirth, a plump, slatternly woman, approached. Her face was prematurely old, sagging in fat wrinkles. Her brown eyes had a defeated look, though there was still something of beauty in them.

"What you got there, Jay?" she asked.

"Tell you later," he said. "Git me some milk, Nora. And an eyedropper or something."

This was done. Kirth fed the reptile, which seemed to like the milk and sucked it down greedily. Its small, glittering eyes stared up unwinkingly.

"Pa," the girl said. "It's bigger. Lots bigger."

"Couldn't be," Kirth said. "Things don't grow that fast. Git out, now, and leave me be."

And in its prison the tiny creature that was to become the Beast drank thirstily of the milk, while in the dim, alien brain, clouded by the mists of centuries, thoughts began to stir. The first faint chords of memory vibrated . . . memory of a previous life, half forgotten. . . .

Kirth's daughter had been right. The reptile grew, abnormally and alarmingly. At the end of the second day, it was six inches long from blunt muzzle to tapering tail. When the week was over, it was more than twice as large. Kirth built a pen for it and was secretly elated.

"I can sell it, all right," he exulted. "Some circus'd pay me plenty. But it might git even bigger. I'll wait a bit."

Meanwhile he tended his Venusian plants. They were sprouting most satisfactorily now, and the beginnings of buds were evident. They were as tall as hollyhocks, but leafless. The thick, rigid stem, pale yellow in hue, was studded with swellings that presently burst into bloom.

At the end of the second week Kirth's garden was a riot of color, and he paid a photographer to take snapshots in color. These he sent to several horticultural gardens, which were immediately interested. A reporter got on the trail and interviewed Kirth.

Kirth was wary and spoke of plant grafting and experiments he had made. A new species of flower it was, and he had grown them. Yes, he had some seeds, and would sell them. . . .

The wrecked spaceship had not yet been discovered. And in its sty the Beast ate enormously of vegetables, and of swill which Kirth refused the reluctant hogs, and drank anything it could get. A scientist would have known, by the shape of the Beast's teeth, that it was carnivorous or at least omnivorous, but Kirth did not know, and the reptile did not appear to object to its menu. It grew, remarkably, and its basal metabolism was so high that its scaly body emitted perceptible heat.

It was as large now as a stallion. But it seemed so gentle that Kirth took no warning, though he kept a revolver in his pocket whenever he approached his bizarre charge.

The dim memories within the Beast's brain stirred into life from time to time. But one factor predominated, drowning them and lulling them to slumber. The Beast knew, somehow, that it was necessary for him to grow. Before anything else, he must attain his full growth and maturity. After that—

The Beast was intelligent, not with the aptitude of a child, but with the mind of a half-drugged adult. And he was not born of Earth. The alien chemistry of his body sent unknown secretions coursing through his veins, and, as he ate and grew, that strange mind worked. . . .

The Beast learned, though as yet he could not take advantage of his knowledge. The Kirths' conversation was clearly audible to him through the open windows of the farmhouse, and their televisor was very often turned on. From observing the humans, he grew to recognize their moods, and in turn came to associate certain word-sounds with those moods.

He learned that certain grimaces accompanied a special set of emotions. He grew to understand laughter and tears.

One thing he did not understand—a look that came into the eyes of Mrs. Kirth and her daughter, and sometimes into Kirth's eyes, as they watched him. It was repugnance and horror, but the Beast did not know that.

Two months passed slowly. Kirth received many checks in his mail. The new flowers had proved tremendously popular, and florists demanded them avidly. Lovelier than orchids they were, and they did not fade for a long time after being cut.

Kirth was not shrewd enough to keep control of the plants in his own hands, and the distribution of them got beyond him. Since the flowers would flourish in any climate, they were grown from California to New York. Fields of them formed a carpet of beauty over America. The fad spread over the world, and in Buenos Aires, London, and Berlin no socialite attended a *dansant* without a corsage of the Rainbows, as the blooms came to be called.

Kirth might have been satisfied with his growing bank account, but he had already got in touch with the owners of several circuses and told them he had a freak to sell. Kirth was becoming apprehensive. The Beast was uncomfortably huge, and people were noticing that scaled, swaying back as it moved about. Kirth, with some trepidation, led the monster into the barn, though it followed willingly enough. But the quarters were cramped. One blow from the mighty tail would have wrecked the structure, and that was scarcely a pleasant thought.

Kirth would have been even more disturbed had he realized what was going on in the monster's brain. The fogs were dissipating as the Beast approached swift maturity. Intelligence and memory were returning. And already the creature could understand many English words.

That was natural enough. A child does the same, over a period of years, by a process of association, experiment, and mental retention of word-sounds. The Beast was not a child. He was a highly intelligent being, and for months he had been in close contact with human beings. At times, he found it hard to concentrate, and would devote himself to feeding and sleeping, in a dull, pleasantly languorous stupor. Then the driving, inexorable force within him would awaken him to life once more.

It was hard to remember. The metamorphosis he had undergone

had altered the psychic patterns of his mind to some degree. But one day he saw, through a crack in the barn, the Venusian flowers, and by a natural process of association thought of long-forgotten things. Then a dull, gray, rainy day occurred. . . .

Rain. Chill, bleak water that splashed on his scaled hide. Thick fogs, through which structures reared. And among those stone buildings moved beings like himself. The Beast remembered. . . .

The hideous, armored head swayed in the dimness of the barn. The saucer eyes stared into vacancy. Tremendous and frightful, the Beast crouched, while its thoughts went far and far into the dusty ages of the past.

Others. There had been others like itself, the ruling race of the second planet Something had happened. Death . . . doom. Many had died. All over the rain-swept, twilit world the mighty reptiles had perished. Nothing could save them from the plague that had come from outer space.

The vast hulk shuddered uneasily in the gloom.

No escape. Yes, there had been one. Despite the beast form of the creatures, they had been intelligent. And they had possessed science of a kind. It was not Earthly science—but it had found an escape.

Not in their own form. Nothing could protect the huge reptilian bodies from the plague. But in another form . . . a form in which the basic energy patterns of their bodies would remain unaltered, though compressed by the creation of atomic stasis . . .

Matter is not solid. Bodies are formed of incredibly tiny solar systems, electrons that swing in wide orbits about their protons. Under the influence of cold this sub-microscopic motion is slowed down, and at the point of absolute zero it ceases. But absolute zero means the cessation of all energy, and is impossible.

Impossible? Not on Venus, ages ago. As an experiment the life energy had been drained from one of the reptiles. As the electrons drew in toward their protons, there had been a shrinkage . . . and a change. A jewel of frozen life, an entity held in absolute stasis, lay before the Venusian scientists, waiting for the heat and solar rays that would waken it to life once more.

Space travel, to those bulky and gigantic forms, was impossible. But if, in different guise, they could flee to another, safer world. . . .

That had been the plan. All the energies of the Venusian survivors were turned toward constructing a spaceship. In this vessel the life-gems were to be stored and, as soon as possible, automatic robot controls would guide the craft across space, to Earth. Once a safe landing had been effected, other robot apparatus would expose the jewels to sunlight and heat, and the Venusians would live again after their cataleptic voyage across the void. But the plan had not been completed. The plague was too deadly. The spaceship's unfinished ruins still lay hidden deep in a Venusian swamp, and it had been an Earth-man, after all, who had brought one of the strange jewels to his own world.

All over Venus the gems were hidden. The Beast had seen the night sky and learned that he was on the third planet. That meant he had been brought here from his own world, and revivified by the energizing rays. He felt gratitude to the Earthmen who had rescued him from the eternal life-in-death.

Perhaps he was not the only one. Perhaps others of his race existed here, on Earth. Well, he would communicate with these humans, now that the fogs were clearing from his brain. Strange creatures they were, bipeds, and hideous to the Beast's alien eyes. But he was grateful to them, nevertheless.

How could he communicate? The Earthmen were intelligent, that was evident enough. His own language would be incomprehensible to them, and though he could understand English after a fashion, his throat and tongue could not form recognizable words. Well, mathematics was a universal language, and that could be the beginning.

There was something he must tell Earthmen—something vitally important. But they were the ruling race on this planet, and it would not be too difficult to establish communication with them.

The Beast moved clumsily. His body lurched against the wall of the barn and, with a crackling crash, timbers gave way. The big structures sagged down, and as the Beast drew back in dismay, he completed the job of ruin. He stood amid the wreck of something that no longer resembled a barn. Impatiently, he shook it off. Things on this world were delicate indeed. The heavy stone structures of Venus were built to withstand normal shocks.

The noise had been heard. Kirth came running out of the farmhouse, carrying a shotgun and holding an electric torch. His wife was beside him. They started toward the barn, and then paused, apprehensive.

"It—it tore it down," Mrs. Kirth said stupidly. "Do you think it'll—Jay! Wait!"

But Kirth went forward, holding the gun ready. In the moonlight the gross bulk of the monster loomed hideously above him.

And the Beast thought: It is time. Time to establish communication. . . .

A huge foreleg lifted and began to trace a design in the dirt of the farmyard. A circle formed, and another. In time, a map of the solar system was clear.

"Look at the way it's pawing," Mrs. Kirth said. "Like a bull getting ready to charge. Jay—watch out!"

"I'm watching," Kirth said grimly. And he lifted the gun.

The Beast drew back, without fear, but waiting for the man to see the design. Yet Kirth's eyes saw only a meaningless maze of concentric circles. He walked slowly forward, his boots obliterating the design.

"He did not notice it," the Beast thought. "I must try again. Surely it will be easy to make him understand. In such a highly organized civilization, only a scientist would have been entrusted with my care."

Remembering the gesture of greeting among Earthmen, the Beast lifted a foreleg and slowly extended it. Shaking hands was fantastically impossible, but Kirth would recognize the significance of the motion.

Instead, Kirth fired. The bullet ripped along the Beast's skull, a painful though not dangerous wound. The Beast instantly withdrew its paw.

The man did not understand. Perhaps it thought harm had been offered, had read menace in the friendly gesture. The Beast lowered its head in a motion of submission.

At sight of that frightful mask swooping down, Mrs. Kirth broke through her paralysis of terror. She shrieked in an agony of fear and turned to flee. Kirth, yelling hysterical oaths, pumped bullet after bullet at the reptile.

The Beast turned clumsily. It was not hurt, but there was danger here. Attempting to escape without damaging the frail structures all around, it managed to step on a pigsty, ruin a silo, and crush in one wall of the farmhouse.

But this could not be helped. The Beast retreated and was lost in the night.

The inhuman brain was puzzled. What had gone wrong now? Earthmen were intelligent, yet they had not understood. Perhaps the fault lay with itself. Full maturity had not been reached; the thought-patterns were still not set in their former matrices. The fogs that shrouded the reptile's mind were not yet completely dissipated. . . .

Growth! Maturity! That was necessary. Once maturity had been achieved, the Beast could meet Earthmen on equal terms and make them understand. But food was necessary. . . .

The Beast lumbered on through the moonlit gloom. It went like a behemoth through fences and plowed fields, leaving a swathe of destruction in its wake. At first it tried to keep to roads, but the concrete and asphalt were shattered beneath the vast weight. So it gave up that plan, and headed for the distant mountains.

A shouting grew behind it. Red light flared. Searchlights began to sweep the sky. But this tumult died as the Beast drove farther and farther into the mountains. For a time, it must avoid men. It must concentrate on—food!

The Beast liked the taste of flesh, but it also understood the rights of property. Animals were owned by men. Therefore they must not be molested. But plants—cellulose—almost anything was fuel for growth. Even the limbs of trees were digestible.

So the colossus roamed the wilderness. Deer and cougars it caught and ate, but mostly vegetation. Once, it saw an airplane droning overhead, and after that more planes came, dropping bombs. But after sundown, the Beast managed to escape.

It grew unimaginably. Some effect of the sun's actinic rays, not filtered as on cloud-veiled Venus, made the Beast grow far beyond the size it had been on Venus eons ago. It grew larger than the vastest dinosaur that ever stalked through the swamps of Earth's dawn, a titanic, nightmare juggernaut out of the Apocalypse. It looked like a walking mountain. And, inevitably, it became clumsier.

The pull of gravity was a serious handicap. Walking was painful work. Climbing slopes, dragging its huge body, was agony. No more could the Beast catch deer. They fleetly evaded the ponderous movements.

Inevitably, such a creature could not escape detection. More planes came, with bombs. The Beast was wounded again, and realized the necessity of communicating with Earthmen without delay. Maturity had been reached. . . .

There was something of vital importance that Earthmen must know. Life had been given to the Beast by Earthmen, and that was a debt to be repaid.

The Beast came out of the mountains. It came by night, and traveled swiftly, searching for a city. There, it knew, was the best chance of finding understanding. The giant's stride shook the earth as it thundered through the dark.

On and on it went. So swift was its progress that the bombers did not find it till dawn. Then the bombs fell, and more than one found its mark.

But the wounds were superficial. The Beast was a mighty, armored Juggernaut, and such a thing may not be easily slain. It felt a pain, however, and moved faster. The men in the sky, riding their air-chariots, did not understand—but somewhere would be men of science. Somewhere. . . .

And so the Beast came to Washington.

Strangely, it recognized the Capitol. Yet it was, perhaps, natural, for the Beast had learned English, and had listened to Kirth's televisor for months. Descriptions of Washington had been broadcast, and the Beast knew that this was the center of government in America. Here, if anywhere on Earth, there would be men who understood. Here were the rulers, the wise men. And despite its wounds, the Beast felt a thrill of exultation as it sped on.

The planes dived thunderously. The aerial torpedoes screamed down. Crashing they came, ripping flesh from that titanic armored body.

"It's stopped!" said a pilot, a thousand feet above the Beast. "I think we've killed it! Thank God it didn't get into the city—"

The Beast stirred into slow movement. The fires of pain bathed it. The reptilian nerves sent their unmistakable messages to the brain, and the Beast knew it had been wounded unto death. Strangely it felt no hate for the men who had slain it.

No—they could not be blamed. They had not known. And, after all, humans had taken the Beast from Venus, restored it to life, tended and fed it for months....

And there was still a debt. There was a message that Earthmen must know. Before the Beast died, it must convey that message, somehow.

The saucer eyes saw the white dome of the Capitol in the distance. There could be found science, and understanding. But it was so far away!

The Beast rose. It charged forward. There was no time to consider the fragility of the man-made structures all around. The message was more important.

The bellow of thunder marked the Beast's progress. Clouds of ruin rose up from toppling buildings. Marble and granite were not the iron-hard stone of Venus, and a trail of destruction led toward the Capitol. The planes followed in uncertainty. They dared not loose bombs above Washington.

Near the Capitol was a tall derricklike tower. It had been built for the accommodation of newscasters and photographers, but now it served a different purpose. A machine had been set up there hastily, and men frantically worked connecting power cables. A lens-shaped projector, gleaming in the sunlight, was swinging slowly to focus on the oncoming monster. It resembled a great eye, high above Washington.

It was a heat ray.

It was one of the first in existence, and if it could not stop the reptile, nothing could.

Still the Beast came on. Its vitality was going fast, but there would still be time. Time to convey its message to the men in the Capitol, the men who would understand.

From doomed Washington arose a cry, from ten thousand panic-strained throats. In the streets men and women fought and struggled and fled from the oncoming monster that towered against the sky, colossal and horrible.

On the tower soldiers worked at the projector, connecting, tightening, barking sharp orders.

The Beast halted. It paused before the Capitol. From the structure, men were fleeing. . . .

The fogs were creeping up to shroud the reptile brain. The Beast fought against increasing lassitude. The message—the message!

A mighty forepaw reached out. The Beast had forgotten Earth's gravity, and the clumsiness of its own gross bulk.

The massive paw crashed through the Capitol's dome!

Simultaneously the heat ray flashed out blindly. It swept up and bathed the Beast in flaming brilliance.

For a heartbeat the tableau held, the colossus towering above the nation's Capitol. Then the Beast fell. . . .

In death, it was terrible beyond imagination. The heat ray crumpled it amid twisted iron girders. The Capitol itself was shattered into utter ruin. For blocks buildings collapsed, and clouds of dust billowed up in a thick, shrouding veil.

The clouds were blinding, like the mists that darkened the sight and the mind of the Beast. For the reptile was not yet dead. Unable to move, the life ebbing swiftly from it, the Beast yet strove to stretch out one monstrous paw. . . .

Darkly it thought: I must give them the message. I must tell them of the plague that destroyed all life on Venus. I must tell them of the virus, borne on the winds, against which there is no protection. Out of space, it came to Venus, spores that grew to flowers. And now, the flowers grow on Earth. In a month, the petals will fall, and from the blossoms the virus will develop. And then, all life on Earth will be destroyed, as it was on Venus, and nothing will exist on all the planet but bright flowers and the ruins of cities. I must warn them to destroy the blossoms now, before they pollinate. . . .

The mists were very thick now. The Beast shuddered convulsively, and lay still. It was dead.

On a rooftop, a man and a woman watched from the distance. The man said: "God, what a horrible thing! Look at it lying there, like the devil himself." He shuddered and glanced away.

The white-faced woman nodded. "It's hard to believe the world can hold so much horror, and yet can give us anything as beautiful as this. . . ." Her slim fingers stroked the velvety petals of the blossom that was pinned to her dress. Radiant, lovely, the flower from Venus glowed in the sunlight.

Already, pollen was forming within its cup.

The Island of the Ud

INTRODUCTION

In his younger days, William Hope Hodgson (1877-1918) was an apprentice seaman. Later he became known for his supernatural stories, many of them eerie tales of the sea, including two yarns about Captain Jat, told from the third person viewpoint of his long-suffering young cabin boy Pibby Tawles. In this one, the not-so-good Captain heads for an unknown island, hoping again to see an old female acquaintance and also to steal a number of valuable pearls. Things get complicated by both the lady friend and the pearls having fearsome guardians who may or may not be altogether human, and another guardian who is definitely not human—and also is very large . . .

❖ ❖ ❖

William Hope Hodgson is now recognized as one of the preeminent fantasy writers of the early twentieth century, particularly his extraordinary novel of the far future, *The Night Land*, set millions of years from now, when the Sun has gone out and the last remnants of humanity huddle in a mountain-sized pyramid, besieged by monsters, many themselves also mountain-sized. Also notable are his novels *The House on the Borderland*, *The Boats of the Glen Carrig*, and *The Ghost Pirates*, as well as the stories of the occult detective Carnaki, and many other short stories. His complete works are available in five omnibus volumes on Baen e-books. While I highly recommend *The*

Night Land, it is written in a pseudo-archaic style which is not for every taste, but his other novels and his short stories of the sea and of Carnaki's exploits have no such stylistic quirks, and I recommend them as well.

The Island of the Ud

by William Hope Hodgson

Pibby Tawles, Cabin-boy and deck-hand stood to lee-ward of the half-poop, and stared silently at the island, incredibly lonely against the translucence of the early dawn—a place of lonesome and mysterious silence, with strange birds of the sea wheeling and crying over it, and making the silence but the more apparent.

A way to wind'ard, Captain Jat, his Master, stood stiff and erect against the growing light, all his leathery length of six feet, five inches, set into a kind of grim attention as he stared at the black shadow upon the sea, that lay off his weather bow.

The minutes passed slowly, and the dawn seemed to dream, stirred to reality only by the far and chill sound of the birds crying so dreely. The small barque crept on, gathering the slight morning airs to her aid, whilst the dawn-shine grew subtly and strengthened up, so that the island darkened the more against it for a little while, and grew stealthily more real. And all the time, above it, the sea birds swung about in noiseless circling against the gold-of-light that hung now in all the lower sky.

Presently, there came the hoarse hail of the lookout man, who must have waked suddenly:—

"Land on the weather bow, Sir!"

But the lean, grim-looking figure to the wind'ard vouchsafed no reply, beyond a low growled "grrrrr!" of contempt.

271

And all the time, Pibby Tawles, the boy, stared, overwhelmed with strange imaginings—treasure, monsters, lovely women, weirdness unutterable, terror brooding beyond all powers of his imagination to comprehend! He had listened to some marvelously strange things, when Captain Jat had been in drink: for it was often then the Captain's whim to make the boy sit at the table with him, and dip his cup likewise in the toddy-bowl.

And presently, when Captain Jat had drunk his toddy steadily out of the big pewter mug, he would begin to talk; rambling on in garrulous fashion from tale to tale; and, at last, as like as not, mixing them quite inextricably. And as he talked, the long, lean man would throw his glance back over his shoulder suspiciously every minute or so, and perhaps bid the boy go up to the little half-poop, and discover the wherabouts of the officer of the watch, and then into the cabin of the officer whose watch it might chance to be below, and so to make sure that neither of his Mates were attending listening ears on the sly.

"Don't never tell the Mates, boy!" he would say to Pibby Tawles, "Or I'll sure maul you! They'd be wantin' profits."

For that was, in the main, the substance of all his talks—treasure, that is to say. To be exact, treasure and women.

"Never a word, boy. I trusts you; but no one else in this packet!"

And truly, Captain Jat did seem to have a trust in the boy; for in his cups, he told him everything that came up in his muddled mind; and always the boy would listen with a vast interest, putting in an odd question this time and that to keep the talk running. And indeed it suited him very well; for though he could never tell how much to believe, or how little, he was very well pleased to be sitting drinking his one cup of toddy slowly in the cabin, instead of being out on the deck, doing ship work.

It is true that the Captain appeared both to like the boy, in his own queer fashion, and to trust him; but for all that, he had with perfect calmness and remorseless intent, shown him the knife with which he would cut his throat, if ever he told a word of anything that his master might say to him during his drinking bouts.

Captain Jat's treatment of the lad was curious in many ways. He had him sleep in a little cabin aback the Mate's where through the open door he could see the boy in his bunk. When he ran out of toddy, he would heave his pewter mug at the lad's head as he lay asleep, and roar to him to turn-out and brew him fresh and stronger; but this trick of the Captain's was no trouble to Pibby; for he rigged a dummy oakum-head to that end of his bunk which showed through the open doorway and slept then the other way about.

And so with this little that I have told you may know something of the life aft in the cabin of the little barque *Gallat*, which vessel belonged, stick-and-keel, to Captain Jat; and some pretty rum doings there were aboard of her, first and last, as you may now have chance to judge.

At times, another side of Captain Jat would break out, and he would spend the whole of a watch having a gorgeous pistol-shooting match against Pibby; and a wonderful good shot the boy was, both by natural eye, and by the training he had this way. In the end, the boy became a better shot than Captain Jat himself, who was an extraordinarily fine marksman; though somewhat unequal. Yet for all that Pibby beat him time after time, this peculiar man showed no annoyance, but persisted in the matches, as if his primary intention were to make the boy an expert with the weapon; and indeed, I have little doubt but that this was his real desire.

Now, although Pibby Tawles had tremendously confused and vague ideas as to what strangeness of mystery was concerned with the island, yet he knew perfectly that it was no chance that had brought them that way; for all the Captain's talks over his toddy had gone to show that the *true* aim of the voyage was to bring up near the island for some purpose that the lad could only guess at in a mystified way, owing to the muddling fashion in which Captain Jat had run his yarns one into another; treasure, women, monsters, and odd times a queer habit of muttering to himself about his little priestess—his little priestess! And once he had broken out into a kind of hazy ramble about the Ud, rolling his eyes at the boy strangely and gesticulating so impressively with his pewter mug that he managed to spread his toddy in an unprejudiced manner over Pibby, the table and the floor generally.

Therefore, having, as I have said, a sure knowledge that the island they approached was the real goal of the voyages, though there was an honest enough cargo below hatches, you may imagine something of Pibby's blank astonishment when Captain Jat allowed the barque to sail quietly past, touching neither brace, sheet nor tack; so that, by the time morning was full come, the island lay upon the weather quarter, and presently far away astern.

Yet, as they had gone past, the lad had studied it very eagerly, and had seen in the light of the coming day that it was wooded almost everywhere, even close down to the shores, with a long, bold reef of stark rock running out in a great sweep upon the South side, so that it was plain a boat could be landed there very safely and easily under its lee. The island, Pibby had noticed, rose towards the centre, into a low, seemingly flat-topped hill, with the forests of great trees very heavy on its slopes.

All the morning the *Gallat* stood to the Southward, until they had sunk the island below the horizon. They hove-to then, and drifted until near evening, when they filled once more on her, and stood back to the Northward. By four bells that night they sighted the island, looking like a doleful smudge in the darkness away to the Northeast.

Presently, the barque was put in irons, and orders given to lower the dingy. When she was in the water, Captain Jat flipped Pibby on the ear, and growled to him to jump down into the boat. The boy climbed over, and Captain Jat followed, after having first directed the Second Mate, whose watch it was, to reach out into the open, and run in again about midnight.

The Captain took the after oar, and rowed standing up, with his face to the bows, whilst Pibby, the boy, took the bow oar and rowed sitting down.

"Easy with that oar, boy!" said Captain Jat presently, after he had pulled awhile. "Put your shirt round it." And this, Pibby had to do, and row naked to the waist, whilst his shirt muffled the sound of his oar between the thole-pins. But, after all, the night was pretty warm.

Meanwhile, the Captain had pulled off his own coat and ripped out one of the sleeves, which he reeved onto his oar, and so made it silent as the lad's. And this was the way, almost as quietly as a shadow boat in the darkness, they came in presently under the shelter of the great barrier reef, and very soon then to the uncomfortable silence of the shore under the dark trees that came down so near to the sea.

Here, before Captain Jat landed, he bid the boy lay on his oar, whilst he listened. But they could hear nothing, except the far dull booming of the sea upon the exposed beach beyond the great reef— the solemn noise of the sea coming very hushed and distant to them, and blending with the dree little sounds that came out of the near forest, as the night airs went wandering on into its gloom.

"Keep her afloat till I come, boy," said Captain Jat, as he stepped ashore. He walked a few paces up the beach, settling a brace of great double-barrelled pistols in his belt. Then he turned sharply and came back:—

"Not a sound, boy, or you're as good as dead," he said grimly, in a low tone. "Not a sound, so what you hears! Keep off there in the shadow of the reef. You'll hear me squark like a catched molley-hawk, when I come. Keep your eyes wide open, boy!" And with that, he slewed round on his heel, and went up pretty quick across the sand into the darkness of the black trees.

Pibby Tawles, the boy, stood in the bows of the boat, and stared after him, listening to the vague sounds of his passage growing ever distant and more distant, but odd-whiles sounding out clear through the dark forests, as some dried kippin snapped under his weight. Then, as Captain Jat went farther and farther, the silence of the island fell again about Pibby, save for the odd whispering of the leaves in the little airs that came off the sea, and the constant solemn booming of the ocean on the far breach that lay exposed upon the outward arc of the great reef.

And so, listening there, and full of the mystery of all the vague and muddled tales that Captain Jat had maundered through so often, over the toddy, is it any matter for surprise that the lad, Pibby, grew suddenly frightened of the loneliness and the silence, and began to think there were pale ovals, among the dark tree-trunks, that peered at him?

He thrust his hand down, inside his trousers, and eased a small double-barrelled pistol out of a canvas pocket he had stitched in there with a palm and needle, and sail-twine for thread. The feel of the small weapon gave him a degree of comfort, and abruptly he remembered that Captain Jat had told him to keep the boat off in the shadow of the reef. He jumped out over the bows, holding the pistol in his right hand, and found to his dismay that the boat was aground. He put his bare shoulder to her stern, and hove madly awhile, sweating; for he felt that Captain Jat was quite capable of knifing him on his return, if he found the boat hard ashore. With a determination, vague but dogged, to protect himself with his pistol if necessary, he made one vast, final effort, and the boat slid afloat.

He jumped in over the bows, ran aft and put his pistol on the stern thwart; then with the boat-hook he pushed out, and so came in a minute under the gloom of the reef, which rose up just there into a chaos of great rocks, weed-hidden at their bases. He thrust the boat-hook into a mass of weed, and anchored the boat temporarily.

Then, with a sudden shiver, he remembered his shirt, and, having freed it, he covered his damp back.

Pibby Tawles had been sitting quietly in the boat for, maybe, half an hour, when he heard something that made him lean forward on the thwart and listen tensely. There was something moving, in among the great rocks and boulders where the reef thrust into the shore; and the sounds were exceedingly curious:— Slither! Slither! click-click, and then a loud squelch and a great splashing, as if some huge thing scrambling over the rocks, had slipped and fallen into one of the pools left by the sea.

There was a little time of silence, and then again came the sharp, click, click, followed by a loud grating noise over the rocks. The noise frightened the boy extraordinarily, and he freed the boat-hook silently from the weed, and began nervously to punt the boat out farther from the shore; but keeping very carefully in the gloom that the shadow of the reef cast.

He held the boat again, some dozen fathoms farther out, and waited. He could hear the strange noises continuing, oddly broken by pauses of profound quiet; then again the slithering and clicking sounds. Abruptly, there was a loud crash—a huge boulder had been moved bodily and sent rolling down from the higher parts of the reef to the shore. The boulder was a big one; for Pibby could see it vaguely through the darkness, where it had bounded out into the soft sand. He thought vividly and horridly of Captain Jat's muddled yarns of grim things, and he began again silently to push the boat farther out.

Even as he loosed the hook of the boat-hook out from the weed, there came a tremendous scrambling noise among the rocks inshore, and something moved out silently onto the vague white sand of the beach. It passed over a darker patch of pebbles, and the lad heard the rounded stones grinding against each other, as if under a vast weight. The pistol seemed only a foolish toy in his hand, and he got down suddenly onto the bottom-boards of the boat and lay flat.

A long while seemed to pass, during which he heard further sounds that told him the thing was moving along the beach. He kept very still, and presently there was only silence of the quiet sea and the island about him again, with the seas booming far and hollowly on the unprotected shore beyond the reef, and the faint stirrings of the forest trees whispering oddly to him across the quiet strip of sea that held the boat off the sand.

He sat up, cautiously, and found that the boat still rose and fell on the gentle heaves of the sea close in under the gloom of the reef. He took the boat-hook and anchored her again, and all the time his gaze searched the vague shore; but he saw nothing and heard nothing, and gradually he grew easier.

A long time passed, whilst he sat, pistol in hand, watching and listening. Everything remained quiet, and slowly he began to nod, drowsing and waking through the minutes, so that he could not be said to be either awake or asleep. And then, in a moment, he was wide awake, for there was a sound breaking the utter stillness. He sat up, gripping his pistol, and stared nervously; and as he stared, the sound came again, a far, faint inhuman howling away up through the dark forests of to the North of him. He stood up in the boat, and, abruptly, a great way off in the night, there came the sound of a shot, and once more the howling, only that now there was a strange screaming as well. There was another shot, and one single, shrill scream that came to him far and attenuated out of the night air; and then, for the best part of an hour, an absolute silence.

Suddenly, far off among the trees, Pibby saw a faint gleam of light, moving here and there, and growing bigger as the minutes passed. Presently, he saw that there were four of these gleams, and then six, and all moving and dancing about strangely; but no sound; at least, not for a time.

All at once, he heard the snapping of a twig, apparently a long way off in the wood, the sound echoing strangely in the quietness. And then, very abrupt and dreadful, the inhuman howling began again, mingled with a wild screaming, seeming to be but a few hundred paces deep in the woods. To the boy, it seemed as though something that was half a woman and half something else, howled and shrieked there among the trees; and he chilled with a very literal fright.

The six lights danced and blended and again separated, and all the time the abominable howling and screaming continued through the grim woods. Then, very sharp and sudden, the noise of one Captain Jat's double-barrelled pistols:—bang! bang! And, almost immediately, Captain Jat's voice shouting, at some distance, to bring the boat in, to bring the boat in.

The lad freed the boat-hook, and started the dinghy in to the shore, and as he did so, he heard the crashing of Captain Jat's footsteps through the rotten wood and leaves; and it was plain to him that the Captain had started to make an undisguised run for the boat.

As Pibby thrust the boat inshore, he realised a number of things:—The Captain was being followed, and those lights and the strange howling had something to do with whatever followed him. The nose of the boat grounded, and Pibby picked up his weapon, and ran forward and stood on the fore thwart, waiting.

The strange lights came nearer, moving swiftly among the trees; and suddenly the lad saw something that was plainly monstrous. He had a clear view up a long vista of dark trees, which the lights had made visible, and he saw the figure of a man, black and immensely tall against the light, running and staggering down towards the beach. He knew it was Captain Jat. The dancing lights, beyond, entered the vista, and came dancing and flaring down through the wood; and abruptly the boy got a clear view of the things that carried them. The lights were great torches, and were carried by a number of wild looking women who were nearly naked, with great manes of hair all loose and wild about them.

But the monstrous and horrid thing that caught the boy's eye was something he saw as the women came nearer, running. They had faces so flat as to be almost featureless. At first, if he thought at all, he supposed that they were wearing some kind of mask; but as they ran, the nearest woman opened her mouth and howled, the same disgusting sound that he had heard earlier that night. As she howled, she brandished both the hand that held the torch, and the other hand, above her head. But she had no hands; her arms ended in enormous claws, like the claws of a great crab. The other women began to howl, and to wave their torches and arms as they ran, and Pibby saw that some of them were like the foremost woman. He stared, with the wide-eyed acceptance of youth of the horrific and monstrous.

Captain Jat came blundering and reeling out of the wood. He stubbed his foot against something, and fell headlong onto the sand, and those extraordinary and brutish things close astern of him. Pibby saw suddenly that three of the women had knives, enormous knives, and somehow the sight of the knives made him feel better—it was more human. In the same moment, he loosed off his right barrel and immediately his left, and with each shot there fell a woman, screaming, their torches flying along the sand, and throwing up great sparks. Captain Jat staggered up, and came on at a heavy run to the boat. He reached it, and fell all his great length in over the bows.

"Put off, boy!" he gasped. "Put off!" And even as he spoke, the boat was away from the shore with the push that he had given it as he came aboard. He scrambled to his feet, seized an oar, and thrust down hard, so that the water boiled under the stern, with the way that he gave the boat. In a moment, they had the oars between the tholes, and were backing the boat madly out into the darkness of the sea; so that in a few minutes they were a good way off the shore, and the quiet and hush of the water about them.

But there danced on the beach, at the edge of the sea, those monstrous-faced and monstrous-armed women, and howled at them across the sea, and a dreadful enough noise to hear. They waved their great torches, and jigged crazily, so that the light splashed redly across the swells; and all the time as they danced, their black manes flew about them, and always they howled.

"Pull, boy!" said Captain Jat, still very hoarse with breathlessness. "Pull, boy!" But indeed, the lad was pulling fit to break his youthful back. There passed a further time of labour and gasping silence, and presently they were out in the open water, where the quiet swells moved big and free under them in the darkness, and the reef lay between them and the shore. But they could still see the mad dancing of the lights at the edge of the sea.

Awhile later, Captain Jat eased, and they put the boat round, after which he lay on his oar, and the boy the same, for he could scarcely breathe. The lights were gone now from the shore, and there was no sound, except the far hollow noise of the breaking seas upon the exposed beaches of the island, to the Eastward.

Now, never a word of thanks said Captain Jat for the way the boy had saved him with the pistol; but presently he pulled his oar in across the boat, and lit his pipe, after which he hove the plug of his tobacco at the lad. That was his way.

"Boy," he said, after smoking a little, "I'm wondering if they knew I was whistlin' to her."

"Who, Sir?" asked Pibby.

But Captain Jat made no answer to this. After smoking a long time, he said suddenly:—"Them was the Ud-women, boy . . . Devil-women . . . Priestesses of the Ud, that's Devil in their talk. I was here a matter of four years gone for water, and I found out somethin' then, boy, about them an' their pearl-fishin' an' devil-worshipping, an' how they've kep' it quiet from all the world. I found one of the priestesses alone one time, a little woman an' pretty, not like *them*!" (He jerked his thumb shorewards.) "I was a week lyin' off here, an' there mightn't have been anyone on the island, the way they kep' hid, boy; not till I found the little priestess down near by the spring. I knew her lingo, a bit, and we got talking. I saw her all that week, every night, secret like. She liked me. I liked her. I had her aboard once, an' she told me a heap. When I put her ashore, I took the Mate with me, Jeremiah Stimple, he was, an' we went prospecting for them pearls I'd learned about; but she'd never told me proper about the Ud an' the Ud-women. She'd never say much that way. That's how we got into trouble. We'd near got to the top of the hill, an' then come some of them devil-women. I was all cut about, an' I guess they likely sacrificed the Mate. I never saw him again.

"There must be hundreds of them devil-women ashore there in them forests. But I always meant to come back, boy. I've seen the pearls this very night. They're down in the bottom of the crater that's inside of yon hill in the middle of the island, all strung round a great carved post; an' I'm going to get 'em too, boy. You sh'd see the pearls them hag women was dressed with. You mustn't be feared of their claws, boy. They'm only cast off claw-shells, or somethin' of that sort. Mind you, the little priestess, she said some of 'em was *real*—growed that way; but I can't think it, scarcely. But you never know what you may find in them sorts of places. What their pet Devil is, I don't know . . ."

"I saw somethin', Sir, after you was gone," began Pibby, interrupting. "It were a 'orrible thing . . ."

"I saw the little Priestess tonight, down in the crater," went on Captain Jat, without taking the least apparent notice of what the boy had begun to tell him. "I was at the top; It's not all of twenty fathom deep. I whistled soft an' gentle to her. She saw me, an' near did faint, boy, by the look of her, an' waved me to go away pretty quick. By the look of things down there, they're in for one of their Devil-Festas. They'd big torches burning—you can see the light of 'em now." And Captain Jat nodded towards the island.

The lad, Pibby, stared away through the darkness, and surely enough there was a faint loom of light in the night above the island.

"I reck'n the festa'll be pretty soon now, boy, at the dark of the moon, an' like there'll be Chiefs from the islands round for a thousand miles, and a sprinklin' of rotten whites, I guess, and devil-work uncounted. I'm hopin' them devil-priestesses didn't see the little woman wavin' me away, or maybe she'll be in bad trouble. They come on me, just after she signed to me to clear out, an' near finished me before I'd time to slew round. They've butcher's knives, some on 'em, as long as your leg, boy, an' one of 'em near ripped me up." He opened his coat, and the lad saw dimly in the gloom that his shirt was all stained dark.

"I settled four of the brutes," Captain Jat continued, "and you outed two. That's six gone to hell, where they come from . . ." He broke off, and puffed meditatively at his pipe for a time, leaning on his oar, which rested on the gunnels. Pibby had never heard him talk so much before when sober.

"The native name for yon island means 'The Island of the Devil,' boy," said Captain Jat, presently. "I heard that years gone from more than one; but none of 'em could tell me anythin', or wouldn't, 'cept it was an almighty unhealthy place for a white man . . . or a native either, for that matter, except, maybe, as I'm thinking, when there's one of their big, secret, damn Ud-Festas on . . ." He broke off short, and slipped his pipe into his pocket.

"Pull, boy, an' break your damn back. There's the ship!" he said.

Ten minutes later they were safe aboard.

All next day, Captain Jat kept the barque away to the Southward of the island; but he sent Pibby aloft, time and again, with his own telescope; and when the youth came down finally in the late afternoon, to report numbers of small craft on the horizon, steering North, he nodded his head, as if the news were what he had expected.

"Native boats, boy," he said. "Keep your mouth shut, an' tell nothin' to no one. They'll hold that festa tonight, an' they'll have all their pearls strung up, an' we'll be there. You clean up all them big double-barr'lled pistols, an' load 'em nice and careful, like I've showed you. Get a move on you now!"

That night, with all lights dowsed, the barque stood again to the Northward, and dropped Captain Jat and the lad in the dingy, off the island. Captain Jat had four great pistols in his belt, and he had spent the dog-watches in mounting an old duck-gun on its swivel, in the bows of the boat. Pibby, the boy, had also two big heavy pistols tucked into his belt, not to mention his own small weapon which reposed snugly in its canvas pocket inside his trousers. They were quite heavily armed. Moreover, he had seen to it, this time, that the oars were properly muffled.

In addition to those preparations, Captain Jat had been very particular concerning the depositing in the boat of a considerable length of chain, with two stout padlocks in the ends.

Captain Jat took the boat round to the North of the island, and, presently, after pulling cautiously for an hour, he bid the lad ease up and lay on his oar a bit, and keep his eyes well skinned. For his part, the Captain lay down on his stomach on the thwarts, and spied along the surface of the quietly heaving sea, with his night-glass. And suddenly, he reached out and caught Pibby a clip with the glass.

"Down under the gunnel, boy, or they'll see you!" he muttered, and Pibby ducked and slid down under his oar, and stared away breathlessly through the darkness to the Northward.

Now that he had his eyes nearer to the surface of the sea, he discovered the thing that Captain Jat had seen with the night-glass. There was a prodigious string of native boats, within two hundred fathoms of them, paddling through the night to the island. Pibby counted them, and numbered eighty; but probably missed some in the darkness.

Captain Jat allowed these craft to get well inshore; then, taking his oar, he shoved it out through a steering-grommet, which he had fixed up in the stern, and began to scull steadily after them; but allowing nothing more than his hand and his forearm to rise above the gunnel of the boat. As the dingy crept into the wake of those silent craft ahead, the boy noticed suddenly that there had come again above the island the strange loom of light that he had seen the night before.

Presently, the heave of the sea had almost died from under the boat, and it was plain that they had come under the lee of some out-jutting "lie" of rocks. The last of the craft ahead vanished into the shadow of the island; but Captain Jat had marked the place, and followed dead on. A minute later, they saw the shore directly ahead, not a score of fathoms away; but there was no beach; only the dark trees of bushes coming right down, apparently to the water's edge. There was no heave at all now under the boat, so that they had evidently been piloted into a perfectly sheltered cove.

Captain Jat kept the boat going straight ahead. He made no attempt to slacken her way, despite the fact that they seemed to be heading straight ashore into the middle of a heavy underwood. The bows of the dingy reached the dank bushes, where they hung out over the water, and Captain Jat took both hands to his oar, and forced her in among them.

For a few moments the overgrowths seemed to smother the boat, all wet and slimy and rank. Then the boat had passed clean through, into open water beyond. Pibby, the lad, stared in front into the darkness; but could see nothing. He looked upward, and saw a narrow, winding ribbon of night-sky far above them, which told him that Captain Jat had discovered the way into a deep-set tidal passage, the mouth of which was completely masked by the undergrowths and overhanging trees. It was, obviously, a huge crack through the side of the low crater, which the sea had turned into a creek.

Very cautiously, Captain Jat sculled ahead. It was like sculling into a pitch-black night, so black that the far upward ribbon of night-sky seemed almost to shine, by comparison. As they went, little hollow sobbing sounds, of the water in the crannies of the unseen rocky sides, came to them, dankly and somehow drearily. But Captain Jat handled the sculling oar so softly that not once did the clinker-built entry of the boat "mutter" on the water. And this way quite half an hour passed; though it seemed much longer, going utterly slow and silent and cautious in that grim dark, and steering by the winding pattern of the night-sky above, and by the odd vague sense which told the Captain when they were come over near to one side or the other, in the darkness.

Once, as they went so quiet and stealthy, there came to them indefinitely out of the night, a far howling, once and then again; and, later, an attenuated, incredibly shrill screaming, that died away and left the boy frightened and holding the stocks of his heavy pistols. But Captain Jat sculled steadily on.

Abruptly, Captain Jat ceased sculling, and stood silent. It was plain to the lad that he was either listening or staring intently; and the boy peered round, every way, nervously. Suddenly, he saw an indefinite glow of light ahead, evidently beyond a bend in the narrow creek. The glow grew rapidly into a bright light, that danced and flickered, and, in the space of a minute, there came round the bend of the creek, upon the left side, two of those brutish things that had followed the Captain the night before. They were running through the stunted trees and bushes, parallel with the course of the creek, but about twenty feet above the level of the water, winding in and out, as they went, among the trees and great bushes that grew up in the steep lower slope of the creek-side. Their agility was incredible; here and there they leaped like goats from rock to rock, their torches dripping and flaring as they ran, one behind the other.

Captain Jat stood motionless in the stern of the dingy, with his oar in one hand, and one of his pistols in the other. He watched the two beastly creatures run by, and the boy—glancing at him swiftly in his fright—saw that his face was perfectly calm; but the lights from the torches seemed to glow in his eyes, so that they shone, almost like the eyes of a wild animal.

The lad's gaze jumped back to the two running brutes. He could not see their hideous flat faces; for their great manes, all loose and wild, hung over them, damp and black and matted, as if they were fresh come up out of the sea; and indeed there was rank, wet weed, all entangled in their hair; for he saw it glisten in the blaze of the torches. Yet, though he could not see their faces, he saw their arms from their naked shoulders downward. The arms of the foremost woman ended in two monstrous claws; but the boy saw plainly that they were no more than cast-off shells of some huge sea reptile, if I may so describe it. He saw where they ended, rough and rude, just below her elbows, and that her right hand came through a hole between the mandibles of the claw, to hold her great torch.

But the second woman gave him a horrible feeling; he could not see where her arms ended and the claws began. He remembered what the little priestess had told Captain Jat. And even as he stared, frightened and horrified, the two creatures were gone past. He saw then that the foremost one had an ugly great knife, stuck naked into the back of a kind of broad belt; and the belt was all stitched with what at first he took to be big shining beads. Then, he realised that perhaps they were not beads, but pearls, as the Captain had told him. Yet it was less of that possible fortune in pearls that Pibby Tawles, the boy, thought in that tense moment, than of the fact he could not see where the arms of the second woman ended and the claws began.

Then the two running, leaping bestial things were gone away down the creek; and a minute after, they were out of sight round one of the rocky bends, and all was dark again about the boat.

The dinghy began to move ahead once more in the darkness, as Captain Jat took up work again with the sculling-oar. A matter of some ten minutes of silence passed, with the water of the creek making odd gurglings and echoes on either hand among the crannies and holes in the rocks, when Pibby realised that the enormous, steep sides of the creek had joined overhead, and that they were moving forward through the complete blackness of an invisible cavern.

And then, even as he realised the fact uneasily, there showed far ahead a small, bright spot of light. The boat began to sway, and a little murmur broke out under her bows, as Captain Jat increased the speed; but he eased it at once, for the faint noise of the water under her entrance made a strangely loud sound in that silence. But still they moved ahead steadily, and that speck of light grew, until the lad saw that it was an inner mouth to the cavern, and beyond it some bright flaring light.

The boat approached, unseen in the darkness of the cavern, to within a dozen fathoms of this newly discovered entrance, and for the last minute, Pibby had been staring with a fixed and astounded interest at what he saw. The arch of the cave mouth must have been fully thirty feet high, and the width of it a little less. And through this great opening, Pibby was looking into a big circular space, apparently several hundred feet across, the walls of which went up out of his sight into the darkness above.

But what fixed both his and Captain Jat's attention was the centre portion of this extraordinary natural amphitheater; for in the centre was a small lake of sea-water, maybe about sixty feet across, and out of the centre of the lake there rose a weed-hung hump of rock, and from the centre of the hump of rock there rose a great pole, maybe fifty feet in height, black through all its length, and polished so highly that it reflected brilliantly the light of six enormous torches that burned on the tops of six great piles that stood up out of the rock all round the central pool or lake. And this pole, from its grotesquely carved head, flat-faced and repulsive, to its base, where it had been cut into the shape of a bunch of huge claws, was banded every few feet with strings of countless beads, that glimmered in a semi-luminous fashion in the flare of the torch-lights. *And every bead was a pearl.*

The water from the cavern in which the dingy floated, ran in a perfectly straight channel into the central pool or lake, and the weeded floor of the ancient crater rose a foot or so on each side, spreading away then in one level, brown, weed-covered reach to the great walls of the inside of the low mountain.

The torches showed that the bottom parts of the mountain walls were all grown with weed, to a height of about six feet above the bottom of the crater, so that it was plain that the sea, entering through the creek and the cavern, rose at high tide to at least that height, in which case there would be only the six great torches and the lofty polished black pole in the centre, with its profusion of strings of pearls, visible when the tide was up, It must have been a strange sight then, even stranger than when Captain Jat and Pibby looked out from the cavern.

And now, but not very distinctly in that light, Pibby saw where all that great line of boats had gone to; for there, so far as he could see all around the bottom of the great natural amphitheatre, were the boats, where they had been drawn up, head to stern upon the weed, and scarcely seen above the weed, out of which they rose only a little, except for their lofty head and stern timbers, which, however, had been so draped with weed as to blend with the weed-grown walls behind.

Over the sides of all these boats, and there were vastly more than the flotilla that they had followed in (for they lay side by side, apparently three or four deep), Captain Jat and the lad saw the heads of hundreds and hundreds of natives; but all vague and indistinct; both because of the uncertain flarings of the great torches, and because each native had dressed her head with a mass of weed. Indeed, it would have been easy to have entered the crater under the impression that there was no more life in it than the blaze of the huge torches.

As Pibby strained his eyes to make out the boats, wondering

whether it had been hard to drag them up out of the creek and across the weed, he felt the dingy beginning to move silently back into the cavern; and, turning, he saw that Captain Jat was using his oar noiselessly, as an Indian uses his paddle, and so fetching the boat gently astern.

In this way they progressed for about a hundred yards, and then Captain Jat set the dingy in to the side, and began to grope along. Presently, he gave out a little grunt of satisfaction, and pushed the boat across to the other side; but was evidently unable to find what he wanted; for he continued to punt the boat astern with his hands, until the great opening of the cave appeared no more than a distant speck of light. Then he grunted again, and immediately sent the boat across once more to the other side. A minute later, he gave out a further note of satisfaction, and suddenly Pibby heard his voice muttering to him to pass up one end of the chain, and one of the padlocks.

He heard the Captain fumbling for a time, and the odd, slight chinking of the chain; then the dinghy was thrust out again, and Captain Jat was bidding him pay out the chain gently without a sound, whilst he paddled the boat once more across. They reached the other side; and Pibby grasped his master's idea, which was obviously to put a chain boom across, slickly, so that if they had to retreat in a hurry, they would pass over it; then tauten it up, and padlock it in position, and so get away easily, whilst all of the boats of the pursuers ran foul of the boom.

The boy ran his hands in along the chain, where the Captain was working, and found that he was "anchoring" it round a huge boulder. Pibby had no doubt but that the other end was quite as efficiently secured, and he began to feel comfortable again in his mind; it was such an efficient retreat. Then, as he sat in the darkness, he fell to wondering just what those natives were waiting for, all hid with weed like they were . . . and the great torches . . . and the huge, carved and polished pole with the fortune of splendid pearls strung around it.

And then, as he worried the thought over nervously in his mind, he thrilled suddenly; for Captain Jat was once more sculling the boat ahead towards the brightly shining arch of the cavern's entrance into the arena.

Abruptly, as the boat forged ahead, there came a queer swirl deep down in the dark water, somewhere astern of the boat, that sent little waves into the sides of the gloomy cavern, breaking in the darkness with a multitudinous chattering of liquid sounds. Something huge passed under the boat, which was now approaching the entrance at a fair speed. They felt the great thing pass under them, deep below the surface, but drawing after it a wave that humped the boat up, stern first, and then the bows.

"My God!" said Captain Jat huskily, aloud . . . "The UD!" His voice came back, husky and dreadful, from a thousand places in the darkness:—"My God! . . . The Ud! My God! . . . The Ud!" And in the same moment, Pibby felt the dingy begin to sway heavily, and heard Captain Jat gasp as he began sculling with a kind of mad violence, whispering:—"The Little Priestess! The Little Priestess! My God! They saw her waving! My . . ."

Pibby never heard any more; for they had come sufficiently near the arch now for him to be able to see again into the crater with some clearness. He stared in complete and dreadful amazement; for though the whole of the great amphitheatre was as silent as when they left it, there was now a little, naked brown woman, lashed by her neck, her waist and her ankles to the great, pearl-stringed central pole that came up out of the hump of rock in the pool. She had been brought there and made fast during the time in which they had been fixing up the chain boom. That was why the weed-hidden boats waited . . . She was the sacrifice . . . The thing that had passed under the boat . . . ! She had been seen waving to the Captain . . . She . . .

The chaos of his thoughts stilled abruptly into a fearful attention. He bent forward from the forthwart, and stared, almost petrified. Something was coming up out of the water, climbing up onto the hump of rock . . . Enormous legs were coming up out of the pool, scrambling at the rock, slipping, slipping, and tearing away great chunks of the weed, and finally effecting a hold. A moment afterwards, a thing like a vast, brown, shell-encrusted dish-cover, as big as an ordinary old-fashioned oval mahogany table, began to rise up out of the pool.

The boy shook as he stared; he did not know that such things existed . . . A crab . . . ! That was no word for it. It was a monster, capable of destroying an elephant . . . He remembered the great thing that had slipped and slithered among the big rocks at the in-shore end of the reef. The thing was rising higher and higher. Nothing could save the woman . . . nothing on earth! They had better get away at once, before it discovered them. The thing was reaching out three of its great, pincer-armed legs towards the little brown woman, who began now to scream in a peculiar, breathless voice. Then Pibby was suddenly caught by the shoulder from behind, and Captain Jat dashed him aft into the stern-sheets of the dingy, out of his way. As he fell, he saw Captain Jat against the light; he had the great duck-gun in his hands. Pibby remembered that it was loaded with the thick end of a broken marlin-spike. There was a rip of fire that coincided with the flashes of light he saw as his head met the stern-thwart; there was a crashing thump of sound that added to the muddle of his fall, and Captain Jat pitched bodily backward onto the top of him, literally felled by the recoil of the big weapon. The boy screamed, and everything went grey for a moment; then Captain Jat rolled free of him, and in the same moment there was a vast thrashing of water, and the boat was cast up a yard into the air by a wave that came travelling down the cavern from the crater. The dingy slewed half round, rolled heavily and shipped several gallons; then steadied.

Pibby staggered to his feet, shaken and sick. He stared towards the pool; the water appeared to be boiling all about the hump of rock; but there was no sign of the thing that had come out of the water. The boiling motion of the water began to ease, and Pibby saw that the little brown woman sagged in her lashings against the carved black pole; but there was no mark on her to show that she had been hurt; she had become unconscious.

The next thing he knew, he had an oar his hand, and Captain Jat had another, and they were out of the great cavern, and pulling madly up the channel that cut across the floor of the crater to the pool. He noticed, with a curious inconsequence, that he could now see trees far up at the top of the walls of the crater, shaking a little in the night-wind against the stars.

The boat bumped into the masses of weed about the hump of rock, and Captain Jat gave one great spring upward, and was onto the rock, having used his oar against the bottom-boards, as a kind of vaulting-pole. His effort forced the boat away; but Pibby grabbed the boat-hook, jabbed it into a mass of the weed, and pulled her back. He saw Captain Jat sawing savagely at the lashings; and was conscious for the first time that the crater was full of wild yelling. He saw his Master pluck the little brown woman loose, and the next moment she was hove down into the boat with a crash. He did not look at her, but at Captain Jat . . . Captain Jat was reaching up, slashing at the lowest string of great pearls. The string gave, and the pearls went spraying and bounding all over the hump of rock, into the water; but Captain Jat had secured a handful.

A spear struck the polished pole, chipping it, and flew off to the side, passing through Captain Jat's sleeve. The boy glanced once now round at the arena, and saw, suddenly, that there were literally hundreds and hundreds of natives, scrambling and slipping and leaping over the weed-covered floor towards them. He saw also another thing; two of the horrible, claw-armed women were slashing at a native with their great knives; it may have been the man who had thrown the spear and chipped the post . . . The post was obviously an incredibly sacred thing.

He heard his own voice shouting strangely to Captain Jat to come; but that indomitable length of man had swarmed a fathom up the polished pole, and was cutting loose another string of pearls. There came a shower of them bounding onto the rock, and into the weed and water; but again Captain Jat had secured a share. He gave one leap to the rock, and another into the boat; then, stern-foremost, they rowed grimly for the opening into the cavern.

One of the savages, a huge fat man, had outdistanced the others, in spite of his fat. Perhaps his fat accounted for it; for he had come across the slippery weed, creeping on hands and feet, and had therefore lost no time in falling. He rose up at the edge of the channel; but as he made to spring at the boat, he slipped and fell squelching on his back, and Captain Jat pistolled him calmly as he lay.

Yet, now the danger was appalling; for scores of the natives were getting near, and a shower of spears came over the boat, four of them striking her starboard quarter, and making it look literally rather like a gigantic pin-cushion; but no one was hurt; though the Captain's clothing was cut in two places. They replied with their heavy pistols, and left a dozen of the natives dead, and so managed to ram the dinghy stern first into the cavern.

Captain Jat put the boat round, as soon as they were well out of sight, and they both settled down to pull. Yet when they had gone about a hundred fathoms they heard a splash, and saw that one of the smaller native boats had already been hauled across the weed, and was now in the water of the channel. They knew that in another few minutes there would be scores of boats after them.

Half a minute later, Pibby's oar stubbed against the slack chain of the boom, and they in oars, and hauled the boat along to the side of the cavern, being now on the seaward side of the boom. Captain Jat worked desperately, and Pibby lighted the chain up to him, so as to get it as taut as possible; yet it took time; for they were in utter darkness; but the chain must be taut, if it were to act as a boom; otherwise the natives would manage either to shove their boats under or over it.

And all the time, as they worked, boats were entering the mouth of the great cavern, with torches held high over their bows to show them the way; while the boat that had been first launched into the creek was now scarcely a hundred and fifty feet away; and still Captain Jat growled to Pibby to "Light up the slack! Light up the slack!"

The small boat came on steadily, until she was not more than seventy or eighty feet away, and suddenly a great shout told Captain Jat and the boy that the light of the distant torches must have picked them out in the blackness. Immediately afterwards, all around them in the water there was *plunk, plunk,* the noise of thrown spears. There came a sharp, chinking sound, as a single spear struck the rocky side. It glanced, gashed along the Captain's face, and took away a part of his ear. He swore grimly, and gave one more pull on the chain; then closed the big padlock and locked it with a swift deliberation.

Immediately afterwards, he fetched a spare pistol out of his side pocket, and loosed off into the approaching boat, with such a good aim that one of his bullets punched a hole in two of the men, who happened to be in a line. Then, dropping his pistol into the bottom of the boat, he sprang to his oar, and a minute later they were away round the bend, bumping heavily in the darkness against the rocky side of the cavern, and listening to the fierce outcry that came echoing along the cavern, as the boom opposed all progress for the time being.

"Done 'em, boy!" said Captain Jat. "Now pull easy! We don't want the boat stove. Back water when I sings out." And therewith the two settled down to work at the oars

Some forty minutes later, they passed through the screen of overhanging bushes and trees that marked the mouth of the creek, and were presently out into the wholesome sweetness of the sea, with the island no more than a shape of darkness astern. Yet, when they came to look for the little brown woman, she had gone. It was evident that she had come-to, and slipped overboard in the darkness, preferring, it appears, to face any risk that the island might contain for her, than to face the facing of the unknown.

"The ship, boy! Pull!" said Captain Jat, a little while afterwards. And indeed, the ship it was; and soon they were safely aboard, steering northward, away from the island, for good this time.

Down in his cabin, with the door safely closed, yet not without more than one suspicious glance towards it, Captain Jat was presently conning over, and exhibiting to Pibby, his spoils. On the table was a jug of very special toddy, and Captain Jat was investigating it with the aid of his big pewter mug. Pibby also, it must be confessed, had adopted a fairish-sized drinking cup for the same purpose; for Captain Jat allowed him only the one, and no more.

It may be that the unusual richness of the toddy developed a latent generosity in the lean Captain; for after a lot of fingering and weighing and examining, he presented Pibby, as his share, one of the smallest of the pearls, which had been somewhat badly chipped.

Pibby Tawles, cabin-boy-deck-hand, call him what you will, took the little, damaged pearl with sufficient evidence of gratitude. He could afford to; for inside his shirt there reposed a number of pearls as fine as any that Captain Jat had brought away with him. The boy had picked them off the bottom-boards of the dingy, where they had fallen when his master cut the strings of pearls about the Sacred Pole.

In short, we may conclude, I think, that whatever else he might be, Pibby Tawles was one who had a very sound eye to the main chance; a conclusion which a further adventure of Captain Jat's has rather impressed upon me.

A Single Samurai

INTRODUCTION

It would be a grave injustice if this book contained no stories set in Japan, home turf of Godzilla/Gojira and other giant monsters, or *kaiju*, to use the Japanese word applied to such formidable creatures. Fortunately, two such are on board, and here's the first, complete with a brave samurai undertaking the impossible task of stopping a monster as big as a mountain.

❖ ❖ ❖

Steven Diamond runs Elitist Book Reviews, which was nominated in 2013 and 2014 for the the Hugo Award. He has several pieces of short fiction published for numerous small publications, and currently writes for Skull Island expeditions, the fiction imprint for Privateer Press' Warmachine/Hordes tabletop/RPG game. He is also currently editing a horror anthology titled *Shared Nightmares*. Steve lives in Utah with his wife and two children, and he is a die-hard fan of the Oakland A's, and New Orleans Saints.

A Single Samurai

by Steven Diamond

My father taught me that the decisions you make are nothing more than the product of who you are. In a way, you could say that the future is all predetermined. Fated. You just have to decide, right from the very beginning, who you are and how far you are willing to go to do what is right. Any early doubts will cause your failure in the end.

So who am I?

Samurai.

It is no easy task to watch your entire land destroyed. Whether real or imagined, I suppose it makes no difference that I can still hear the screams coming from the throats of thousands as they died. I could do nothing at the time. No, I suppose that is untrue. I could have hid my eyes. Covered my ears. But how would my ancestors have regarded me then?

No, I watched. I listened. I took in every death. Every scream of terror and pain.

How did I escape the devastation, you wonder? I could comment that, in a way, I didn't. That I was right there in the thick of it, and that I am still experiencing it. But I don't think that is the answer being requested of me.

The truth of the matter is that I escaped my certain death by *riding*

297

on the creature—the *kaiju*—that was in fact the instrument of the destruction and chaos left behind me.

It is hard to describe a monster the size of the one I currently ride. It is a mountain. Massive. Unyielding. Indestructible. Imagine if the mountain nearest you suddenly began moving. Imagine if, one day, it slowly began unfolding itself like a bear emerging from hibernation. What is a village to a mountain? More, what is a *person* to a mountain?

Nothing.

This is not the first time *kaiju* have been stirred from the depths of their slumber into our world. My ancestors fought them, though those monsters were nothing compared to the one upon which I traveled. To compare myself to a flea on a dog would not do justice to the scale of the monstrosity. It had no definitive form that I could identify. It was simply too big, and my view too limited.

All I know is the *kaiju* utterly obliterates anything that crosses its path. Armies have tried to stop it with cannon. Other samurai have tried with blades. Nothing causes even the most subtle of reaction from the beast.

Yet here I am, riding the *kaiju*. It heads south, where in a matter of weeks, if not days, it will reduce my entire country into little more than rubble. I have one goal. Climb the *kaiju*, and kill it. How does one kill a mountain?

Somehow.

What is a true samurai without a *daisho*? There are many myths and legends surrounding a samurai and the two blades he carries. Wearing a *daisho* not only marks a samurai for all to see, but it innately conjures the whispers of heroic deeds, demonic opponents, and traditional duels.

In public, in the rare event that a samurai is asked the question, a samurai will brush aside the myth. We don't brag. We don't boast. It accomplishes nothing to let the common masses know what we truly protect them from. We kill the demons before they can do untold levels of harm, and then we tell the people that nothing untoward has happened. We keep the darkness at bay while most people struggle to even understand that there *is* an encroaching darkness.

The katana and wakizashi—or whichever desired combination of blades the samurai chooses to wear—are sacred weapons. They are more than just status symbols. They are physical representations of what we should all be spiritually. There are some blades that are passed from father to son, but these are a different sort of katana. They have not been forged in the old way. The secret way.

My katana and its matching short sword are different than those weapons wielded by regular samurai. Like myself, with their appearance, they don't brag. They don't boast. The scabbards for both are simple and lacquered black. The hilts are wood wrapped in gray sharkskin. The blades stone-polished.

It is not the look of them that makes the blades special. Again, it is *how* the blade is made. It is what is inside the blade that makes it different. When blades are forged in the old way, that forging is done literally with a piece of the samurai's soul inside. How it is done is a mystery even unto the samurai and a secret kept by the monks who forge our blades. A unique bond is formed between the samurai and his weapons. Should the blade break—which is rare in the extreme— a samurai's soul breaks with it, and dies. Likewise—and far more common—when a samurai dies, his sword crumbles to dust.

What is a true samurai without a *daisho*?

Soulless.

I was not truly expecting the carnage I stumbled upon. It could be argued that it was luck that led me to the clearing in which I now stood. I would not be the one to argue that point, for I do not believe in luck. I believe in my ancestors and the guidance they give me should I be worthy to hear it.

As the *kaiju* moved, crushing everything in its path, it began shedding the stone and foliage that covered it. Up the great beast I traveled, along a faint animal trail with the monster's back my goal. How long must this *kaiju* have rested in its one place for it to have grown trees? To have these animal paths crossing its surface? And not just the evidence of their passing, but those creatures themselves with their homes? More than once I saw the passing deer, or heard the distant growling of predators.

Every step the *kaiju* took shook loose the debris—some of my *country*—that clung to it. Great rockslides cascaded down the monster's sides. Trees three times my age would rip free from where they had rooted and tumble away. More than once I sought shelter in small caves to wait out the upheaval surrounding me.

It was after waiting out a particularly violent series of earthquakes upon the *kaiju*—likely nothing more than a sequence of quick steps from the abomination that resounded upwards—that I found the path I had been following completely gone. It had been swept away, and there was no clear route for me to follow to reach the top of the monster. I backtracked for the better part of a day until I found another, steeper path that I never recalled previously passing. Climbing it took the remander of that day, and that was when I found myself in a clearing of sorts as the sun was falling.

The first thing I noticed was the coppery smell of blood.

It assaulted my nose, and I could tell without seeing it that the quantity of spilt blood was enormous. I could tell that it was human blood.

I drew my katana.

In the center of the small clearing I quietly turned in a slow circle, taking in the picture. The clearing was more of a hollow set between large rocks. The trees were sparse, and I began picking out smallish pools of darkness that I realized were caves. In the middle of the clearing were the scattered remains of a small contingent of soldiers.

It was impossible to tell just how many had been here. Heads lay like discarded and rotting fruits that the peasants had neglected to harvest. Arms and legs lay strewn about the clearing, and I soon saw even more hanging in the few trees surround me. Blood arced and streaked everywhere. I picked a point of reference and turned again in a slow circle, this time counting legs I could see. When I arrived back at my starting point, I had counted twenty-five legs. At least thirteen soldiers had died here. I saw signs of gunfire, but nothing that suggested what the men had been firing at.

Samurai have a sense of when events have turned perilous. A shift in the breeze. A sudden stillness. An icy chill that slips insidiously into the heart. There was something here. Watching me.

I do not claim to never be afraid. That is foolishness. My father taught me that lesson when I was very young. He taught me that fear is a tool; perhaps even the most valuable tool a samurai can have. When controlled, that fear can serve as an extra sense of protection. But it does not rule me. I rule it.

I pivoted to my left and carved upward with my blade before I even had time to register the nearness of the danger. My katana bit deep into . . . something. I used my momentum to pull the blade clear and felt the spray of liquid—blood?—cover me. I did not pause to look at the thing I had, hopefully, killed. As I spun back to my unguarded flank, I caught the briefest glimpse of a vaguely cat-shaped animal bounding toward me.

Diving to the left, I rolled and came back to my feet with my katana held at the ready. The thing was the size of a mountain cat, only it looked to have rocks covering its back for protection. I had never seen a monster like this, nor heard of the like. As the creature and I circled, I wondered if the appearance of these small creatures had anything to do with the sudden awakening of the *kaiju*.

I feinted a strike at the thing, then pulled back, looking for a weakness. I now saw four eyes, vertically slit, that gleamed in the waning light. Claws retracted into the thing's paws. It did not make any further move to attack me. Almost as if it were waiting—

I threw myself to the side and felt claws rake my left shoulder from behind.

Pain is nothing. It is simply a feeling, like hunger, or worry. It can be tolerated and banished with proper discipline. There are demons that live off that pain, that thrive off their victims succumbing to it. So I feel no pain. I do not just ignore it, for that implies a recognition that it was there to begin with.

Two more of the cat-things had emerged from their caves, making four that faced me. They moved to surround me, sniffing the air, and likely smelling my blood. But not my fear.

One leapt at me, and I drew my wakizashi and buried it in the thing's neck. Its momentum wrenched the short blade from my grasp. I took three running steps at the nearest of the other three cat-things and swung low with my katana, cutting off the two legs on its right side. It bellowed in pain, a sound somewhere between a wolf's howl and a cat's shriek.

I turned, keeping the thrashing beast between me and the other two. I reached out and tapped my blade on the wounded monster's rocky hide. It clinked like it would against stone. I needed to send the creatures a message. I needed them to understand that they were not the predator here. I was.

I stepped quickly around to where I had easy access to the cat-thing's unprotected belly, and drove my blade into it. I did not make the cut quick. I slowly dragged my blade, gutting the monster. I felt the connection between the monster and myself. I felt it as the bit of my soul in the blade eradicated the soul in the creature. I had only felt this a few times before, and only when necessity had forced me to kill an oni slowly. Through my katana, I felt the creature die.

When I withdrew my blade, the other two creatures were gone. I had not seen them flee, but I knew they would not trouble me further. I retrieved my wakizashi, cleaned my blades on a strip of cloth from my robes, and continued through the clearing and up toward the spine of the *kaiju*.

If it was not luck that saw me through my encounter with the cat-things, what was it? To me the answer was simple.

Guidance.

I was barely fifteen when my father committed ritual *hara-kiri*. Had he given offense to some lord? Had he given offense to some lord's wife? No. My father was the most honorable of all men. At least, that is how I remember him. And is not that what truly matters?

"Son," he said that morning. "I must do something that you will find hard to understand today."

I was very confused, and said, "What do you mean, father?"

"Today, my son, is the day I must task you with watching over the family."

"Where are you going?" I was still confused, but looking back on that day, my father did not regard me with a look of indignation or impatience at my questions.

"I go to join our ancestors."

"Why?"

"Because sometimes sacrifices are needed to protect those we love."

A few hours later, I served as my father's second. The katana I held then was not the one I hold now, but I remember that blade in every detail. From the way the grip was ever so slightly uneven beneath my grip. How the sun reflected off the polished blade. There was the smallest of nicks near the end of the blade's edge. I never was able to learn how that had come to be there.

In front of our local magistrate, my father shrugged off the top of his robe and let it fall to the ground. He slipped his wakizashi from the scabbard, reversed his grip on the blade, and settled the point against his flesh.

I glanced at the magistrate and saw the sadness that filled his eyes.

My father had not been the one to cause offense. My father's lord had been the one to do that. But even with his faults, our lord was the best person to lead. The best person to see our people through difficult times. My father knew this.

So he offered to cleanse his lord's honor with his own life.

I lifted the katana, poised to end my father's suffering.

My father took one calming breath, and plunged the blade into his flesh. I could hear the wet tearing and cutting as he gutted himself. Just the sound of it was nearly too much for me. I remember blackness encroaching at the edge of my vision. My hands shook.

My father looked up over his left shoulder at me, pain and sweat streaking his face. He managed a small smile.

"Learn from me," he said, his voice a bloody whisper. Then nodded his head once.

My vision cleared. My nerves calmed. I lifted the katana high, then brought it down and gave my father the one thing he deserved and had earned with his sacrifice.

Peace.

I could see beauty for leagues upon leagues.

In front of me, and in the path of the *kaiju*, the landscape of my country unfolded like the secrets of an origami crane. I could pick out dozens of individual villages, and several walled fortresses. The land was green and full of life. I took in a deep breath of crisp air, savoring the sharpness of it. For a moment, I let myself become lost in the beauty.

I exhaled. Turned.

Behind me lay destruction for leagues upon leagues.

Had there ever been life in this beast's wake? Had I not personally traveled these lands in the past, I would not have believed it. There was no green in the path of violence the creature had wrought. What was left was inhospitable wasteland. It was not unlike when a nervous horse paws at the ground, gouging it. Only this was on the magnitude of a mountain. Gouges the size of lakes. Great rents in the earth that I doubted would ever heal.

If there had been villages in that devastation, they no longer existed. As high as I was, it was impossible to actually see if anything had survived. But I did not need to see to know. Nothing lived. Nothing would have survived the *kaiju*'s passage.

I turned again to the front and looked at the beauty of my country. If I did not stop the *kaiju*, it would all be gone. All of it. Every village, town, pasture, samurai, woman, peasant, and child. They would not just die or be destroyed. After the *kaiju* passed, it would be like they never existed, and their futures would be murdered as surely as if they too had been caught in the path of the monster.

I resumed my journey.

I had been climbing this monster for days, and with each of those passing days, more of the creature was revealed. It sloughed off rock and vegetation like a snake discards old skin. I could discern a tail, and the head would wave from side to side. There was something distinctly reptilian about its head and the way its eyes seemed to regard the world which it annihilated.

The *kaiju* moved forward, unabated.

I had little time if I was to stop it from crushing the rest of my country.

My path was virtually unobstructed now, and I was able to keep at a run for hours. The head of the monster grew steadily larger in my view. There was a clarity within my mind as I ran, and I pondered how I could kill the beast.

I had hoped that my ancestors would have given me a sign by now, but they had been silent thus far. Perhaps it was not time yet for them to give me direction. Or perhaps they had no direction to give. Could it be that my ancestors were as overwhelmed as I was? What if they did not know how to kill this monster, and I was running to my death?

Well, that is the purpose of samurai, is it not? To make the sacrifices—regardless of how difficult or contrary to what logic declares—that no one else will make.

I ran on.

The catlike creatures followed me at a considerable distance. Did they know my intentions? If they did, they made no move to attack me. They only stalked, no doubt waiting for me to do something careless. Why bother attacking me if I would do them the favor of dying on my own?

Crossing the neck of the *kaiju* was treacherous, but of no great challenge. The biggest worry was not the shifting terrain, but what lay ahead. I could see major landholdings. From this unfamiliar vantage it was hard to say whose land the monster approached, but I knew what would happen once the *kaiju* reached it. Everyone living there would be crushed and buried. I could almost hear the terrified wails of the children as I imagined the ground being broken and churned under the beast's passing.

Ahead, after crossing the neck, I spotted a cave.

It was below me, with no clear path to it. A look ahead showed me how much closer the beast was to the city. The city would be crushed within an hour. The ground—I still thought of it as ground even though this was the *kaiju*'s head—shifting beneath my feet, I began climbing down. Rock crumbled beneath my left hand, and suddenly I was falling. My knee struck an outcropping, and I felt the wet snap of my leg breaking. I would have screamed in pain, but the impact of my back against the floor of the cave stole my breath.

I rested there for several minutes, fighting for breath and trying to cope with the pain I felt in my back and leg. I hesitantly moved my back, and while sore, it had not been broken in the fall. My leg was another matter entirely. When I managed to sit up partially to look at myself, I noticed my leg bent sharply away from me at an angle impossible in nature.

There would be no more walking for me.

I turned myself so my back was facing the inside of the cave and began dragging myself farther in. The floor of the cavern was smooth, keeping the jostling of my wounded leg to a minimum. Soon the cave began to change. The ground gave beneath me slightly more, and a faint green light steadily grew more and more pronounced as I moved into the cave's depths.

I blacked out for an unknown amount of time. The ground pitched beneath me and I tumbled, striking my wounded leg. The pain was the worst I had ever felt previously. It was a pain that, even as a samurai, I was unable to ignore. When I regained consciousness, I was in a glowing green room, giant and smooth along every visible wall. The space was not hollow, but at its center was a massive, green, pulsing clump of flesh. From it, hundreds of darker green, stringy, muscle lines connected the flesh to the walls of the cavern.

I have killed thousands of monsters in my life. Oni. Undead. Gaki. Other demons. It did not take me long to realize I was in the *kaiju*'s head and that the pulsing bit of flesh the size of a house was the monster's brain. I could hack at it for days, and while the monster would be hurt, it would still crush everything that stood in its path. Cutting the muscle fibers holding the brain suspended could also work, but it too would take too much time.

It took most of my remaining strength, but I pulled myself until I was right next to the brain. I closed my eyes and begged for my ancestors' guidance. Nothing. I opened my eyes and gritted my teeth to keep from yelling in frustration. Why had I come all this way if I was to fail? The journey had nearly killed me, but here I was with no clear way to quickly kill the beast.

The journey.

The thought floated into my mind like a gentle breeze. My father taught me that who I am is nothing more than the product of where I have been and the decisions I have made. What is that if not a journey?

Who am I?

Samurai.

In a single motion, I drew my katana and plunged it into the brain of the *kaiju*.

I doubt it even felt what I did. But I could feel it. First in just a trickle, and soon in a torrent. Just like in the past when I had killed oni, and earlier when killing the catlike creatures, I felt a connection to the *kaiju* through my katana. The bit of my soul forged into my sword connected to the soul of the monster. I felt every animalistic desire, and I saw through its eyes.

Ahead was the city.

Fleeing humans, not even like ants.

No anger. No desire to kill.

Ambivalence.

Apathy.

The *kaiju* did not care.

It did not even notice the world it destroyed.

The flood of thought and emotion coursed through me, burying me. It was like an avalanche, and I had no way of surviving it. I tried to push the thoughts away. I tried to pull the blade from the *kaiju*'s brain. It was impossible.

Learn from me.

I felt tears fill my eyes at the sound of my father's voice. It was as if he were right next to me, whispering in my ear. It had been so long since a boy had heard his father's words.

Learn from me.

Smiling, I drew the wakizashi with my left hand. I truly was a product of all my past choices.

I barely felt the blade of my wakizashi as I stabbed myself. But I felt the shock and pain of the *kaiju*. It knew something was wrong, and it ground to a halt. As my right hand still grasped the hilt of my katana—blade buried in the monster's brain—my left hand pulled the wakizashi across in one, fluid motion. I felt my insides tearing and parting. Blood poured over my hand and pooled in my lap.

I pulled the blade out, and stabbed myself again.

The *kaiju* bellowed, and the resonance of it burst my eardrums. I cut across my middle again, and then my left hand ceased to work. My wakizashi was still sunk into my flesh, but my grip slipped from it. As this happened I also felt the *kaiju* collapse. Confusion surged through it.

Blood still leaked from me, spreading in a pool around me. I had mere moments left, but I knew that when I died, the connection of my life to the *kaiju*'s would remain. When I died, it would die. My ancestors would be proud. I smiled again, and felt myself slipping away.

Today, a single samurai killed a mountain.

Planet of Dread

INTRODUCTION

Here's another case where I suspect that the story was written around a pre-existing cover painting, in this case the cover of *Fantastic*, May 1962, showing a spaceship and men in space suits trapped in a gigantic web while an appropriately-sized spider is attacking them. Hugo-winner Murray Leinster (1896-1975) was a natural for the story, having written two classic novellas in the 1930s set in a far-future world where insects and spiders have grown to a huge size and humans have descended back to the stone age level. He later wrote a third novella, changing the location to another planet where a terraforming operation had gone terribly wrong, then published all three as a novel, *The Forgotten Planet* (included in the Baen e-book *Planets of Adventure*). In "Planet of Dread," a crippled spaceship lands on a planet of giant creepy-crawlers. Repairing the ship to escape seems hopeless, but never underestimate the ingenuity of a Leinster hero, even one who's apparently a criminal.

❊ ❊ ❊

William F. Jenkins (1986-1975) was a prolific and successful writer, selling stories to magazines of all sorts, from pulps like *Argosy* to the higher-paying slicks such as *Collier's* and *The Saturday Evening Post*, writing stories ranging from westerns, to mysteries, to science fiction. However, for SF he usually used the pen name of Murray Leinster, and he used it often. Even though SF was a less lucrative field than other categories of fiction, he enjoyed writing it (fortunately for SF readers everywhere) and wrote a great deal of it, including such classics as "Sidewise in Time," "First Contact," and "A Logic Named Joe," the last being a story you should keep in mind the next time someone repeats the canard that SF never predicted the home computer or the internet. Leinster did it (though under his real name, this time) in *Astounding Science-Fiction* in 1946! His first SF story was "The Runaway Skyscraper," published in 1919, and his last was the third of three novelizations of the *Land of the Giants* TV show in 1969. For the length of his career, his prolificity, and his introduction of original concepts into SF, fans in the 1940s began calling him the Dean of Science Fiction, a title he richly deserved.

Planet of Dread

by Murray Leinster

❊ I ❊

Moran, naturally, did not mean to help in the carrying out of the plans which would mean his destruction one way or another. The plans were thrashed out very painstakingly, in formal conference on the space-yacht *Nadine*, with Moran present and allowed to take part in the discussion. From the viewpoint of the *Nadine*'s ship's company, it was simply necessary to get rid of Moran. In their predicament he might have come to the same conclusion; but he was not at all enthusiastic about their decision. He would die of it.

The *Nadine* was out of overdrive and all the uncountable suns of the galaxy shone steadily, remotely, as infinitesimal specks of light of every color of the rainbow. Two hours since, the sun of this solar system had been a vast glaring disk off to port, with streamers and prominences erupting about its edges. Now it lay astern, and Moran could see the planet that had been chosen for his marooning. It was a cloudy world. There were some dim markings near one lighted limb, but nowhere else. There was an ice-cap in view. The rest was—clouds.

The ice-cap, by its existence and circular shape, proved that the planet rotated at a not unreasonable rate. The fact that it was water-ice told much. A water-ice ice-cap said that there were no poisonous gases in the planet's atmosphere. Sulfur dioxide or chlorine, for example, would not allow the formation of water-ice. It would have to be sulphuric-acid or hydrochloric-acid ice. But the ice-cap was simple snow. Its size, too, told about temperature-distribution on the planet. A large cap would have meant a large area with arctic and sub-arctic temperature, with small temperate and tropical climate-belts. A small one like this meant wide tropical and sub-tropical zones. The fact was verified by the thick, dense cloud-masses which covered most of the surface—all the surface, in fact, outside the ice-cap. But since there were ice-caps there would be temperate regions. In short, the ice-cap proved that a man could endure the air and temperature conditions he would find.

Moran observed these things from the control-room of the *Nadine,* then approaching the world on planetary drive. He was to be left here, with no reason ever to expect rescue. Two of the *Nadine's* four-man crew watched out the same ports as the planet seemed to approach. Burleigh said encouragingly;

"It doesn't look too bad, Moran!"

Moran disagreed, but he did not answer. He cocked an ear instead. He heard something. It was a thin, wabbling, keening whine. No natural radiation sounds like that. Moran nodded toward the all-band speaker.

"Do you hear what I do?" he asked sardonically.

Burleigh listened. A distinctly artificial signal came out of the speaker. It wasn't a voice-signal. It wasn't an identification beacon, such as are placed on certain worlds for the convenience of interstellar skippers who need to check their courses on extremely long runs. This was something else.

Burleigh said;

"Hm . . . Call the others, Harper."

Harper, prudently with him in the control-room, put his head into the passage leading away. He called. But Moran observed with grudging respect that he didn't give him a chance to do anything drastic. These people on the *Nadine* were capable. They'd managed to recapture the *Nadine* from him, but they were matter-of-fact about it. They didn't seem to resent what he'd tried to do, or that he'd brought them an indefinite distance in an indefinite direction from their last landing-point, and they had still to relocate themselves.

They'd been on Coryus Three and they'd gotten departure clearance from its space-port. With clearance-papers in order, they could land unquestioned at any other space-port and take off again—provided the other spaceport was one they had clearance for. Without rigid control of space-travel, any criminal anywhere could escape the consequences of any crime simply by buying a ticket to another world. Moran couldn't have bought a ticket, but he'd tried to get off the planet Coryus on the *Nadine*. The trouble was that the *Nadine* had clearance papers covering five persons aboard—four men and a girl Carol. Moran made six. Wherever the yacht landed, such a disparity between its documents and its crew would spark an investigation. A lengthy, incredibly minute investigation. Moran, at least, would be picked out as a fugitive from Coryus Three. The others were fugitives too, from some unnamed world Moran did not know. They might be sent back where they came from. In effect, with six people on board instead of five, the *Nadine* could not land anywhere for supplies. With five on board, as her papers declared, she could. And Moran was the extra man whose presence would rouse space-port officials' suspicion of the rest. So he had to be dumped.

He couldn't blame them. He'd made another difficulty, too. Blaster in hand, he'd made the *Nadine* take off from Coryus III with a trip-tape picked at random for guidance. But the trip-tape had been computed for another starting-point, and when the yacht came out of overdrive it was because the drive had been dismantled in the engine-room. So the ship's location was in doubt. It could have travelled at almost any speed in practically any direction for a length of time that was at least indefinite. A liner could re-locate itself without trouble. It had elaborate observational equipment and tri-di star-charts. But smaller craft had to depend on the Galactic Directory.

The process would be to find a planet and check its climate and relationship to other planets, and its flora and fauna against descriptions in the Directory. That was the way to find out where one was, when one's position became doubtful. The *Nadine* needed to make a planet-fall for this.

The rest of the ship's company came into the control-room. Burleigh waved his hand at the speaker.

"Listen!"

They heard it. All of them. It was a trilling, whining sound among the innumerable random noises to be heard in supposedly empty space.

"That's a marker," Carol announced. "I saw a costume-story tape once that had that sound in it. It marked a first-landing spot on some planet or other, so the people could find that spot again. It was supposed to be a long time ago, though."

"It's weak," observed Burleigh. "We'll try answering it." Moran stirred, and he knew that every one of the others was conscious of the movement. But they didn't watch him suspiciously. They were alert by long habit. Burleigh said they'd been Underground people, fighting the government of their native world, and they'd gotten away to make it seem the revolt had collapsed. They'd go back later when they weren't expected, and start it up again. Moran considered the story probable. Only people accustomed to desperate actions would have remained so calm when Moran had used desperate measures against them.

Burleigh picked up the transmitter-microphone.

"Calling ground," he said briskly. "Calling ground! We pick up your signal. Please reply."

He repeated the call, over and over and over. There was no answer. Cracklings and hissings came out of the speaker as before, and the thin and reedy wabbling whine continued. The *Nadine* went on toward the enlarging cloudy mass ahead.

Burleigh said;

"Well?"

"I think," said Carol, "that we should land. People have been here.

If they left a beacon, they may have left an identification of the planet. Then we'd know where we are and how to get to Loris."

Burleigh nodded. The *Nadine* had cleared for Loris. That was where it should make its next landing. The little yacht went on. All five of its proper company watched as the planet's surface enlarged. The ice-cap went out of sight around the bulge of the globe, but no markings appeared. There were cloud-banks everywhere, probably low down in the atmosphere. The darker vague areas previously seen might have been highlands.

"I think," said Carol, to Moran, "that if it's too tropical where this signal's coming from, we'll take you somewhere near enough to the ice-cap to have an endurable climate. I've been figuring on food, too. That will depend on where we are from Loris because we have to keep enough for ourselves. But we can spare some. We'll give you the emergency-kit, anyhow."

The emergency kit contained antiseptics, seeds, and a weapon or two, with elaborate advice to castaways. If somebody were wrecked on an even possibly habitable plane, the especially developed seed-strains would provide food in a minimum of time. It was not an encouraging thought, though, and Moran grimaced.

She hadn't said anything about being sorry that he had to be marooned. Maybe she was, but rebels learn to be practical or they don't live long. Moran wondered, momentarily, what sort of world they came from and why they had revolted, and what sort of set-back to the revolt had sent the five off in what they considered a strategic retreat but their government would think defeat. Moran's own situation was perfectly clear.

He'd killed a man on Coryus III. His victim would not be mourned by anybody, and somebody formerly in very great danger would now be safe, which was the reason for what Moran had done. But the dead man had been very important, and the fact that Moran had forced him to fight and killed him in fair combat made no difference. Moran had needed to get off-planet, and fast. But space-travel regulations are especially designed to prevent such escapes.

He'd made a pretty good try, at that. One of the controls on space-traffic required a ship on landing to deposit its fuel-block in the space-port's vaults. The fuel-block was not returned until clearance for departure had been granted. But Moran had waylaid the messenger carrying the *Nadine*'s fuel-block back to that space-yacht. He'd knocked the messenger cold and presented himself at the yacht with the fuel. He was admitted. He put the block in the engine's gate. He duly took the plastic receipt-token the engine only then released, and he drew a blaster. He'd locked two of the *Nadine's* crew in the engine-room, rushed to the control-room without encountering the others, dogged the door shut, and threaded in the first trip-tape to come to hand. He punched the take-off button and only seconds later the overdrive. Then the yacht—and Moran— was away. But his present companions got the drive dismantled two days later and once the yacht was out of overdrive they efficiently gave him his choice of surrendering or else. He surrendered, stipulating that he wouldn't be landed back on Coryus; he still clung to hope of avoiding return—which was almost certain anyhow. Because nobody would want to go back to a planet from which they'd carried away a criminal, even though they'd done it unwillingly. Investigation of such a matter might last for months.

Now the space-yacht moved toward a vast mass of fleecy whiteness without any visible features. Harper stayed with the direction-finder. From time to time he gave readings requiring minute changes of course. The wabbling, whining signal was louder now. It became louder than all the rest of the space-noises together.

The yacht touched atmosphere and Burleigh said;
"Watch our height, Carol."
She stood by the echometer. Sixty miles. Fifty. Thirty. A correction of course. Fifteen miles to surface below. Ten. Five. At twenty-five thousand feet there were clouds, which would be particles of ice so small that they floated even so high. Then clear air, then lower clouds, and lower ones still. It was not until six thousand feet above the surface that the planet-wide cloud-level seemed to begin. From there on down it was pure opacity. Anything could exist in that dense, almost palpable grayness. There could be jagged peaks.

The *Nadine* went down and down. At fifteen hundred feet above the unseen surface, the clouds ended. Below, there was only haze. One could see the ground, at least, but there was no horizon. There was only an end to visibility. The yacht descended as if in the center of a sphere in which one could see clearly nearby, less clearly at a little distance, and not at all beyond a quarter-mile or so.

There was a shaded, shadowless twilight under the cloudbank. The ground looked like no ground ever seen before by anyone. Off to the right a rivulet ran between improbable-seeming banks. There were a few very small hills of most unlikely appearance. It was the ground, the matter on which one would walk, which was strangest. It had color, but the color was not green. Much of it was a pallid, dirty-yellowish white. But there were patches of blue, and curious veinings of black, and here and there were other colors, all of them unlike the normal color of vegetation on a planet with a sol-type sun.

Harper spoke from the direction-finder;

"The signal's coming from that mound, yonder."

There was a hillock of elongated shape directly in line with the *Nadine*'s course in descent. Except for the patches of color, it was the only considerable landmark within the half-mile circle in which anything could be seen at all.

The *Nadine* checked her downward motion. Interplanetary drive is rugged and sure, but it does not respond to fine adjustment. Burleigh used rockets, issuing great bellowings of flame, to make actual contact. The yacht hovered, and as the rocket-flames diminished slowly she sat down with practically no impact at all. But around her there was a monstrous tumult of smoke and steam. When the rockets went off, she lay in a burned-out hollow some three or four feet deep with a bottom of solid stone. The walls of the hollow were black and scorched. It seemed that at some places they quivered persistently.

There was silence in the control-room save for the whining noise which now was almost deafening. Harper snapped off the switch. Then there was true silence. The space-yacht had come to rest possibly a hundred yards from the mound which was the source of the space-signal. That mound shared the peculiarity of the ground as far as they could see through the haze. It was not vegetation in any ordinary sense. Certainly it was no mineral surface! The landing-rockets had burned away three or four feet of it, and the edge of the burned area smoked noisesomely, and somehow it looked as if it would reek. And there were places where it stirred.

Burleigh blinked and stared. Then he reached up and flicked on the outside microphones. Instantly there was bedlam. If the landscape was strange, here, the sounds that came from it were unbelievable.

There were grunting noises.

There were clickings, uncountable clickings that made a background for all the rest. There were discordant howls and honkings. From time to time some thing unknown made a cry that sounded very much like a small boy trailing a stick against a picket fence, only much louder. Something hooted, maintaining the noise for an impossibly long time. And persistently, sounding as if they came from far away, there were booming noises, unspeakably deep-bass, made by something alive. And something shrieked in lunatic fashion and something else still moaned from time to time with the volume of a steam-whistle. . . .

"This sounds and looks like a nice place to live," said Moran with fine irony.

Burleigh did not answer. He turned down the outside sound.

"What's that stuff there, the ground?" he demanded. "We burned it away in landing. I've seen something like it somewhere, but never taking the place of grass!"

"That," said Moran as if brightly, "that's what I'm to make a garden in. Of evenings I'll stroll among my thrifty plantings and listen to the delightful sounds of nature."

Burleigh scowled. Harper flicked off the direction-finder.

"The signal still comes from that hillock yonder," he said with finality.

Moran said bitingly;

"That ain't no hillock, that's my home!"

Then, instantly he'd said it, he recognized that it could be true. The mound was not a fold in the ground. It was not an up-cropping of the ash-covered stone on which the *Nadine* rested. The enigmatic, dirty-yellow-dirty-red-dirty-blue-and-dirty-black ground-cover hid something. It blurred the shape it covered, very much as enormous cobwebs made solid and opaque would have done. But when one looked carefully at the mound, there was a landing-fin sticking up toward the leaden skies. It was attached to a large cylindrical object of which the fore part was crushed in. The other landing-fins could be traced.

"It's a ship," said Moran curtly. "It crash-landed and its crew set up a signal to call for help. None came, or they'd have turned the beacon off. Maybe they got the lifeboats to work and got away. Maybe they lived as I'm expected to live until they died as I'm expected to die."

Burleigh said angrily;

"You'd do what we are doing if you were in our shoes!"

"Sure," said Moran, "but a man can gripe, can't he?"

"You won't have to live here," said Burleigh. "We'll take you somewhere up by the ice-cap. As Carol said, we'll give you everything we can spare. And meanwhile we'll take a look at that wreck yonder. There might be an indication in it of what solar system this is. There could be something in it of use to you, too. You'd better come along when we explore."

"Aye, aye, sir," said Moran with irony. "Very kind of you, sir. You'll go armed, sir?"

Burleigh growled;

"Naturally!"

"Then since I can't be trusted with a weapon," said Moran, "I suggest that I take a torch. We may have to burn through that loathsome stuff to get in the ship."

"Right," growled Burleigh again. "Brawn and Carol, you'll keep ship. The rest of us wear suits. We don't know what that stuff is outside."

Moran silently went to the space-suit rack and began to get into a suit. Modern space-suits weren't like the ancient crudities with bulging metal casings and enormous globular helmets. Non-stretch fabrics took the place of metal, and constant-volume joints were really practical nowadays. A man could move about in a late-model space-suit almost as easily as in ship-clothing. The others of the landing-party donned their special garments with the brisk absence of fumbling that these people displayed in every action.

"If there's a lifeboat left," said Carol suddenly, "Moran might be able to do something with it."

"Ah, yes!" said Moran. "It's very likely that the ship hit hard enough to kill everybody aboard, but not smash the boats!"

"Somebody survived the crash," said Burleigh, "because they set up a beacon. I wouldn't count on a boat, Moran."

"I don't!" snapped Moran.

He flipped the fastener of his suit. He felt all the openings catch. He saw the others complete their equipment. They took arms. So far they had seen no moving thing outside, but arms were simple sanity on an unknown world. Moran, though, would not be permitted a weapon. He picked up a torch. They filed into the airlock. The inner door closed. The outer door opened. It was not necessary to check the air specifically. The suits would take care of that. Anyhow the ice-cap said there were no water-soluble gases in the atmosphere, and a gas can't be an active poison if it can't dissolve.

They filed out of the airlock. They stood on ash-covered stone, only slightly eroded by the processes which made life possible on this planet. They looked dubiously at the scorched, indefinite substance which had been ground before the *Nadine* landed. Moran moved scornfully forward. He kicked at the burnt stuff. His foot went through the char. The hole exposed a cheesy mass of soft matter which seemed riddled with small holes.

Something black came squirming frantically out of one of the openings. It was eight or ten inches long. It had a head, a thorax, and an abdomen. It had wing-cases. It had six legs. It toppled down to the stone on which the *Nadine* rested. Agitatedly, it spread its wing-covers and flew away, droning loudly. The four men heard the sound above even the monstrous cacophony of cries and boomings and grunts and squeaks which seemed to fill the air.

"What the devil—"

Moran kicked again. More holes. More openings. More small tunnels in the cheese-like, curdlike stuff. More black things squirming to view in obvious panic. They popped out everywhere. It was suddenly apparent that the top of the soil, here, was a thick and blanket-like sheet over the whitish stuff. The black creatures lived and thrived in tunnels under it.

Carol's voice came over the helmet-phones.

"They're—bugs!" she said incredulously. *"They're beetles! They're twenty times the size of the beetles we humans have been carrying around the galaxy, but that's what they are!"*

Moran grunted. Distastefully, he saw his predicament made worse. He knew what had happened here. He could begin to guess at other things to be discovered. It had not been practical for men to move onto new planets and subsist upon the flora and fauna they found there. On some new planets life had never gotten started. On such worlds a highly complex operation was necessary before humanity could move in. A complete ecological complex had to be built up; microbes to break down the rock for soil, bacteria to fix nitrogen to make the soil fertile; plants to grow in the new-made dirt and insects to fertilize the plants so they would multiply, and animals and birds to carry the seeds planet-wide. On most planets, to be sure, there were local, aboriginal plants and animals. But still terrestrial creatures had to be introduced if a colony was to feed itself. Alien plants did not supply satisfactory food. So an elaborate adaptation job had to be done on every planet before native and terrestrial living things settled down together. It wasn't impossible that the scuttling things were truly beetles, grown large and monstrous under the conditions of a new planet. And the ground . . .

"This ground stuff," said Moran distastefully, "is yeast or some sort of toadstool growth. This is a seedling world. It didn't have any life on it, so somebody dumped germs and spores and bugs to make it ready for plants and animals eventually. But nobody's come back to finish up the job."

Burleigh grunted a somehow surprised assent. But it wasn't surprising; not wholly so. Once one mentioned yeasts and toadstools and fungi generally, the weird landscape became less than incredible. But it remained actively unpleasant to think of being marooned on it.

"Suppose we go look at the ship?" said Moran unpleasantly. "Maybe you can find out where you are, and I can find out what's ahead of me."

He climbed up on the unscorched surface. It was elastic. The parchment-like top skin yielded. It was like walking on a mass of springs.

"We'd better spread out," added Moran, "or else we'll break through that skin and be foundering in this mess."

"I'm giving the orders, Moran!" said Burleigh shortly. "But what you say does make sense."

He and the others joined Moran on the yielding surface. Their footing was uncertain, as on a trampoline. They staggered. They moved toward the hillock which was a covered-over wrecked ship.

The ground was not as level as it appeared from the *Nadine*'s control-room. There were undulations. But they could not see more than a quarter-mile in any direction. Beyond that was mist. But Burleigh, at one end of the uneven line of advancing men, suddenly halted and stood staring down at something he had not seen before. The others halted.

Something moved. It came out from behind a very minor spire of whitish stuff that looked like a dirty sheet stretched over a tall stone. The thing that appeared was very peculiar indeed. It was a—worm. But it was a foot thick and ten feet long, and it had a group of stumpy legs at its fore end—where there were eyes hidden behind bristling hair-like growths—and another set of feet at its tail end. It progressed sedately by reaching forward with its fore-part, securing a foothold, and then arching its middle portion like a cat arching its back, to bring its hind part forward. Then it reached forward again. It was of a dark olive color from one end to the other. Its manner of walking was insane but somehow sedate.

Moran heard muffled noises in his helmet-phone as the others tried to speak. Carol's voice came anxiously;

"What's the matter? What do you see?"

Moran said with savage precision;

"We're looking at an inch-worm, grown up like the beetles only more so. It's not an inch-worm any longer. It's a yard-worm." Then he said harshly to the men with him; "It's not a hunting creature on worlds where it's smaller. It's not likely to have turned deadly here. Come on!"

He went forward over the singularly bouncy ground. The others followed. It was to be noted that Hallet, the engineer, avoided the huge harmless creature more widely than most.

They reached the mound which was the ship. Moran unlimbered his torch. He said sardonically;

"This ship won't do anybody any good. It's old-style. That thick belt around its middle was dropped a hundred years ago, and more." There was an abrupt thickening of the cylindrical hull at the middle. There was an equally abrupt thinning, again, toward the landing-fins. The sharpness of the change was blurred over by the revolting ground-stuff growing everywhere. "We're going to find that this wreck has been here a century at least!"

Without orders, he turned on the torch. A four-foot flame of pure blue-white leaped out. He touched its tip to the fungoid soil. Steam leaped up. He used the flame like a gigantic scalpel, cutting a square a yard deep in the whitish stuff, and then cutting it across and across to destroy it. Thick fumes arose, and quiverings and shakings began. Black creatures in their labyrinths of tunnels began to panic. Off to the right the blanket-like surface ripped and they poured out. They scuttled crazily here and there. Some took to wing. By instinct the other men—the armed ones—moved back from the smoke. They wore space-helmets but they felt that there should be an intolerable smell.

Moran slashed and slashed angrily with the big flame, cutting a way to the metal hull that had fallen here before his grandfather was born. Sometimes the flame cut across things that writhed, and he was sickened. But above all he raged because he was to be marooned here. He could not altogether blame the others. They couldn't land at any colonized world with him on board without his being detected as an extra member of the crew. His fate would then be sealed. But they also would be investigated. Official queries would go across this whole sector of the galaxy, naming five persons of such-and-such description and such-and-such fingerprints, voyaging in a space-yacht of such-and-such size and registration. The world they came from would claim them as fugitives. They would be returned to it. They'd be executed.

Then Carol's voice came in his helmet-phone. She cried out;

"Look out! It's coming! Kill it! Kill it—"

He heard blast-rifles firing. He heard Burleigh pant commands. He was on his way out of the hollow he'd carved when he heard Harper cry out horribly.

He got clear of the newly burned-away stuff. There was still much smoke and stream. But he saw Harper. More, he saw the thing that had Harper.

It occurred to him instantly that if Harper died, there would not be too many people on the *Nadine.* They need not maroon him. In fact, they wouldn't dare. A ship that came in to port with too few on board would be investigated as thoroughly as one that had too many. Perhaps more thoroughly. So if Harper were killed, Moran would be needed to take his place. He'd go on from here in the *Nadine,* necessarily accepted as a member of her crew.

Then he rushed, the flame-torch making a roaring sound.

❋ II ❋

They went back to the *Nadine* for weapons more adequate for encountering the local fauna when it was over. Blast-rifles were not effective against such creatures as these. Torches were contact weapons but they killed. Blast-rifles did not. And Harper needed to pull himself together again, too. Also, neither Moran nor any of the others wanted to go back to the still un-entered wreck while the skinny, somehow disgusting legs of the thing still kicked spasmodically—quite separate—on the whitish ground-stuff. Moran had disliked such creatures in miniature form on other worlds. Enlarged like this. . . .

It seemed insane that such creatures, even in miniature, should painstakingly be brought across light-years of space to the new worlds men settled on. But it had been found to be necessary. The ecological system in which human beings belonged had turned out to be infinitely complicated. It had turned out, in fact, to be the ecological system of Earth, and unless all parts of the complex were present, the total was subtly or glaringly wrong. So mankind distastefully ferried pests as well as useful creatures to its new worlds as they were made ready for settlement. Mosquitoes throve on the inhabited globes of the Rim Stars. Roaches twitched nervous antennae on the settled planets of the Coal-sack. Dogs on Antares had fleas, and scratched their bites, and humanity spread through the galaxy with an attendant train of insects and annoyances. If they left their pests behind, the total system of checks and balances which make life practical would get lopsided. It would not maintain itself. The vagaries that could result were admirably illustrated in and on the landscape outside the *Nadine*. Something had been left out of the seeding of this planet. The element—which might be a bacterium or a virus or almost anything at all—the element that kept creatures at the size called "normal" was either missing or inoperable here. The results were not desirable.

Harper drank thirstily. Carol had watched from the control-room. She was still pale. She looked strangely at Moran. "You're sure it didn't get through your suit?" Burleigh asked insistently of Harper.

Moran said sourly;

"The creatures have changed size. There's no proof they've changed anything else. Beetles live in tunnels they make in fungus growths. The beetles and the tunnels are larger, but that's all. Inch worms travel as they always did. They move yards instead of inches, but that's all. Centipedes—"

"It was—" said Carol unsteadily. "It was thirty feet long!"

"Centipedes," repeated Moran, "catch prey with their legs. They always did. Some of them trail poison from their feet. We can play a blowtorch over Harper's suit and any poison will be burned away. You can't burn a space-suit!"

"We certainly can't leave Moran here!" said Burleigh uneasily.

"He kept Harper from being killed!" said Carol. "Your blast-rifles weren't any good. The—creatures are hard to kill."

"Very hard to kill," agreed Moran. "But I'm not supposed to kill them. I'm supposed to live with them! I wonder how we can make them understand they're not supposed to kill me either?"

"I'll admit," said Burleigh, "that if you'd let Harper get killed, we'd have been forced to let you take his identity and not be marooned, to avoid questions at the spaceport on Loris. Not many men would have done what you did."

"Oh, I'm a hero," said Moran. "Noble Moran, that's me! What the hell would you want me to do? I didn't think! I won't do it again, I promise!"

The last statement was almost true. Moran felt a squeamish horror at the memory of what he'd been through over by the wrecked ship. He'd come running out of the excavation he'd made. He had for a weapon a four-foot blue-white flame, and there was a monstrous creature running directly toward him, with Harper lifted off the ground and clutched in two gigantic, spidery legs. It was no less than thirty feet long, but it was a centipede. It travelled swiftly on grisly, skinny, pipe-thin legs. It loomed over Moran as he reached the surface and he automatically thrust the flame at it. The result was shocking. But the nervous systems of insects are primitive. It is questionable that they feel pain. It is certain that separated parts of them act as if they had independent life. Legs—horrible things—sheared off in the flame of the torch, but the grisly furry thing rushed on until Moran slashed across its body with the blue-white fire. Then it collapsed. But Harper was still held firmly and half the monster struggled mindlessly to run on while another part was dead. Moran fought it almost hysterically, slicing off legs and wanting to be sick when their stumps continued to move as if purposefully, and the legs themselves kicked and writhed rhythmically. But he bored in and cut at the body and ultimately dragged Harper clear.

Afterward, sickened, he completed cutting it to bits with the torch. But each part continued nauseatingly to move. He went back with the others to the *Nadine*. The blast-rifles had been almost completely without effect upon the creature because of its insensitive nervous system.

"I think," said Burleigh, "that it is only fair for us to lift from here and find a better part of this world to land Moran in."

"Why not another planet?" asked Carol.

"It could take weeks," said Burleigh harassedly. "We left Coryus three days ago. We ought to land on Loris before too long. There'd be questions asked if we turned up weeks late! We can't afford that! The space-port police would suspect us of all sorts of things. They might decide to check back on us where we came from. We can't take the time to hunt another planet!"

"Then your best bet," said Moran caustically, "is to find out where we are. You may be so far from Loris that you can't make port without raising questions anyhow. But you might be almost on course. I don't know! But let's see if that wreck can tell us. I'll go by myself if you like."

He went into the airlock, where his suit and the others had been sprayed with a corrosive solution while the outside air was pumped out and new air from inside the yacht admitted. He got into the suit. Harper joined him.

"I'm going with you," he said shortly. "Two will be safer than one—both with torches."

"Too, too true!" said Moran sardonically.

He bundled the other suits out of the airlock and into the ship. He checked his torch. He closed the inner lock door and started the pump. Harper said;

"I'm not going to try to thank you—"

"Because," Moran snapped, "you wouldn't have been on this planet to be in danger if I hadn't tried to capture the yacht. I know it!"

"That wasn't what I meant to say!" protested Harper.

Moran snarled at him. The lock-pump stopped and the ready for exit light glowed. They pushed open the outer door and emerged.

Again there was the discordant, almost intolerable din. It made no sense. The cries and calls and stridulations they now knew to be those of insects had no significance. The unseen huge creatures made them without purpose. Insects do not challenge each other like birds or make mating-calls like animals. They make noises because it is their nature. The noises have no meaning. The two men started toward the wreck to which Moran had partly burned a passage-way. There were clickings from underfoot all around them. Moran said abruptly;

"Those clicks come from the beetles in their tunnels underfoot. They're practically a foot long. How big do you suppose bugs grow here—and why ?"

Harper did not answer. He carried a flame-torch like the one Moran had used before. They went unsteadily over the elastic, yielding stuff underfoot. Harper halted, to look behind. Carol's voice came in the helmet-phones.

"We're watching out for you. We'll try to warn you if—anything shows up."

"Better watch me!" snapped Moran. "If I should kill Harper after all, you might have to pass me for him presently!"

He heard a small, inarticulate sound, as if Carol protested. Then he heard an angry shrill whine. He'd turned aside from the direct line to the wreck. Something black, the size of a fair-sized dog, faced him belligerently. Multiple lensed eyes, five inches across, seemed to regard him in a peculiarly daunting fashion. The creature had a narrow, unearthly, triangular face, with mandibles that worked from side to side instead of up and down like an animal's jaws. The head was utterly unlike any animal such as breed and raise their young and will fight for them. There was a small thorax, from which six spiny, glistening legs sprang. There was a bulbous abdomen.

"This," said Moran coldly, "is an ant. I've stepped on them for no reason, and killed them. I've probably killed many times as many without knowing it. But this could kill me."

The almost yard-long enormity, standing two and a half feet high, was in the act of carrying away a section of one of the legs of the giant centipede Moran had killed earlier. It still moved. The leg was many times the size of the ant. Moran moved toward it. It made a louder buzzing sound, threatening him.

Moran cut it apart with a slashing sweep of the flame that a finger-touch sent leaping from his torch. The thing presumably died, but it continued to writhe senselessly.

"I killed this one," said Moran savagely, "because I remembered something from my childhood. When one ant finds something to eat and can't carry it all away, it brings back its friends to get the rest. The big thing I killed would be such an item. How'd you like to have a horde of these things about us? Come on!"

Through his helmet-phone he heard Harper breathing harshly. He led the way once more toward the wreck.

Black beetles swarmed about when he entered the cut in the mould-yeast soil. They popped out of tunnels as if in astonishment that what had been subterranean passages suddenly opened to the air. Harper stepped on one, and it did not crush. It struggled frantically and he almost fell. He gasped. Two of the creatures crawled swiftly up the legs of Moran's suit, and he knocked them savagely away. He found himself grinding his teeth in invincible revulsion.

They reached the end of the cut he'd made in the fungus-stuff. Metal showed past burned-away soil. Moran growled;

"You keep watch. I'll finish the cut."

The flame leaped out. Dense clouds of smoke and steam poured out and up. With the intolerably bright light of the torch overwhelming the perpetual grayness under the clouds and playing upon curling vapors, the two space-suited men looked like figures in some sort of inferno.

Carol's voice came anxiously into Moran's helmet-phone;

"Are you all right?"

"So far, both of us," said Moran sourly. "I've just uncovered the crack of an airlock door."

He swept the flame around again. A mass of undercut fungus toppled toward him. He burned it and went on. He swept the flame more widely. There was carbonized matter from the previously burned stuff on the metal, but he cleared all the metal. Carol's voice again;

"*There's something flying . . . It's huge! It's a wasp! It's—monstrous!*"

Moran growled;

"Harper, we're in a sort of trench. If it hovers, you'll burn it as it comes down. Cut through its waist. It won't crawl toward us along the trench. It'd have to back toward us to use its sting."

He burned and burned, white light glaring upon a mass of steam and smoke which curled upward and looked as if lightning-flashes played within it.

Carol's voice;

"*It—went on past. . . . It was as big as a cow!*"

Moran wrenched at the port-door. It partly revolved. He pulled. It fell outward. The wreck was not standing upright on its fins. It lay on its side. The lock inside the toppled-out port was choked with a horrible mass of thread-like fungi. Moran swept the flame in. The fungus shriveled and was not. He opened the inner lock-door. There was pure blackness within. He held the torch for light.

For an instant everything was confusion, because the wreck was lying on its side instead of standing in a normal position. Then he saw a sheet of metal, propped up to be seen instantly by anyone entering the wrecked space-vessel.

Letters burned into the metal gave a date a century and a half old. Straggly torch-writing said baldly;

> "*This ship the* Malabar *crashed here on Tethys II a week ago. We cannot repair. We are going on to Candida III in the boats. We are carrying what bessendium we can with us. We resign salvage rights in this ship to its finders, but we have more bessendium with us. We will give that to our rescuers. Jos. White, Captain.*"

Moran made a peculiar, sardonic sound like a bark.

"Calling the *Nadine!*" he said in mirthless amusement. "This planet is Tethys Two. Do you read me? Tethys II! Look it up!"

A pause. Then Carol's voice, relieved;

"Tethys is in the Directory! That's good!" There was the sound of murmurings in the control-room behind her. *"Yes! . . . Oh— wonderful! It's not far off the course we should have followed! We won't be suspiciously late at Loris! Wonderful!"*

"I share your joy," said Moran sarcastically. "More information! The ship's name was the *Malabar*. She carried bessendium among her cargo. Her crew went on to Candida III a hundred and fifty years ago, leaving a promise to pay in more bessendium whoever should rescue them. More bessendium! Which suggests that some bessendium was left behind."

Silence. The bald memorandum left behind the vanished crew was, of course, pure tragedy. A ship's lifeboat could travel four light-years, or possibly even six. But there were limits. A castaway crew had left this world on a desperate journey to another in the hope that life there would be tolerable. If they arrived, they waited for some other ship to cross the illimitable emptiness and discover either the beacon here or one they'd set up on the other world. The likelihood was small, at best. It had worked out zero. If the lifeboats made Candida III, their crews stayed there because they could go no farther. They'd died there, because if they'd been found this ship would have been visited and its cargo salvaged.

Moran went inside. He climbed through the compartments of the toppled craft, using his torch for light. He found where the cargo-hold had been opened from the living part of the ship. He saw the cargo. There were small, obviously heavy boxes in one part of the hold. Some had been broken open. He found scraps of purple bessendium ore dropped while being carried to the lifeboats. A century and a half ago it had not seemed worthwhile to pick them up, though bessendium was the most precious material in the galaxy. It couldn't be synthesized. It had to be made by some natural process not yet understood, but involving long-continued pressures of megatons to the square inch with temperatures in the millions of degrees. It was purple. It was crystalline. Fractions of it in blocks of other metals made the fuel-blocks that carried liners winging through the void. But here were pounds of it dropped carelessly. . . .

Moran gathered a double handful. He slipped it in a pocket of his space-suit. He went clambering back to the lock.

He heard the roaring of a flame-torch. He found Harper playing it squeamishly on the wriggling fragments of another yard-long ant. It had explored the trench burned out of the fungus soil and down to the rock.

Harper'd killed it as it neared him.

"That's three of them I've killed," said Harper in a dogged voice. "There seem to be more."

"Did you hear my news?" asked Moran sardonically.

"Yes," said Harper. "How'll we get back to the *Nadine?*"

"Oh, we'll fight our way through," said Moran, as sardonically as before. "We'll practice splendid heroism, giving battle to ants who think we're other ants trying to rob them of some fragments of an over-sized dead centipede. A splendid cause to fight for, Harper!"

He felt an almost overpowering sense of irony. The quantity of bessendium he'd seen was riches incalculable. The mere pocketful of crystals in his pocket would make any man wealthy if he could get to a settled planet and sell them. And there was much, much more back in the cargo-hold of the wreck. He'd seen it.

But his own situation was unchanged. Bessendium could be hidden somehow—perhaps between the inner and outer hulls of the *Nadine.* But it was not possible to land the *Nadine* at any space-port with an extra man aboard her. In a sense, Moran might be one of the richest men in the galaxy in his salvagers' right to the treasure in the wrecked *Malabar*'s hold. But he could not use that treasure to buy his way to a landing on a colonized world.

Carol's voice; she was frightened.

"Something's coming! It's—terribly big! It's coming out of the mist!"

Moran pushed past Harper in the trench that ended at the wreck's lock-door. He moved on until he could see over the edge of that trench as it shallowed. Now there were not less than forty of the giant ants about the remnants of the monstrous centipede Moran had killed. They moved about in great agitation. There was squabbling. Angry, whining stridulations filled the air beneath the louder and more gruesome sounds from farther away places. It appeared that scouts and foragers from two different ant-cities had come upon the treasure of dead—if twitching—meat of Moran's providing. They differed about where the noisome booty should be taken. Some ants pulled angrily against each other, whining shrilly. He saw individual ants running frantically away in two different directions. They would be couriers, carrying news of what amounted to a frontier incident in the city-state civilization of the ants.

Then Moran saw the giant thing of which Carol spoke. It was truly huge, and it had a gross, rounded body, and a ridiculously small thorax, and its head was tiny and utterly mild in expression. It walked with an enormous, dainty deliberation, placing small spiked feet at the end of fifteen-foot legs very delicately in place as it moved. Its eyes were multiple and huge, and its forelegs, though used so deftly for walking, had a horrifying set of murderous, needle-sharp sawteeth along their edges.

It looked at the squabbling ants with its gigantic eyes that somehow appeared like dark glasses worn by a monstrosity. It moved primly, precisely toward them. Two small black creatures tugged at a hairy section of a giant centipede's leg. The great pale-green creature—a mantis; a praying mantis twenty feet tall in its giraffe-like walking position—the great creature loomed over them, looking down as through sunglasses. A foreleg moved like lightning. An ant weighing nearly as much as a man stridulated shrilly, terribly, as it was borne aloft. The mantis closed its arm-like forelegs upon it, holding it as if piously and benignly contemplating it. Then it ate it, very much as a man might eat an apple, without regard to the convulsive writhings of its victim.

It moved on toward the denser fracas among the ants. Suddenly it raised its ghastly sawtoothed forelegs in an extraordinary gesture. It was the mantis' spectral attitude, which seemed a pose of holding out its arms in benediction. But its eyes remained blind-seeming and enigmatic—again like dark glasses.

Then it struck. Daintily, it dined upon an ant. Upon another. Upon another and another and another.

From one direction parties of agitated and hurrying black objects appeared at the edge of the mist. They were ants of a special caste—warrior-ants with huge mandibles designed for fighting in defense of their city and its social system and its claim to fragments of dead centipedes. From another direction other parties of no less truculent warriors moved with the swiftness and celerity of a striking task-force. All the air was filled with the deep-bass notes of something huge, booming beyond visibility, and the noises as of sticks trailed against picket fences, and hootings which were produced by the rubbing of serrated leg-joints against chitinous diaphragms. But now a new tumult arose.

From forty disputatious *formicidae,* whining angrily at each other over the stinking remains of the monster Moran had killed, the number of ants involved in the quarrel became hundreds. But more and more arrived. The special caste of warriors bred for warfare was not numerous enough to take care of the provocative behavior of foreign foragers. There was a general mobilization in both unseen ant-city states. They became nations in arms. Their populations rushed to the scene of conflict. The burrows and dormitories and eating-chambers of the underground nations were swept clean of occupants. Only the nurseries retained a skeleton staff of nurses—the nurseries and the excavated palace occupied by the ant-queen and her staff of servants and administrators. All the resources of two populous ant-nations were flung into the fray.

From a space of a hundred yards or less, containing mere dozens of belligerent squabblers, the dirty-white ground of the fungus-plain became occupied by hundreds of snapping, biting combatants. They covered—they fought over—the half of an acre. There were contending battalions fighting as masses in the center, while wings of fighting creatures to right and left were less solidly arranged. But reinforcements poured out of the mist from two directions, and momently the situation changed. Presently the battle covered an acre. Groups of fresh fighters arriving from the city to the right uttered shrill stridulations and charged upon the flank of their enemies. Simultaneously, reinforcements from the city to the left flung themselves into the fighting-line near the center.

Formations broke up. The battle disintegrated into an indefinite number of lesser combats; troops or regiments fighting together often moved ahead with an appearance of invincibility, but suddenly they broke and broke again until there was only a complete confusion of unorganized single combats in which the fighters rolled over and over, struggling ferociously with mandible and claw to destroy each other. Presently the battle raged over five acres. Ten. Thousands upon thousands of black, glistening, stinking creatures tore at each other in murderous ferocity. Whining, squealing battle-cries arose and almost drowned out the deeper notes of larger but invisible creatures off in the mist.

Moran and Harper got back to the *Nadine* by a wide detour past warriors preoccupied with each other just before the battle reached its most savage stage. In that stage, the space-yacht was included in the battleground. Fights went on about its landing-fins. Horrifying duels could be followed by scrapings and bumpings against its hull. From the yacht's ports the fighting ants looked like infuriated machines, engaged in each other's destruction. One might see a warrior of unidentified allegiance with its own abdomen ripped open, furiously rending an enemy without regard to its own mortal wound. There were those who had literally been torn in half, so that only1 head and thorax remained, but they fought on no less valiantly than the rest.

At the edges of the fighting such cripples were more numerous. Ants with antennae shorn off or broken, with legs missing, utterly doomed—they sometimes wandered forlornly beyond the fighting, the battle seemingly forgotten. But even such dazed and incapacitated casualties came upon each other. If they smelled alike, they ignored each other. Every ant-city has its particular smell which its inhabitants share. Possession of the national odor is at once a certificate of citizenship in peacetime and a uniform in war. When such victims of the battle came upon enemy walking wounded, they fought.

And the giant praying mantis remained placidly and invulnerably still. It plucked single fighters from the battle and dined upon them while they struggled, and plucked other fighters, and consumed them. It ignored the battle and the high purpose and self-sacrificing patriotism of the ants. Immune to them and disregarded by them, it fed on them while the battle raged.

Presently the gray light overhead turned faintly pink, and became a deeper tint and then crimson. In time there was darkness. The noise of battle ended. The sounds of the day diminished and ceased, and other monstrous outcries took their place.

There were bellowings in the blackness without the *Nadine*. There were chirpings become baritone, and senseless uproars which might be unbelievable modifications of once-shrill and once-tranquil night-sounds of other worlds. And there came a peculiar, steady, unrhythmic pattering sound. It seemed like something falling upon the blanket-like upper surface of the soil.

Moran opened the airlock door and thrust out a torch to see. Its intolerably bright glare showed the battlefield abandoned. Most of the dead and wounded had been carried away. Which, of course, was not solicitude for the wounded or reverence for the dead heroes. Dead ants, like dead centipedes, were booty of the only kind the creatures of this world could know. The dead were meat. The wounded were dead before they were carried away.

Moran peered out, with Carol looking affrightedly over his shoulder. The air seemed to shine slightly in the glare of the torch. The pattering sound was abruptly explained. Large, slow, widely-separated raindrops fell heavily and steadily from the cloudbanks overhead. Moran could see them strike. Each spot of wetness glistened briefly. Then the raindrop was absorbed by the ground.

But there were other noises than the ceaseless tumult on the ground. There were sounds in the air; the beating of enormous wings. Moran looked up, squinting against the light. There were things moving about the black sky. Gigantic things.

Something moved, too, across the diminishingly lighted surface about the yacht. There were glitterings. Shining armor. Multifaceted eyes. A gigantic, horny, spiked object crawled toward the torch-glare, fascinated by it. Something else dived insanely. It splashed upon the flexible white surface twenty yards away, and struggled upward and took crazily off again. It careened blindly.

It hit the yacht, a quarter-ton of night-flying beetle. The air seemed filled with flying things. There were moths with twenty-foot wings and eyes which glowed like rubies in the torch's light. There were beetles of all sizes from tiny six-inch things to monsters in whom Moran did not believe even when he saw them. All were drawn by the light which should not exist under the cloud-bank. They droned and fluttered and performed lunatic evolutions, coming always closer to the flame.

Moran cut off the torch and closed the lock-door from the inside.

"We don't load bessendium tonight," he said with some grimness. "To have no light, with what crawls about in the darkness, would be suicide. But to use lights would be worse. If you people are going to salvage the stuff in that wreck, you'll have to wait for daylight. At least then you can see what's coming after you."

They went into the yacht proper. There was no longer any question about the planet's air. If insects which were descendants of terrestrial forms could breathe it, so could men. When the first insect-eggs were brought here, the air had to be fit for them if they were to survive. It would not have changed.

Burleigh sat in the control-room with a double handful of purple crystals before him.

"This," he said when Moran and Carol reentered, "this is bessendium past question. I've been thinking what it means."

"Money," said Moran drily. "You'll all be rich. You'll probably retire from politics."

"That wasn't exactly what I had in mind," said Burleigh distastefully. "You've gotten us into the devil of a mess, Moran!"

"For which," said Moran with ironic politeness, "there is a perfect solution. You kill me, either directly or by leaving me marooned here."

Burleigh scowled.

"We have to land at spaceports for supplies. We can't hope to hide you, it's required that landed ships be sterilized against infections from off-planet. We can't pass you as a normal passenger. You're not on the ship's papers and they're alteration-proof. Nobody's ever been able to change a ship's papers and not be caught! We could land and tell the truth, that you hijacked the ship and we finally overpowered you. But there are reasons against that."

"Naturally!" agreed Moran. "I'd be killed anyhow and you'd be subject to intensive investigation. And you're fugitives as much as I am."

"Just so," admitted Burleigh, Moran shrugged.

"Which leaves just one answer. You maroon me and go on your way."

Burleigh said painfully;

"There's this bessendium. If there's more—especially if there's more—we can leave you here with part of it. When we get far enough away, we charter a ship to come and get you. It'll be arranged. Somebody will be listed as of that ship's company, but he'll slip away from the spaceport and not be on board at all. Then you're picked up and landed using his name."

"If," said Moran ironically, "I am alive when the ship gets here. If I'm not, the crew of the chartered ship will be in trouble, short one man on return to port. You'll have trouble getting anybody to run that risk!"

"We're trying to work out a way to save you!" insisted Burleigh angrily. "Harper would have been killed but for you. And—this bessendium will finance the underground work that will presently make a success of our revolution. We're grateful! We're trying to help you!"

"So you maroon me," said Moran. Then he said; "But you've skipped the real problem! If anything goes wrong, Carol's in it! There's no way to do anything without risk for her! That's the problem! I could kill all you characters, land somewhere on a colonized planet exactly as you landed here, and be gone from the yacht on foot before anybody could find me! But I have a slight aversion to getting a girl killed or killing her just for my own convenience. It's settled. I stay here. You can try to arrange the other business if you like. But it's a bad gamble."

Carol was very pale. Burleigh stood up.

"You said that, I didn't. But I don't think we should leave you here. Up near the ice-cap should be infinitely better for you. We'll load the rest of the bessendium tomorrow, find you a place, leave you a beacon, and go."

He went out. Carol turned a white face to Moran.

"Is that—is that the real trouble? Do you really—"

Moran looked at her stonily. "I like to make heroic gestures," he told her. "Actually, Burleigh's a very noble sort of character himself. He proposes to leave me with treasure that he could take. Even more remarkably, he proposes to divide up what you take, instead of applying it all to further his political ideals. Most men like him would take it all for the revolution!"

"But—but—"

Carol's expression was pure misery. Moran walked deliberately across the control-room. He glanced out of a port. A face looked in. It filled the transparent opening. It was unthinkable. It was furry. There were glistening chitinous areas. There was a proboscis like an elephant's trunk, curled horribly. The eyes were multiple and mad.

It looked in, drawn and hypnotized by the light shining out on this nightmare world from the control-room ports.

Moran touched the button that closed the shutters.

❖ III ❖

When morning came, its arrival was the exact reversal of the coming of night. In the beginning there was darkness, and in the darkness there was horror.

The creatures of the night untiringly filled the air with sound, and the sounds were discordant and gruesome and revolting. The creatures of this planet were gigantic. They should have adopted new customs appropriate to the dignity of their increased size. But they hadn't. The manners and customs of insects are immutable. They feed upon specific prey—spiders are an exception, but they are not insects at all—and they lay their eggs in specific fashion in specific places, and they behave according to instincts which are so detailed as to leave them no choice at all in their actions. They move blindly about, reacting like automata of infinite complexity which are capable of nothing not built into them from the beginning. Centuries and millenia do not change them. Travel across star-clusters leaves them with exactly the capacities for reaction that their remotest ancestors had, before men lifted off ancient Earth's green surface.

The first sign of dawn was deep, deep, deepest red in the cloud-bank no more than fifteen hundred feet overhead. The red became brighter, and presently was as brilliant as dried blood. Again presently it was crimson over all the half-mile circle that human eyes could penetrate. Later still—but briefly—it was pink. Then the sky became gray. From that color it did not change again.

Moran joined Burleigh in a survey of the landscape from the control-room. The battlefield was empty now. Of the thousands upon thousands of stinking combatants who'd rent and torn each other the evening before, there remained hardly a trace. Here and there, to be sure, a severed saw-toothed leg remained. There were perhaps as many as four relatively intact corpses not yet salvaged. But something was being done about them.

There were tiny, brightly-banded beetles hardly a foot long which labored industriously over such frayed objects. They worked agitatedly in the yeasty stuff which on this world took the place of soil. They excavated, beneath the bodies of the dead ants, hollows into which those carcasses could descend. They washed the yeasty, curdy stuff up and around the sides of those to-be-desired objects. The dead warriors sank little by little toward oblivion as the process went on. The up-thrust, dug-out material collapsed upon them as they descended. In a very little while they would be buried where no larger carrion-eater would discover them, and then the brightly-colored sexton beetles would begin a banquet to last until only fragments of chitinous armor remained.

* * *

But Moran and Burleigh, in the *Nadine's* control-room, could hardly note such details.

"You saw the cargo," said Burleigh, frowning. "How's it packed? The bessendium, I mean."

"It's in small boxes too heavy to be handled easily," said Moran. "Anyhow the *Malabar's* crew broke some of them open to load the stuff on their lifeboats."

"The lifeboats are all gone?"

"Naturally," said Moran. "At a guess they'd have used all of them even if they didn't need them for the crew. They could carry extra food and weapons and such."

"How much bessendium is left?"

"Probably twenty boxes unopened," said Moran. "I can't guess at the weight, but it's a lot. They opened six boxes." He paused. "I have a suggestion."

"What?"

"When you've supplied yourselves," said Moran, "leave some spaceport somewhere with papers saying you're going to hunt for minerals on some plausible planet. You can get such a clearance. Then you can return with bessendium coming out of the *Nadine's* waste-pipes and people will be surprised but not suspicious. You'll file for mineral rights, and cash your cargo. Everybody will get busy trying to grab off the mineral rights for themselves. You can clear out and let them try to find the bessendium lode. You'll be allowed to go, all right, and you can settle down somewhere rich and highly respected."

"Hmmm," said Burleigh. Then he said uncomfortably; "One wonders about the original owners of the stuff."

"After a hundred and fifty years," said Moran, "who'd you divide with? The insurance company that paid for the lost ship? The heirs of the crew? How'd you find them?" Then he added amusedly, "Only revolutionists and enemies of governments would be honest enough to worry about that!"

Brawn came into the control-room. He said broodingly that breakfast was ready. Moran had never heard him speak in a normally cheerful voice. When he went out, Moran said;

"I don't suppose he'll be so gloomy when he's rich!"

"His family was wiped out," said Burleigh curtly, "by the government we were fighting. The girl he was going to marry, too."

"Then I take back what I said," said Moran ruefully.

They went down to breakfast.

Carol served it. She did not look well. Her eyes seemed to show that she'd been crying. But she treated Moran exactly like anyone else. Harper was very quiet, too. He took very seriously the fact that Moran had saved his life at the risk of his on the day before. Brawn breakfasted in a subdued, moody fashion. Only Hallet seemed to have reacted to the discovery of a salvageable shipment of bessendium that should make everybody rich—everybody but Moran, who was ultimately responsible for the find.

"Burleigh," said Hallet expansively, "says the stuff you brought back from the wreck is worth fifty thousand credits, at least. What's the whole shipment worth?"

"I've no idea," said Moran. "It would certainly pay for a fleet of space-liners, and I'd give all of it for a ticket on one of them."

"But how much is there in bulk?" insisted Hallet.

"I saw that half a dozen boxes had been broken open and emptied for the lifeboat voyagers," Moran told him. "I didn't count the balance, but there were several times as many untouched. If they're all full of the same stuff, you can guess almost any sum you please."

"Millions, eh?" said Hallet. His eyes glistened. "Billions? Plenty for everybody?"

"There's never plenty for more than one," said Moran mildly. "That's the way we seem be made."

Burleigh said suddenly;

"I'm worried about getting the stuff aboard. We can't afford to lose anybody, and if we have to fight the creatures here, every time we kill one its carcass draws others."

Moran took a piece of bread. He said;

"I've been thinking about survival-tactics for myself as a castaway. I think a torch is the answer. In any emergency on the yeast surface, I can burn a hole and drop down in it. The monsters are stupid. In most cases they'll go away because they stop seeing me. In the others, they'll come to the hole and I'll burn them. It won't be pleasant, but it may be practical."

Burleigh considered it.

"It may be," he admitted. "It may be."

Hallet said;

"I want to see that work before I trust the idea."

"Somebody has to try it," agreed Moran. "Anyhow my life's going to depend on it."

Carol left the room. Moran looked after her as the door closed.

"She doesn't like the idea of our leaving you behind," said Burleigh. "None of us do."

"I'm touched."

"We'll try to get a ship to come for you, quickly," said Burleigh.

"I'm sure you will," said Moran politely.

But he was not confident. The laws governing space-travel were very strict indeed, and enforced with all the rigor possible. On their enforcement, indeed, depended the law and order of the planets. Criminals had to know that they could not escape to space whenever matters got too hot for them aground. For a spaceman to trifle with interstellar-traffic laws meant at the least that they were grounded for life. But the probabilities were much worse than that. It was most likely that Burleigh or any of the others would be reported to spaceport police instantly they attempted to charter a ship for any kind of illegal activity. Moran made a mental note to warn Burleigh about it.

By now, though, he was aware of a very deep irritation at the idea of being killed, whether by monsters on this planet or men sent to pick him up for due process of law. When he made the grand gesture of seizing the *Nadine*, he'd known nothing about the people on board, and he hadn't really expected to succeed. His real hope was to be killed without preliminary scientific questioning. Modern techniques of interrogation were not torture, but they stripped away all concealments of motive and to a great degree revealed anybody who'd helped one. Moran had killed a man in a fair fight the other man did not want to engage in. If he were caught on Coryus or returned to it, his motivation could be read from his mind. And if that was done the killing—and the sacrifice of his own future and life—would have been useless. But he'd been prepared to be killed. Even now he'd prefer to die here on Tethys than in the strictly painless manner of executions on Coryus. But he was now deeply resistant to the idea of dying at all. There was Carol . . .

He thrust such thoughts aside.

Morning was well begun when they prepared to transfer the wreck's treasure to the *Nadine*. Moran went first. At fifteen-foot intervals he burned holes in the curd-like, elastic ground-cover. Some of the holes went down only four feet to the stone beneath it. Some went down six. But a man who jumped down one of them would be safe against attack except from directly overhead, which was an unlikely direction for attack by an insect. Carol had seen a wasp fly past the day before. She said it was as big as a cow. A sting from such a monster would instantly be fatal. But no wasp would have the intelligence to use its sting on something it had not seized. A man should be safe in such a fox-hole. If a creature did try to investigate the opening, a torch could come into play. It was the most practical possible way for a man to defend himself on this world.

Moran made more than a dozen such holes of refuge in the line between the *Nadine* and the wreck. Carol watched with passionate solicitude from a control-room port as he progressed. He entered the wreck through the lock-doors he'd uncovered. Harper followed doggedly, not less than two fox-holes behind. Carol's voice reassured them, the while, that within the half-mile circle of visibility no monster walked or flew.

Inside the wreck, Moran placed emergency-lanterns to light the dark interior. He placed them along the particularly inconvenient passageways of a ship lying on its side instead of standing upright. He was at work breaking open a box of bessendium when Harper joined him. Harper said heavily;

"I've brought a bag. It was a pillow. Carol took the foam out."

"We'll fill it," said Moran. "Not too full. The stuff's heavy." Harper watched while Moran poured purple crystals into it from his cupped hands.

"There you are," said Moran. "Take it away."

"Look!" said Harper. "I owe you plenty—."

"Then pay me," said Moran, exasperatedly, "by shutting up! By making Burleigh damned careful about who he tries to hire to come after me! And by getting this cargo-shifting business in operation! The *Nadine*'s almost due on Loris. You don't want to have the space-port police get suspicions. Get moving!"

Harper clambered over the side of doorways. He disappeared. Moran was alone in the ship. He explored. He found that the crew that had abandoned the *Malabar* had been guilty of a singular oversight for a crew abandoning ship. But, of course, they'd been distracted not only by their predicament but by the decision to carry part of the ship's precious cargo with them, so they could make it a profitable enterprise to rescue them. They hadn't taken the trouble to follow all the rules laid down for a crew taking to the boats.

Moran made good their omission. He was back in the cargo-hold when Brawn arrived. Burleigh came next. Then Harper again. Hallet came last of the four men of the yacht. They did not make a continuous chain of men moving back and forth between the two ships. Three men came, and loaded up, and went back. Then three men came again, one by one. There could never be a moment when a single refuge-hole in the soil could be needed by two men at the same time.

Within the first hour of work at transferring treasure, the bolt-holes came into use. Carol called anxiously that a gigantic beetle neared the ship and would apparently pass between it and the yacht. At the time, Brawn and Harper were moving from the *Malabar* toward the *Nadine,* and Hallet was about to leave the wreck's lock.

He watched with wide eyes. The beetle was truly a monster, the size of a hippopotamus as pictured in the culture-books about early human history. Its jaws, pronged like antlers, projected two yards before its huge, faceted eyes. It seemed to drag itself effortfully over the elastic surface of the ground. It passed a place where red, foleated fungus grew in a fantastic absence of pattern on the surface of the ground. It went through a streak of dusty-blue mould, which it stirred into a cloud of spores as it passed. It crawled on and on. Harper popped down into the nearest bolt-hole, his torch held ready. Brawn stood beside another refuge, sixty feet away.

Carol's voice came to their helmet-phones, anxious and exact. Hallet, in the lock-door, heard her tell Harper that the beetle would pass very close to him and to stay still. It moved on and on. It would be very close indeed. Carol gasped in horror.

The monster passed partly over the hole in which Harper crouched. One of its clawed feet slipped down into the opening. But the beetle went on, unaware of Harper. It crawled toward the encircling mist upon some errand of its own. It was mindless. It was like a complex and highly decorated piece of machinery which did what it was wound up to do, and nothing else.

Harper came out of the bolthole when Carol, her voice shaky with relief, told him it was safe. He went doggedly on to the *Nadine*, carrying his bag of purple crystals. Brawn followed, moodily.

Hallet, with a singularly exultant look upon his face, ventured out of the airlock and moved across the fungoid world. He carried a king's ransom to be added to the riches already transferred to the yacht.

Moving the bessendium was a tedious task. One plastic box in the cargo-hold held a quantity of crystals that three men took two trips each to carry. In mid-morning the bag in Hallet's hand seemed to slip just when Moran completed filling it. It toppled and spilled half its contents on the cargo-hold floor, which had been a sidewall. He began painstakingly to gather up the precious stuff and get it back in the bag. The others went on to the *Nadine*. Hallet turned off his helmet-phone and gestured to Moran to remove his helmet. Moran, his eyebrows raised, obeyed the suggestion.

"How anxious," asked Hallet abruptly, gathering up the dropped crystals, "how anxious are you to be left behind here?"

"I'm not anxious at all," said Moran.

"Would you like to make a deal to go along when the *Nadine* lifts? —*If* there's a way to get past the space-port police?"

"Probably," said Moran. "Certainly! But there's no way to do it."

"There is," said Hallet. "I know it. Is it a deal?"

"What is the deal?"

"You do as I say," said Hallet significantly. "Just as I say! Then . . ."

The lock-door opened, some distance away. Hallet stood up and said in a commanding tone;

"Keep your mouth shut. I'll tell you what to do and when."

He put on his helmet and turned on the phone once more. He went toward the lock-door. Moran heard him exchange words with Harper and Brawn, back with empty bags to fill with crystals worth many times the price of diamonds. But diamonds were made in half-ton lots, nowadays.

Moran followed their bags. He was frowning. As Harper was about to follow Brawn, Moran almost duplicated Hallet's gestures to have him remove his helmet.

"I want Burleigh to come next trip," he told Harper, "and make some excuse to stay behind a moment and talk to me without the helmet-phones picking up everything I say to him. Understand?"

Harper nodded. But Burleigh did not come on the next trip. It was not until near midday that he came to carry a load of treasure to the yacht.

When he did come, though, he took off his helmet and turned off the phone without the need of a suggestion.

"I've been arranging storage for this stuff," he said. "I've opened plates between the hulls to dump it in. I've told Carol, too, that we've got to do a perfect job of cleaning up. There must be no stray crystals on the floor."

"Better search the bunks, too," said Moran drily, "so nobody will put aside a particularly pretty crystal to gloat over. Listen!"

He told Burleigh exactly what Hallet had said and what he'd answered. Burleigh looked acutely unhappy.

"Hallet isn't dedicated like the rest of us were," he said distressedly. "We brought him along partly out of fear that if he were captured he'd break down and reveal what he knows of the Underground we led, and much of which we had to leave behind. But I'll be able to finance a real revolt, now!"

❖ ❖ ❖

Moran regarded him with irony. Burleigh was a capable man and a conscientious one. It would be very easy to trust him, and it is all-important to an Underground that its leaders be trusted. But it is also important that they be capable of flintlike hardness on occasion. To Moran, it seemed that Burleigh had not quite the adamantine resolution required for leadership in a conspiracy which was to become a successful revolt. He was—and to Moran it seemed regrettable—capable of the virtue of charity.

"I've told you," he said evenly. "Maybe you'll think it's a scheme on my part to get Hallet dumped and myself elected to take his identity. But what happens from now on is your business. Beginning this moment, I'm taking care of my own skin. I've gotten reconciled to the idea of dying, but I'd hate for it not to do anybody any good."

"Carol," said Burleigh unhappily, "is much distressed."

"That's very kind," said Moran sarcastically. "Now take your bag of stuff and get going."

Burleigh obeyed. Moran went back to the business of breaking open the strong plastic boxes of bessendium so their contents could be carried in forty-pound lots to the *Nadine*.

Thinking of Carol, he did not like the way things seemed to be going. Since the discovery of the bessendium, Hallet had been developing ideas. They did not look as if they meant good fortune for Moran without corresponding bad fortune for the others. Obviously, Moran couldn't be hidden on the *Nadine* during the space-port sterilization of the ship which prevented plagues from being carried from world to world. Hallet could have no reason to promise such a thing. Before landing here, he'd urged that Moran simply be dumped out the air-lock. This proposal to save his life. . . .

Moran considered the situation grimly while the business of ferrying treasure to the yacht went on almost monotonously. It had stopped once during the forenoon while a giant beetle went by. Later, it stopped again because a gigantic flying thing hovered overhead. Carol did not know what it was, but its bulging abdomen ended in an organ which appeared to be a sting. It was plainly hunting. There was no point in fighting it. Presently it went away, and just before it disappeared in the circular wall of mist it dived headlong to the ground. A little later it rose slowly into the air, carrying something almost as large as itself. It went away into the mist.

Again, once a green-and-yellow caterpillar marched past upon some mysterious enterprise. It was covered with incredibly long fur, and it moved with an undulating motion of all its segments, one after another. It seemed well over ten yards in length, and its body appeared impossibly massive. But a large part of the bulk would be the two-foot-long or longer hairs which stuck out stiffly in all directions. It, too, went away.

But continually and constantly there was a bedlam of noises. From underneath the yielding skin of the yeast-ground, there came clickings. Sometimes there were quiverings of the surface as if it were alive, but they would be the activities of ten and twelve-inch beetles who lived in subterranean tunnels in it. There were those preposterous noises like someone rattling a stick along a picket fence—only deafening—and there were baritone chirpings and deep bass boomings from somewhere far away. Moran guessed that the last might be frogs, but if so they were vastly larger than men.

Shortly after what was probably midday, Moran brushed off his hands. The bessendium part of the cargo of the wrecked *Malabar* had been salvaged. It was hidden between the twin hulls of the yacht. Moran had, quite privately, attended to a matter the wreck's long-dead crew should have done when they left it. Now, in theory, the *Nadine* should lift off and take Moran to some hastily scouted spot not too far from the ice-cap. It should leave him there with what food could be spared, and the kit of seeds that might feed him after it was gone, and weapons that might but probably wouldn't enable him to defend himself, and with a radio-beacon to try to have hope in. Then—that would be that.

"Calling," said Moran sardonically into his helmet-phone. "Everything's cleaned up here. What next?"

"*You can come along,*" said Hallet's voice from the ship. It was shivery. It was gleeful. "*Just in time for lunch!*"

Moran went along the disoriented passages of the *Malabar* to the lock. He turned off the beacon that had tried uselessly during six human generations to call for help for men now long dead. He went out the lock and closed it behind him. It was not likely that this planet would ever become a home for men. If there were some strangeness in its constitution that made the descendents of insects placed upon it grow to be giants, humans would not want to settle on it. And there were plenty of much more suitable worlds. So the wrecked space-ship would lie here, under deeper and ever deeper accumulations of the noisome stuff that passed for soil. Perhaps millenia from now, the sturdy, resistant metal of the hull would finally rust through, and then—nothing. No man in all time to come would ever see the *Malabar* again.

Shrugging, he went toward the *Nadine*. He walked through bedlam. He could see a quarter-mile in one direction, and a quarter-mile in another. He could not see more than a little distance upward. The Nadine had landed upon a world with tens of millions of square miles of surface, and nobody had moved more than a hundred yards from its landing-place, and now it would leave and all wonders and all horrors outside this one quarter of a square mile would remain unknown. . . .

He went to the airlock and shed his suit. He opened the inner door. Hallet waited for him.

"Everybody's at lunch," he said. "We'll join them."

Moran eyed him sharply. Hallet grinned widely.

"We're going to take off to find a place for you as soon as we've eaten," he said.

There was mockery in the tone. It occurred abruptly to Moran that Hallet was the kind of person who might, to be sure, plan complete disloyalty to his companions for his own benefit. But he might also enjoy betrayal for its own sake. He might, for example, find it amusing to make a man under sentence of death or marooning believe that he would escape, so Hallet could have the purely malicious pleasure of disappointing him. He might look for Moran to break when he learned that he was to die here after all.

Moran clamped his lips tightly. Carol would be better off if that was the answer. He went toward the yacht's mess-room. Hallet followed close behind. Moran pushed the door aside and entered. Burleigh and Harper and Brawn looked at him, Carol raised her eyes. They glistened with tears.

Hallet said gleefully;

"Here goes!"

Standing behind Moran, he thrust a hand-blaster past Moran's body and pulled the trigger. He held the trigger down for continuous fire as he traversed the weapon to wipe out everybody but Moran and himself.

❖ IV ❖

Moran responded instantly.

His hands flew to Hallet's throat, blind fury making him unaware of any thought but a frantic lust to kill. It was very strange that Moran somehow noticed Hallet's hand insanely pulling the trigger of the blast-pistol over and over and over without result. He remembered it later. Perhaps he shared Hallet's blank disbelief that one could pull the trigger of a blaster and have nothing at all happen in consequence. But nothing did happen, and suddenly he dropped the weapon and clawed desperately at Moran's fingers about his throat. But that was too late.

There was singularly little disturbance at the luncheon-table. The whole event was climax and anticlimax together. Hallet's intention was so appallingly murderous and his action so shockingly futile that the four who were to have been his victims tended to stare blankly while Moran throttled him.

Burleigh seemed to recover first. He tried to pull Moran's hands loose from Hallet's throat. Lacking success he called to the others. "Harper! Brawn! Help me!"

It took all three of them to release Hallet. Then Moran stood panting, shaking, his eyes like flames.

"He—he—" panted Moran. "He was going to kill Carol!"

"I know," said Burleigh, distressedly. "He was going to kill all of us. You gave me an inkling, so while he was packing bessendium between the hulls, and had his space-suit hanging in the airlock, I doctored the blaster in the space-suit pocket." He looked down at Hallet. "Is he still alive?"

Brawn bent over Hallet. He nodded.

"Put him in the airlock for the time being," said Burleigh. "And lock it. When he comes to, we'll decide what to do."

Harper and Brawn took Hallet by the arms and hauled him along the passageway. The inner door of the lock clanged shut on him.

"We'll give him a hearing, of course," said Burleigh conscientiously. "But we should survey the situation first."

To Moran the situation required no survey, but he viewed it from a violently personal viewpoint which would neither require or allow discussion. He knew what he meant to do about Hallet. He said harshly;

"Go ahead. When you're through I'll tell you what will be done."

He went away. To the control-room. There he paced up and down, trying to beat back the fury which rose afresh at intervals of less than minutes. He did not think of his own situation, just then. There are more important things than survival.

He struggled for coolness, with the action before him known. He didn't glance out the ports at the half-mile circle in which vision was possible. Beyond the mist there might be anything; an ocean, swarming metropoli of giant insects, a mountain-range. Nobody on the *Nadine* had explored. But Moran did not think of such matters now. Hallet had tried to murder Carol, and Moran meant to take action, and there were matters which might result from it. The matter the crew of the *Malabar* had forgotten to attend to—.

He searched for paper and a pen. He found both in a drawer for the yacht's hand-written log. He wrote. He placed a small object in the drawer. He had barely closed it when Carol was at the control-room door. She said in a small voice;

"They want to talk to you."

He held up the paper.

"Read this later. Not now," he said curtly. He opened and closed the drawer again, this time putting the paper in it. "I want you to read this after the Hallet business is settled. I'm afraid that I'm not going to look well in your eyes."

She swallowed and did not speak. He went to where the others sat in official council. Burleigh said heavily;

"We've come to a decision. We shall call Hallet and hear what he has to say, but we had to consider various courses of action and decide which were possible and which were not."

Moran nodded grimly. He had made his own decision. It was not too much unlike the one that, carried out, had made him seize the *Nadine* for escape from Coryus. But he'd listen. Harper looked doggedly resolved. Brawn seemed moody as usual.

"I'm listening," said Moran.

"Hallet," said Burleigh regretfully, "intended to murder all of us and with your help take the *Nadine* to someplace where he could hope to land without spaceport inspection."

Moran observed;

"He didn't discuss that part of his plans. He only asked if I'd make a deal to escape being marooned."

"Yes," said Burleigh, nodding. "I'm sure—"

"My own idea," said Moran, "when I tried to seize the *Nadine*, was to try to reach one of several newly-settled planets where things aren't too well organized. I'd memos of some such planets. I hoped to get to ground somewhere in a wilderness on one of them and work my way on foot to a new settlement. There I'd explain that I'd been hunting or prospecting or something of the sort. On a settled planet that would be impossible. On a brand-new one people are less fussy and I might have been accepted quite casually."

"Hallet may have had some such idea in his mind," agreed Burleigh. "With a few bessendium crystals to show, he would seem a successful prospector. He'd be envied but not suspected. To be sure!"

"But," said Moran drily, "he'd be best off alone. So if he had that sort of idea, he intended to murder me too."

Burleigh nodded. "Undoubtedly. But to come to our decision.

We can keep him on board under watch—as we did you—and leave you here. This has disadvantages. We owe you much. There would be risk of his taking someone unawares and fighting for his life. Even if all went as we wished, and we landed and dispersed, he could inform the spaceport officials anonymously of what had happened, leading to investigation and the ruin of any plans for the future revival of our underground. Also, it would destroy any hope for your rescue."

Moran smiled wryly. He hadn't much hope of that, if he were marooned.

"We could leave him here," said Burleigh unhappily, "with you taking his identity for purposes of landing. But I do not think it would be wise to send a ship after him. He would be resentful. If rescued, he would do everything possible to spoil all our future lives, and we are fugitives."

"Ah, yes!" said Moran, still more wryly amused.

"I am afraid," said Burleigh reluctantly, "that we can only offer him his choice of being marooned or going out the airlock. I cannot think of any other alternative."

"I can," said Moran. "I'm going to kill him."

Burleigh blinked. Harper looked up sharply.

"We fight," said Moran grimly. "Armed exactly alike. He can try to kill me. I'll give him the same chance I have. But I'll kill him. They used to call it a duel, and they came to consider it a very immoral business. But that's beside the point. I won't agree to marooning him here. That's murder. I won't agree to throwing him out the air-lock. That's murder, too. But I have the right to kill him if it's in fair fight. That's justice! You can bring him in and let him decide if he wants to be marooned or fight me. I think he's just raging enough to want to do all the damage he can, now that his plans have gone sour."

Burleigh fidgeted. He looked at Harper. Harper nodded grudgingly. He looked at Brawn. Brawn nodded moodily.

Burleigh said fretfully, "Very well . . . Harper, you and Brawn bring him here. We'll see what he says. Be careful!"

Harper and Brawn went down the passageway. Moran saw them take out the blasters they'd worn since he took over the ship. They were ready. They unlocked and opened the inner airlock door.

There was silence. Harper looked shocked. He went in the airlock while Brawn stared, for once startled out of moodiness. Harper came out.

"He's gone," he said in a flat voice. "Out the airlock."

All the rest went instantly to look. The airlock was empty. By the most natural and inevitable of oversights, when Hallet was put in it for a temporary cell, no one had thought of locking the outer door. There was no point in it. It only led out to the nightmare world. And out there Hallet would be in monstrous danger; he'd have no food. At most his only weapon would be the torch Moran had carried to the *Malabar* and brought back again. He could have no hope of any kind. He could feel only despair unthinkable and horror undiluted.

There was a buzzing sound in the airlock. A space-suit hung there. The helmet-phone was turned on. Hallet's voice came out, flat and metallic and desperate and filled with hate:

"What're you going to do now? You'd better think of a bargain to offer me! You can't lift off! I took the fuel-block so Moran couldn't afford to kill me after the rest of you were dead. You can't lift off the ground! Now give me a guarantee I can believe in or you stay here with me!"

Harper bolted for the engine-room. He came back, his face ashen. "He's right. It's gone. He took it."

Moran stirred. Burleigh wrung his hands. Moran reached down the space-suit from whose helmet the voice came tinnily. He began to put it on. Carol opened her lips to speak, and he covered the microphone with his palm.

"I'm going to go out and kill him," said Moran very quietly. "Somebody else had better come along just in case. But you can't make a bargain with him. He can't believe in any promise, because he wouldn't keep any."

Harper went away again. He came back, struggling into a space-suit. Brawn moved quickly. Burleigh suddenly stirred and went for a suit.

"We want torches," said Moran evenly, "for our own safety, and blasters because they'll drop Hallet. Carol, you monitor what goes on. When we need to come back, you can use the direction finder and talk us back to the yacht."

"But—but—"

"What are you going to do?" rasped the voice shrilly. *"You've got to make a bargain! I've got the fuel-block! You can't lift off without the fuel-block! You've got to make a deal."*

The other men came back. With the microphone still muffled by his hand, Moran said sharply, "He has to keep talking until we answer, but he won't know we're on his trail until we do. We keep quiet when we get the helmets on. Understand?" Then he said evenly to Carol. "Look at that paper I showed you if—if anything happens. Don't forget! Ready?"

Carol's hands were clenched. She was terribly pale. She tried to speak, and could not. Moran, with the microphone still covered by the palm of his hand, repeated urgently;

"Remember, no talking! He'll pick up anything we say. Use gestures. Let's go!"

He swung out of the airlock. The others followed. The one certain thing about the direction Hallet would have taken was that it must be away from the wreck. And he'd have been in a panic to get out of sight from the yacht.

Moran saw his starting-point at once. Landing, the *Nadine* had used rockets for easing to ground because it is not possible to make delicate adjustments of interplanetary drive. A take-off, yes. But to land even at a spaceport one uses rockets to cushion what otherwise might be a sharp impact. The *Nadine*'s rockets had burned away the yeasty soil when she came to ground. There was a burnt-away depression down to bedrock in the stuff all around her. But Hallet had broken the scorched, crusty edge of the hollow as he climbed up to the blanket-like surface-skin.

Moran led the way after him. He moved with confidence. The springy, sickeningly uncertain stuff underfoot was basically white-that-had-been-soiled. Between the *Nadine*'s landing-spot and the now-gutted wreck, it happened that only that one color showed. But, scattered at random in other places, there were patches of red mould and blue mould and black dusty rust and greenish surface-fungi. Twenty yards from the depression in which the *Nadine* lay, Hallet's footprints were clearly marked in a patch of orange-yellow ground-cover which gave off impalpable yellow spores when touched. Moran gestured for attention and pointed out the trail. He gestured again for the others to spread out.

Hallet's voice came again. He'd left the *Nadine's* lock because he could make no bargain for his life while in the hands of his companions. He could only bargain for his life if they could not find him or the precious fuel-block without which the *Nadine* must remain here forever. But from the beginning he knew such terror that he could not contrive, himself, a bargain that could possibly be made.

He chattered agitatedly, not yet sure that his escape had been discovered. At times he seemed almost hysterical. Moran and the others could hear him pant, sometimes, as a fancied movement aroused his panic. Once they heard the noise of his torch as he burned a safety-hole in the ground. But he did not use it. He hastened on. He talked desperately. Sometimes he boasted, and sometimes he tried cunningly to be reasonable. But he hadn't been prepared for the absolute failure of what should have been the simplest and surest form of multiple murder. Now in a last ditch stand, he hysterically abused them for taking so long to realize that they had to make a deal.

His four pursuers went grimly over the elastic surface of this world upon his trail. The *Nadine* faded into the mist. Off to the right a clump of toadstools grew. They were taller than any of the men, and their pulpy stalks were more than a foot thick. Hallet's trail in the colored surface-moulds went on. The giant toadstools were left behind. The trail led straight toward an enormous object the height of a three-storey house. When first glimpsed through the mist, it looked artificial. But as they drew near they saw that it was a cabbage; gigantic, with leaves impossibly huge and thick. There was a spike in its middle on which grew cruciform faded flowers four feet across.

Then Hallet screamed. They heard it in their helmet-phones. He screamed again. Then for a space he was silent, gasping, and then he uttered shrieks of pure horror. But they were cries of horror, not of pain.

Moran found himself running, which was probably ridiculous. The others hastened after him. And suddenly the mistiness ahead took on a new appearance. The ground fell away. It became evident that the *Nadine* had landed upon a plateau with levels below it and very possibly mountains rising above. But here the slightly rolling plateau fell sheer away. There was a place where the yeasty soil—but here it was tinted with a purplish overcast of foleate fungus—where the soil had given way. Something had fallen, here.

It would have been Hallet. He'd gone too close to a precipice, moving agitatedly in search of a hiding-place in which to conceal himself until the people of the *Nadine* made a deal he could no longer believe in.

His cries still came over the helmet-phones. Moran went grimly to look. He found himself gazing down into a crossvalley perhaps two hundred feet deep. At the bottom there were the incredible, green growing things. But they were not trees. They were some flabby weed with thick reddish stalks and enormous pinnate leaves. It grew here to the height of oaks. But Hallet had not dropped so far.

From anchorages on bare rock, great glistening cables reached downward to other anchorages on the valley floor. The cables crossed each other with highly artificial precision at a central point. They formed the foundation for a web of geometrically accurate design and unthinkable size. Crosscables of sticky stuff went round and round the center of the enormous snare, following a logarithmic spiral with absolute exactitude. It was a spider's web whose cables stretched hundreds of feet; whose bird-limed ropes would trap and hold even the monster insects of this world. And Hallet was caught in it.

He'd tumbled from the cliff-edge as fungoid soil gave way under him. He'd bounced against a sloping, fungus-covered rocky wall and with fragments of curdy stuff about him had been flung out and into the snare. He was caught as firmly as any of the other creatures on which the snare's owner fed.

His shrieks of horror began when he realized his situation. He struggled, setting up insane vibrations in the fabric of the web. He shrieked again, trying to break the bonds of cordage that clung the more horribly as he struggled to break free. And the struggling was most unwise.

"We want to cut the cables with torches," said Moran sharply. "If we can make the web drop we'll be all right. Webspiders don't hunt on the ground. Go ahead! Make it fast!"

Burleigh and the others hastened to what looked like a nearly practicable place by which to descend. Moran moved swiftly to where one cable of the web was made fast at the top. It was simple sanity to break down the web—by degrees, of course—to get at Hallet. But Hallet did not cooperate. He writhed and struggled and shrieked.

His outcry, of course, counted for nothing in the satanic cacophony that filled the air. All the monsters of all the planet seemed to make discordant noises. Hallet could add nothing. But his struggles in the web had meaning to the owner of the trap.

They sent tiny tremblings down the web-cables. And this was the fine mathematical creation of what was quaintly called a "garden spider" on other worlds. *Epeira fasciata*. She was not in it. She sat sluggishly in a sheltered place, remote from her snare. But a line, a cord, a signal-cable went from the center of the web to the spider's retreat. She waited with implacable patience, one foreleg—sheathed in ragged and somehow revolting fur—resting delicately upon the line. Hallet's frantic struggles shook the web. Faintly, to be sure, but distinctively. The vibrations were wholly unlike the violent, thrashing struggles of a heavy beetle or a giant cricket. They were equally unlike those flirtatious, seductive pluckings of a web-cable which would mean that an amorous male of her own species sought the grisly creature's affection.

Hallet made the web quiver as small prey would shake it. The spider would have responded instantly to bigger game, if only to secure it before the vast snare was damaged by frenzied plungings. Still, though there was no haste, the giant rose and in leisurely fashion traversed the long cable to the web's center. Moran saw it.

"Hallet!" he barked into his helmet-phone, "Hallet! Hold still! Don't move!"

He raced desperately along the edge of the cliff, risking a fall more immediately fatal than Hallet's. It was idiotic to make such an attempt at rescue. It was sheer folly. But there are instincts one has to obey against all reason. Moran did not think of the fuel-block. Typically, Hallet did.

"I've got the fuel-block," he gasped between screams. *"If you don't help me—"*

But then the main cable nearest him moved in a manner not the result of his own struggles. It was the enormous weight of the owner of the web, moving leisurely on her own snare, which made the web shake now. And Hallet lost even the coherence of hysteria and simply shrieked.

Moran came to a place where a main anchor-cable reached bed-rock. It ran under yeasty ground-cover to an anchorage. He thrust his torch deep, feeling for the cable. It seared through. The web jerked wildly as one of its principal supports parted. The giant spider turned aside to investigate the event. Such a thing should happen only when one of the most enormous of possible victims became entangled.

Moran went racing for another cable-anchorage. But when he found where the strong line fastened, it was simply and starkly impossible to climb down to it. He swore and looked desperately for Burleigh and Brawn and Harper. They were far away, hurrying to descend but not yet where they could bring the web toppling down by cutting other cables.

The yellow-banded monster came to the cut end of the line. It swung down. It climbed up again. Hallet shrieked and kicked.

The spider moved toward him. Of all nightmarish creatures on this nightmare of a planet, a giant spider with a body eight feet long and legs to span as many yards was most revolting. Its abdomen was obscenely swollen. As it moved, its spinnerets paid out newly-formed cord behind it. Its eyes were monstrous and murderously intent. The ghastly, needle-sharp mandibles beside its mouth seemed to move lustfully with a life of their own. And it was somehow ten times more horrible because of its beastly fur. Tufts of black hairiness, half-yards in length, streamed out as its legs moved.

There was another cable still. Moran made for it. He reached it where it stretched down like a slanting tight-rope. He jerked out his torch to sever it—and saw that to cut it would be to drop the spider almost upon Hallet. It would seize him then because of his writhings. But not to cut it—

He tried his blaster. He fired again and again. The blaster-bolts hurt. The spider reacted with fury. The blaster would have killed a man at this distance, though it would have been ignored by a chitin-armored beetle. But against the spider the bolts were like bites. They made small wounds, but not serious ones. The spider made a bubbling sound which was more daunting than any cry would have been. It flung its legs about, fumbling for the thing that it believed attacked it. It continued the bubbling sounds. Its mandibles clashed and gnashed against each other. They were small noises in the din which was the norm on this mad world, but they were more horrible than any other sounds Moran had ever heard.

The spider suddenly began to move purposefully toward the spot where Hallet jerked insanely and shrieked in heart-rending horror.

Moran found himself attempting the impossible. He knew it was impossible. The blast-pistol hurt but did not injure the giant because the range was too long. So—it was totally unjustifiable—he found himself slung below the downward-slanting cable and sliding down its slope. He was going to where the range would be short enough for his blast-pistol to be effective. He slid to a cross-cable, and avoided it and went on.

Burleigh and Brawn and Harper were tiny figures, very far away. Moran hung by one hand and used his free hand to fire the blaster once more. It hurt more seriously, now. The spider made bubbling noises of infinite ferocity. And it moved with incredible agility toward the one object it could imagine as meaning attack.

It reached Hallet. It seized him.

Moran's blast-pistol could not kill it. It had to be killed. Now! He drew out his torch and pressed the continuous-flame stud. Raging, he threw it at the spider.

It spun in the air, a strange blue-white pinwheel in the gray light of this planet's day. It cut through a cable that might have deflected it. It reached the spider, now reared high and pulling Hallet from the sticky stuff that had captured him.

The spinning torch hit. The flame burned deep. The torch actually sank into the spider's body.

And there was a titanic flame and an incredible blast and Moran knew nothing.

A long time later he knew that he ached. He became aware that he hurt. Still later he realized that Burleigh and Brawn and Harper stood around him. He'd splashed in some enormous thickness of the yeasty soil, grown and fallen from the cliff-edge, and it was not solid enough to break his bones. Harper, doubtless, had been most resolute in digging down to him and pulling him out.

He sat up, and growled at innumerable unpleasant sensations.

"That," he said painfully, "was a very bad business."

"It's all bad business," said Burleigh in a flat and somehow exhausted tone. "The fuel-block burned. There's nothing left of it or Hallet or the spider."

Moran moved an arm. A leg. The other arm and leg. He got unsteadily to his feet.

"It was bessendium and uranium," added Burleigh hopelessly. "And the uranium burned. It wasn't an atomic explosion, it just burned like sodium or potassium would do. But it burned fast! The torch-flame must have reached it." He added absurdly. "Hallet died instantly, of course. Which is better fortune than we are likely to have."

"Oh, that . . ." said Moran. "We're all right. I said I was going to kill him. I wasn't trying to at the moment, but I did. By accident." He paused, and said dizzily; "I think he should feel obliged to me. I was distinctly charitable to him!"

Harper said grimly;

"But we can't lift off. We're all marooned here now."

Moran took an experimental step. He hurt, but he was sound.

"Nonsense!" he said. "The crew of the *Malabar* went off without taking the fuel-block from the wreck's engines. It's in a drawer in the

Nadine's control-room with a note to Carol that I asked her to read should something happen to me. We may have to machine it a little to make it fit the Nadine's engines. But we're all right!"

Carol's voice came in his helmet-phone. It was shaky and desperately glad.

"We're on the way," said Moran.

He was pleased with Carol's reaction. He also realized that now there would be the right number of people on the *Nadine;* they would take off from this world and arrive reasonably near due-time at Loris without arousing the curiosity of space-port officials.

He looked about him. The way the others had come down was a perfectly good way to climb up again. On the surface, above, their trail would be clear on the multi-colored surface rusts. There were four men together, all with blast-pistols and three with torches. They should be safe.

Moran talked cheerfully, climbing to the plateau on which the *Nadine* had landed, trudging with the others across a world on which it was impossible to see more than a quarter-mile in any direction. But the way was plain. Beyond the mist Carol waited.

An Epistle to the Thessalonians

INTRODUCTION

Normally, I disapprove of the practice of including an excerpt from a novel in an anthology as if it were a short story, but as Sturgeon's Law puts it, "Nothing is always absolutely so,"* and this excerpt actually *is* a self-contained short story. Moreover, Damon Knight reprinted this same excerpt as a short story in his early 1950s SF magazine, *Worlds Beyond*, so there's formidable precedent for doing this. Philip Wylie's novel *Finnley Wren* was, as part of its long subtitle had it, "A Novel in a New Manner," and at one point the narrator is reading a story that the title character has written titled, "An Epistle to the Thessalonians," about an apparently human (he wears pants with cuffs!), but very, *very* big giant who descends from space, stays for a time, indifferent to the destruction he causes, then departs into the sky. Not surprisingly for the author of *Generation of Vipers*, Wylie's focus is on satire, as he casts a jaundiced eye on the human reaction to the titanic visitor.

✣ ✣ ✣

Philip Wylie (1902-1971) may be remembered mostly for his best-selling nonfiction work of social criticism, *Generation of Vipers*, but he was very much a prolific writer of science fiction. His early novel *Gladiator* was probably an influence in the creation of Superman, and his collaborative novels with Edwin Balmer, *When Worlds Collide* and *After Worlds Collide*, were national best-sellers in a time when science fiction was seldom published in book form. *When Worlds Collide* was sold to the movies and almost became a Cecil B. DeMille production in the 1930s, but instead languished until 1951 when George Pal brought it to the screen as his follow-up to *Destination Moon*. Wylie's fantasy novel *The Disappearance*, another best seller, was cited by Theodore Sturgeon as one of his favorite novels. In the 1960s, his novel of atomic war, *Triumph*, was a best seller, as well as being serialized in *The Saturday Evening Post*, a triumph in itself. While *Finnley Wren*, from which "Epistle to the Thessalonians" is taken, is in no way either fantasy or SF, I recommend it highly, and I'm glad to see that Dalkey Archive is bringing the novel out in a new edition.

*Yes, that is Sturgeon's *Law*. While "Ninety percent of *everything* is crud" is often mistakenly called Sturgeon's Law, Theodore Sturgeon's preferred name for the latter quip was "Sturgeon's *Revelation*" when he presented it in his book review column in the March 1958 issue of the SF magazine *Venture*.

An Epistle to the Thessalonians

by Philip Wylie

Comerade Nikolai Dimitri Eisenstein, the renowned Leninist incendiary and pickpocket, having heisted the keister of Mrs. Benjamin Bissel, housewife, of 1594 East Orchid Street, the Bronx, reviewed its meager interior as he stood beneath the elevated on Sixth Avenue. He was quite unaware of the lacy pattern described on the trolley track by the sun in conjunction with the elevated ties until the phenomenon was blotted out, some say rudely, some say politely and gradually.

We will now drop Comrade Nikolai Dimitri Eisenstein.

The cause of the shadow which fell over the whole city of New York and many other cities besides on that halcyon July morning was an obstruction of Old Sol in the form of a giant one thousand miles high.

The giant, appearing from no one knows where and unannounced by the world's observatories which, at the time, were jammed with hawk-eyed astronomers whose data tabulated in light-years about matters of less consequence than the visitor to our planet was always available while on this pertinent matter their information was nil, dropped rapidly from a strategic position behind the moon. As he entered the gravitational sphere of earth's influence he picked up our rotary motion so that his descent upon the sea was not accompanied by embarrassing tidal waves. Indeed, he stepped onto the waters of the Atlantic so circumspectly that the lay notion he had jumped through space was absurd.

The lower two hundred miles of him penetrated our atmosphere between eleven-six and eleven-twenty A.M., Eastern Standard Time, and came to rest on the sea about an hour later, as he manifestly appreciated the danger of stamping upon the water.

However, his advent caused trouble enough, in spite of his elaborate caution. The sea rose in a slow surge which drenched the populous fringes of New York Bay and the lower portion of the Hudson River. His descending feet set in motion currents of air that roared and twisted over New York, Long Island, New Jersey and Connecticut, causing property damage later totaled by the Associated Press at one hundred and seventeen million, loss of life to eighty-three persons and accidents of varying seriousness to a number estimated at two hundred twelve.

A minor earthquake was reported from the seismographs of several stations, the most remote of them located at Butte, Montana, and one Torrence Bemis cabled an interesting story to the *New York Telegram* headed, "Malaise among Inhabitants of Mombasa, Kenya, Africa," with time corrections.

These geological eccentricities, however, were mere twaddle and fluff in comparison to the effect of the giant and his appearance upon mankind in general. No complete record will ever be made. Witness, for example, the following: at a time as recently removed from the incident as the present, no less than seven hundred three volumes have been published relating to the monstrous man and ranging in scope from Glover's authoritative *Economic Consequences of the Giant's Visitation* to *Love in Giant Land,* by Jacqueline Chiffon, an opus from the typewriter of a young Cleveland woman so saturated with sentimentality, so saccharine, and so illiterate that one Amos Golf, after reading it, went stark mad (to his infinite glory) and assassinated not only Miss Chiffon but the eleven other most famous American lady authors.

Twenty-six religions were founded during the stay of the giant or are now identified with his sojourn. Bouncerism, originating in

Georgia, attempted to drive away the giant, claimed sole credit for his departure (which is widely believed to have been voluntary) and now holds as its major tenet the prevention of further visits. The devotees of Bouncerism pray in pig Latin while jumping up and down in each others' arms. The Arrivalists, now segregated in Toledo, live in metal shacks, wear only garments woven of human beard hair, and celebrate July 19th as Giantmas. The Church of the Holy Nut, venerating a brown seed thirty-seven feet long which fell from the giant's person and is assumed to be a spore from the stranger's world, believe that their deity was Christ in his Second Coming. Legal process was necessary to keep the members of the Church of the Holy Nut from worshiping Him by blowing up mountains—a form of veneration doubtless appropriate, but unduly hazardous to the skeptical, of whom there were luckily hundreds of millions.

And so it went. While a draft blew over the cities of New Jersey—cities named by persons with minds as poisoned as the imagination of their architects (Belcher has listed them in his "Inverse Lyrics": Hackensack, Trenton, Newark, Hoboken, Red Bank, Jersey City, Weehawken, Nutley, Ten Eyck, New Brunswick, Paterson, Camden, Perth Amboy, Boonton, Elizabeth, etc., *ad naus.*) and while the waters rose in the shipping focus of the world—the necks of the western hemisphere bent upward to behold the wonder in the sky. Millions were frightened. Millions sought for methods of turning the phenomenon into cash. Millions ignored the giant.

Fields and housetops were at a premium.

Telescopes swung from their patient routines.

Scientists hopped to long distance telephones.

The War Department drew in a lungful of air and bleated it out in its usual vain ignorance.

The President's lunch was spoiled.

But one fact—or perhaps it was a condition—dominated all others. Nobody—nobody in Hoboken and nobody in New York, nobody in Washington and nobody in Europe—knew what in hell to do.

Standing in the Atlantic Ocean, southeast of New York, was a giant one thousand miles high.

Incredible.

Ominous.

Unprecedented.

Indubitable.

There he was.

The sun beat upon him.

The sea laved the soles of his shoes.

His trouser cuffs, seen longitudinally through the earth's atmosphere, disappeared in haze. But the higher portions of him reemerged. His head, a thousand miles out in space, was boldly visible. Through telescopes mounted on the loftier summits, even his expression could be observed. It was speculative, absorbed, and yet bland. He had gray eyes (which shone like moons in the late afternoon sun) and chestnut-colored hair which revealed a distinct tendency to curl. Lowell Wertzberg, of Ohio Wesleyan, located at Delaware, Ohio, was first to report the mole on his left cheek. His age was promptly put at thirty-five—although when an editor of an evening paper asked, "Thirty-five what?" no answer was forthcoming.

During the afternoon following his arrival the giant was seen to blink seven times. The process required about fifteen minutes (15 min. 36.9006 sec. average for twenty-four winks—Ed.). His head turned downward sixteen degrees between noon and four P.M. His arms swung forward eighty miles (Westcliffe and Leadbecker) and his eyebrows lifted seven thousand six hundred and five meters (Finch). The most proximate position of the sole of his left shoe was accurately determined by the United States Coast Guard and afterward substantiated by the Geodetic Survey at one hundred eleven miles east southeast of Sandy Hook.

Photographs taken by Binnel at seven-fifty show that the sun had set on his lower extremities, but his face was vividly illuminated and, in fact, it became clearer as terrestrial darkness increased. Equally interesting are Gukel's lens studies of the moon partially eclipsed by the giant's buttocks, Gukel's credit being shared by the enterprising University of Southern Illinois.

Before nightfall on that memorable First Day, Lieutenant Charles Windbuck had returned from his epochal flight to the giant's toe.

Although subsequent observations demonstrated that the monster moved with a slowness which suggested either consideration of the human beings below or, more probably, a desire to avoid setting fire to his clothing by atmospheric friction, Windbuck's flight was regarded at the time as a heroic venture.

"I discovered," Windbuck said that night over the radio to an audience of millions, "that the material of the giant's shoe is granular and resembles at close range a rough, conglomerate cliff. The sole of the shoe itself, although submerged in the Atlantic, rises to such a height from the water that its upper edge was above the ceiling of my airplane. A few dead fish floated around the shoe, which appeared to be motionless. I cannot describe the feeling I had staring at the precipice which had dropped into the sea, or looking eastward where the giant's shadow stretched over the broad ocean."

On the night of July nineteenth to twentieth, the uproar caused by the strange visit had spread over the globe. Hindus and Brahmins were praying as shriekingly as Presbyterians, and only remote Australian Bushmen shared tranquility with a few Senegalese, Eskimos, and the like.

The morning of the twentieth, hot and cloudless in Eastern U.S., was marked by a partial evacuation of the seaboard, a Stock Exchange panic, the declaration of martial law, and innumerable other mass reactions.

Professor Grover Rigg, with a corps of university volunteers, endeavored to communicate with the giant by laying out thousands of yards of white muslin on the fields south of Princeton in varying mathematical configurations. Nothing happened. A fighting fleet consisting of six battleships, four submarines, three cruisers, twelve destroyers, four blimps and the dirigible *Akron* moved out to the toe, stripped for action. Nothing happened. A Gloucester fisherman approached the right shoe and detached some of its material with axes and an acetylene torch brought for the purpose. Still nothing happened.

General Trumpley Clutt made before the House of Congress his celebrated "survival of the fittest" address, parts of which were published on the front pages of every American daily. "The man," said the general, "is human, obviously hostile, patently an enemy scout. We must declare war on him, gentlemen. We must annihilate him. Otherwise he will return whence he came and carry the news that we are a defenseless rabble. He will bring back a host of his fellows and we shall be doomed."

His speech was greeted by a tumult. When Representative Smith of Connecticut stood up afterward and said, briefly, "How are we to annihilate him? What shall we do with a carcass weighing billions of tons?" he was booed down by the members of the House, who make it a rule to prefer any idiocy, so long as it is noisome, to the most obvious common sense.

The result of Clutt's bombast was the immediate formation of eighteen committees and commissions.

On the morning of the twenty-first it was perceived that the giant was bending at the waist, knees, and hips. His shadow slipped sidewise across eastern U.S., moving out of Ohio entirely. The afternoon newspapers carried the banner, "GIANT SQUATTING."

And squat he did, all during the hectic night that followed. At dawn, he was within seventy-four miles of the surface of the sea at certain hitherto unapproached points. Otherwise his behavior was innocuous.

War was declared on him twelve hours later, as his hands swung forward. Clutt and an expeditionary force spent the night mining his shoe with eighty tons of high explosive. It was detonated at daybreak on the twenty-third.

With the explosion, vast chunks of the giant's shoe were ripped away, but when an animated drawing showing the relative amount of damage done was displayed in the New York newsreel theaters later in the day, public confidence in our military strength and resourcefulness diminished. The damage to the shoe was equivalent to the bite of a very small ant on a number twelve hiking boot. There was a brief wave of ridicule launched against Clutt. Editors pointed out that the giant could scarcely be called a military scout, as he wore not a uniform, but tweeds of the most informal sort. Clutt retorted that he would shoot any puppy who wrote a line about him and asked what scouts were presumed to wear in the giant's homeland.

Thus the whole controversy was soon at loggerheads.

During the night of the twenty-fourth, the giant put his fingertips down in New Jersey and New York and leaned forward on them.

Small cities and towns were wiped out. Thousands upon thousands were slain. Hundreds of millions of dollars' worth of property damage was done.

Higgle's report that the material resembling pudding or cobblestone retrieved by the Gloucester fisherman was cell tissue, interested few. His assertion that the possession of those vastly magnified, dry leather cells would advance the study of biology, physics, and chemistry farther than all the research in those subjects hitherto conducted, fell on deaf ears. Ryelin's amazing "Initial Remarks" referring to his inspection of material taken from one of the mighty, inverted canyons which were the whorls and patterns in the skin of the giant's fingers appeared in but two or three newspapers.

On the twenty-fifth, the giant stood up again. Nearly every cabinet in the world had collapsed. Half the people on the eastern coast of the United States had fled to the interior. Crime and lawlessness had surpassed the powers of the military authorities and there had been several mutinies among the troops closest to the giant.

General Trumpley Clutt had committed suicide.

It rained, generally, on the twenty-sixth and the blotting out of the shape in the sky had a salubrious effect on the population of the eastern states. This effect was lost, however, when it was observed as the storm cleared that the giant was standing on his right foot and had drawn back his left.

What happened after that appalls the most sanguine and capacious imagination. The giant stood for three hours like a football player about to kick a goal. Then his majestic toe descended in a slow arc. It connected with the earth at Fire Island. It rushed northward at a speed of forty-three miles an hour and scuffed out of existence the five Boroughs of New York, the cities of New Jersey, the Hudson River Valley and much of the region between it and the Connecticut River, leaving behind a smooth channel of polished rock and stacking up in a line between the Adirondack Mountains and Augusta, Maine, the surface material thus collected which included not only the forests, fields, farms, slums and skyscrapers of the region, but the corpses of eighteen million persons and which made a range of loosely integrated mountains rising at their highest elevation to fifty-six thousand four hundred and eight feet. By some absurd mischance the steel steeple of the Empire State Building protruded from the highest escarpment of the unnatural range.

After that devastating act, the giant departed. He seemed to float away into space, gathering speed as he went. He wore on his face a faintly annoyed expression, such as might be found on the countenance of a man who had come upon an anthill and kicked it out of existence.

Daçoit, however, and other Europeans, agree that the scientific knowledge of molecular and atomic structure and of cell function derived from a consideration of the skin and leather snippings are worth more than the lives lost and the property destroyed.

Who knows?

The Monster of Lake Lametrie

INTRODUCTION

Here's the oldest story in this book (though not all that old in comparison with such giants of unpleasant appearance and habits as Polyphemus and Grendel), published in the September 1899 issue of *Pearson's Magazine*, according to some sources, though *The Encyclopedia of Science Fiction*, edited by John Clute and Peter Nichols, confirms the year of 1899, but gives the title of the publication as *The Windsor Magazine*. That invaluable book describes the tale as, "a short story about a brain transplant . . . in which the brain is human and the recipient body that of a prehistoric survival from a bottomless lake that may lead into a hollow earth." In the website, *Tellers of Weird Tales*, Terence E. Hanley quoted the same description, then added, "If that description doesn't make you want to read the story, I don't know what will." He's right, you know . . .

❖ ❖ ❖

Wardon Allan Curtis (1867-1940) was a journalist for several newspapers, including the *Chicago Daily News*, the *Boston Herald*, and the *Manchester Herald*, and wrote a number of stories with fantastic elements, including "The Fate of the 'Senegambian Queen'" in a 1900 issue of *The Black Cat*, reprinted in *Weird Tales* in 1973, "The Seal of Solomon the Great" in *The Argosy* in 1901, and "The Mahoosalem Boys" in *All-Story Weekly* in 1920, as well as a 1903 book of stories, *The Strange Adventures of Mr. Middleton*.

The Monster of Lake Lametrie

by Wardon Allan Curtis

Being the narration of James McLennegan, M.D., Ph.D.

LAKE LAMETRIE, WYOMING,

APRIL 1ST, 1899.

Prof. Wilhelm G. Breyfogle,
University of Taychobera.

DEAR FRIEND,—Inclosed you will find some portions of the diary it has been my life-long custom to keep, arranged in such a manner as to narrate connectedly the history of some remarkable occurrences that have taken place here during the last three years. Years and years ago, I heard vague accounts of a strange lake high up in an almost inaccessible part of the mountains of Wyoming. Various incredible tales were related of it, such as that it was inhabited by creatures which elsewhere on the globe are found only as fossils of a long vanished time.

The lake and its surroundings are of volcanic origin, and not the least strange thing about the lake is that it is subject to periodic disturbances, which take the form of a mighty boiling in the centre, as if a tremendous artesian well were rushing up there from the bowels of the earth. The lake rises for a time, almost filling the basin of black rocks in which it rests, and then recedes, leaving on the shores mollusks and trunks of strange trees and bits of strange ferns which no longer grow—on the earth, at least—and are to be seen elsewhere only in coal measures and beds of stone. And he who casts hook and line into the dusky waters, may haul forth, ganoid fishes completely covered with bony plates.

All of this is described in the account written by Father LaMetrie years ago, and he there advances the theory that the earth is hollow, and that its interior is inhabited by the forms of plant and animal life which disappeared from its surface ages ago, and that the lake connects with this interior region. Symmes' theory of polar orifices is well known to you. It is amply corroborated. I know that it is true now. Through the great holes at the poles, the sun sends light and heat into the interior.

Three years ago this month, I found my way through the mountains here to Lake LaMetrie accompanied by a single companion, our friend, young Edward Framingham. He was led to go with me not so much by scientific fervor, as by a faint hope that his health might be improved by a sojourn in the mountains, for he suffered from an acute form of dyspepsia that at times drove him frantic.

Beneath an overhanging scarp of the wall of rock surrounding the lake, we found a rudely-built stone-house left by the old cliff dwellers. Though somewhat draughty, it would keep out the infrequent rains of the region, and serve well enough as a shelter for the short time which we intended to stay.

The extracts from my diary follow:

APRIL 29TH, 1896.

I have been occupied during the past few days in gathering specimens of the various plants which are cast upon the shore by the waves of this remarkable lake. Framingham does nothing but fish, and claims that he has discovered the place where the lake communicates with the interior of the earth, if, indeed, it does, and there seems to be little doubt of that. While fishing at a point near the centre of the lake, he let down three pickerel lines tied together, in all nearly three hundred feet, without finding bottom. Coming ashore, he collected every bit of line, string, strap, and rope in our possession, and made a line five hundred feet long, and still he was unable to find the bottom.

MAY 2ND, EVENING.

The past three days have been profitably spent in securing specimens, and mounting and pickling them for preservation. Framingham has had a bad attack of dyspepsia this morning and is not very well. Change of climate had a brief effect for the better upon his malady, but seems to have exhausted its force much sooner than one would have expected, and he lies on his couch of dry water weeds, moaning piteously. I shall take him back to civilisation as soon as he is able to be moved.

It is very annoying to have to leave when I have scarcely begun to probe the mysteries of the place. I wish Framingham had not come with me. The lake is roaring wildly without, which is strange, as it has been perfectly calm hitherto, and still more strange because I can neither feel nor hear the rushing of the wind, though perhaps that is because it is blowing from the south, and we are protected from it by the cliff. But in that case there ought to be no waves on this shore. The roaring seems to grow louder momentarily. Framingham—

MAY 3RD, MORNING.

Such a night of terror we have been through. Last evening, as I sat writing in my diary, I heard a sudden hiss, and, looking down, saw wriggling across the earthen floor what I at first took to be a serpent of some kind, and then discovered was a stream of water which, coming in contact with the fire, had caused the startling hiss. In a moment, other streams had darted in, and before I had collected my senses enough to move, the water was two inches deep everywhere and steadily rising.

Now I knew the cause of the roaring, and, rousing Framingham, I half dragged him, half carried him to the door, and digging our feet into the chinks of the wall of the house, we climbed up to its top. There was nothing else to do, for above us and behind us was the unscalable cliff, and on each side the ground sloped away rapidly, and it would have been impossible to reach the high ground at the entrance to the basin.

After a time we lighted matches, for with all this commotion there was little air stirring, and we could see the water, now half-way up the side of the house, rushing to the west with the force and velocity of the current of a mighty river, and every little while it hurled tree-trunks against the house-walls with a terrific shock that threatened to batter them down. After an hour or so, the roaring began to decrease, and finally there was an absolute silence. The water, which reached to within a foot of where we sat, was at rest, neither rising nor falling.

Presently a faint whispering began and became a stertorous breathing, and then a rushing like that of the wind and a roaring rapidly increasing in volume, and the lake was in motion again, but this time the water and its swirling freight of tree-trunks flowed by the house toward the east, and was constantly falling, and out in the centre of the lake the beams of the moon were darkly reflected by the sides of a huge whirlpool, streaking the surface of polished blackness down, down, down the vortex into the beginning of whose terrible depths we looked from our high perch.

This morning the lake is back at its usual level. Our mules are drowned, our boat destroyed, our food damaged, my specimens and some of my instruments injured, and Framingham is very ill. We shall have to depart soon, although I dislike exceedingly to do so, as the disturbance of last night, which is clearly like the one described by Father LaMetrie, has undoubtedly brought up from the bowels of the earth some strange and interesting things. Indeed, out in the middle of the lake where the whirlpool subsided, I can see a large quantity of floating things; logs and branches, most of them probably, but who knows what else?

Through my glass I can see a tree-trunk, or rather stump, of enormous dimensions. From its width I judge that the whole tree must have been as large as some of the Californian big trees. The main part of it appears to be about ten feet wide and thirty feet long. Projecting from it and lying prone on the water is a limb, or root, some fifteen feet long, and perhaps two or three feet thick. Before we leave, which will be as soon as Framingham is able to go, I shall make a raft and visit the mass of driftwood, unless the wind providentially sends it ashore.

MAY 4TH, EVENING.

A day of most remarkable and wonderful occurrences. When I arose this morning and looked through my glass, I saw that the mass of driftwood still lay in the middle of the lake, motionless on the glassy surface, but the great black stump had disappeared. I was sure it was not hidden by the rest of the driftwood, for yesterday it lay some distance from the other logs, and there had been no disturbance of wind or water to change its position. I therefore concluded that it was some heavy wood that needed to become but slightly waterlogged to cause it to sink.

Framingham having fallen asleep at about ten, I sallied forth to look along the shores for specimens, carrying with me a botanical can, and a South American machete, which I have possessed since a visit to Brazil three years ago, where I learned the usefulness of this sabre-like thing. The shore was strewn with bits of strange plants and shells, and I was stooping to pick one up, when suddenly I felt my clothes plucked, and heard a snap behind me, and turning about I saw—but I won't describe it until I tell what I did, for I did not fairly see the terrible creature until I had swung my machete round and sliced off the top of its head, and then tumbled down into the shallow water where I lay almost fainting.

❖   ❖   ❖

Here was the black log I had seen in the middle of the lake, a monstrous elasmosaurus, and high above me on the heap of rocks lay the thing's head with its long jaws crowded with sabre-like teeth, and its enormous eyes as big as saucers. I wondered that it did not move, for I expected a series of convulsions, but no sound of a commotion was heard from the creature's body, which lay out of my sight on the other side of the rocks. I decided that my sudden cut had acted like a stunning blow and produced a sort of coma, and fearing lest the beast should recover the use of its muscles before death fully took place, and in its agony roll away into the deep water where I could not secure it, I hastily removed the brain entirely, performing the operation neatly, though with some trepidation, and restoring to the head the detached segment cut off by my machete, I proceeded to examine my prize.

In length of body, it is exactly twenty-eight feet. In the widest part it is eight feet through laterally, and is some six feet through from back to belly. Four great flippers, rudimentary arms and feet, and an immensely long, sinuous, swan-like neck, complete the creature's body. Its head is very small for the size of the body and is very round, and a pair of long jaws project in front much like a duck's bill. Its skin is a leathery integument of a lustrous black, and its eyes are enormous hazel optics with a soft, melancholy stare in their liquid depths. It is an elasmosaurus, one of the largest of antediluvian animals. Whether of the same species as those whose bones have been discovered, I cannot say.

My examination finished, I hastened after Framingham, for I was certain that this waif from a long past age would arouse almost any invalid. I found him somewhat recovered from his attack of the morning, and he eagerly accompanied me to the elasmosaurus. In examining the animal afresh, I was astonished to find that its heart was still beating and that all the functions of the body except thought were being performed one hour after the thing had received its death blow, but I knew that the hearts of sharks have been known to beat hours after being removed from the body, and that decapitated frogs live, and have all the powers of motion, for weeks after their heads have been cut off.

I removed the top of the head to look into it and here another surprise awaited me, for the edges of the wound were granulating and preparing to heal. The colour of the interior of the skull was perfectly healthy and natural, there was no undue flow of blood, and there was every evidence that the animal intended to get well and live without a brain. Looking at the interior of the skull, I was struck by its resemblance to a human skull; in fact, it is, as nearly as I can judge, the size and shape of the brain-pan of an ordinary man who wears a seven and an eighth hat. Examining the brain itself, I found it to be the size of an ordinary human brain, and singularly like it in general contour, though it is very inferior in fibre and has few convolutions.

MAY 5TH, MORNING.

Framingham is exceedingly ill and talks of dying, declaring that if a natural death does not put an end to his sufferings, he will commit suicide. I do not know what to do. All my attempts to encourage him are of no avail, and the few medicines I have no longer fit his case at all.

MAY 5TH, EVENING.

I have just buried Framingham's body in the sand of the lake shore. I performed no ceremonies over the grave, for perhaps the real Framingham is not dead, though such speculation seems utterly wild. To-morrow I shall erect a cairn upon the mound, unless indeed there are signs that my experiment is successful, though it is foolish to hope that it will be.

At ten this morning, Framingham's qualms left him, and he set forth with me to see the elasmosaurus. The creature lay in the place where we left it yesterday, its position unaltered, still breathing, all the bodily functions performing themselves. The wound in its head had healed a great deal during the night, and I daresay will be completely healed within a week or so, such is the rapidity with which these reptilian organisms repair damages to themselves. Collecting three or four bushels of mussels, I shelled them and poured them down the elasmosaurus's throat. With a convulsive gasp, they passed down and the great mouth slowly closed.

"How long do you expect to keep the reptile alive?" asked Framingham.

"Until I have gotten word to a number of scientific friends, and they have come here to examine it. I shall take you to the nearest settlement and write letters from there. Returning, I shall feed the elasmosaurus regularly until my friends come, and we decide what final disposition to make of it. We shall probably stuff it."

"But you will have trouble in killing it, unless you hack it to pieces, and that won't do. Oh, if I only had the vitality of that animal. There is a monster whose vitality is so splendid that the removal of its brain does not disturb it. I should feel very happy if someone would remove my body. If I only had some of that beast's useless strength."

"In your case, the possession of a too active brain has injured the body," said I. "Too much brain exercise and too little bodily exercise are the causes of your trouble. It would be a pleasant thing if you had the robust health of the elasmosaurus, but what a wonderful thing it would be if that mighty engine had your intelligence."

I turned away to examine the reptile's wounds, for I had brought my surgical instruments with me, and intended to dress them. I was interrupted by a burst of groans from Framingham and turning, beheld him rolling on the sand in an agony. I hastened to him, but before I could reach him, he seized my case of instruments, and taking the largest and sharpest knife, cut his throat from ear to ear.

"Framingham, Framingham," I shouted and, to my astonishment, he looked at me intelligently. I recalled the case of the French doctor who, for some minutes after being guillotined, answered his friends by winking.

"If you hear me, wink," I cried. The right eye closed and opened with a snap. Ah, here the body was dead and the brain lived. I glanced at the elasmosaurus. Its mouth, half closed over its gleaming teeth, seemed to smile an invitation. The intelligence of the man and the strength of the brain. The living body and the living brain. The curious resemblance of the reptile's brain-pan to that of a man flashed across my mind.

"Are you still alive, Framingham?"

The right eye winked. I seized my machete, for there was no time for delicate instruments. I might destroy all by haste and roughness, I was sure to destroy all by delay. I opened the skull and disclosed the brain. I had not injured it, and breaking the wound of the elasmosaurus's head, placed the brain within. I dressed the wound and, hurrying to the house, brought all my store of stimulants and administered them.

For years the medical fraternity has been predicting that brain-grafting will some time be successfully accomplished. Why has it never been successfully accomplished? Because it has not been tried. Obviously, a brain from a dead body cannot be used and what living man would submit to the horrible process of having his head opened, and portions of his brain taken for the use of others?

The brains of men are frequently examined when injured and parts of the brain removed, but parts of the brains of other men have never been substituted for the parts removed. No uninjured man has ever been found who would give any portion of his brain for the use of another. Until criminals under sentence of death are handed over to science for experimentation, we shall not know what can be done in the way of brain-grafting. But public opinion would never allow it.

Conditions are favourable for a fair and thorough trial of my experiment. The weather is cool and even, and the wound in the head of the elasmosaurus has every chance for healing. The animal possesses a vitality superior to any of our later day animals, and if any organism can successfully become the host of a foreign brain, nourishing and cherishing it, the elasmosaurus with its abundant vital forces can do it. It may be that a new era in the history of the world will begin here.

MAY 6TH, NOON.

I think I will allow my experiment a little more time.

MAY 7TH, NOON.

It cannot be imagination. I am sure that as I looked into the elasmosaurus's eyes this morning there was expression in them. Dim, it is true, a sort of mistiness that floats over them like the reflection of passing clouds.

MAY 8TH, NOON.

I am more sure than yesterday that there *is* expression in the eyes, a look of troubled fear, such as is seen in the eyes of those who dream nightmares with unclosed lids.

MAY 11TH, EVENING.

I have been ill, and have not seen the elasmosaurus for three days, but I shall be better able to judge the progress of the experiment by remaining away a period of some duration.

MAY 12TH, NOON.

I am overcome with awe as I realise the success that has so far crowned my experiment. As I approached the elasmosaurus this morning, I noticed a faint disturbance in the water near its flippers. I cautiously investigated, expecting to discover some fishes nibbling at the helpless monster, and saw that the commotion was not due to fishes, but to the flippers themselves, which were feebly moving.

"Framingham, Framingham," I bawled at the top of my voice. The vast bulk stirred a little, a very little, but enough to notice. Is the brain, or Framingham, it would perhaps be better to say, asleep, or has he failed to establish connection with the body? Undoubtedly he has not yet established connection with the body, and this of itself would be equivalent to sleep, to unconsciousness. As a man born with none of the senses would be unconscious of himself, so Framingham, just beginning to establish connections with his new body, is only dimly conscious of himself and sleeps. I fed him, or it—which is the proper designation will be decided in a few days—with the usual allowance.

MAY 17TH, EVENING.

I have been ill for the past three days, and have not been out of doors until this morning. The elasmosaurus was still motionless when I arrived at the cove this morning. Dead, I thought; but I soon detected signs of breathing, and I began to prepare some mussels for it, and was intent upon my task, when I heard a slight, gasping sound, and looked up. A feeling of terror seized me. It was as if in response to some doubting incantations there had appeared the half-desired, yet wholly-feared and unexpected apparition of a fiend. I shrieked, I screamed, and the amphitheatre of rocks echoed and re-echoed my cries, and all the time the head of the elasmosaurus raised aloft to the full height of its neck, swayed about unsteadily, and its mouth silently struggled and twisted, as if in an attempt to form words, while its eyes looked at me now with wild fear and now with piteous intreaty.

"Framingham," I said.

The monster's mouth closed instantly, and it looked at me attentively, pathetically so, as a dog might look.

"Do you understand me?"

The mouth began struggling again, and little gasps and moans issued forth.

"If you understand me, lay your head on the rock."

Down came the head. He understood me. My experiment was a success. I sat for a moment in silence, meditating upon the wonderful affair, striving to realise that I was awake and sane, and then began in a calm manner to relate to my friend what had taken place since his attempted suicide.

"You are at present something in the condition of a partial paralytic, I should judge," said I, as I concluded my account. "Your mind has not yet learned to command your new body. I see you can move your head and neck, though with difficulty. Move your body if you can. Ah, you cannot, as I thought. But it will all come in time. Whether you will ever be able to talk or not, I cannot say, but I think so, however. And now if you cannot, we will arrange some means of communication. Anyhow, you are rid of your human body and possessed of the powerful vital apparatus you so much envied its former owner. When you gain control of yourself, I wish you to find the communication between this lake and the under-world, and conduct some explorations. Just think of the additions to geological knowledge you can make. I will write an account of your discovery, and the names of Framingham and McLennegan will be among those of the greatest geologists."

I waved my hands in my enthusiasm, and the great eyes of my friend glowed with a kindred fire.

JUNE 2ND, NIGHT.

The process by which Framingham has passed from his first powerlessness to his present ability to speak, and command the use of his corporeal frame, has been so gradual that there has been nothing to note down from day to day. He seems to have all the command over his vast bulk that its former owner had, and in addition speaks and sings. He is singing now. The north wind has risen with the fall of night, and out there in the darkness I hear the mighty organ pipe-tones of his tremendous, magnificent voice, chanting the solemn notes of the Gregorian, the full throated Latin words mingling with the roaring of the wind in a wild and weird harmony.

To-day he attempted to find the connection between the lake and the interior of the earth, but the great well that sinks down in the centre of the lake is choked with rocks and he has discovered nothing. He is tormented by the fear that I will leave him, and that he will perish of loneliness. But I shall not leave him. I feel too much pity for the loneliness he would endure, and besides, I wish to be on the spot should another of those mysterious convulsions open the connection between the lake and the lower world.

He is beset with the idea that should other men discover him, he may be captured and exhibited in a circus or museum, and declares that he will fight for his liberty even to the extent of taking the lives of those attempting to capture him. As a wild animal, he is the property of whomsoever captures him, though perhaps I can set up a title to him on the ground of having tamed him.

JULY 6TH.

One of Framingham's fears has been realised. I was at the pass leading into the basin, watching the clouds grow heavy and pendulous with their load of rain, when I saw a butterfly net appear over a knoll in the pass, followed by its bearer, a small man, unmistakably a scientist, but I did not note him well, for as he looked down into the valley, suddenly there burst forth with all the power and volume of a steam calliope, the tremendous voice of Framingham, singing a Greek song of Anacreon to the tune of "Where did you get that hat?" and the singer appeared in a little cove, the black column of his great neck raised aloft, his jagged jaws wide open.

That poor little scientist. He stood transfixed, his butterfly net dropped from his hand, and as Framingham ceased his singing, curvetted and leaped from the water and came down with a splash that set the whole cove swashing, and laughed a guffaw that echoed among the cliffs like the laughing of a dozen demons, he turned and sped through the pass at all speed.

I skip all entries for nearly a year. They are unimportant.

JUNE 30TH, 1897.

A change is certainly coming over my friend. I began to see it some time ago, but refused to believe it and set it down to imagination. A catastrophe threatens, the absorption of the human intellect by the brute body. There are precedents for believing it possible. The human body has more influence over the mind than the mind has over the body. The invalid, delicate Framingham with refined mind, is no more. In his stead is a roistering monster, whose boisterous and commonplace conversation betrays a constantly growing coarseness of mind.

No longer is he interested in my scientific investigations, but pronounces them all bosh. No longer is his conversation such as an educated man can enjoy, but slangy and diffuse iterations concerning the trivial happenings of our uneventful life. Where will it end? In the absorption of the human mind by the brute body? In the final triumph of matter over mind and the degradation of the most mundane force and the extinction of the celestial spark? Then, indeed, will Edward Framingham be dead, and over the grave of his human body can I fittingly erect a headstone, and then will my vigil in this valley be over.

FORT D. A. RUSSELL, WYOMING,

APRIL 15TH, 1899.

Prof. William G. Breyfogle.

DEAR SIR,—the inclosed intact manuscript and the fragments which accompany it, came into my possession in the manner I am about to relate and I inclose them to you, for whom they were intended by their late author. Two weeks ago, I was dispatched into the mountains after some Indians who had left their reservation, having under my command a company of infantry and two squads of cavalrymen with mountain howitzers. On the seventh day of our pursuit, which led us into a wild and unknown part of the mountains, we were startled at hearing from somewhere in front us a succession of bellowings of a very unusual nature, mingled with the cries of a human being apparently in the last extremity, and rushing over a rise before us, we looked down upon a lake and saw a colossal, indescribable thing engaged in rending the body of a man.

Observing us, it stretched its jaws and laughed, and in saying this,

I wish to be taken literally. Part of my command cried out that it was the devil, and turned and ran. But I rallied them, and thoroughly enraged at what we had witnessed, we marched down to the shore, and I ordered the howitzers to be trained upon the murderous creature. While we were doing this, the thing kept up a constant blabbing that bore a distinct resemblance to human speech, sounding very much like the jabbering of an imbecile, or a drunk trying to talk. I gave the command to fire and to fire again, and the beast tore out into the lake in its death-agony, and sank.

With the remains of Dr. McLennegan, I found the foregoing manuscript intact, and the torn fragments of the diary from which it was compiled, together with other papers on scientific subjects, all of which I forward. I think some attempt should be made to secure the body of the elasmosaurus. It would be a priceless addition to any museum.

Arthur W. Fairchild,
Captain U.S.A.

The Giant Cat of Sumatra

INTRODUCTION

I still have reservations about the respectability of an editor anthologizing one of his own stories, but I'll consider respectability as honored in the breach this time. Besides, in these pages I've briefly brought back my truly amazing cat Neutron, named after the feline in the movie of *This Island Earth,* who chased dogs with vigor and frequently attempted to operate doorknobs with her paws (without success, but she kept trying) and died much too soon (1965-1971), and what could be more respectable than that? I'll add that if you're looking for a *serious* story here, you're in the wrong part of the book. You may also complain that R'lyeh is beneath the Pacific, not the Atlantic—or is that what They *want* you to think?

❈ ❈ ❈

Hank Davis is an editor emeritus at Baen Books. While a naïve youth in the early 1950s (yes, he's *old!*), he was led astray by SF comic books, and then by A. E. van Vogt's *Slan,* which he read in the Summer 1952 issue of *Fantastic Story Quarterly* while in the second grade, sealing his fate. He has had stories published mumble-mumble years ago in *Analog, If, F&SF,* and Damon Knight's *Orbit* anthology series. (There was also a story sold to *The Last Dangerous Visions,* but let's not go there.) A native of Kentucky, he currently lives in North Carolina to avoid a long commute to the Baen office.

The Giant Cat of Sumatra

by Hank Davis

The mayor was looking at my face, unlike his assistant in the outer office, who mostly hadn't looked that high, so I took a moment to seem to inspect his office, while looking for a reflecting surface to make sure I still had the right head on my shoulders.

There was no mirror in sight, but a metal plaque on the wall commemorating something or other gave enough of a blurred reflection for me to be relieved. The silhouette looked good, and the ears looked human, and they were on the sides of my head. Couldn't get a good look at the eyes, though. The eyes change if I'm not careful.

The body parts that had captured his assistant's gaze also require care and concentration to keep from developing extra helpings. Humans normally only have one pair, the poor things.

I looked back at His Honor, and he was still looking at my face. Maybe the eyes *had* slipped. Then he said, "Probably people are always telling you that you look strikingly like Julie Andrews."

"All the time," I said, wondering who Julie Andrews was. I'd have to have a very serious talk with Udjut, my makeup demon. Maybe a talk with a little show-and-tell involving red-hot instruments. At least Udjut'd followed my firm instructions not to make me look like Diana Rigg again, no matter how feline (for a human) he thought she was.

Not when I was going to be where her face was familiar. So, he'd given me another famous face.

Maybe white-hot instead of just red-hot . . .

"But don't worry, Ms. Bastion. I won't make any jokes about Mary Poppins or the Trapp Family. You've probably heard them all."

More names that didn't mean anything to me, but I thanked him and nodded knowingly while I considered a few more ways to make life more interesting for Udjut.

"Please sit," he said, and we both did. "How can I help you and the Environmental Protection Agency?"

Before yesterday, the EPA had never heard of me, but now I'm in their hard files and databases as if I'd been there for years. Anyone who doubts my official-looking I.D. and gives them a phone call will get a confirmation. It amuses me to spread falsehoods through a bureaucracy which was initiated by Richard M. Nixon.

"Mr. Mayor, we have reports that your city has an unusual rat problem."

I'd thought he already had his politician's face on, affable with a twinkle in his eye, with somehow an undertone of seriousness and competence, but my remark extinguished the twinkle and brought out a strong touch of would-I-lie-to-you? (Speaking of Nixon.) I'm sometimes impressed with what humans can do with their faces, and without the help of makeup demons, too.

"Ms. Bastion, New York certainly does have a rat problem. It's unavoidable, when you have so many people in a relatively small space, and garbage can only be hauled away so fast. Where does the EPA come in? Rats haven't been declared an endangered species, have they?" he asked, smiling slightly to let me know that that last comment was a joke, but not quite smiling enough to hide that he was worried it might *not* be a joke.

"Well, quite frankly," and I wasn't *completely* fibbing, "we've had reports of rats of an unusual size. Some reports say they're big as a Labrador retriever." If he asked me where I got my information, I definitely was not going to tell him that a cat mummy (an old friend of mine) in the Metropolitan Museum of Art's Egyptian display had seen the big rodents running by in the wee small hours and alerted me.

This time, the smile didn't quite hit five out of ten. "Ms. Bastion, some of the rats might be large for a rodent, but rats as big as a Lab? Certainly not—"

At which point he noticed the rising commotion outside his door, and stopped. I'd heard it earlier, of course, and was wondering when his mortal's ears would pick it up. People shouting and sounds of running. Somebody screamed. It sounded like the assistant who had ogled me, and I couldn't help smiling.

Then the door opened, and a rat loped into the room. Big one. His Honor hadn't quite been fibbing, either, at least about rats as big as a Lab, since this one was at least half again as big as a Lab. I wondered if it had turned the doorknob by itself, or if it had help. It did have another kind of help with it, since four more rats, not quite as big, followed it in.

The mayor had a desk between him and the uninvited guests, but he pushed his chair back until it hit the wall, then seemed to consider whether or not standing up was a good idea, particularly since the rats weren't heading for him—yet. I was the object of their attentions.

I was already standing and had raised my chair over my head. I bonked the biggest one on the nose (they *hate* it when that happens) with the chair and said, "Do you have an appointment?" Then I got down on all fours, not easy to do in high heels and a short skirt, reached under my blouse, pulled out the ankh that was on a chain around my neck, and snarled at them. It wasn't really just a snarl, but no living human would know the language. I wanted to drive them out as unspectacularly as possible, so when the ankh grew warm in my hand, only the roots of their tails caught fire. Opening my mouth wide so that the fangs showed, I gave them a drawn-out hiss with plenty of attitude, and they beat a retreat. I wondered how they got in and if they could operate the elevator to get out.

Since they'd gone for me as soon as they came in the door, it was obvious that someone knew I was in town. And I was getting closer to being certain who that someone was.

I stood up and looked at the mayor, who was standing up now, looking at the open door. Then he looked at me, said, "How did you drive them—" and stopped, staring at my eyes. Oops.

In the excitement, I had let them slip. I needed to get to the real reason for my visit, anyway. I'd been about to say, "It's a secret hypnotic power I learned long ago in the Orient," but instead I just used my own genuine secret power to calm him down while I made my eyes look human again, without slit pupils. Just call me round eyes.

I tucked the ankh back under my blouse. Men seeing it might think I was wearing it as a sign of being open to indecent proposals, and I didn't need any such distractions. Round eyes *and* round heels. Speaking of distractions, I glanced down the front of my blouse. Good. Still only two to a customer.

Two cops came through the door, guns drawn. "Are you all right, sir?" the older one asked, then noticed me. "Are you okay, ma'am?" He didn't stare at my eyes, so I must have fixed that problem.

I glanced at his name tag and said, "We're fine, officer Chandler." Looking intently at His Honor, I added, "Aren't we, Mr. Mayor?"

"I'm . . . uh, we're fine. They ran back out, and we're fine." His voice was a little slurred and his own eyes had a glassy look, but I hoped the cops would attribute that to mild shock.

Chandler looked like he was going to say something else, but then sounds of shots came, not very close but still inside the building. All he said was, "Maybe you should lock the door, sir," and, "Let's go, Ray," to the other cop. They left and I did as advised. I didn't want anyone coming through the door for a few minutes, cops, rats, or staff.

I tried standing my chair back up, but a leg fell off and I gave up on that. "Mr. Mayor, did you see anything odd about me a few minutes ago?"

"Your eyes. They had slit pupils, like a snake. Or a cat."

I decided not to slug him for mentioning snakes before cats. "Anything else?"

"When you got down on the floor. You had a great behind."

Okay, I definitely wouldn't slug him. This time. "You're going to forget about the eyes. And—sorry—the other thing, too." He'd sounded less slurred when he mentioned my second attribute. That might have been the habits of a professional hand-shaker and B.S. artist taking over, but he also might be coming out of the trance, so I slapped a fresh one on him, then asked him for his computer password. He told me, and I told him to take a little nap standing up. He complied, so I moved his chair away from the wall and attended to his computer.

It was handy that the mayor could use his own computer—smart for a politician, particularly a Democrat. I had to ask him for a couple more passwords, but I soon had stored all the information the city had about the oversized rats on a flash drive (shaped like a reclining cat—so, sue me!). Once the mayor was reinstalled behind the desk and given a final prep on what he would and wouldn't remember, I thanked him and left.

On the way out, I had to detour around a dead rat on the ground floor. Bullets stopped them, or at least this one, which was good news. But once dead it hadn't returned to standard rat size, which was bad. The top rat was as powerful as I'd expected.

I hadn't brought a laptop along. Even turned off, they don't respond well to being carried through a spacetime anomaly. I located a Kinko's and took over a computer for most of an hour. It took my charge card without complaint, not that I'd expected anything different. Money was such a handy invention by the mortals. They think it's real, but we know better.

I closed down the computer and headed back to the street. Reports of giant rats were increasing on a steep slope, and I probably didn't have much time. From the data, I thought I now had an idea where the source of the problem was hanging out, but I'd need help. Unfortunately, the most likely source for help was iffy, likely to deny everything (again I thought of Nixon), so I needed to find something out first.

I hadn't done much hopping around for a couple of days, so my energy level wasn't low and I should be able to get there and back again with no problem. There weren't as many people on the street as usual—maybe the rumors about giant rat attacks were getting around in spite of the secrecy—so I didn't have trouble finding a spot with no one looking, and I left, changing my apparel (a *much* longer skirt) en route.

Since I was not just crossing the Atlantic but also doing a considerable time hop, I arrived feeling a momentary dizziness, not to mention being hungry, like I could eat a whole tuna. Later, maybe. I'm just not the gal I was three or four millennia ago. Fortunately, I was right outside my destination, on Baker Street.

I trotted up the stairs (17 steps—I counted them) and knocked on the door. The doctor opened it and, right away, sneezed in my face. Poor guy, he's allergic to cats and won't admit it.

"I'm terribly sorry, miss. I must have a cold coming on."

Bad diagnosis, Doc. "That's quite all right. Perhaps the cause might be all the tobacco smoke in here. Maybe you should go out for a walk and get some fresh air," I said, applying a touch of influence. Actually, London air wasn't all that fresh this late in the Industrial Revolution, but it would be less murky than the apartment was at that moment. The man I'd come to see was sitting in a chair and going full blast, incinerating shag tobacco by the pipeful. There were many ways in which he and the twenty-first century wouldn't fit together, and the rules laid down by the anti-smoking zealots wouldn't be the least of them.

Stifling another sneeze, the good doctor steered me to a chair while his friend silently studied me through a blue tobacco haze. Then he put on his hat, apologized once more, and departed. The detective continued to examine me, waiting for me to speak. Once again, his hawklike features reminded me of Horus, and I wondered if he might have had an immortal for one of his ancestors.

I said, "My name is—"

The hawklike features softened, and his gaze was no longer so intent. "Very good. The voice is different as well as the face. I congratulate you, Miss Bastoli. Or is it Helliwell? Or—"

Busted again! "Call me Bastion, please. Toffee Bastion. You think we've met before?" Dammit, I didn't think he could possibly recognize me, after once having seen me looking like Diana Rigg, and the next time like Sophia Loren (I'd picked those two seemings myself, unlike the present one).

"My dear Miss Bastion—and since we *have* met before, I hope you'll permit me that small informality of address—you somehow have changed your voice and your face, and I am impressed with the latter, since I can see no sign of makeup or a mask, yet it is very different from your previous three visits. Even the bone structure looks different. But to the observant eye, the way you move, even the way you sit is unmistakably similar to your motions I saw those other times. Actually, I explained this on your last appearance—please pardon the double meaning—and you gave it an interesting name then."

Oh, well. No point in denying who I was. "Yes, body language," I said.

"A singular phrase," he said. "I haven't been able to uncover an appearance of it in any journals. Did you coin it?"

"No, but you're not likely to come across it this, ah, soon. I was trying to move differently—"

"That, too, was evident. But sometimes the more one tries to hide a characteristic, the more obvious it becomes. And while you've just arrived, and we've scarcely begun to converse, I'm sure that any discussion we have will once again bring to light the strikingly unusual word combinations and usages you sometimes employ. Since your last visit, I've often wondered what 'jet-propelled' could mean. Or why anyone would use the word 'issue' as if it were a synonym for 'problem' or 'defect.' But, in any case, it's scarcely a deduction worthy of the word for me to notice that you are the only visitor to these rooms whose arrival inevitably precipitates a fit of sneezing on the part of my friend."

"He's allergic to cats, very strongly. That's why he sneezes."

"Interesting. To have such an overpowering effect, you must be closely involved with a large number of cats."

"I am involved with cats. And you could say it's a large number of them." Like, all of the ones on the planet who are no bigger than a breadbox.

"And yet, your clothes seem very clean, as if they were newly purchased, and I see no sign of cat hair on your apparel. An interesting problem."

"Please, no three-pipe problems right now. I need to know something about one of the untold stories."

"I must confess that there are a great many of my cases which the doctor has not written up. Some would cause irreparable harm to the reputations of innocent people no matter how the names and places were disguised. And there are cases which I could not solve, and my Boswell prefers that I continue to appear all but infallible—or, as you pronounced it on your first visit, 'infallibibble.' An odd mispronunciation for someone whose speech could be taken for that of a native English speaker who obviously has spent much time in America, and probably also in other countries such as— But I suspect that I am growing garrulous while you are growing anxious. Obviously, you refer to one of the cases to which my friend has made an oblique reference in his accounts. Perhaps the Giant Rat of Sumatra?"

That *was* the case that I urgently needed to know something about, but it scares me when he seems to read my mind. "Why do you think I'm referring to that one? Why not the matter of the aluminium crutch"—I was careful to give it the Brit pronunciation—"or the steamer *Friesland*, or—"

"As you yourself put it, Ms., ah, Bastion, you are involved with cats, and, while I might with difficulty imagine some connection between a crutch made of a then-expensive metal, or a prehistoric flying reptile—"

"A prehistoric *what*?" I said, in spite of myself.

"Some other time, perhaps. As I was about to say, there is an obvious connection between the unusually large rodent vaguely alluded to and a cat. An even more unusual cat. The good doctor made a brief reference to the case, though he didn't mention the cat, and wrote that the world was not yet ready for the tale to be told. More accurately, the world wouldn't believe it, and would call us—even me—insane. "

I had the feeling that I was about to be told that I wouldn't believe it, either, so I said, "But surely, with your reputation—"

"Reputations are very fragile things, Miss, ah, Bastion. Why on earth did you choose *that* for an alias? But no matter. If I may have your assurance that you will not repeat the story—"

"Not to anyone in this century," I assured him.

"And neither of us will be around to see the century after that, eh," he said, then gave me an odd look, making me wonder for the *n*th time how much about me he suspected.

"Well, I'll spare you a recitation of the more tedious details of what the doctor and I were doing on the docks in the middle of the night, except to say that the crew of the *Matilda Briggs*, a ship just in from Sumatra, had deserted the vessel as soon as it had docked, and refused to go anywhere near it again, let alone unload the cargo. Apparently they had been talking around, since the ship's owner couldn't find anyone else willing to go on board, either. The owner asked me to look into what was happening, so the doctor and I were watching the ship from behind some crates, when a watchman came down the dock on his midnight round. I thought he would discover us and was preparing to retreat, when I noticed that something had appeared on the deck of the ship.

"It was a gigantic rat, the size of a horse, and it leaped down to the dock and came at the watchman. He was firing his pistol at it, and the doctor also opened fire with his service revolver—did you know that he's a crack shot?—yet the rat showed no sign that it had been peppered with bullets, but just stopped long enough to stare at all three of us, as if trying to make up its mind where to begin its midnight snack. I dashed toward the watchman to seize his lantern and smash it on the rat's head, hoping to set it afire. And then the story became completely unbelievable."

He had been neglecting his pipe, so he took a few puffs before continuing.

"What happened next was that an eruption of water splashed everywhere, on all of us, as something even bigger, much bigger, than the rat came out of the water, grabbed the rat in its mouth, then leaped back off the dock into the water, and both were gone."

I was sure I knew what it was—and *who* it was—but I asked, "What was it that came out of the water?"

"Miss Bastion, it was a cat. It looked like an ordinary housecat. But it must have been fifty feet long. As the cliché goes, if I hadn't been there myself, I wouldn't have believed it. Nobody who wasn't there will believe it. Which is why the world isn't ready for it. The doctor had a little joke by mentioning it in the account of a case where we investigated a supposed vampire, which turned out to be nothing of the kind. But the giant rat and cat were real. And even that was not the most fantastic part of the event."

I waited through a few more puffs of the pipe, then asked, "What was more fantastic, then?"

"First, the cat's eyes were wrong." He seemed to be looking intently into my eyes when he said that, and I started worrying again about keeping them human. "Consider the laws of optics, Miss Bastion. An elephant is much larger than a man, yet its eyes are far smaller in proportion to its head than a man's eyes are in proportion to his. The elephant doesn't need a proportionately larger eye. Yet the eyes of this creature that looked like a huge housecat were of a size to its head in the same proportion that a normal-sized housecat would have. The eyes were huge, bigger then a football—the British football, I mean. The optics would have been all wrong. And there was the other thing." Puff, puff, puff.

"And that was?"

"As soon as the giant cat had landed on the dock, it spoke to the rat. It wasn't a language that I recognized, but it was definitely a language, not mere animal growls and grunts. And the rat answered it, in what sounded like the same language. And both spoke with human voices. Much deeper, but otherwise human."

"Could you repeat what the cat said?"

He gave me an odd look. "Testing me, are you?"

"Oh, no. I'm curious what it sounded like."

"I have a well-trained memory, and can recall part of it. Let's see . . . I remember it as . . ." And he made sounds that meant nothing to him, but I understood them, allowing for his pronunciation being a little off in spots. And I knew who had said them.

"Thank you, sir," I said. "I suppose once again, you won't accept payment—"

"For telling you an unbelievable story? You brought no intriguing problem before me to stir my interest and relieve the tedium—" He paused and gave me another piercing look, then said, "Except perhaps the mystery of yourself. But you haven't engaged me to investigate that. Perhaps I should accept my own curiosity as a client, but instead I'll respect your privacy."

I stood and said, "I appreciate that. But please accept this small gift," I said, handing him a tin of tobacco.

He was also standing. "Interesting," he said, opening the lid and sniffing it. "Not a commercial product, I gather."

"Definitely not." It was a strain that was long extinct, cut and cured by a tribe who were equally extinct, but I wasn't going to tell him that. "Thank you for telling me about the rat—"

"Not to mention what the cat did in the night-time," he said.

I got the joke. "You've been very kind, sir. But I need to be going. Thank you."

"You are very welcome, and thank you for the intriguing gift. I look forward to our next meeting, and will anticipate seeing what new face you will be wearing then. And in that time to come, perhaps you will again be purring."

Yikes! I realized that I was purring, and didn't know how long I'd been doing it. I'd done it on previous visits, too. Something about him put me in a purring mood. As before, I thought that if he wasn't an immortal, he ought to be, in *some* pantheon, even if not in ours.

"It's a nervous habit that I have . . . um, of humming tunelessly," I said, knowing he didn't believe me. We shook hands, and I left, running into the returning doctor on the stairs (still 17 steps), who had stopped sneezing, but now resumed it with vigor. Poor fellow.

Outside, night was falling and it was foggy. Unlikely to be seen disappearing, I hopped forward to the twenty-first century, and into a short skirt again. This time, I was going in the direction of entropy, so it was like running downhill instead of uphill and consumed less energy. I came out, still in London, and went into a phone booth. I was going to make a person-to-person call, but wouldn't actually be using the phone, though I would seem to be talking into the handset. Certainly, I would look less odd than if I were outside, talking to nobody visible.

"Sekhmet!" I said. "Hey, Sekhmet! I know you're there, I can hear you growling." No response. "Sekhmet, you have a problem and we need to talk. Either you answer, or I'll take it up with the boss."

A voice came into the booth, but not from the phone receiver I was holding. "Okay, Buzz, what's your problem this time?"

I answer to Bastet and also Bast, but from Sekhmet I have to put up with Buzz, grrr. "It's *your* problem, Sekkie-poo. You were charged with keeping Pinowa under control for five hundred years. Your shift's not up yet, and you've let him escape twice. Maybe even more times that I don't know about."

A leonine growl echoed in the booth, which caused some of the people in the street to stop, look around, then move on with a quicker step. "I don't know what you're talking about, fuzzball. He's locked away—"

"Like he was locked away in the early twentieth century? Back when you caught up to him in the form of a giant housecat, and dragged him underwater in London?"

Another growl, not as loud this time. At least, she didn't roar, which would really have stopped traffic. Sometimes, I wish I could roar, but if you can purr, you can't roar, which strikes me as poor design, and I'd like to take it up with the boss's boss sometime, but we don't hear much from Him.

"Okay, so he got away back then, but I nabbed him before he could do any harm. Are you just calling to berate me for a little slip-up? Gonna tell the boss?"

"Not unless I have to, in order for you to get your butt in gear. Pinowa's loose again, and up to something in Manhattan. If you don't believe me, go check where you think he's stashed."

She didn't answer and broke the connection. At some point in Egypt, they got confused and thought we were the same goddess, but really, we're just good friends. Or as good friends as two cats can be. Or as two cranky immortals can be.

Hoping that she was checking up on Pinowa's whereabouts and not just sulking, I took the time to put through a call to Anapa. Lately he's been preferring his older name to the Greek version, Anubis, which I think sounds much cooler. Kebechet answered at first, and wanted to gossip and complain about her latest spat with her parents, but I told her this was an emergency, and she put Anapa on the line. He was dubious about my idea, but agreed to see if he could manage it. For someone with a canine aspect, he's not a bad immortal.

Bang! Sekkie was back and loud, rattling the booth. "Crap! He's gone. Left a Mouseketeer ears-cap in the cage. Probably thought it was funny. Where is he? Never mind, you said he was in Manhattan. Where in Manhattan?"

"Calm down," I said. "I think I know where he is, but we've gotta move fast. Can you get over here—?"

The connection was broken again, and she appeared a couple of yards away in a cloud of red smoke (she's such a showoff), though she was using her influence so that the mortals passing her didn't notice the special effects. She was a redhead, which was nothing new, with an explosion of hair framing her face. Lionesses don't have manes, and when she's in human-seeming, she makes up for that oversight of nature (or Somebody) with an abundant ape equivalent. She looked at me, rocked her head back and forth, and said, "I tawt I taw a puddy tat."

She's very big on movies and TV shows, and animated cartoons in particular. I'll take a book instead. Even better if it's a big, heavy book, and I can always slam someone on the head with it. Someone who really deserves it.

Sekkie looked around and complained, "This isn't Manhattan, Buzz. I homed in on your lifeforce without checking your location. I just jumped from Egypt and now I've got to jump again? It's exhausting, traveling across the Atlantic under my own power. But I don't like taking a ship—all that water, in every direction but up. And suppose the stars happened to be right when I was over where you-know-who is sleeping. *That is not dead which can eternal lie—*" she began.

"And if he wakes up, even immortals may fry," I said.

"Frying might be preferable. Besides, the big C may like his food raw."

"Everyone's a critic or a rewrite man," I grumbled.

"Who're you calling a man? Or a human?" She did a low-volume roar, but not low enough. Several people didn't stop, but did look around uneasily, then walked on, once again at a brisker pace. Sekhmet was proving to be a great stimulus to burning calories.

"Save the sound effects for the rats," I said. "We don't have time to take a ship. I said this was an emergency."

"What do you mean, rats? Has Pinowa got friends?"

"Scads of friends, bigger than life and twice as ratty. We've gotta move, now. Let's hop."

"Taking a plane across is more restful than hopping, and most of the way, the water way down there doesn't look like water. Might be a desert."

"A blue desert? With blue sand?"

"If there's a blue Nile, why not a blue desert? You have no imagination, Buzz."

We needed to move, but she was getting silly, so I decided to be silly, too, and started humming "Beyond the Blue Horizon." People started looking around. Not at my humming, surely, I thought, then realized I was purring again, and keeping time with the tune at that. I stopped.

"You really need to get that kitty noise under control," Sekkie said.

"We'll worry about that later. Right now we have to hop to Manhattan."

"Rush, rush, rush!" Sekhmet said. "You ought to have a nice long lie-down in the veldt, sometime. Just the thing after a little snack of wildebeest." She was still doing a soft growl as she talked that sounded like a bass rumble, a sign that she was in a stubborn mood, but when I hopped, she followed me.

I'd aimed for the Empire State Building, but we landed a block and change away (I was getting tired), just as a mob of people was frantically pouring out of a subway entrance, yelling and stepping on each other. I hoped it was just a typical rush-hour crowd, but once they'd managed to get clear of the entrance, a gang of rats came out right after them. They were at least twice as big as the ones I'd seen in the mayor's office.

"Damn, he *has* been busy," Sekkie said. "Where is he?"

"We'll worry about that in a minute. First, I need backup." Nobody was paying attention to anything but the rats and hauling ass, pariularly the latter, so I didn't worry about anybody noticing me talking to thin air. "Anapa, turn 'em loose *now*!"

Then we were surrounded by housecats, thousands of them. They were transparent at first, then translucent, then as solid-looking as when they'd been alive. And they started growing.

One gray cat, with a dash of red in her fur, ran up to me and meowed like a friendly foghorn. I knew her right away, though she was elephant-sized now. She'd been one of my favorites when she was alive, and afterwards, though she had trouble running off dogs five times her size after she'd quit breathing. "Hi, Neutron," I greeted her. "Good to see you, too. Now, go get 'em."

She growled and took off. Everywhere I looked, the rats were too busy running from outrageously enlarged examples of *Felis domesticus* to chase humans. Anapa had been worried that he might not be able to coax them out of the underworld. "You know what the mortals say about herding cats," he'd said. "And they don't get more cooperative after they're dead."

I'd told him just to mention the rats to them. Lots and lots of rats. "Tell 'em it's a target-rich environment," I'd added.

"Okay, so the cavalry is here," Sekkie said. "Now, how about the diabolical mastermind?"

I pointed at the Empire State Building. "I think he's in there somewhere. We need to triangulate on his location," I said, and hopped fifty yards down the street. I got out my ankh, and waved to Sekkie to do the same. But triangulation wasn't necessary. My arm jerked upwards, and pointed at the top of the building.

Sekkie appeared beside me and said, "He made it, Ma! Top of the world." That was probably another movie reference, but I didn't ask.

"Are you too tired from the ocean hop to get up there?" I asked her.

"Hopping is for wimps," she said. She reformed and enlarged, becoming a housecat at least fifty feet long; not counting the tail, which twitched sideways and knocked me over. "Sorry," she said, then grabbed me up in her mouth and galloped toward the building. People, rats, and not-as-large ghost cats saw us coming and scattered.

"Put me down!" I yelled. "You're getting me soaked. At least stop drooling!"

"Mmmph, murrrram," she said. I'm sure she would have been understandable if she hadn't had a really p.o.ed immortal in her mouth. Then she did what I was afraid she was going to do and started climbing the building.

"You're scratching the building. It's a historic structure, and you're leaving scars in the outside." She was also smashing in a lot of the windows. She reached the top, taking out part of the framework and netting put there to discourage would-be suicides, put her head over the edge of the top and dropped me there. "Oof," I grunted. I looked at my soaking-wet clothes and yelled, "I'm sending you the dry-cleaning bill."

Pinowa was there, all right, a rat bigger than any of his rodent minions, hanging on to the broadcast antenna above us. Sekkie reached up a paw and swatted him loose. He came down, but the antenna now looked the worse for wear, and I hoped it wouldn't fall over. Big as a horse, as he'd been described, he snarled, then started growing bigger. But Sekkie grew bigger, faster, and loomed over him. "This town isn't big enough for both of us," she said. Sometimes I think humans shouldn't have invented movies.

She roared at him, and his concentration slipped, and he shrank somewhat. Sometimes a roar is a handy thing to have, though I wouldn't want to give up my purrability.

He switched from inarticulate snarling to human speech, though it was in a thoroughly dead language. "I'm the rat-god," he yelled. "I deserve to have worshippers. Stop interfering or I'll tear you ridiculous cats to pieces."

"Balderdash!" I cried, aiming my ankh at him. "You're just a stupid, pathetic demon with an overblown ego. We'll let you know if you get promoted to godhood, but don't hold your breath." I was sending an influence through the ankh, keeping him from moving, or growing again. "Hit him with your ankh," I yelled to Sekhmet. "It'll take both of us." She'd have to get out of cat form to do that.

Instead, she put her front feet on the column, and craned her head around. "I thought that there'd surely be biplanes by now. There ought to be biplanes."

Even I had seen *that* movie. "Next time, we can do this in D.C.," I said. "They can probably pull some out of the Air and Space Museum. If you stick around here much longer, though, you'll probably attract some helicopter gunships."

"Oh well, back to the salt mines," she said and changed back to human form—almost. She now had a lioness's head on her human shoulders. "Thought you wouldn't want to be the odd god out," she said.

I realized that I had lost control in all the excitement, and a cat's head was on *my* shoulders. "Let's wrap this up and go home," I said.

"Close, but no cigar," Sekkie said. "It's, 'Let's blow this thing and go home.'"

I must have been almost quoting a movie, but I wasn't going to ask. "Put some emphasis on the *go home* part. Or at least, let's get off this building!" I waved my ankh around, but without letting Pinowa out of its influence.

Sekkie got her ankh out, and we shrank the rat demon back to normal rat-size. He was still yelling and threatening us until we turned him to stone. It would only last a few weeks, but Sekkie would have time to put him away again. She pulled a purse out of a hole in the air and dropped the lifelike rat statuette into it. The purse was spellproof, and with the demon shut up in it, all the rats in the city would return to normal size. I sent a message to Anapa to bring the ghost cats back to his domain. He grumbled something about now comes the hard part, and broke the connection.

"Taking him back to his cage?" I asked, starting for the exit.

"No, he's gotten out of two cages. I think I'll do some rodent research and put him in a maze."

"Think that'll hold him?" I was wondering if the elevators were still working. "Some rats are good at solving mazes using ordinary rat brains."

"This one will be a four-dimensional maze. And a big one. I'll leave his Mouseketeer cap in it in case he needs something to chew on, heh, heh." She was mispronouncing "heh," but I was too tired to twit her about it.

"I hope the boss doesn't hear about this mess," she said. "Too bad I can't go back in time and keep the little creep from escaping in the first place."

"You know we can't change the past, even the recent past."

"Yeah, it's against the rules, and we don't want to get the boss upset, because he's—"

"Amun-Ra, whose anger can shatter the world," I said in unison with her. I do see *some* movies, even ones that get so much wrong about the old homestead. Tana leaves and the cult of Arkhan, hah! No such things.

"Something that's been bothering me," I said, changing my head back to that of the apparently famous human, Julie Andrews, and making a mental note to find out more about her. I filed it next to the note about Udjut and red-hot implements. "Both times that you apprehended Pinowa, you took the form of a giant housecat. Why not a lioness?"

"Lionesses don't bother themselves with puny rats and mice," she said. "That's a job for the B-team. Which reminds me . . ." She aimed her ankh at a bare concrete surface and burned the words (in English) *This Building Protected by a Trained Attack Cat* into it. "Hey, Buzz, as long as you're looking like America's sweetheart, let's rent *Mary Poppins* and *The Sound of Music* and watch a double feature."

Actually, that didn't sound like a completely bad idea, but I wasn't going to watch any movies with Sekkie. She already knows them all by heart, and acts out all the dialogue. And— "That second movie is a musical, isn't it?"

"Yes. One of the most popular ever. And the other one's a musical, too."

Which meant she would be doing all the songs, too. No way. "No thanks. I think I'll look in the bookstores for something to read."

"Well, if you're gonna be a party pooper, I'll take in the big town before going home. I hear the new musical version of *Somewhere in Time* is a hot ticket."

"It's sold out for months," I said, trying not to sound pleased about it.

"Oh, come now, Buzz. They'll have a ticket for me, one that somehow was completely overlooked. Just one of the perks of being a god."

"Unless the show is cancelled because of the great rat panic," I said. "I wonder if the building's elevators are working?"

"Your glass is always half empty, isn't it, Buzz? Since you look like Mary Poppins, why don't you just grab an umbrella and fly down?"

There was that name again. I refused to ask her for an explanation.

"Planning on reading anything in particular?" she asked. "They have great adult bookstores here."

"No, I think I'll reread an old friend. Maybe I can find a copy of *The Swords of Lankhmar*. That book has a terrific kitten in it."

"And you want to be just like it when you grow up, eh?" she said.

"Do immortals ever grow up? I haven't noticed any of us doing that. Present company definitely included," I said.

"Meow!"

"Nice try, but you should stick to roaring," I said. Nuts to the elevators, I'd leave while I had the last word. I was purring again as I hopped down to the street, still wondering why Sekkie thought I should have an umbrella. There was no sign of rain.

Greenface

INTRODUCTION

Aside from being an exciting story with solid characters, "Greenface" stands out in several ways. It was the first published story by James H. Schmitz, and it's unusual for a beginning writer to write something at such a length, let alone to produce such a masterful performance. Another striking point is that, while the story is certainly science fiction, rather than fantasy, it appeared in the August 1943 issue of the great fantasy magazine *Unknown Worlds*, which had changed its name from *Unknown* a bit earlier. Admittedly, *Unknown* did publish SF on several other occasions, notably in its first issue, with Eric Frank Russell's Fortean novel, *Sinister Barrier*, but one wonders why the magazine's editor, John W. Campbell, didn't include the story in *Unknown*'s older sister, *Astounding Science-Fiction*. Probably we should just be thankful that this tale of the vegetable kingdom striking back *was* published and is still around for anyone who needs an adrenaline charge.

❖   ❖   ❖

James H. Schmitz (1911-1981) was a master of action-adventure science fiction, notably in his stories of the Hub, a loosely-bound confederation of star systems. His most popular characters, both female, were Telzey Amberdon, the spunky teenage telepath, and Trigger Argee, a crack shot with a gun and reflexes that make lighting look lethargic. His most popular novel, *The Witches of Karres*, though not part of the Hub universe, is a classic space opera. Many of his SF adventure tales have scary moments, and this one has them in abundance.

Greenface

by James H. Schmitz

"What I don't like," the fat sport—his name was Freddie Something—said firmly, "is snakes! That was a whopping mean-looking snake that went across the path there, and I ain't going another step nearer the icehouse!"

Hogan Masters, boss and owner of Masters Fishing Camp on Thursday Lake, made no effort to conceal his indignation.

"What you don't like," he said, his voice a trifle thick, "is work! That little garter snake wasn't more than six inches long. What you want is for me to carry all the fish up there alone, while you go off to the cabin and take it easy—"

Freddie already was on his way to the cabin. "I'm on vacation!" he bellowed back happily. "Gotta save my strength! Gotta 'cuperate!"

Hogan glared after him, opened his mouth and shut it again. Then he picked up the day's catch of bass and walleyes and swayed on toward the icehouse. Usually a sober young man, he'd been guiding a party of fishermen from one of his light-housekeeping cabins over the lake's trolling grounds since early morning. It was hot work in June weather and now, at three in the afternoon, Hogan was tanked to the gills with iced beer.

He dropped the fish between chunks of ice under the sawdust, covered them up and started back to what he called the lodge—an

417

old two-story log structure reserved for himself and a few campers too lazy even to do their own cooking.

When he came to the spot where the garter snake had given Freddie his excuse to quit, he saw it wriggling about spasmodically at the edge of a clump of weeds, as if something hidden in there had caught hold of it.

Hogan watched the tiny reptile's struggles for a moment, then squatted down carefully and spread the weeds apart. There was a sharp buzzing like the ghost of a rattler's challenge, and something slapped moistly across the back of his hand, leaving a stinging sensation as if he had reached into a cluster of nettles. At the same moment, the snake disappeared with a jerk under the plants.

The buzzing continued. It was hardly a real sound at all—more like a thin, quivering vibration inside his head, and decidedly unpleasant. Hogan shut his eyes tight and shook his head to drive it away. He opened his eyes again, and found himself looking at Greenface.

Nothing even faintly resembling Greenface had ever appeared before in any of Hogan's weed patches, but at the moment he wasn't greatly surprised. It hadn't, he decided at once, any real face. It was a shiny, dark-green lump, the size and shape of a goose egg standing on end among the weeds; it was pulsing regularly like a human heart; and across it ran a network of thin, dark lines that seemed to form two tightly shut eyes and a closed, faintly smiling mouth.

Like a fat little smiling idol in green jade—Greenface it became for Hogan then and there.... With alcoholic detachment, he made a mental note of the cluster of fuzzy strands like hair roots about and below the thing. Then—somewhere underneath and blurred as though seen through milky glass—he discovered the snake, coiled up in a spiral and still turning with labored writhing motions as if trying to swim in a mass of gelatin.

Hogan put out his hand to investigate this phenomenon, and one of the rootlets lifted as if to ward off his touch. He hesitated, and it flicked down, withdrawing immediately and leaving another red line of nettle-burn across the back of his hand.

In a moment, Hogan was on his feet, several yards away. A

belated sense of horrified outrage overcame him—he scooped up a handful of stones and hurled them wildly at the impossible little monstrosity. One thumped down near it; and with that, the buzzing sensation in his brain stopped.

Greenface began to slide slowly away through the weeds, all its rootlets wriggling about it, with an air of moving sideways and watching Hogan over a nonexistent shoulder. He found a chunk of wood in his hand and leaped in pursuit—and it promptly vanished.

He spent another minute or two poking around in the vegetation with his club raised, ready to finish it off wherever he found it lurking. Instead, he discovered the snake among the weeds and picked it up.

It was still moving, though quite dead, the scales peeling away from the wrinkled flabby body. Hogan stared at it, wondering. He held it by the head; and at the pressure of his finger and thumb, the skull within gave softly, like leather. It became suddenly horrible to feel and then the complete inexplicability of the grotesque affair broke in on him.

He flung the dead snake away with a wide sweep of his arm, went back of the icehouse and was briefly but thoroughly sick.

Julia Allison was leaning on her elbows over the kitchen table studying a mail-order catalogue when Hogan walked unsteadily into the lodge. Julia had dark-brown hair, calm gray eyes, and a wicked figure. She and Hogan had been engaged for half a year. Hogan didn't want to get married until he was sure he could make a success of Masters Fishing Camp, which was still in its first season.

Julia glanced up, smiling. The smile became a stare. She closed the catalogue.

"Hogan," she stated, in the exact tone of her pa, Whitey Allison, refusing a last one to a customer in Whitey's bar and liquor store in town, "you're plain drunk! Don't shake your head—it'll slop out your ears."

"Julia—" Hogan began excitedly.

She stepped up to him and sniffed, wrinkling her nose. "*Pfaah!* Beer! Yes, darling?"

"Julia, I just saw something—a sort of crazy little green spook—"

Julia blinked twice.

"Look, infant," she said soothingly, "that's how people get talked about! Sit down and relax while I make up coffee, black. There's a couple came in this morning, and I put them in the end cabin. They want the stove tanked with kerosene, ice in the icebox, and coal for a barbecue—I fixed them up with linen."

"Julia," Hogan inquired hoarsely, "are you going to listen to me or not?"

Her smile vanished. "Now you're yelling!"

"I'm *not* yelling. And I don't need coffee. I'm trying to tell you—"

"Then do it without shouting!" Julia replaced the coffee can with a whack that showed her true state of mind, and gave Hogan an abused look which left him speechless.

"If you want to stand there and sulk," she continued immediately, "I might as well run along—I got to help Pa in the store tonight." That meant he wasn't to call her up.

She was gone before Hogan, struggling with a sudden desire to shake his Julia up and down like a cocktail for some time, could come to a decision. So he went instead to see to the couple in the end cabin. Afterwards he lay down bitterly and slept it off.

When he woke up, Greenface seemed no more than a vague and very uncertain memory, an unaccountable scrap of afternoon nightmare. Due to the heat, no doubt. *Not* to the beer—on that point Hogan and Julia remained in disagreement, however completely they became reconciled otherwise. Since neither wanted to bring the subject up again, it didn't really matter.

The next time Greenface was seen, it wasn't Hogan who saw it.

In mid-season, on the twenty-fifth of June, the success of Masters Fishing Camp looked pretty well assured. Whitey Allison was hinting he'd be willing to advance money to have the old lodge rebuilt, as a wedding present. When Hogan came into camp for lunch, everything seemed peaceful and quiet; but before he got to the lodge steps, a series of piercing feminine shrieks from the direction of the north end cabin swung him around, running.

Charging up to the cabin with a number of startled camp guests strung out behind him, Hogan heard a babble of excited talk shushed suddenly and emphatically within. The man who was vacationing there with his wife appeared at the door.

"Old lady thinks she's seen a ghost, or something!" he apologized with an embarrassed laugh. "Nothing you can do. I . . . I'll quiet her down, I guess. . . ."

Hogan waved the others back, then ducked around behind the cabin, and listened shamelessly. Suddenly the babbling began again. He could hear every word.

"I did so see it! It was sort of blue and green and wet—and it had a green face, and it s-s-smiled at me! It f-floated up a tree and disappeared! Oh-G-G-Georgie!"

Georgie continued to make soothing sounds. But before nightfall, he came into the lodge to pay his bill.

"Sorry, old man," he said. He still seemed more embarrassed than upset. "I can't imagine what the little woman saw, but she's got her mind made up, and we gotta go home. You know how it is. I sure hate to leave, myself!"

Hogan saw them off with a sickly smile. Uppermost among his feelings was a sort of numbed vindication. A ghost that was blue and green and wet and floated up trees and disappeared was a far from exact description of the little monstrosity he'd persuaded himself he *hadn't* seen—but still too near it to be a coincidence. Julia, driving out from town to see him next day, didn't think it was a coincidence, either.

"You couldn't possibly have told that hysterical old goose about the funny little green thing you thought you saw? She got confidential in the liquor store last night, and her hubby couldn't hush her. Everybody was listening. That sort of stuff won't do the camp any good, Hogan!"

Hogan looked helpless. If he told her about the camp haunt again, she wouldn't believe him, anyhow. And if she did believe him, it might scare her silly.

"Well?" she urged suspiciously.

Hogan sighed. "Never spoke more than a dozen words with the woman. . . ."

Julia seemed doubtful, but puzzled. There was a peculiar oily hothouse smell in the air when Hogan walked up to the road with her and watched her start back to town in her ancient car; but with a nearly sleepless night behind him, he wasn't as alert as he might have been. He was recrossing the long, narrow meadow between the road and the camp before the extraordinary quality of that odor struck him. And then, for the second time, he found himself looking at Greenface—at a bigger Greenface, and not a better one.

About sixty feet away, up in the birches at the end of the meadow, it was almost completely concealed: a vague oval of darker vegetable green in the foliage. Its markings were obscured by the leaf shadows among which it lay motionless except for that sluggish pulsing.

Hogan stared at it for long seconds while his scalp crawled and his heart hammered a thudding alarm into every fiber of his body. What scared him was its size—that oval was as big as a football! It had been growing at a crazy rate since he saw it last.

Swallowing hard, he mopped sweat off his forehead and walked on stiffly towards the lodge, careful to give no sign of being in a hurry. He didn't want to scare the thing away. There was an automatic shotgun slung above the kitchen door for emergencies; and a dose of No. 2 shot would turn this particular emergency into a museum specimen. . . .

Around the corner of the lodge he went up the entrance steps four at a time. A few seconds later, with the gun in his hand and reaching for a box of shells, he shook his head to drive a queer soundless buzzing out of his ears. Instantly, he remembered where he'd experienced that sensation before, and wheeled towards the screened kitchen window.

The big birch trembled slightly as if horrified to see a huge spider with jade-green body and blurred cluster of threadlike legs flow down along its trunk. Twelve feet from the ground, it let go of the tree and dropped, the long bunched threads stretched straight down before it. Hogan grunted and blinked.

It had happened before his eyes: at the instant the bunched tips hit the ground, Greenface was jarred into what could only be called a higher stage of visibility. There was no change in the head, but the legs abruptly became flat, faintly greenish ribbons, flexible and semi-transparent. Each about six inches wide and perhaps six feet long, they seemed attached in a thick fringe all around the lower part of the head, like a Hawaiian dancer's grass skirt. They showed a bluish gloss wherever the sun struck them, but Greenface didn't wait for a closer inspection.

Off it went, swaying and gliding swiftly on the ends of those foot ribbons into the woods beyond the meadow. And for all the world, it *did* look almost like a conventional ghost, the ribbons glistening in a luxurious winding sheet around the area where a body should have been, but wasn't! No wonder that poor woman—

Hogan found himself giggling helplessly. He laid the gun on the kitchen table, then tried to control the shaking of his hands long enough to get a cigarette going.

Long before the middle of July, every last tourist had left Masters Fishing Camp. Vaguely, Hogan sensed it was unfortunate that two of his attempts to dispose of Greenface had been observed while his quarry remained unseen. Of course, it wasn't his fault if the creature chose to exercise an uncanny ability to become almost completely invisible at will—nothing more than a tall glassy blur which flickered off through the woods and was gone. And it wasn't until he drove into town one evening that he realized just how unfortunate that little trick was, nevertheless, for him.

Whitey Allison's greeting was brief and chilly. Then Julia delayed putting in an appearance for almost half an hour. Hogan waited patiently enough.

"You might pour me a Scotch," he suggested at last.

Whitey passed him a significant look.

"Better lay off the stuff," he advised heavily. Hogan flushed.

"What do you mean by that?"

"There's plenty of funny stories going around about you right now!" Whitey told him, blinking belligerently. Then he looked past Hogan, and Hogan knew Julia had come into the store behind him; but he was too angry to drop the matter there.

"What do you expect me to do about them?" he demanded.

"That's no way to talk to Pa!"

Julia's voice was sharper than Hogan had ever heard it—he swallowed hard and tramped out of the store without looking at her. Down the street he had a couple of drinks; and coming past the store again on the way to his car, he saw Julia behind the bar counter, laughing and chatting with a group of summer residents. She seemed to be having a grand time; her gray eyes sparkled and there was a fine high color in her cheeks.

Hogan snarled out the worst word he knew and went on home. It was true he'd grown accustomed to an impressive dose of whiskey at night, to put him to sleep. At night, Greenface wasn't abroad, and there was no sense in lying awake to wonder and worry about it. On warm clear days around noon was the time to be alert; twice Hogan caught it basking in the treetops in full sunlight and each time took a long shot at it, which had no effect beyond scaring it into complete visibility. It dropped out of the tree like a rotten fruit and scudded off into the bushes, its foot ribbons weaving and flapping all about it.

Well, it all added up. Was it surprising if he seemed constantly on the watch for something nobody else could see? When the camp cabins emptied one by one and stayed empty, Hogan told himself that he preferred it that way. Now he could devote all his time to tracking down that smiling haunt and finishing it off. Afterwards would have to be early enough to repair the damage it had done his good name and bank balance.

He tried to keep Julia out of these calculations. Julia hadn't been out to the camp for several weeks; and under the circumstances he didn't see how he could do anything at present to patch up their misunderstanding.

After being shot at the second time, Greenface stayed out of sight for so many days that Hogan almost gave up hunting for it. He was morosely cleaning out the lodge cellar one afternoon; and as he shook out a box he was going to convert to kindling, a small odd-looking object tumbled out to the floor. Hogan stared at the object a moment, then frowned and picked it up.

It was the mummified tiny body of a hummingbird, some tropical species with a long curved beak and long ornamental tail feathers. Except for beak and feathers, it would have been unrecognizable; bones, flesh, and skin were shriveled together into a small lump of doubtful consistency, like dried gum. Hogan, remembering the dead snake from which he had driven Greenface near the icehouse, turned it around in fingers that trembled a little, studying it carefully.

The origin of the camp spook seemed suddenly explained. Some two months ago, he'd carried the box in which the hummingbird's body had been lying into the lodge cellar. In it at the time had been a big cluster of green bananas he'd got from the wholesale grocer in town. . . .

Greenface, of course, was carnivorous, in some weird, out-of-the-ordinary fashion. Small game had become rare around the camp in recent weeks; even birds now seemed to avoid the area. When that banana cluster was shipped in from Brazil or some island in the Caribbean, Greenface—a seedling Greenface, very much smaller even than when Hogan first saw it—had come along concealed in it, clinging to its hummingbird prey.

And then something—perhaps simply the touch of the colder North—had acted to cancel the natural limits on its growth; for each time he'd seen it, it had been obvious that it still was growing rapidly. And though it apparently lacked solid parts that might resist decomposition after death, creatures of its present size, which conformed to no recognizable pattern of either the vegetable or the animal kingdom, couldn't very well exist anywhere without drawing human attention to themselves. While if they grew normally to be only a foot or two high, they seemed intelligent and alert enough to escape observation in some luxuriant tropical forest—even discounting that inexplicable knack of turning transparent from one second to the next.

His problem, meanwhile, was a purely practical one. The next time he grew aware of the elusive hothouse smell near the camp, he had a plan ready laid. His nearest neighbor, Pete Jeffries, who provided Hogan with most of his provisions from a farm two miles down the road to town, owned a hound by the name of Old Battler—a large, surly brute with a strong strain of Airedale in its make-up, and reputedly the best trailing nose in the county.

Hogan's excuse for borrowing Old Battler was a fat buck who'd made his headquarters in the marshy ground across the bay. Pete had no objection to out-of-season hunting; he and Old Battler were the slickest pair of poachers for a hundred miles around. He whistled the hound in and handed him over to Hogan with a parting admonition to keep an eye peeled for snooping game wardens.

The oily fragrance under the birches was so distinct that Hogan almost could have followed it himself. Unfortunately, it didn't mean a thing to the dog. Panting and rumbling as Hogan, cradling the shotgun, brought him up on a leash, Old Battler was ready for any type of quarry from rabbits to a pig-stealing bear; but he simply wouldn't or couldn't accept that he was to track that bloodless vegetable odor to its source. He walked off a few yards in the direction the thing had gone, nosing the grass; then, ignoring Hogan's commands, he returned to the birch, sniffed carefully around its base and paused to demonstrate in unmistakable fashion what he thought of the scent. Finally he sat on his haunches and regarded Hogan with a baleful, puzzled eye.

There was nothing to do but take him back and tell Pete Jeffries the poaching excursion was off because a warden had put in an appearance in the area. When Hogan got back to the lodge, he heard the telephone ringing above the cellar stairs and hurried towards it with an eagerness that surprised himself.

"Hello?" he said into the mouthpiece. "Hello? Julia? That you?"

There was no answer from the other end. Hogan, listening, heard voices, several of them, people laughing and talking. Then a door slammed faintly and someone called out: "Hi, Whitey! How's the old man?" She had phoned from the liquor store, perhaps just to see what he was doing. He thought he could even hear the faint fluttering of her breath.

"Julia," Hogan said softly, scared by the silence. "What's the matter, darling? Why don't you say something?"

Now he did hear her take a quick, deep breath. Then the receiver clicked down, and the line was dead.

The rest of the afternoon he managed to keep busy cleaning out the cabins which had been occupied. Counting back to the day the last of them had been vacated, he decided the reason nobody had arrived since was that a hostile Whitey Allison, in his strategic position at the town bus stop, was directing all tourist traffic to other camps. Not—Hogan assured himself again—that he wanted anyone around until he had solved his problem; it would only make matters more difficult.

But why had Julia called up? What did it mean?

That night, the moon was full. Near ten o'clock, with no more work to do, Hogan settled down wearily on the lodge steps. Presently he lit a cigarette. His intention was to think matters out to some conclusion in the quiet night air, but all he seemed able to do was to keep telling himself uselessly that there must be some way of trapping that elusive green horror.

He pulled the sides of his face down slowly with his fingertips. "I've got to do something!"—the futile whisper seemed to have been running through his head all day: "Got to *do* something! Got to . . ." He'd be having a mental breakdown if he didn't watch out.

The rumbling barks of Jeffries' Old Battler began to churn up the night to the east—and suddenly Hogan caught the characteristic tinny stutter of Julia's little car as it turned down into the road from Jeffries' farm and came on in the direction of the camp.

The thrill that swung him to his feet was tempered at once by fresh doubts. Even if Julia was coming to tell him she'd forgiven him, he'd be expected to explain what was making him act like this. And there was no way of explaining it. She'd think he was crazy or lying. No, he couldn't do it, Hogan decided despairingly. He'd have to send her away again. . . .

He took the big flashlight from its hook beside the door and started off forlornly to meet her when she would bring the car bumping along the path from the road. Then he realized that the car, still half a mile or so from the lodge, had stopped.

He waited, puzzled. From a distance he heard the creaky shift of its gears, a brief puttering of the motor—another shift and putter. Then silence. Old Battler was also quiet, probably listening suspiciously, though he, too, knew the sound of Julia's car. There was no one else to hear it. Jeffries had gone to the city with his wife that afternoon, and they wouldn't be back till late next morning.

Hogan frowned, flashing the light on and off against the moonlit side of the lodge. In the quiet, three or four whippoorwills were crying to each other with insane rapidity up and down the lake front. There was a subdued shrilling of crickets everywhere, and occasionally the threefold soft call of an owl dropped across the bay. He started reluctantly up the path towards the road.

The headlights were out, or he would have been able to see them from here. But the moon rode high, and the road was a narrow silver ribbon running straight down through the pines towards Jeffries' farmhouse.

Quite suddenly he discovered the car, pulled up beside the road and turned back towards town. It was Julia's car all right; and it was empty. Hogan walked slowly towards it, peering right and left, then jerked around with a start to a sudden crashing noise among the pines a hundred yards or so down off the road—a scrambling animal rush which seemed to be moving toward the lake. An instant later, Old Battler's angry roar told him the hound was running loose and had prowled into something it disapproved of down there.

He was still listening, trying to analyze the commotion, when a girl in a dark sweater and skirt stepped out quietly from the shadow of the roadside pines beyond him. Hogan didn't see her until she crossed the ditch to the road in a beautiful reaching leap. Then she was running like a rabbit for the car.

He shouted: "Julia!"

For just an instant, Julia looked back at him, her face a pale scared blur in the moonlight. Then the car door slammed shut behind her, and with a shiver and groan the old machine lurched into action. Hogan made no further attempt to stop her. Confused and unhappy, he watched the headlights sweep down the road until they swung out of sight around a bend.

Now what the devil had she been poking about here for?

Hogan sighed, shook his head and turned back to the camp. Old Battler's vicious snarling had stopped; the woods were quiet once more. Presently a draft of cool air came flowing up from the lake across the road, and Hogan's nostrils wrinkled. Some taint in the breeze—

He checked abruptly. Greenface! Greenface was down there among the pines somewhere. The hound had stirred it up, discovered it was alive and worth worrying, but lost it again, and was now casting about silently to find its hiding place.

Hogan crossed the ditch in a leap that bettered Julia's, blundered into the wood and ducked just in time to avoid being speared in the eye by a jagged branch of aspen. More cautiously, he worked his way in among the trees, went sliding down a moldy incline, swore in exasperation as he tripped over a rotten trunk and was reminded thereby of the flashlight in his hand. He walked slowly across a moonlit clearing, listening, then found himself confronted by a dense cluster of evergreens and switched on the light.

It stabbed into a dark-green oval, more than twice the size of a human head, fifteen feet away.

He stared in fascination at the thing, expecting it to vanish. But Greenface made no move beyond a slow writhing among the velvety foot ribbons that supported it. It had shot up again since he'd seen it last, stood taller than he now and was stooping slightly towards him. The lines on its pulsing head formed two tightly shut eyes and a wide, thin-lipped, insanely smiling mouth.

Gradually it was borne in on Hogan that the thing was asleep. Or had been asleep . . . for now he became aware of a change in the situation through something like the buzzing escape of steam, a sound just too high to be audible that throbbed through his head. Then he noticed that Greenface, swaying slowly, quietly, had come a foot or two closer, and he saw the tips of the foot ribbons grow dim and transparent as they slid over the moss toward him. A sudden horror of this stealthy approach seized him. Without thinking of what he did, he switched off the light.

Almost instantly, the buzzing sensation died away, and before Hogan had backed off to the edge of the moonlit clearing, he realized that Greenface had stopped its advance. Suddenly he understood.

Unsteadily, he threw the beam on again and directed it full on the smiling face. For a moment, there was no result; then the faint buzzing began once more in his brain, and the foot ribbons writhed and dimmed as Greenface came sliding forward. He snapped it off; and the thing grew still, solidifying.

Hogan began to laugh in silent hysteria. He'd caught it now! Light brought Greenface alive, let it act, move, enabled it to pull off its unearthly vanishing stunt. At high noon, it was as vital as a cat or hawk. Lack of light made it still, dulled, though perhaps able to react automatically.

Greenface was trapped.

He began to play with it, savagely savoring his power over the horror, switching the light off and on. Perhaps it wouldn't even be necessary to kill the thing now. Its near-paralysis in darkness might make it possible to capture it, cage it securely alive, as a stunning justification of everything that had occurred these past weeks. He watched it come gliding toward him again, and seemed to sense a dim rising anger in the soundless buzzing. Confidently, he turned off the light. But this time Greenface didn't stop.

In an instant, Hogan realized he had permitted it to reach the edge of the little clearing. Under the full glare of the moon, it was still advancing on him, though slowly. Its outlines grew altogether blurred. Even the head started to fade.

He leaped back, with a new rush of the instinctive horror with which he had first detected it coming toward him. But he retreated only into the shadows on the other side of the clearing.

The ghostly outline of Greenface came rolling on, its nebulous leering head swaying slowly from side to side like the head of a hanged and half-rotted thing. It reached the fringe of shadows and stopped, while the foot ribbons darkened as they touched the darkness and writhed back. Dimly, it seemed to be debating this new situation.

Hogan swallowed hard. He had noticed a blurred shapeless something which churned about slowly within the jellylike shroud beneath the head; and he had a sudden conviction that he knew the reason for Old Battler's silence . . . . Greenface had become as dangerous as a tiger!

But he had no intention of leaving it in the moonlight's releasing spell. He threw the beam on the dim oval mask again, and slowly, stupidly, moving along that rope of light, Greenface entered the shadows; and the light flicked out, and it was trapped once more.

Trembling and breathless after his half-mile run, Hogan stumbled into the lodge kitchen and began stuffing his pockets with as many shells as they would take. Then he took down the shotgun and started back toward the spot where he had left the thing, keeping his pace down to a fast walk. If he made no blunders now, his troubles would be over. But if he did blunder . . . Hogan shivered. He hadn't quite realized before that the time was bound to come when Greenface would be big enough to lose its fear of him. His notion of trying to capture it alive was out—he might wind up inside it with Old Battler. . . .

Pushing down through the ditch and into the woods, he flashed the light ahead of him. In a few more minutes, he reached the place where he had left Greenface. And it wasn't there.

Hogan glared about, wondering wildly whether he had missed the right spot and knowing he hadn't. He looked up and saw the tops of the jack pines swaying against the pale blur of the sky; and as he stared at them, a ray of moonlight flickered through the broken canopy and touched him and was gone again, and then he understood. Greenface had crept up along such intermittent threads of light into the trees.

One of the pine tips appeared blurred and top-heavy. Hogan studied it carefully; then he depressed the safety button on the shotgun, cradled the weapon, and put the flashlight beam dead-center on that blur. In a moment, he felt the familiar mental irritation as the blur began to flow down through the branches toward him. Remembering that Greenface didn't mind a long drop to the ground, he switched off the light and watched it take shape among the shadows, and then begin a slow retreat toward the treetops and the moon.

Hogan took a deep breath and raised the gun.

The five reports came one on top of the other in a rolling roar, while the pine top jerked and splintered and flew. Greenface was plainly visible now, still clinging, twisting and lashing in spasms like a broken snake. Big branches, torn loose in those furious convulsions, crashed ponderously down toward Hogan. He backed off hurriedly, flicked in five new shells and raised the gun again.

And again.

And again . . .

Greenface and what seemed to be the whole top of the tree came down together. Dropping the gun, Hogan covered his head with his arms. He heard the sodden, splashy thump with which Greenface landed on the forest mold half a dozen yards away. Then something hard and solid slammed down across his shoulders and the back of his skull.

There was a brief sensation of diving headlong through a fire-streaked darkness. For many hours thereafter, no sort of sensation reached Hogan's mind at all.

"Haven't seen you around in a long time!" bellowed Pete Jeffries across the fifty feet of water between his boat and Hogan's. He pulled a flapping whitefish out of the illegal gill net he was emptying, plunked it down on the pile before him. "What you do with yourself—sleep up in the woods?"

"Times I do," Hogan admitted.

"Used to myself, your age. Out with a gun alla time!" Pete's face drew itself into mournful folds. "Not much fun now any more . . . not since them damn game wardens got Old Battler."

Hogan shivered imperceptibly, remembering the ghastly thing he'd buried that July morning six weeks back, when he awoke, thinking his skull was caved in, and found Greenface had dragged itself away, with what should have been enough shot in it to lay out half a township. At least, it had felt sick enough to disgorge what was left of Old Battler, and to refrain from harming Hogan. And perhaps it had died later of its injuries. But he didn't really believe it was dead. . . .

"Think the storm will hit before evening?" he asked out of his thoughts, not caring particularly whether it stormed or not. But Pete was sitting there, looking at him, and it was something to say.

"Hit the lake in half an hour," Pete replied matter-of-factly. "I know two guys who are going to get awful wet."

"Yeah?"

Pete jerked his head over his shoulder. "That little bay back where the Indian outfit used to live. Two of the drunkest mugs I seen on Thursday Lake this summer—fishing from off a little duck boat. . . . They come from across the lake somewhere."

"Maybe we should warn them."

"Not me!" Jeffries said emphatically. "They made some smart cracks at me when I passed there. Like to have rammed them!" He grunted, studied Hogan with an air of puzzled reflection. "Seems there was something I was going to tell you . . . well, guess it was a lie." He sighed. "How's the walleyes hitting?"

"Pretty good." Hogan had picked up a stringerful trolling along the lake bars.

"Got it now!" Pete exclaimed. "Whitey told me last night. Julia got herself engaged with a guy in the city-place she's working at. Getting married next month."

Hogan bent over the side of his boat and began to unknot the fish stringer. He hadn't seen Julia since the night he last met Greenface. A week or so later he heard she'd left town and taken a job in the city.

"Seemed to me I ought to tell you," Pete continued with remorseless neighborliness. "Didn't you and she used to go around some?"

"Yeah, some," Hogan agreed. He held up the walleyes. "Want to take these home for the missis, Pete? I was just fishing for the fun of it."

"Sure will!" Pete was delighted. "Nothing beats walleyes for eating, 'less it's whitefish. But I'm going to smoke these. Say, how about me bringing you a ham of buck, smoked, for the walleyes? Fair enough?"

"Fair enough," Hogan smiled.

"Can't be immediate. I went shooting the north side of the lake three nights back, and there wasn't a deer around. Something's scared 'em all out over there."

"Okay," Hogan said, not listening at all. He got the motor going, and cut away from Pete with a wave of his hand. "Be seeing you, Pete!"

Two miles down the lake, he got his mind off Julia long enough to find a possible significance in Pete's last words.

He cut the motor to idling speed, and then shut it off entirely, trying to get his thoughts into some kind of order. Since that chunk of pine slugged him in the head and robbed him of his chance of finishing off Greenface, he'd seen no more of the thing and heard nothing to justify his suspicion that it was still alive somewhere, perhaps still growing. But from Thursday Lake northward to the border of Canada stretched two hundred miles of bush-trees and water, with only the barest scattering of farms and tiny towns. Hogan sometimes pictured Greenface prowling about back there, safe from human detection, and a ghastly new enemy for the harried small life of the bush, while it nourished its hatred for the man who had so nearly killed it.

It wasn't a pretty picture. It made him take the signs indicating Masters Fishing Camp from the roads, and made him turn away the occasional would-be guest who still found his way to the camp in spite of Whitey Allison's unrelenting vigilance in town. It also made it impossible for him even to try to get in touch with Julia and explain what couldn't have been explained, anyway.

A rumbling of thunder broke through his thoughts. The sky in the east hung black with clouds now; and the boat was drifting in steadily toward shore with the wind and waves behind it. Hogan started the motor and came around in a curve to take a direct line toward camp. As he did so, a pale object rose sluggishly on the waves not a hundred yards ahead of him. With a start, he realized it was the upturned bottom of a small boat, and remembered the two fishermen he'd intended warning against the approach of the storm.

The little bay Pete Jeffries had mentioned lay half a mile behind; in his preoccupation he'd passed it without becoming conscious of the fact. There was no immediate reason to assume the drunks had met with an accident; more likely they'd landed and neglected to draw the boat high enough out of the water, so that it drifted off into the lake again on the first eddy of wind. Circling the derelict to make sure it was what it appeared to be, Hogan turned back to pick up the stranded sportsmen and take them to his camp until the storm was over.

When he reached the relatively smooth water of the tree-ringed bay, he throttled the motor and moved in slowly because the bay was shallow and choked with pickerel grass and reeds. There was surprisingly little breeze here; the air seemed almost oppressively hot and still after the free race of wind across the lake. Hogan realized it was darkening rapidly.

He stood up in the boat and stared along the shoreline over the tops of the reeds, wondering where the two had gone—and whether they mightn't have been in their boat anyway when it overturned.

"Anyone around?" he yelled uncertainly.

His voice echoed back out of the creaking shore pines. From somewhere near the end of the bay sounded a series of splashes—probably a big fish flopping about in the reeds. When that stopped, the stillness turned almost tangible; and Hogan drew a quick, deep breath, as if he found breathing difficult here.

Again the splashing in the shallows—closer now. Hogan faced the sound, frowning. The frown became a puzzled stare. That certainly was no fish, but some large animal—a deer, a bear, possibly a moose. The odd thing was that it should be coming *toward* him . . . Craning his neck, he saw the reed tops bend and shake about a hundred yards away, as if a slow, heavy wave of air were passing through them in his direction. There was nothing else to be seen.

Then the truth flashed on him—a rush of horrified comprehension.

Hogan tumbled back into the stern and threw the motor on, full power. As the boat surged forwards, he swung it around to avoid an impenetrable wall of reeds ahead, and straightened out toward the mouth of the bay. Over the roar of the motor and the rush and hissing of water, he was aware of one other sensation: that shrilling vibration of the nerves, too high to be a sound, which had haunted him in memory all summer. Then there was a great splash behind the boat, shockingly close; another, a third. How near the thing actually came to catching him as he raced through the weedy traps of the bay, he never knew. Only after he was past the first broad patch of open water, did he risk darting a glance back over his shoulder—

He heard someone screaming. Raw, hoarse yells of animal terror. Abruptly, he realized it was himself.

He was in no immediate danger at the time. Greenface had given up the pursuit. It stood, fully visible among the reeds, a hundred yards or so back. The smiling jade-green face was turned toward Hogan, lit up by strange reflections from the stormy sky, and mottled with red streaks and patches he didn't remember seeing there before. The glistening, flowing mass beneath it writhed like a cloak of translucent pythons. It towered in the bay, dwarfing even the trees behind it in its unearthly menace.

It *had* grown again. It stood all of thirty feet tall. . . .

The storm broke before Hogan reached camp and raged on through the night and throughout the next day. Since he would never be able to find the thing in that torrential downpour, he didn't have to decide whether he must try to hunt Greenface down or not. In any case, he told himself, staring out of the lodge windows at the tormented chaos of water and wind, he wouldn't have to go looking for it. It had come back for him, and presently it was going to find its way to the familiar neighborhood of the camp.

There seemed to be a certain justice in that. He'd been the nemesis of the monster as much as it had been his. It had become time finally for the matter to end in one way or another.

Someone had told him—now he thought of it, it must have been Pete Jeffries, plodding up faithfully through the continuing storm one morning with supplies for Hogan—that the two lost sportsmen were considered drowned. Their boat had been discovered; and as soon as the weather made it possible, a search would be made for their bodies. Hogan nodded, saying nothing. Pete studied him as he talked, his broad face growing increasingly worried.

"You shouldn't drink so much, Hogan!" he blurted out suddenly. "It ain't doing you no good! The missis told me you were really keen on Julia. I should've kept my trap shut . . . but you'd have found out, anyhow."

"Sure I would," Hogan said promptly. It hadn't occurred to him that Pete believed he'd shut himself up here to mourn for his lost Julia.

"Me, I didn't marry the girl I was after, neither," Pete told him confidentially. "Course the missis don't know that. Hit me just about like it's hit you. You just gotta snap outta it, see?"

Something moved, off in the grass back of the machine shed. Hogan watched it from the corner of his eye through the window until he was sure it was only a big bush shaking itself in the sleety wind.

"Eh?" he said. "Oh, sure! I'll snap out of it, Pete. Don't you worry."

"Okay." Pete sounded hearty but not quite convinced. "And drive over and see us one of these evenings. It don't do a guy no good to be sitting off here by himself all the time."

Hogan gave his promise. He might, in fact, have been thinking about Julia a good deal. But mostly his mind remained preoccupied with Greenface—and he wasn't touching his store of whiskey these nights. The crisis might come at any time; when it did, he intended to be as ready for it as he could be. Shotgun and deer rifle were loaded and close at hand. The road to town was swamped and impassable now, but as soon as he could use it again, he was going to lay in a stock of dynamite.

Meanwhile, the storm continued day and night, with only occasional brief lulls. Hogan couldn't quite remember finally how long it had been going on; he slept fitfully at night, and a growing bone-deep fatigue gradually blurred the days. But it certainly was as long and bad a wet blow as he'd ever got stuck in. The lake water rolled over the main dock with every wave, and the small dock down near the end cabins had been taken clean away. Trees were down within the confines of the camp, and the ground everywhere was littered with branches.

While this lasted, he didn't expect Greenface to put in an appearance. It, too, was weathering the storm, concealed somewhere in the dense forests along the lake front, in as much shelter as a thing of that size could find, its great head nodding and pulsing slowly as it waited.

❖ ❖ ❖

By the eighth morning, the storm was ebbing out. In mid-afternoon the wind veered around to the south; shortly before sunset the cloud banks began to dissolve while mists steamed from the lake surface. A few hours earlier, Hogan had worked the car out on the road to see if he could make it to town. After a quarter of a mile, he turned back. The farther stretches of the road were a morass of mud, barricaded here and there by fallen trees. It would be days before anyone could get through.

Near sunset, he went out with an ax and hauled in a number of dead birches from a windfall over the hill to the south of the lodge. He felt chilled and heavy all through, unwilling to exert himself; but his firewood was running low and had to be replenished. As he came back to the lodge dragging the last of the birches, he was startled into a burst of sweat by a pale, featureless face that stared at him out of the evening sky between the trees. The moon had grown nearly full in the week it was hidden from sight; and Hogan remembered then that Greenface was able to walk in the light of the full moon.

He cast an anxious look overhead. The clouds were melting toward the horizon in every direction; it probably would be an exceptionally clear night. He stacked the birch logs to dry in the cellar and piled the wood he had on hand beside the fireplace in the lodge's main room. Then he brewed up the last of his coffee and drank it black. A degree of alertness returned to him.

Afterwards he went about, closing the shutters over every window except those facing the south meadow. The tall cottonwoods on the other three sides of the house should afford a protective screen, but the meadow would be flooded with moonlight. He tried to calculate the time the moon should set, and decided it didn't matter—he'd watch till it had set and then sleep.

He pulled an armchair up to an open window, from where, across the sill, he controlled the whole expanse of open ground over which Greenface could approach. The rifle lay on the table beside him; the shotgun, in which he had more faith, lay across his knees. Open shell boxes and the flashlight were within reach on the table.

❖ ❖ ❖

With the coming of night, all but the brightest of stars were dimmed in the gray gleaming sky. The moon itself stood out of Hogan's sight above the lodge roof, but he could look across the meadow as far as the machine shed and the icehouse.

He got up twice to replenish the fire which made a warm, reassuring glow on his left side. The second time, he considered replacing the armchair with something less comfortable. The effect of the coffee had begun to wear off; he was becoming thoroughly drowsy. Occasionally, a ripple of apprehension brought him bolt upright, pulses hammering; but the meadow always appeared quiet and unchanged and the night alive only with familiar, heartening sounds: the crickets, a single whippoorwill, and now and then the dark wail of a loon from the outer lake.

Each time, fear wore itself out again; and then, even thinking of Julia, it was hard to stay awake. She was in his mind tonight with almost physical vividness, sitting opposite him at the kitchen table, raking back her unruly hair while she leafed through the mail-order catalogues; or diving off the float he'd anchored beyond the dock, a bathing cap tight around her head and the chin strap framing her beautiful stubborn little face like a picture.

Beautiful but terribly stubborn, Hogan thought, nodding drowsily. Like one evening, when they'd quarreled again and she hid among the empty cabins at the north end of the camp. She wouldn't answer when Hogan began looking for her, and by the time he discovered her, he was worried and angry. So he came walking through the half-dark toward her without a word; and that was one time Julia got a little scared of him. "Now wait, Hogan!" she cried breathlessly. "Listen, Hogan—"

He sat up with a jerky start, her voice still ringing in his mind.

The empty moonlit meadow lay like a great silver carpet before him, infinitely peaceful; even the shrilling of the tireless crickets was withdrawn in the distance. He must have slept for some while, for the shadow of the house formed an inky black square on the ground immediately below the window. The moon was sinking.

Hogan sighed, shifted the gun on his knees, and immediately grew still again. There'd been something . . . and then he heard it clearly: a faint scratching on the outside of the bolted door behind him, and afterwards a long, breathless whimper like the gasp of a creature that has no strength to cry out.

Hogan moistened his lips and sat very quiet. In the next instant, the hair at the back of his neck rose hideously of its own accord.

"Hogan . . . Hogan . . . oh, please! Hogan!"

The toneless cry might have come out of the shadowy room behind him, or over miles of space, but there was no mistaking that voice. Hogan tried to say something, and his lips wouldn't move. His hands lay cold and paralyzed on the shotgun.

"Hogan . . . *please!* Hogan!"

He heard the chair go over with a dim crash behind him. He was moving toward the door in a blundering, dreamlike rush, and then struggling with numb fingers against the stubborn resistance of the bolt.

"That awful thing! That awful thing! Standing there in the meadow! I thought it was a . . . *tree!* I'm not crazy, am I, Hogan?"

The jerky, panicky whispering went on and on, until he stopped it with his mouth on hers and felt her relax in his arms. He'd bolted the door behind them, picked Julia up and carried her to the fireplace couch. But when he tried to put her on it, she clung to him hard, and he settled down with her, instead.

"Easy! Easy!" He murmured the words. "You're not crazy . . . and we'd better not make much noise. How'd you get here? The road's—"

"By boat. I had to find out." Her voice was steadier. She stared up at his face, eyes huge and dark, jerked her head very slightly in the direction of the door. "Was that what—"

"Yes, the same thing. It's a lot bigger now." Greenface must be standing somewhere near the edge of the cottonwoods if she'd seen it in the meadow as she came up from the dock. He went on talking quickly, quietly, explaining it all. Now Julia was here, there was no question of trying to stop the thing with buckshot or rifle slugs. That idea had been some kind of suicidal craziness. But they could get away from it, if they were careful to keep to the shadows.

The look of nightmare grew again in Julia's eyes as she listened, fingers digging painfully into his shoulder. "Hogan," she interrupted, "it's so big—big as the trees, a lot of them!"

He frowned at her uncomprehendingly a moment. Then, as she watched him, Julia's expression changed. He knew it mirrored the change in his own face.

She whispered: "It could come right through the trees!"

Hogan swallowed.

"It could be right outside the house!" Julia's voice wasn't a whisper any more; and he put his hand over her mouth.

"Don't you smell it?" he murmured close to her ear.

It was Greenface, all right; the familiar oily odor was seeping into the air they breathed, growing stronger moment by moment, until it became the smell of some foul tropical swamp, a wet, rank rottenness. Hogan eased Julia off his knees.

"The cellar," he whispered. "Dark—completely dark. No moonlight; nothing. Understand? Get going, but quietly!"

"What are you—"

"I'm putting the fire out first."

"I'll help you!" All Julia's stubbornness seemed concentrated in the three words, and Hogan clenched his teeth against an impulse to slap her face hard. Like a magnified echo of that impulse was the vast soggy blow which smashed at the outer lodge wall above the entrance door.

They stared, motionless. The whole house had shaken. The log walls were strong, but a prolonged tinkling of glass announced that each of the shuttered windows on that side had broken simultaneously. The damn thing, Hogan thought. It's really come for me! If it hits the door—

The ability to move returned to them together. They left the couch in a clumsy, frenzied scramble and reached the head of the cellar stairs not a step apart. A second shattering crash—the telephone leaped from its stand beside Hogan. He checked, hand on the stair railing, looking back.

He couldn't see the entry door from there. The fire roared and danced in the hearth, as if it enjoyed being shaken up so roughly. The head of the eight-point buck had bounced from the wall and lay beside the fire, glass eyes fixed in a red baleful glare on Hogan. Nothing else seemed changed.

"Hogan!" Julia cried from the darkness at the bottom of the stone stairs. He heard her start up again, turned to tell her to wait there.

Then Greenface hit the door.

Wood, glass, metal flew inward together with an indescribable explosive sound. Minor noises followed; then there was stillness again. Hogan heard Julia's choked breathing from the foot of the stairs. Nothing else seemed to stir.

But a cool draft of air was flowing past his face. And now there came heavy scraping noises, a renewed shattering of glass.

"Hogan!" Julia sobbed. "Come down! It'll get in!"

"It can't!" Hogan breathed.

As if in answer, the lodge's foundation seemed to tremble beneath him. Wood splintered ponderously; there was the screech of parting timbers. The shaking continued and spread through the entire building. Just beyond the corner of the wall which shut off Hogan's view of the entry door, something smacked heavily and wetly against the floor. Laboriously, like a floundering whale, Greenface was coming into the lodge.

At the bottom of the stairs, Hogan caught his foot in a roll of wires, and nearly went headlong over Julia. She clung to him, shaking.

"Did you see it?"

"Just a glimpse of its head!" Hogan was steering her by the arm along the dark cellar passage, then around a corner. "Stay there. . . ." He began fumbling with the lock of the cellar exit.

"What will we do?" she asked.

Timbers creaked and groaned overhead, cutting off his reply. For seconds, they stared up through the dark in frozen expectation, each sensing the other's thoughts. Then Julia gave a low, nervous giggle.

"Good thing the floor's double strength!"

"That's the fireplace right above us," Hogan said. I wonder—" He opened the door an inch or two, peered out. "Look over there!"

The dim, shifting light of the fireplace outlined the torn front of the lodge. As they stared, a shadow, huge and formless, blotted out the light. They shrank back.

"Oh, Hogan! It's horrible!"

"All of that," he agreed, with dry lips. "You feel something funny?"

"Feel what?"

He put his fingertips to her temples. "Up there! Sort of buzzing? Like something you can almost hear."

"Oh! Yes, I do! What is it?"

"Something the thing does. But the feeling's usually stronger. It's been out in the cold and rain all week. No sun at all. I should have remembered. It *likes* that fire up there. And it's getting livelier now— that's why we feel the buzz."

"Let's run for it, Hogan! I'm scared to death here! We can make it to the boat."

"We might," Hogan said. "But it won't let us get far. If it hears the outboard start, it can cut us off easily before we're out of the bay."

"Oh, no!" she said, shocked. She hesitated. "But then what can we *do*?"

Hogan said, "Right now it's busy soaking up heat. That gives us a little time. I have an idea. Julia, will you promise that—just once— you'll stay here, keep quiet, and not call after me or do anything else you shouldn't?"

"Why? Where are you going?"

"I won't leave the cellar," Hogan said soothingly. "Look, darling, there's no time to argue. That thing upstairs may decide at any moment to start looking around for us—and going by what it did to the front wall, it can pull the whole lodge apart. . . . Do you promise, or do I lay you out cold?"

"I promise," she said, after a sort of frosty gasp.

Hogan remained busy in the central areas of the cellar for several minutes. When he returned, Julia was still standing beside the exit door where he'd left her, looking out cautiously.

"The thing hasn't moved much," she reported, her tone

somewhat subdued. She looked at him in the gloom. "What were you doing?"

"Letting out the kerosene tank—spreading it around."

"I smelled the kerosene." She was silent a moment. "Where are *we* going to be?"

Hogan opened the door a trifle wider, indicated the cabin immediately behind the cottonwood stand. "Over there. If the thing can tell we're around, and I think it can, we should be able to go that far without starting it after us."

Julia didn't answer; and he moved off into the dark again. Presently she saw a pale flare light up the chalked brick wall at the end of the passage, and realized Hogan was holding a match to papers. Kerosene fumes went off with a dim BOO-ROOM! and a glare of yellow light. Other muffled explosions followed in quick succession in various sections of the cellar. Then Hogan stepped out of a door on the passage, closed the door and turned toward her.

"Going up like pine shavings!" he said. "I guess we'd better leave quietly. . . ."

"It looks almost like a man in there, doesn't it, Hogan? Like a huge, sick, horrible old man!"

Julia's whisper was thin and shaky, and Hogan tightened his arms reassuringly about her shoulders. The buzzing sensation in his brain was stronger, rising and falling, as if the energies of the thing that produced it were gathering and ebbing in waves. From the corner of the cabin window, past the trees, they could see the front of the lodge. The frame of the big entry door had been ripped out and timbers above twisted aside, so that a good part of the main room was visible in the dim glow of the fireplace. Greenface filled almost all of that space, a great hunched dark bulk, big head bending and nodding slowly at the fire. In that attitude, there was in fact something vaguely human about it, a nightmarish caricature.

But most of Hogan's attention was fixed on the two cellar windows of the lodge which he could see. Both were alight with the flickering glare of the fires he had set; and smoke curled up beyond the cottonwoods, rising from the far side of the lodge, where he had opened other windows to give draft to the flames. The fire had a voice, a soft growing roar, mingled in his mind with the soundless rasping that told of Greenface's returning vitality.

It was like a race between the two: whether the fire, so carefully placed beneath the supporting sections of the lodge floor, would trap the thing before the heat kindled by the fire increased its alertness to the point where it sensed the danger and escaped. If it did escape—

It happened then, with blinding suddenness.

The thing swung its head around from the fireplace and lunged hugely backward. In a flash, it turned nearly transparent. Julia gave a choked cry. Hogan had told her about that disconcerting ability; but seeing it was another matter.

And as Greenface blurred, the flooring of the main lodge room sagged, splintered, and broke through into the cellar, and the released flames leaped bellowing upwards. For seconds, the vibration in Hogan's mind became a ragged, piercing shriek—became pain, brief and intolerable.

They were out of the cabin by that time, running and stumbling down toward the lake.

A boat from the ranger station at the south end of Thursday Lake chugged into the bay forty minutes later, with fire-fighting equipment. Pete Jeffries, tramping through the muddy woods on foot, arrived at about the same time to find out what was happening at Hogan's camp. However, there wasn't really much to be done. The lodge was a raging bonfire, beyond salvage. Hogan pointed out that it wasn't insured, and that he'd intended to have it pulled down and replaced in the near future, anyway. Everything else in the vicinity of the camp was too sodden after a week of rain to be in the least endangered by flying sparks. The fire fighters stood about until the flames settled down to a sullen glow. Then they smothered the glow, and the boat and Pete left. Hogan and Julia had been unable to explain how the fire got started; but, under the circumstances, it hardly seemed to matter. If anybody had been surprised to find Julia Allison here, they didn't mention it. However, there undoubtedly would be a good many comments made in town.

"Your Pa isn't going to like it," Hogan observed, as the sounds of the boat engine faded away on the lake.

"Pa will have to learn to like it!" Julia replied, perhaps a trifle grimly. She studied Hogan a moment. "I thought I was through with you, Hogan!" she said. "But then I had to come back to find out."

"Find out whether I was batty? Can't blame you. There were times these weeks when I wondered myself."

Julia shook her head.

"Whether you were batty or not didn't seem the most important point," she said.

"Then what was?"

She smiled, moved into his arms, snuggled close. There was a lengthy pause.

"What about your engagement in the city?" Hogan asked finally.

Julia looked up at him. "I broke it when I knew I was coming back."

It was still about an hour before dawn. They walked back to the blackened, twisted mess that had been the lodge building, and stood staring at it in silence. Greenface's funeral pyre had been worthy of a Titan.

"Think there might be anything left of it?" Julia asked, in a low voice.

"After that? I doubt it. Anyway, we won't build again till spring. By then, there'll be nothing around we might have to explain, that's for sure. We can winter in town, if you like."

"One of the cabins here will do fine."

Hogan grinned. "Suits me!" He looked at the ruin again. "There was nothing very solid about it, you know. Just a big poisonous mass of jelly from the tropics. Winter would have killed it, anyway. Those red spots I saw on it—it was already beginning to rot. It never really had a chance here."

She glanced at him. "You aren't feeling sorry for the thing?"

"Well, in a way." Hogan kicked a cindered two-by-four apart, and stood there frowning. "It was just a big crazy freak, shooting up all alone in a world where it didn't fit in, and where it could only blunder around and do a lot of damage and die. I wonder how smart it really was and whether it ever understood the fix it was in."

"Quit worrying about it!" Julia ordered.

Hogan grinned down at her. "Okay," he said.

"And kiss me," said Julia.

Tokyo Raider

INTRODUCTION

Now to close with the second story set in Japan, the *kaiju* capitol of the world, this one by *New York Times* best-selling author Larry Correia. The tale is part of his Grimnoir universe. For those who've wondered what happened to the characters after the conclusion of *Warbound*, the third novel in the Grimnoir trilogy, this yarn will provide some of the answers, along with exciting action scenes and—at no extra cost— the giant robot to end all giant robots.

❈ ❈ ❈

Best-selling author and Hugo Award finalist Larry Correia is hopelessly addicted to two things: guns and B-horror movies. He has been a gun dealer, firearms instructor, accountant, and is now a very successful writer. He shoots competitively and is a certified concealed weapons instructor. Larry resides in Utah with his very patient wife and family. His first novel, *Monster Hunter International*, is now in its fourth printing. In addition to the four novels in the best-selling Monster Hunter International series, he has written the popular Grimnoir trilogy, *Hard Magic*, *Spellbound* and the Hugo Award nominated *Warbound*, combining alternate history, urban fantasy, and the hard-boiled private eye genre in one delirious mixture.

Tokyo Raider

by Larry Correia

Adak, Alaska
1954

"You wanted to see me, sir?"

The Colonel of the 2nd Raider Battalion was pouring himself a cup of coffee and looking a bit more surly than usual. He returned the salute and gestured at the chair on the other side of his desk. "Take a seat, Lieutenant."

The building was quiet. The office walls around them were covered in maps of the Imperium. If—or more likely, *when*—there was war with the Japanese, this place was going to be hopping, but until then the Marines on the island of Adak had to watch and wait, train, freeze, and shoo caribou out of the barracks. The colonel was normally in a rotten mood before he had his coffee, so Joe got ready for another ass-chewing. He was the new guy, and he didn't fit in. Those made for a bad combination.

Luckily, the colonel got right down to business. "We got a priority magical transmission. Since everybody forgets about us stationed out here on the ass end of nowhere, the commo boys get excited when their window actually starts talking to them. They woke me up, telling me that the Commander in Chief of the Pacific Fleet himself had special orders for one of my butter bars."

So much for keeping his head down.

"Turns out my new junior platoon leader is some big shot back in the states. I knew you were a Heavy. File says you're really good at manipulating gravity, and you're qualified on a Heavy Suit, but nobody told me you were supposed to be some sort of genius wizard."

"I wouldn't say genius. It's all in my file. I have a degree in magical engineering from MIT and a master's from the Otis Institute."

"You went to college at what, twelve?"

"I graduated when I was nineteen, then I joined the Marine Corps, sir."

"Why the hell you ended up . . . Never mind. Whatever you've done impressed somebody. Congratulations, Lieutenant, you're going to Japan."

That was certainly unexpected. "Japan, sir?"

"Tokyo, to be exact. You'll be leaving immediately. An airship is being prepped now."

Joe took a deep breath. The ceasefire had held for a few years. There'd been some skirmishes and the usual saber rattling, but the Japanese had been too busy fighting the Soviets to cause any trouble for the American forces in the Pacific. The peace process must have broken down. If they were sending Raiders to Tokyo, that meant a full-blown war. A Marine Raider's job was to be dropped behind enemy lines to cause as much chaos as possible. Tokyo wasn't just behind their lines: it was the enemy heart. Joe wasn't sure if he was scared, eager, or a combination of both, but he'd signed up, so he'd do whatever needed to be done. "Are we jumping in?"

"I believe you'll just be landing at the air station."

Now he was really confused, but Raiders were trained to be flexible. "My platoon is ready for anything."

"No, Lieutenant, they're not. Your platoon is made up of Marines who are still trying to decide if they trust their newly assigned half-Jap officer to fight the Japanese. Frankly, I'm not sure if they'd follow you or frag you. Can you blame them? You speak the enemy's language, know their culture, and you even kind of look like one of them. I've heard of black Irish, but never yellow Irish."

"The men don't know if they should stick with rice or potato jokes, sir, but I carry on."

"Don't be a wiseass. Hell, I've been told you've got kanji brands on your body like one of their Iron Guards."

"No, sir. Those spells are a family recipe. They were inspected and approved by the War Department when I joined."

"I've been trying to decide what to do with you."

Joe appreciated the colonel's honesty. "My mother was born in the Imperium, but she was a *slave*. I may have been too young to make the last war, but I hate the Imperium as much as any man who's fought them, and I'll be here for the next."

The colonel sighed. "I believe you, but I'm not some dumb private who's going to be tempted to roll a grenade into your tent while you're sleeping because he's thinking he's doing his country a favor. I've no doubt you'll prove yourself to them eventually, but luckily, this assignment is just you."

There were limits to a Raider's flexibility, and Joe wasn't feeling up to invading the Imperium by himself. "I'm kind of hazy on the nature of my orders."

"Me, too. Per the peace treaty, you're to be a military observer. I neglected to mention that the radio man was mistaken. Turns out it wasn't the Commander in Chief of the Pacific Fleet calling, but *the* Commander in Chief."

"The president?"

"Yeah. I even voted for the man. I'll tell you, that was an unexpected way to start my day. I was a little concerned about being told to send one of my junior officers off by himself to the Imperium capital with orders to *help* those bastards, but the president spoke rather highly of your aptitude. How come you never told anybody you're buddies with President Stuyvesant?"

"Our families are acquainted."

"He said that you would be too humble, but that you were the best man for the job. That sounds fairly acquainted to me."

"Well, the First Lady does insist I call her Aunt Faye."

"Uh-huh . . ." The colonel took a drink of his coffee. "He said your presence as an observer was requested by the high commander of the entire Imperium military, General Toru Tokugawa. You know, the man in charge of our enemies, who rules over an evil empire with an iron fist. You're supposed to do him a favor for diplomacy's sake. I take it you're acquainted with him, too?"

He shrugged. "He and my father once worked together. It's complicated."

"Well, then, I can't imagine why your men don't have complete faith in you. Good luck in Japan, Lieutenant Sullivan."

Tokyo, Japan

Immediately after landing, Joe Sullivan had been met with a lot of ceremony by the Imperium Diplomatic Corps and then picked up by an armored car and some Iron Guard who didn't seem nearly so big on polite conversation. The Imperium elites had driven him directly to an ancient palace surrounded by cherry trees. The trip confirmed that Japan really was as pretty as Mom had made it out to be. They'd escorted him through the castle, to an ultramodern military command bunker beneath it. Then he'd stood there, waiting in his dress uniform, being eyeballed by a bunch of Japanese soldiers as they talked all sorts of shit about the *gaijin*, until somebody who'd been briefed told those idiots that he spoke Japanese, and they'd shut up.

The Imperium didn't seem to be hiding anything. The red markings on the wall maps told him that the Russians were pushing back against the Imperium in Asia. The unit markers were either true, or it was an elaborate setup for his benefit. Either way he memorized every unit and location so he could put it all in his report when he got home and let the intel types decide.

There was only one marker he didn't understand. It was shaped like a dragon, was red like the rest of the communist forces, and it had to represent something naval because it was tracking up the east coast of the island, heading for Tokyo bay, and several Japanese naval units had been destroyed along its path, including an entire carrier battle group. Several submarines were marked as missing. The kanji on the marker identified it with the code name: *Gorilla Whale*.

The Imperium were big on treating guests with respect, so the lack of respect had to be meant as an insult. After half an hour of waiting, without being offered so much as a chair, there was some shouting in the hall. Several military aides fled as a big, stocky, thickset Japanese man stomped into the bunker. He'd heard a lot about Toru Tokugawa growing up. Even though they'd been opponents, his dad had held more respect for this Imperium warrior than he did for most of the men supposedly on their side. The recent war had proven him to be one of best tacticians in the world, and in his youth he'd been one of the strongest Brutes to ever live.

Toru Tokugawa didn't disappoint in person.

"Damn those wretched Soviet pig dogs!" the general shouted as he stormed across the command center. The rest of the Imperium army staff remained quiet and polite as expected, as Tokugawa, on the other hand, was not. "Stalin has no honor!" He punched one of the bunker's walls, cracking the concrete. Tokugawa may have been in his fifties, but he still possessed an impressive connection to burn Power like that. "They fight like cowards!"

As their supreme commander flipped over a map table, the Japanese officers exchanged nervous glances. Having a visitor witness their leader acting in such a passionate manner was a loss of face. Tokugawa stood there, seething and glowering at the shower of falling papers, until one of the staffers broke the awkward silence. "Pardon me, General, the American observer you requested has arrived."

"Already? That was fast . . ." He composed himself, adjusted his uniform, then turned around and switched to English. "Present our guest."

"Second Lieutenant Joseph Sullivan of the United States Marine Corps," announced one of the Iron Guard.

"General Tokugawa." Sullivan bowed, careful to keep the gesture to the appropriate respectful level of a visiting dignitary of *equal* stature.

Tokugawa snorted. "You look more like your father than I expected. American Heavies are all so blocky and . . . corn fed . . . You're not quite so doughy as most of your fat countrymen. You could almost pass for a proper Imperium soldier, if you'd been lucky and taken a bit more after your mother, that is."

"I'd suggest leaving my parents out of this," Joe stated.

"Why would I do that? Your parents are the reason I asked for you. If I were to inadvertently insult them, what would you do about it?"

"I know you changed a lot of the Imperium's laws after the Chairman died, especially the ones about torture, slavery, and experimenting on prisoners, which all reasonable men can appreciate, but you've still got that thing where you can duel over insults, right?"

The Iron Guards shared nervous glances, but Tokugawa smiled. "Ha! Excellent. That is the defiant attitude I was hoping for. You will do. I was hoping you'd inherited your father's fearlessness, not to mention his sense of diplomacy. This will save time." Toru glanced at the assembled command staff. "All of you, leave us." They complied, rapidly shuffling out the door. The two Iron Guard escorts remained standing behind Sullivan. "You may leave as well."

"Our Finder believes he bears seven kanji, General. The Grimnoir knight is dangerous."

"They're not kanji," Joe said, as if he'd stoop to copying the spells of Imperium butchers. "And I'm not Grimnoir."

"I'm not worried," Toru stated. "Go." The Iron Guards bowed and left without another word. Toru waited for the bunker's door to be closed. "Not Grimnoir . . . Curious. You do not wish to follow in your father's footsteps?"

He'd had a bit of a disagreement with the Society, but that was none of Tokugawa's business.

"Interesting . . . An American who has barely lived there, who chose to join a military where he will never be accepted because of his half-breed race, refuses to join the one organization that must surely want him. Where do you *belong*, Sullivan?"

He was still working on that question himself. "My orders say I'm supposed to help. What do you want?"

"It pains me to admit it, but I require your assistance. In a show of mutual cooperation, your president has seen fit to grant my request. Apparently, your old friend Francis sees the Soviets as the greater threat at this time. This agreement should be beneficial to both of our nations. America and Imperium have been enemies in the past, but today we are . . . temporarily on the same side."

"Why in the world would he want me to help you? Once the Imperium finishes off the Russians, you'll go back to trying to conquer the rest of the world."

"I prefer the term *liberate*, but if you do not help, then we will be forced to use Tesla weapons to stop this threat, which will cause the deaths of hundreds of thousands of innocent civilians . . . Ah, your face betrays your emotions, young Sullivan. You'll need to work on that if you expect to make it long in this world. You might not wear the ring, but it appears you still have a Grimnoir knight's morals. I need an Active of your particular skills."

"I'm only a Gravity Spiker. We're a dime a dozen."

Tokugawa chuckled. "I believe I've heard that line before. Yet, according to my sources, despite your youth, your ability to manipulate gravity is unmatched."

"I learned from the best."

"Of course. We all stand upon the shoulders of those who came before us. Your father was self-taught. You benefit from his discoveries. We are alike in that way. I understand what is required to be the son of a great man. It is a burden, but also an incredible honor." Considering who Toru's father had been, that was probably one hell of a compliment around these parts. "There are many of your kind among the Iron Guard, some of whom are incredibly strong, far stronger than you, no doubt, but strength alone does not make a warrior great. That also requires awareness and will."

"Most folks chosen by the Power to control gravity aren't the sharpest knives in the drawer."

"I intended to be polite and say they lack nuance, but yes, most of them are stupid oxen good only for lifting things or throwing their bodies at the enemy. I've yet to find one among my army capable of the subtle manipulations of gravity your father was. Are you up to the task?"

Joe didn't actually know the answer to that. Those were some big shoes to fill. "What's the mission?"

Toru walked to the biggest wall map and pointed at the red

dragon symbol. "Trust me, the monster is far more impressive in person."

As the Iron Guard moved their general and his guest across Tokyo in a convoy of armored vehicles, Toru Tokugawa had continued his briefing. "They have sent giant demons against us before, but nothing like this. The soviets have been experimenting with increasing the abilities of their Summoners ever since they saw what happened to Washington D.C. in 1933."

"If I recall correctly, you were there for that," Joe said.

"The god of demons swatted me as if I were an annoying insect. We were only able to stop it because it was new and not yet fully formed. Luckily for all of mankind, even Stalin is not foolish enough to Summon anything that mighty. It would be too dangerous, too uncontrollable. However, they have made great strides over the last twenty years. This one is extremely resilient, far more armored than the last. The fact that they are still able to direct a demon this powerful is astounding."

"It's already destroyed a chunk of your navy."

"Correct."

"So that part was real, but I'm guessing everything else on those maps was probably wrong so I'd provide bad intel?"

"You are a perceptive man, Sullivan." Which didn't confirm or deny anything. Joe figured the temper tantrum earlier had been some sort of test as well. "The Summoned is approximately fifty meters tall and apparently still growing. Its capabilities are a mystery. It is amphibious and has been walking along the sea bed, only emerging every few days to attack. It has already damaged several cities along the coast."

"Civilian casualties?"

"I'm surprised you care."

"They didn't ask to be born under tyranny," Joe answered.

"Perhaps you may get that duel after all . . ."

Joe figured he would lose, but he wasn't in the mood to put up with nonsense. "I control gravity, so when we pick weapons, I vote telephone poles."

"As your people say, the apple does not fall far from the tree.

Twenty years ago I would have taken you up on that duel. I'd enjoy knocking the smug off your face, but we do not have time for that. There are over one hundred thousand dead so far, but we are still pulling bodies from the rubble."

Joe gave a low whistle.

"Intelligence predicts the demon will be here within the week. Iron Guard have been unable to defeat it. Our own greater Summoned have been stepped on. Conventional weapons harm it, but then once sufficiently wounded it retreats back out to sea to hide and heal for a few days before striking again. Depth charges have done nothing. My forces have been unable to track it in the sea. Every submarine I have sent after it has been lost. Aerial bombing has stung it, but has caused more harm to the city it was attacking than the beast itself."

"Have you tried Tesla weapons?"

"Once. A low powered firing to minimize collateral damage, but it did not work as expected. The demon's hide does not react like human flesh. I destroyed an entire town only to chase it back into hiding." The Imperium was far more casual about sacrificing its people than the west, but unlike his predecessor, it seemed this Tokugawa actually cared.

The general was staring out the narrow slit of the window at his capital city. They drove into a tunnel and Tokyo disappeared. "Our defense force is prepared to intercept it. We have moved the emperor somewhere safe. Anyone who is not vital to the war effort is being evacuated from the city. The *Yamamoto* is our newest airship and carries our most powerful Tesla weapon. It is on station above us and its Peace Ray is charged. If the demon cannot be stopped I will have no choice but to fire upon it at full power."

That would obliterate a good chunk of Tokyo in the process. "So what's the plan?"

The general didn't answer. The armored car came to a stop. The doors were opened, revealing that they'd parked inside some sort of vast hanger. Tokugawa climbed out, and Joe followed. His first thought was *Why are they building a skyscraper underground?* Then he realized they weren't actually underground, as much as they'd hollowed out an entire hill and covered the top to protect the interior from spy planes. The place was crowded with soldiers and engineers, and they began to panic when they saw who their distinguished visitor was. The Iron Guards snapped at them to get back to work. Hundreds of men were scrambling about on this level, and in the several floors of scaffolding overhead.

"There is my plan, Lieutenant Sullivan."

Directly in front of them was an armored metal rectangle, painted olive drab. His first thought was that it was a train car missing its wheels. Then he realized it was a *foot*.

"Behold, the Nishimura Super *Gakutensoku*. It has taken over a decade to build. It is the most daring feat of magical engineering ever attempted by Cog science."

He looked up, and up, and *up*. It was hard to wrap his brain around the size of the thing. "That's one *big* robot."

"Forty-six meters tall and nearly two thousand tons, it would destroy itself if it tried to move . . ."

"Galileo called it. That square cube law is a real stickler," Joe agreed.

"Which is why it must be piloted by someone who can break the rules."

"I'm good, but I'm not that good."

"The spells bound upon it will increase an Active's connection to the Power by an order of magnitude. It has a crew of seventy Actives, and the Turing machines inside control all of the minor systems. In theory, it should be as easy to drive as a suit of Nishimura combat armor. *If* the *Gakutensoku* works as projected, we should be able to defeat the demon and send Stalin a message."

He couldn't figure out what kind of spells they'd carved onto that thing to get it to work. Even powered down he could feel it pulling magic from the air around him. It was hard to tell through all the scaffolding, but it was shaped like a broad-shouldered man, with two arms that were too long and two legs that were too short. He couldn't even imagine this thing moving.

Then he realized that there were craters on the concrete floor from where the thing had fallen. He glanced around the vast hanger. There were a lot of craters.

"I will speak plainly. As you can see from the dents on my giant robot, every other Heavy has lacked the will necessary to control it. We are still repairing the damage from yesterday's test. I had hope for the last test pilot, since he was very intelligent for a Heavy. Sadly Captain Nakamura lacked finesse, tripped over his own feet within two hundred meters, and the Super Gakutensoku fell on its head."

"I imagine it takes practice."

"Feedback from the spell caused him to have an aneurism and die."

"Great." Helping his sworn enemies work the bugs out of a super weapon sure as hell wasn't what he'd joined the Marines for. "So now that you're running out of time, you asked for me."

"Deciding between asking for American help or blowing up our capital with a Tesla weapon was a very difficult decision."

Considering the fact that Joe had less than a week to learn how to drive a mechanical man the size of a 12-story building . . . "Keep that Peace Ray warmed up, General, because I'm not making any promises."

"If it is any consolation, Lieutenant Sullivan, the Super Gakutensoku is purely a defensive weapon system," Hikaru told him. "Since you are helping us—as you Americans say—*work out the kinks,* there is no way we could bring this magnificent device to America to lay waste to your cities and crush your armies beneath its massive steel feet. How would we get it there?"

"Good point," Joe muttered, resisting the urge to drop a few extra gravities on the annoyingly helpful Cog's head. It turned out that the Japanese Actives capable of magical bursts of intellectual brilliance were just as squirrely as their western counterparts.

Hikaru continued talking while fastening electrodes to Joe's freshly shaved head. "There is no airship that could carry it. Moving a machine of this size via sea would be too dangerous. Not to mention we've not solved the deep-water pressure problems of walking it across the ocean floor yet."

"Yet?"

"Uh . . . I . . . Never mind." The Cog spoke English better than Joe spoke Japanese, and he knew the Super *Gakutensoku* inside and out, so he'd been appointed Joe's assistant. Hikaru taped down the last wire. "There you go. The Turing machines are now monitoring your brain. The spells have been activated. The crew is ready. We are ready to test."

Joe glanced across the control center. He knew how to fly an airplane. This was way worse. He'd spent the last twenty hours memorizing every control, and they'd skipped all the *unimportant* ones. There were four pedals beneath each foot, friction sticks directly in front of him, and half a dozen levers for each arm. Cables and pulleys were attached to bands around his abdomen, chest, biceps, and wrists. It was bad enough that he needed to tell each "muscle group" what to do physically; he had to simultaneously tell gravity what to do magically.

"It looks more complicated than it is. This should be no worse than controlling a Heavy Suit."

"Have you ever driven a Heavy Suit, Hikaru?"

"No, Lieutenant. I have not personally, but that is what it says in the manual."

"Then do me a favor and shut up." Joe looked out the armored portholes. Cranes were lifting away the scaffolding to the front, and the workers were taking cover. The row of gauges told him that all twenty of their diesel engines were running. The indicator board was all green lights. There were Fixers on board making sure everything was working, Torches for damage control and weapons systems, Iceboxes making sure nothing overheated and taking care of the ridiculous amount of friction generated by their movement, Brutes to manhandle shells and guns, and other Gravity Spikers just to help channel enough magic into the machine's spells to keep them balanced.

Joe checked his own connection to the Power. The magic was gathered up in his chest, waiting to be directed. He used a bit of it to test the world around him. Spells had been carved all over the interior of the Super *Gakutensoku*. They magnified his connection but also distorted it. It was like looking through a microscope that was just a little bit out of focus. Maybe it was because he was running on coffee and determination at this point, but it was already starting to give him a headache. No wonder the last guy had a stroke.

He put his right foot down on a pedal while simultaneously pushing forward with the right friction stick. At the same time he called upon his magic, imagining the pull of the earth against his own leg, and easing that *just* enough. He'd never tried to change gravity over such a gigantic space. It was like magic was being ripped from the Power and channeled through his body out into the great machine. Joe ground his teeth and held on.

A hundred tons of foot scraped along the concrete before rising a few dozen feet and then slamming back down with an impact that shook the whole world.

There were ten other men in the *Gakutensoku*'s head. They began rattling off readings and stats from their CRTs and gauges. This was requiring such focus that Joe only barely heard them. He pushed down with his left foot and repeated the process. The robot lurched forward, but stayed balanced and upright. The crew let up a cheer. They'd gone *two* whole steps.

"How are you feeling, Lieutenant?" Hikaru asked.

In actuality he felt like he'd just been mule-kicked in the head. The Power draw made his teeth hurt, and he wanted to vomit. "Are you asking because you've bought into that propaganda about how soft Westerners are?"

"Quite the contrary. On our first test, at this point blood shot from the test pilot's ears. I just wanted to make sure I had the spells calibrated correctly."

It was taking effort simply to keep from sinking into the floor. Joe lifted one hand to wipe the sweat that had instantly formed on his brow. The unconscious movement caused one giant robot arm to rise up and crash through the scaffolding, tearing it all to pieces. Luckily he froze before swatting the cockpit and decapitating them. The noise of cascading, crashing metal could barely be heard through their thick armor, but it still went on for several painful seconds. Joe slowly lowered the arm, then pushed the disconnect button so he could turn enough to look out the side porthole. Yep. The scaffolding was just gone. Hopefully they'd had the sense to get everybody off of it before starting the test.

"Perhaps that is enough for your first day?" Hikaru asked hesitantly. "The physical and magical strain is considerable."

Iron Guard weren't the only ones around here taught to never show weakness. "I'm just getting warmed up." Joe looked up at the bank of CRT screens. Since the robot couldn't turn its head and their footprint took up a city block, those cameras were as close as he was going to get to peripheral vision. He found the exit out of the hillside. "Buckle up, Hikaru. Let's see what this baby can do."

Five days later, the second biggest demon to ever walk the earth attacked Tokyo.

General Toru Tokugawa stood on the observation deck of the tallest building in the city, watching out the window with his hands folded behind his back. He'd moved his command center here temporarily for this very view. It was a beautiful, clear day. Twenty miles to the southwest he could see buildings falling and smoke rising.

One of his aides entered the room in a hurry. "General, the demon is crossing Yokohama."

"I am aware," Toru stated.

"We have begun the mass evacuation as instructed. The coastal defense cannons were engaging before we lost contact with them. The Iron Guard are moving into position now. The air force is scrambling. The *Yamamoto* is awaiting your orders."

Nearly ten million people lived in the wards that would be directly affected by the Peace Ray. Those who would be instantly incinerated were the lucky ones. The burns and radiation sickness were far more painful ways to die. "And the Super *Gakutensoku*?"

"It is in the hills to the west. A message has been sent." From his aide's tone, Toru could tell the officer had very little faith in that option working.

He'd understated the danger to the American, Sullivan. This demon's presence and constant raids were crippling his country and endangering the entire war effort. Demons could be banished from this world, but they were not as easy to kill as a mortal being. Their bodies were artificial magical constructs. They had no internal organs to wound or bones to break. They were filled with magical substances that best resembled ink and smoke, and the only way to end one this powerful was to bleed it dry. That took time.

"Tell the *Yamamoto* to hold its fire for now. The Iron Guard must fall back. Draw it in, farther onto land, and then we will strike. Wait for the demon to be distracted by the *Gakutensoku*, then we will hit it with every conventional weapon at our disposal. If we cannot fell it, only then will we fire the Peace Ray. Better to raze the greatest city in the world than to endanger the whole Imperium." It would either be a scalpel or a tetsubo, but one way or the other, Stalin's demon died today.

"We should get you to the *Yamamoto* immediately, General."

"No." Toru looked back toward the growing pillars of black smoke. If this city died, then he deserved to die with it. "I believe that I'd like to watch the fight from here."

They were making excellent time. The robot's legs were too short to call it a run, but when you covered this much ground with each stride, a shuffling jog still got them to fifty miles an hour. The fact that there wasn't much they had to go around meant they could travel in a straight line. Joe had gotten good enough that he even managed to step *over* individual houses. Mostly.

Hikaru was giving him directions based upon roads, power lines, and compass directions. They'd quickly discovered that when you were twelve stories up you couldn't give directions based on street signs, and local landmarks meant nothing when your pilot had never been here before. Joe's entire knowledge of Japan's geography came from stories his mother had told him and maps he'd studied in the off chance the Marines got to invade the place.

"The demon is tracking north. To the east is an orchard, after you cross it there is a railway. Follow that toward the city," Hikaru told him.

"Got it." He couldn't see the Cog or the rest of the crew sitting behind him. Joe had learned the hard way not to turn his head enough to look back over his shoulder because the Turing machines read that the wrong way. The first time he'd done it they'd face-planted in a field. On the bright side, that had been a few days ago, and it had taught him how to stand this thing back up without waiting for multiple construction cranes to come save them.

Moving was fairly instinctive at this point. There was a rhythm to it. *Clomp. Clomp. Clomp.* It made sense that the cockpit was where the robot's head should have been, since that was how the human body's control center was wired, and once you were magically connected, he was the brain and it was all a matter of scale. He'd spent the last few days learning to move about with a modicum of grace, and slugging boulders, and it really wasn't that much different than working a punching bag with his own fists . . . Except for the part where he could punch through mountains.

The buildings were getting taller and the neighborhoods more populated. Joe had to step carefully to keep from landing on any moving cars. He was burning a lot of magic trying to keep a light step, but they still weighed so much that each footstep left an impact crater, so he wasn't sure how many of those automobiles unwittingly drove into the suddenly created holes they'd left in the roads.

One armored foot clipped the edge of a warehouse, but it was enough to rip one wall off. "I wish you people would've built wider streets!"

"I'll have you know Tokyo is the most advanced city in the world," Hikaru snapped.

"Horseshit. We've got an interstate highway system in America you could drive an aircraft carrier down. Hang on, I see smoke." The buildings here were already smashed flat or knocked over. A giant lizard-shaped footprint was clear as day in the middle of a park. "I've got the demon's trail." Joe guided the robot toward the path of carnage. Since everything here was already destroyed, he might as well take it up a notch. Joe pushed both friction sticks forward. "Hang on!"

ClompClompClomp!

The trail was easy to follow, what with all the spreading fires and collapsed buildings. Hundreds of civilians were down there. He could lie to himself and say they looked like bugs from up here, but they still looked like people, and he tried his best not to land on any of them. They might have just had a war, but that was no excuse to be an asshole.

Following in the demon's wake gave him a good glimpse into how the creature thought. If he'd been down there at ground level, he would have missed it. The scene would have just been too damned big to take in, but from up here, from the perspective of somebody twelve stories tall and nearly indestructible, he could tell that the demon was angry. It was heading toward the capital, but it was meandering about, swatting down anything that stood out along the way. A temple had been kicked over. Ornate wooden arches had been stepped on. It had gone three blocks out of its way to chase down a bus. It had picked up a passenger train and tossed it out into the ocean. The miles went by, showing an ever-increasing amount of spite. This Summoned was an engine of destruction.

It was enjoying itself.

"I can't believe this," Hikaru whispered as he looked out over the devastation. "This is nearly as bad as when the Americans firebombed the city."

"That was different," Joe snapped.

"How?"

"You started it. Now zip your lip. I'm concentrating."

An alarm horn sounded. There was some shouting in Japanese. Joe had thought he was fairly fluent, but polite Japanese was different than the profanity-laced military exclamations you got when one of the techs spotted a giant demon. Joe eased back on the sticks to slow them down.

They were in an open campus of large, ornate buildings, probably a university. The opposite end of the space was covered in black smoke, and through it, something truly *vast* moved. Long spines appeared, cutting ripples through the smoke, and there was a tremendous crash as a clock tower was knocked off its foundations to topple to the ground. The spines froze, then swiftly turned and disappeared, as the demon sensed the approaching footfalls.

Four brilliant beams of red light appeared in the smoke, about even with the *Gakutensoku*'s cockpit. Those were its *eyes*. It was watching them.

"All weapons, prepare to fire," Joe said with far more calm than he actually felt. Hikaru relayed the order. The gravitational magic lurched as a dozen other forms of Power were channeled through the spells carved on the great machine. "Let's hit this son of bitch with everything we've got."

The wind shifted. The smoke parted and the Summoned revealed itself. It was reptilian, with a dark, glistening hide perforated by random shards of black bone. It was thick-set, muscular, with a long spiked tail, two squat, powerful legs, and arms that ended in claws that looked like they could do a number on even the *Gakutensoku*'s armor. The demon stepped full into view, lowered its dragon-shaped head, and roared. It was so loud that it vibrated through their hull. Humans on the ground probably had their eardrums ruptured from the blast. The screech dragged on until it threatened to blot out the world. Then it snapped its razor jaws closed, spread its arms, and raised itself to its full height to meet this new challenge.

It was *far* bigger than they were.

"I believe that the greater Summoned may be significantly taller than the specified fifty meters," Hikaru stated.

It didn't matter what country you were in, military intelligence was always wrong.

"Put that record I gave you on the player, Hikaru. I want it blasting at full volume over the PA system."

"Lieutenant, despite your intentions, I truly do not believe that music really soothes the savage beast. That is just a colloquialism."

"Put my record on the player or I'm getting out of this chair." He waited until he heard the scratch of the record and the whine of the intercom. "That's better." Joe flipped open the safety cover and put his finger on the trigger. "Fire on my command."

Toru watched as the two titans faced each other. To the north was the Summoned, a horrible alien creature, its spirit torn from another realm and given form here. On the bony plates of its chest the soviet Cogs had engraved a hammer and sickle, and then filled it in with molten bronze so that it would never heal. To the south was the Super *Gakutensoku*. It was rather impressive, though not nearly as intimidating as the demon. Though it made no sense to camouflage a walking mountain, they'd painted it brown and olive drab, except for the glorious rising sun painted on its shoulder plates. Both sides of this duel were proud to claim their champions, each one representing their mighty nation. There was a certain dignity to this event.

A deadly silence covered the city after the demon's roar. It had been loud enough to break windows a mile away, and Toru could smell the smoke through the open wound in the building's side. There was a new sound, tinny, and much quieter than the demon's bellow. It was coming from the Super *Gakutensoku*. The machine had been equipped with a bank of loudspeakers for psychological warfare purposes. Now it was playing a song.

"What is that noise?" asked one of his aides.

So much for dignity. Toru sighed. "I believe that is the American National Anthem."

Magical energy was building in the air. A bolt of lightning erupted from the clear blue sky and struck the *Gakutensoku*. Thunder rolled across the city. The mighty robot lifted one arm. Brilliant orange fire danced along that hand. Then the other arm came up, shimmering with reflected light as ice formed along that limb. Hatches opened on the giant robot's torso as cannon barrels extended outward.

Toru stuck his fingers in his ears. This was going to be very loud.

"Open fire!" Joe shouted. A dozen 120mm anti-tank cannons went off simultaneously. Expanding gray clouds appeared across the demon's body.

"Spells are charged," Hikaru said.

"Magic up!" The Actives released their magic, and Joe hurled it at the enemy. He slammed the far right stick forward. Normally a Torch could direct a stream of magical fire or cause small objects to combust, but, magically augmented by the *Gakutensoku*'s spells, that same magic now caused a super-heated ball of plasma the size of an automobile to shoot across the campus, melting everything beneath it, before crashing into the demon in a shower of sparks and smoking demon flesh.

The demon charged. He'd been expecting that. That's what an aggressive beast would do when confronted by a seeming equal rather than being stung by hundreds of ants.

Joe cranked on the left stick. A wave of magical cold shot forth. It was absolute zero at the release point, and not a whole lot warmer when the wave struck the demon's hide. It shuddered as molecules slowed, tissues became inflexible and cracked. Then Joe activated one of the right sticks to throw a punch. The *Gakutensoku* responded a second later by slamming its steel knuckles into the monster's side. The frozen layers of hide shattered. Flaming ink ruptured from the hole.

There was an impact that shook the entire *Gakutensoku*. The shift in gravity told him that they'd been hit low, in the legs. *The tail!* Joe directed gravity to pull them back from tripping while he worked the foot pedals. They slid across the campus, through a four-story building and out the other side, but they didn't fall.

"Damage to the secondary servos and the port accumulator," Hikaru reported.

"I don't even know what those things are," Joe said, trying to concentrate on not killing them all while the Power surging through him felt like it was going to yank his heart out of his chest.

The forest of spines was visible through the port holes, and then it was gone. The demon was circling to the side faster than they could turn. One of the CRTs had gone black, the camera lens covered in demon sludge. The others told him that it was about to grab hold of them. There was a lot to keep track of, especially on a system this complex that he hadn't had time to properly learn, but Joe was a Sullivan, and Sullivans didn't get rattled.

"Cracklers. Release on my signal," Joe ordered, and Hikaru repeated it to their Actives who could direct electricity. The *Gakutensoku* shuddered and metal groaned as the demon collided with them. "Now!"

The stored energy leapt between the two huge bodies, and a billion volts blasted the demon off of them. It flew back, across the street, through several apartments, and disappeared in a cloud of dust at the base of a large office building.

There was a terrible burning smell inside the cockpit. Smoke drifted in front of his face.

"That's horrible!" Then Hikaru began to gag. "One of our electricians is on fire. The augmented spell was too much."

Joe couldn't turn to see right now, he was trying to turn the robot to keep track of the demon. "Have one of the Torches put him out. I'm busy," Joe snarled. The magical strain was really getting to him. "Get another Crackler in that chair. Charge our magic. Get those guns reloaded. I want them to fire every time they've got a shot. Pour it on!"

The demon lifted itself off the ground. The *Gakutensoku* covered the distance in a few strides and caught it on the way up. As the big fist came down, Joe threw as much extra gravity as possible to haul it down faster. The blow hit so hard that it blew demon ink out one of the demon's eye sockets.

It hit them around the midsection, wrapping its arms around their center of mass and squeezing. Cannon shells fired at point-blank range. A few floors below, one of their Brutes died screaming as flaming demon ink poured through the gun hatch, and then the noise stopped as it washed him away.

Joe acted on instinct, the robot an extension of his own body, as he pummeled the demon. There was an awful grinding noise, and the stick wouldn't pull back. That arm wouldn't retract; it was stuck. It took a moment to find the right CRT screen to see that their wrist was stuck on a horn. So Joe reached across with their other hand, grabbed that horn, and squeezed. The diesels powering those hydraulics redlined and it still wouldn't break, so Joe changed gravity's direction to the side and basically hung tons of extra weight on that horn. It tore free with a sick crack that they probably heard back in China.

The Summoned lurched away, spraying flaming blood everywhere. Joe still had the horn, and it was pretty stout, so he went about beating the beast about the head with it. Their movements were powerful, but slow. The demon was organic, fluid, and far faster. It caught the descending horn with one hand, turned it aside, and then bit down on their shoulder.

It was distant and down a floor, but he could hear the grinding of metal, breaking of welds, and the scream of men as they were torn from their seats and flung to their deaths. More smoke filled the air, and this time it smelled like burning wires. More CRTs had gone black. Half the lights on the warning panel had gone red. He tried to hit it with the horn again, but couldn't tell if it worked. Feedback through the electrodes told him that hand was now empty.

"Torch magic is charged," Hikaru said.

Joe drove their right fist deep into the monster's side. "Fire!"

The contact point between them was briefly hotter than the surface of the sun. The explosion rocked them. A wave of heat flashed through the robot.

"Right arm is not responding," Hikaru warned. "Repeat, right arm down!"

Joe could have told him that by the way the control had frozen up. "Get the Fixers on it, now." The demon lurched away, so Joe lowered their uninjured shoulder and pushed both of the friction sticks all the way forward.

ClompClompClompClomp!

They collided, a wall of steel meeting a wall of meat. One of the armored portholes shattered. A thick chunk of glass spun over and hit Joe in the jaw. It hurt; he could feel the cut leaking blood, but he sure as hell didn't have time to check it. He jerked back on both sticks, stomped on the pedals to plant their feet, and even let gravity return to normal for an instant to drag them down into the ground to stop their forward momentum. Their feet dug a hundred-foot-long trench through the road, tearing up water mains, but they came to a full stop.

The demon wasn't so lucky. It hit the next building, a big twenty-story affair, and went *through* it, to crash across the next street, trip on a bridge, and then roll over to shatter a canal.

Joe drove them around the collapsing building. The demon was already getting up. Cannon shells were falling around it like rain. "Where's my ice magic? Come on!"

"Still charging. Two of our Iceboxes were in the shoulder. They are not responding."

There were more explosions around the demon than could be

accounted for with just the *Gakutensoku*'s 120mms. Tanks were rolling down the street. Several fast moving aircraft buzzed by just overhead, strafing cannon shells into the monster before veering off. Tokugawa had sent in the cavalry.

Black demon ink was pouring from its wounds, down the gutters, pooling on top of the canals to shimmer like oil, but it charged them anyway. It leapt across the distance, and the only thing he could see through the portholes was a forest of spines. "Brace for impac—"

BOOM!

No amount of gravity manipulation was going to keep them on their feet this time.

They hit a building, and then another building, and another. Joe couldn't tell what was going on. They were changing direction too fast. The demon had ahold of them, and was swinging them back and forth. It was hitting them over and over again. Magical energy was flowing back through the electrodes, and each impact was like getting hit directly in the brain with a hammer. Every warning light on the panel was red, and then the panel disappeared entirely as the demon ripped the *Gakutensoku*'s face off.

The black, slimy claw, big as a bulldozer blade, was thrashing back and forth, only a foot in front of him. It should have been terrifying, but all Joe could think of at the time was that it smelled like the ocean. And then the claw vanished as fast as it had come, and they were falling forward.

The view through the hole was of rapidly approaching ground. Joe slammed the main left arm stick forward and mashed the button to open their hand. He called upon all his magic at once, reversing gravity, trying to pull them upwards, but even the spells on this thing couldn't reverse two thousand tons once it was in motion.

Their hand hit, and that took most of the impact. They froze in place for a moment, leaving Joe hanging by the straps on his chair, staring down into a pile of debris and squirting pipes. Somebody had unbuckled their harness and fell past him, screaming, to disappear out the face hole. He hoped that hadn't been Hikaru, because he needed the little guy to relay orders.

Then a big hydraulic cylinder in the arm burst, and they were falling. Joe stomped on the pedals to kick out, pushing them so they'd land on their shoulder rather than flat. Facedown—assuming he didn't just get impaled on some rebar or smashed like a mouse beneath a boot heel—they wouldn't be able to get back up as easily, especially with one working arm. Besides, everybody in that shoulder was probably already dead.

On the upside, they landed like he'd hoped. On the downside, he smashed his head against the controls hard enough to knock himself stupid. Joe came back to reality a moment later dangling sideways about thirty feet over a ruined street. The moisture on his face was from a broken fire hydrant spraying upward.

It hurt to think. Talking was worse. "Hikaru, you still alive?"

"Yes, Lieutenant."

"Good, because we're not done yet." His voice was ragged. He didn't know if it was because he was breathing in clouds of dust, or if all the magic he was burning had damaged his vocal cords somehow. They were at a really awkward angle and looking out a jagged hole, but from the noise and shadows, it appeared the demon was trying to get away. If Tokugawa thought it was going to make it back to the ocean to heal, he'd light it up with the Peace Ray. "Get those Fixers to work. I want my arm and my ice magic, and I want them now."

"I'll do my best."

"If you don't, we're going to get flash-fried." Joe very gently tested the pedals. He'd gotten this thing stood up before, but he'd had both arms and a whole bunch of monitors to keep him informed then. This was going to take some finesse and a whole lot of screwing with gravity. "On that thought, get me a radio. This might take a minute."

"The *Gakutensoku* appears to be disabled, General. The beast is severely wounded, but it is merely fleeing back toward the bay. They have failed to stop it." The aide presented him with a radio. "The *Yamamoto* awaits your orders."

Toru took the radio with a heavy heart. He grieved for his nation, and gave no thought to his own life. The greater Summoned had to be stopped. If not now, then it would simply heal in the depths and then return to finish the job, even stronger than before. "This is General

Tokugawa granting permission to fire the Peace Ray. Authorization code one five three tw—"

"General!" Another staff officer rushed forward. "Please wait."

Normally Toru was very unforgiving of rude interruptions, but since he was about to obliterate them all, he was allowed to hope for a bit of good news. "Hold on that authorization . . . What is it?" He was handed another radio.

"It is the Super *Gakutensoku!*"

"—*hear me, Tokugawa, you son of a bitch! Don't you dare touch that thing off. I can still do this.*"

Toru keyed the radio. "This is General Tokugawa."

The young Sullivan sounded exhausted. "*We're not out of the fight yet. We're getting back up. I can still stop it before it gets back to the ocean.*"

One of his aides warned, "Time is of the essence, sir. It will be at Minato soon. Once it is out to sea, we will lose it."

"What is your status, Sullivan?"

"*Just peachy.*" There was something that sounded like a groan of metal and a loud clang. "*Couldn't be better.*"

"There! The *Gakutensoku* rises." A spotter was pointing at the financial district.

Broken glass crunching underfoot, he moved over to see. In the distance the mighty mechanical man was swaying, badly charred on one side, and missing an arm . . . but *standing*. The men began to cheer.

"There is no time, General!" the aide shouted.

"*Give us one more shot.*"

Toru had once trusted this man's father and he'd not been disappointed. He keyed the radio. "Sullivan, go southeast as fast as possible. You can cut it off at the port."

"*Got it. Sullivan out.*"

The *Gakutensoku* began an awkward limping jog through the city.

"That is our only chance. Do everything we can to slow the monster down. When it reaches the ocean, we will have no choice." He handed back the radio that offered hope and took up the one that could only dispense doom. "*Yamamoto,* await my signal."

✧ ✧ ✧

Joe didn't worry about the landscape now. It was better to bounce off a building to keep up speed than to move carefully if the whole place was minutes from being vaporized anyway. Since the robot was missing half of its head, wind was blowing freely through the cockpit. He'd not thought he'd need to wear goggles. On the bright side, now that they had a convertible, they all had a lot better view.

"Demon sighted!" Hikaru shouted.

The forest of spines was visible on the other side of some buildings to their left. It had gotten turned around and slowed down while being harassed by the Imperium military and not taken the most direct route to the bay. So they'd caught up before reaching the ocean, and judging by the numerous cargo cranes in front of them, just in the nick of time.

"Radio your air force to back off for a minute." With them all hanging in the breeze, one unlucky hit and shrapnel would kill them all. Then what good was their fancy robot? Joe had both friction sticks all the way forward and was running the foot pedals as fast as he could. He veered them to the side and tracked directly toward the demon.

The magic draw was intense. His personal Power had long since been exhausted. He was only a conduit now, a circuit between the Power itself and the hungry spells on this machine. The other Gravity Spikers aboard had either been killed or incapacitated, because it felt like he was on his own. He knew he was probably going to die here, but that just made him want to make sure this thing didn't get away even more.

The demon heard them coming. It had to be severely weakened, because rather than turn to meet them, it kept on moving toward ocean. The demon was stumbling as bombs kept going off around it, leaving a smoking trail of lost tissue. They were almost on top of it.

"Cold magic ready." Hikaru had to shout to be heard over the wind.

"About damned time. I've got an idea. Hold on."

They were both in the open, smashing their way through stacks of cargo containers and trucks. He realized what was really slowing down the demon. The horn that he'd ripped off earlier had wound up impaled through one of its legs, causing it to limp. *So I did stick it. Nice.* Joe pulled back on the friction sticks, slowing them just a bit, allowing the demon to reach the water first.

"What're you doing?" Hikaru probably thought Joe had decided to throw in the towel.

"Trust me."

The demon reached a moored freighter and began clambering over it. Waves crashed as the ship capsized and the beast hit the water. Joe lifted their remaining arm. The crosshairs used for aiming earlier were long gone, but he wasn't shooting at the monster: he was shooting at the ocean around it. "Release the ice magic now!"

He'd not realized how well insulated they'd been before. The cold that blasted through the cockpit was a shock to the system, but it was far, far worse on the receiving end. The ocean around the monster turned solid instantly. Partially submerged, the creature could no longer move its legs or tail, and fell forward. Its snout smashed into the suddenly hard surface, and it flailed about through the slush and breaking ice.

Joe plowed ahead, only there was no longer ground ahead of him, only man made dock facilities, and those came apart beneath their weight. It took all of his skill and concentration to keep them from falling over in the mud, but below that was bedrock, and that was solid enough to get some gravity-assisted purchase on. Waist deep, they slogged forward as water came rushing through the fresh holes in their robot.

The demon was sliding, trying to gain purchase. The loss of smoke and ink was shrinking it. The thing was no longer so massive and imposing, and Joe drove straight into the monster, crushing it back into another ship. Once he was sure they were partially on top of it, and there was solid rock beneath, Joe cut his Power and let gravity return to normal.

There was an unholy screech as the giant monster's legs were crushed, but demons didn't have bones to break, so there was still work to be done.

Its head was far beneath them, jaws snapping, so Joe lifted their remaining arm, pushed the button to form a fist, and then let the thing have it right in the teeth. He kept hitting it, arm rising and falling like a jackhammer. Each blow caused the head to deform further, spraying burning ink in every direction. The second of its four eyes went out, and then a third, and Joe just kept on hitting it.

The monster was shrieking and thrashing, A claw caught the rest of their cockpit and tore that away, but the controls were still connected, so Joe just kept on plugging away. There was so much black floating on the waves that it looked like the ship they'd rolled over had been an oil tanker, but that was just demon ink.

There was a gleam of bronze through the churning salt water. It was the giant hammer and sickle embedded on the demon's chest. Joe opened the palm and reached down, plunging the robot's fingers through the thick hide until they were around the symbol. Then he hit the button to make a fist. Satisfied that the crunch meant he'd caught it, he yanked back on the controls, ripping it from the demon's body.

The demon opened its mouth to screech one last time, and this time Joe slammed the hammer and sickle right down its throat and through the back of its head.

The vast Summoned body began to dissolve, but so did Joe's consciousness. The pain was making it hard to think. He was leaning forward, and as he lost it, so did the robot.

The dark ocean rushed up to meet him.

Joe woke up in a hospital bed. General Tokugawa was sitting in a chair next to him.

"You know, if I ran this Imperium the same way my father did, I would simply notify your president that you perished in the battle and your body was lost in the harbor. Even his best spies would not be able to discern the truth. I have thousands of witnesses who saw the ruined Super *Gakutensoku* sink into the bay. Then you would be experimented upon, your will broken, and your impressive Power utilized for the greater good."

"Lucky for me you're not like your father," Joe croaked.

"And lucky for my city, you are very much like yours . . . I have named you an honorary Iron Guard and awarded you the Order of the Golden Kite. Wear the medal with pride."

"The Marine Corps is gonna *love* that."

"You may stay here if you wish, and I will gladly change that from honorary to official . . . From your expression I shall take that as a no? Oh well . . . My Healers have repaired your wounds. All that remains is the exhaustion. Soon, you will be returned to your country, whether to a hero's welcome or to the shame of having aided an enemy, I do not know. Your people are fickle and unpredictable."

"Yep, but they're *my* people."

"Indeed." Tokugawa smiled. "It is good for a warrior to know where he belongs."